SUNDAY KIND OF LOVE

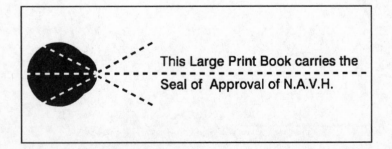

This Large Print Book carries the
Seal of Approval of N.A.V.H.

Sunday Kind of Love

Dorothy Garlock

THORNDIKE PRESS
A part of Gale, Cengage Learning

Farmington Hills, Mich • San Francisco • New York • Waterville, Maine
Meriden, Conn • Mason, Ohio • Chicago

Copyright © 2016 by Dorothy Garlock.
Thorndike Press, a part of Gale, Cengage Learning.

Thorndike Press® Large Print Basic.
The text of this Large Print edition is unabridged.
Other aspects of the book may vary from the original edition.
Set in 16 pt. Plantin.

LIBRARY OF CONGRESS CATALOGING-IN-PUBLICATION DATA

Names: Garlock, Dorothy, author.
Title: Sunday kind of love / by Dorothy Garlock.
Description: Large print edition. | Waterville, Maine : Thorndike Press, 2016. |
  Series: Thorndike Press large print basic
Identifiers: LCCN 2016022337 | ISBN 9781410491480 (hardcover) | ISBN
  141049148X (hardcover)
Subjects: LCSH: Large type books. | GSAFD: Love stories.
Classification: LCC PS3557.A71645 S857 2016 | DDC 813/.54—dc23
LC record available at https://lccn.loc.gov/2016022337

Published in 2016 by arrangement with Grand Central Publishing, a division of Hachette Book Group, Inc.

Printed in the United States of America
1 2 3 4 5 6 7 20 19 18 17 16

Dedicated in loving memory to
Rex McChesney

PROLOGUE

Buckton, Indiana
May 1946

The first thing Gwen Foster noticed was the man's angry scowl. From where she sat in the back of her family's car, thumbing through the book she'd just checked out from the library, with warm spring sunshine falling across her dress and faint music coming from the radio, his expression was so out of place, so ugly on an otherwise beautiful day, that it grabbed her attention. At ten years old, Gwen knew it wasn't polite to stare, but she just couldn't stop looking.

Running a hand through his unruly hair, the man looked impatient as he paced back and forth like an animal in a cage. He kept glancing toward the mercantile, at the door he'd just exited. He pulled out a pack of cigarettes, shook one loose, lit it from a book of matches, and began to puff furiously.

The woman who followed him out of the store couldn't have looked more different. She smiled brightly, one hand holding a stylish purse, the other waving good-bye to someone inside. But her good humor vanished the instant the man grabbed her arm, squeezing so tightly that her skin went white as bone; he moved so quickly, so violently, that Gwen flinched in surprise.

"What in the hell'd you say that for?" he hissed, pulling her close, his face inches from hers. "You know I hate that!"

The woman's eyes were wide with shock and pain. She shook her head slowly, cowering in the glare of the man's anger. "I was just making conversation, Billy," she told him, her tone pleading. "I didn't mean to —"

"That's 'cause you don't think!" he snapped, yanking her arm hard enough to cause her purse to fall to the sidewalk; some of what was inside spilled out, clattering around at her feet. Abruptly, he let go of her, returning his attention to his cigarette as she began to hurriedly pick up her things.

"A man like that is nothing but trouble."

Gwen turned at the sound of her mother's voice. Meredith Foster sat behind the wheel of the car. Normally her expression was friendly and inviting; now her eyes were cold and narrow as she watched the couple.

"When the time comes for you to find a husband, don't end up with someone like him," her mother said. "Do you understand?"

Gwen nodded.

"You want someone who will stand by your side, not tower over you."

On the sidewalk, the woman had finished picking up her things. When she stood up, Gwen noticed that she had tears in her eyes; one broke free, leaving a trail of mascara down her cheek before the woman wiped at it, smudging it across her skin. Nervously, she looked up and down the street, clearly hoping that no one was watching. She was so out of sorts that she didn't notice Gwen or her mother sitting in their car only twenty feet away.

With a practiced flip of his finger, Billy sent the smoldering butt of his cigarette flying, then turned back to the woman.

"I swear, Sally, if you ever pull that crap again . . ." he snarled, the threat unfinished but nevertheless clear.

"I won't, Billy," she said, trying to placate him. "I promise."

"Stupid bitch," he grumbled, then once again grabbed her arm, giving it another squeeze as if to show her he meant business.

Gwen felt sick to her stomach. She'd seen couples arguing on the big screen at the Crown Theater, but that was Hollywood make-believe. This was real. Her own father, recently returned from the war, was always smiling and laughing, kissing his wife on the cheek when he came home from the bakery, and doting on his only child. Warren Foster was *nothing* like this man. Truth be told, Gwen was worried about what might happen next.

Her mother must have felt the same.

Meredith opened her car door, as if she meant to intervene. Gwen wanted to stop her, afraid her mother might suffer the same mistreatment as the other woman, but before she could do anything, she noticed the couple looking right at them; they must've heard the squeak of the door's hinges. The woman wore an expression of embarrassment, while the man seethed with anger.

"Come on," he spat, yanking the woman roughly down the sidewalk. "Let's get somethin' to eat. I'm starvin'."

As they walked away, the man moved with a noticeable limp; Gwen wondered if he had been wounded during the war, like dozens of other men from Buckton, or if he'd always had it, if it was something he had been born with.

Either way, Gwen was glad to see him go.

Once beneath the awning of the hardware store, the woman looked back at them. Her eyes were still wet, but she offered a weak smile, as if she was apologizing for something, though it vanished when the man started in on her again. Moments later, they rounded the corner and were lost to sight.

When Meredith shut the car door, she and Gwen were both quiet, the only sound coming from the radio, where Perry Como sang "Prisoner of Love."

Listening to the song's lyrics, Gwen thought about the troubled couple. Were they in love? How did they meet? Was he *ever* sweet to her? Did he buy her flowers, write love letters, or take her to the movies? Would she spend the rest of her life with him, or would there come a day when she would leave?

"That wasn't love," Meredith suddenly said. Gwen thought that her mother must have been listening to the song, too.

She nodded. "I know what real love is."

"You do?" her mother asked with a curious expression.

"It's what you have with Daddy."

Meredith smiled. "You're right. What your father and I have *is* love, but every relationship is different. No two people are the same, whether they're together or separate," she explained.

Gwen's brow furrowed. It was all so confusing. "Then how will I know who's the right person for me?"

"Be true to yourself. Set your own path. Don't let someone drag you down theirs if you don't want to go," her mother said, then she paused to look at the now-empty sidewalk. "If you do, you'll never know true happiness."

Before Gwen could reply, the door to the mercantile opened again and her aunt Samantha, her father's younger sister, stepped outside, her arms full of bundles of fabric. Somehow she managed to drop into the passenger seat, spilling her new purchases across her lap.

"You didn't tell me you were making clothes for an army," Meredith teased with a playful laugh.

"I couldn't make up my mind," Samantha answered. "There I was, convinced that I'm going to use satin, and the next thing I know, I'm intrigued by plain old cotton. Then there's the choice between a flowered pattern or plaid, to say nothing of sequins!

In the end, I figured it was just easier to get them all."

"You'll spend so much time making these clothes that you won't have a chance to actually wear them!"

Ignoring her sister-in-law's sassy comment, Samantha turned around in her seat and held up two pieces of fabric, one green and the other a shiny red. "What do you think, kiddo?" she asked her niece. "Which one catches your fancy?"

"I like the red better," Gwen replied.

"You're probably right," her aunt agreed. "It's flashier. More likely to grab a good-looking fella's attention."

"Men," Meredith commented, turning the key in the ignition. "You have a one-track mind. Don't you think about anything else?"

Samantha laughed. "What else *is* there to think about?"

But by then, as her mother pulled away from the curb and headed for home, Gwen was no longer listening. When they passed the corner where the couple had turned, she craned her neck for one last glimpse, but they were already gone.

Leaning back in her seat, Gwen couldn't stop thinking about love and relationships. It was all so much more complicated than she'd thought. On the one hand there was the man and woman on the sidewalk, arguing, crying, and even becoming physically violent. On the other was her parents: partners in building a business, raising a family, and loving each other as best they could. But Gwen now understood that there was an awful lot of ground in between; this included her aunt, flamboyant and a bit eccentric, still searching for just the right man to share her life.

So what about me? Will I make the right choice?

Right then and there, Gwen vowed that she would never let herself be treated like the woman on the sidewalk. She'd find someone who would encourage her, a man to stand beside her, who'd let her chase her dreams rather than yank her where he wanted to go. They would be partners, like her mother and father.

They would be in love, forever and ever.

When the right man finally came along, Gwen would be ready.

CHAPTER ONE

Chicago, Illinois
July 1955

"I've never been so insulted in all my life! How dare you treat me this way! Don't you know who I am?!"

"But, sir, I'm afraid that we don't have —"

"I don't want to hear any more of your pathetic excuses! I want this fixed immediately or heads are going to roll!"

Gwen Foster put down her book, unable to ignore the ugly scene unfolding in front of her. The train station was crowded with travelers, but from where she sat, opposite the ticket booth so that she could keep an eye on the departure board, she'd heard every word. Other nearby passengers turned away, as uncomfortable with what was happening as the train station employee. But not Gwen. Her eyes never left the irate businessman.

"I demand to speak to whoever's in charge!" he shouted.

"Sir, like I was telling you, I'm afraid that it's too late for us to —"

"Now!"

A few minutes earlier, the man and his wife had approached the ticket counter. Even from her first quick glance, Gwen could tell the man considered himself to be important. He was dressed expensively, his pin-striped suit cut in the latest fashion, a gold watch chain hanging from his pocket, his shoes impeccably shined. In the beginning, he'd been friendly enough, if a little curt, but the moment he discovered that something was wrong with his reservation, it was as if a curtain had been pulled back, revealing the man's true, uglier personality.

"What are you still standing here for?" he barked at the clearly distressed employee. "I demand satisfaction!"

The ticket agent hurried away in search of help.

Through it all, the businessman's wife didn't look put out or embarrassed. She stood off to the side, absently inspecting her nails, acting as if this wasn't the first time she'd seen her husband give someone a piece of his mind. On second thought, Gwen wasn't sure the couple was married.

The woman was young, far closer to Gwen's age than that of her traveling companion. She was pretty; curvy in all the right places, with hair dyed a blond so platinum that it was almost white. As Gwen watched, the woman yawned, looking more than a little bored.

By now, another man had appeared behind the counter; the previous employee, the one who'd already gotten an earful, stood a ways back, more than happy to let someone else take the brunt of the businessman's ire.

"What seems to be the trouble, sir?" the new arrival asked.

"The trouble is that your incompetent company lost our reservations!" the man shouted. He then proceeded to recite the same list of grievances as before, peppered with plenty of his own bona fides, as if he was giving an encore performance.

Gwen was enthralled. She absorbed every detail: the flecks of spittle that flew from the man's mouth as he yelled; the crimson hue of his cheeks; the sweat beading on the employee's forehead as well as how he nervously shifted his weight from one foot to the other, then back; the whispers drifting through the crowd. Gwen considered getting out her notebook to write it all down, but she didn't want to look away, not even for a moment.

"I'm terribly sorry for the inconvenience, sir," the employee apologized. "I'll make certain that you have your compartment."

"See that you do!" the businessman snapped. He folded his arms across his chest and smiled smugly, clearly pleased that his outburst had been successful. Glancing over his shoulder, he nodded to his traveling companion, but she was busy admiring her reflection in her compact.

Now that the show was over, the attention of the couple's fellow travelers drifted away. Gwen went back to worrying.

For what felt like the tenth time, she looked at the enormous clock ticking away high above the concourse. Her train left in half an hour.

Kent was late.

Rising from her seat, Gwen looked in every direction for some sign of him in the crowd: a hand raised in greeting, a glimpse of his blond hair, anything that would mean she wasn't going home to see her parents by herself.

But he was nowhere to be seen.

So when her train's track was called over the loudspeaker, Gwen sighed, picked up her suitcase, and trudged off to board it, alone.

As the train readied to leave the station, the platform was abuzz with activity. From her seat at the window, Gwen watched all the commotion. Porters pushed carts weighed down by dozens of bags; one had tipped, spilling its load, and several men were hurriedly restacking it. The conductor smiled broadly as he ushered passengers to their cars, periodically checking his watch to make sure they were on time for their scheduled departure. People said their good-byes: some shared a laugh and a wave; young couples held each other in tender embraces, wanting their final moment together to last as long as it could; and some partings were sad, tearful farewells for a loved one's leaving.

And I know just *what that's like . . .*

Four years ago, when Gwen had left Indiana to become a student at the Worthington Academy for Girls, a private school in Evanston, just outside Chicago, she'd been heartbroken. Saying good-bye to her mother and father at the train depot had been the hardest thing she'd ever done. Wrapped tightly in her blankets as if they were a cocoon, she had cried herself to sleep every night for a week. It didn't matter that her parents had scrimped and saved to give her this opportunity, sending her away in the belief that it would lead to a better life for their only child; Gwen was convinced that her life was ruined.

But then things slowly began to change.

Gwen thrived. She made friends, many of whom had been sent to the big city for the same reason, other girls just as lost and lonely as she was. In the classroom, she received high marks, studying literature, history, Latin, and mathematics. On the weekends, she took the train into the city to walk among the sky-scraping buildings, marvel at all the people, gawk at the goods in the store windows, eat at nice restaurants, and occasionally go to a play or the movies. Gwen understood that a door had been opened for her, and even though she'd had to be forced through, once over the threshold, she didn't want to go back.

Still looking out the window, Gwen caught sight of her reflection. When she was a child, she'd thought she looked plain, but now, at nineteen years old, she could recognize some of the reasons men's heads turned when she walked down the sidewalk: almond-shaped eyes a piercing blue as deep in color as a sapphire stone, curly dark hair long enough to drape across her shoulders, skin as smooth and unblemished as a spring apple, and a friendly smile that held within its curve just a hint of mischievousness.

Gwen knew she was pretty, but it was a knowledge with which she wasn't entirely comfortable. Some of the other girls at school wore their beauty as if it was a badge of honor, flaunting it for all it was worth. Doing so meant they attracted plenty of attention, most of it from the opposite sex. Gwen had had her share of suitors, boys from nearby academies as well as young men she'd met on her trips into the city. She had gone to a few movies, shared a milkshake or two, and even stolen a kiss here and there, but nothing had ever blossomed into something more.

Until the day she met Kent Brookings.

Speaking of whom . . .

Where was he? Gwen took another look up and down the platform, growing more convinced by the second that he wasn't going to make it.

I swear, if I have to go by myself, there will be —

"Excuse me, miss, but is this seat taken?"

Gwen spun around to find Kent standing in the aisle. His smile was impeccable, like something you'd expect to see on a billboard over Michigan Avenue. His blue eyes practi-

21

cally sparkled. But the fact that his blond hair was slightly mussed, his cheeks were flushed, and his chest rose and fell beneath his tailor-made suit and expensive tie meant that he'd had to run to catch the train.

"I was starting to think I'd be leaving without you," she admitted.

Kent sat down beside her, leaned over, and placed a soft kiss on her forehead. "I can't believe you doubted me."

"It wouldn't be the first time," Gwen said with a smirk.

"Only once or twice, surely."

"More like six or seven times," she answered. "There was the night I had tickets to see *Oklahoma!* at the Biltmore Theater and ended up missing the whole first act waiting in the lobby. Then last year at Christmas, when I made reservations at —"

"Okay, okay," Kent surrendered with a laugh. "You've made your point. So maybe I'm not as punctual as you'd like me to be, but for this special occasion, I would've made it even if I'd had to run down the tracks after you."

"Now, that I would've liked to see."

Once again, Kent laughed good-naturedly, then he lifted his briefcase into his lap and undid the clasps. Seeing it made Gwen frown.

"You said you weren't going to bring work with you," she told him, trying to hold back the worry teasing at the edges of her thoughts.

Kent paused, the lid only half-open. He turned to her.

"I know I did," he said. "But Caruthers came into my office just as I was getting ready to leave last night and dropped the Atwood case in my lap. He said that Burns wasn't making any headway with it and that now it was my turn. They're such important clients for the firm that I couldn't turn it down. This is my big chance to grab the partners' attention, sweetheart! If I win this one, it might not be long before my name is on the masthead. I was up half the night working on it and overslept. That's why I had to run to catch the train."

Just then, the engine gave a short, loud toot of its whistle. With a jolt, they began to leave the station. Gwen glanced out the window, watching the crowds slowly fall from view; a man ran alongside the platform, fervently waving his hand, his goodbye lasting until he could no longer keep up.

She looked back at Kent, trying to smile, but from his expression, she knew that she'd

23

done a poor job of hiding her disappointment.

He reached over and took her hand. "How about if I agree to work only while we're on the train?" he asked. "When we get to Buckton, I'll put everything away and won't touch it again until we leave." He gave her hand a gentle squeeze. "Would that make you happy?"

Gwen nodded, but her heart wasn't in it. She'd heard these promises before. They were a lot like his vows to arrive on time.

He rarely kept them.

From the moment Gwen met Kent Brookings, she'd been captivated by him. While it didn't hurt that she found him devastatingly handsome, she was surprised to also find him to be polite, well-mannered, and easy to talk to. He seemed to know something about everything, whether it be politics, music, books, the popular fashions, or even subjects she knew next to nothing about, like sports cars or wine. That he'd shown an interest in her was, to Gwen, the biggest surprise of all.

So when he asked her to dinner, she didn't hesitate to accept.

It didn't take long for Gwen to see that for all Kent's many attributes, he was fiercely driven to succeed. He was the son of Thomas Brookings, a wealthy industrialist, but rather than coast along on his father's coattails, Kent desperately wanted to make his own way. After earning his law degree and passing the bar exam, he'd joined the firm of Woodrell, Hamilton, Carr & Wilkinson, one of the most successful, prestigious outfits in all of Chicago. Soon Kent was working impossible hours, burning the candle at both ends, doing whatever was asked of him in order to make a strong impression.

Through it all, Gwen had tried to remain supportive. Every time she got stood up for dinner, was left standing alone outside a movie theater, or felt a bit lonely because of his absence, she tried to put it all in perspective. Besides, it wasn't as if they did *nothing* together: they attended the lavish parties thrown by Kent's firm, where Gwen wore pretty dresses and strings of pearls; they boated on Lake Michigan with his friends; and they drove through the city in his Oldsmobile 98 Starfire, fresh off the assembly line.

Kent was aware of her hurt feelings. Often, when he was forced to work late, he would apologize by sending a bouquet of flowers or by writing the sweetest letters.

Gwen knew that he truly cared for her, that he loved her; Kent Brookings was the first and only man who had spoken those three magical words to her. But Gwen still couldn't help but wonder what came first in his life, her or his career. Sometimes she suspected that she didn't really want to know the answer.

But *his* wasn't the only career causing problems between them.

When Gwen had started taking classes at Worthington, she'd liked most of her subjects, math and piano lessons notwithstanding. But writing had been her absolute favorite from her very first attempt at telling a story. Gwen had marveled at how easily she could make her characters fall in love, lie through their teeth, fight for what they believed in, even live or die. She agonized over getting each word just right; sometimes she couldn't sleep until everything was exactly how she wanted it.

From the beginning, Gwen had had encouragement. Her English teacher, Dwight Wirtz, was a balding man with a bright red beard and a habit of quoting Shakespeare in a deep, theatrical voice. He pushed Gwen to get better with a word of praise here, a criticism there. During her second year in his class, Mr. Wirtz suggested that she submit a short story to a magazine.

"I . . . I can't . . ." she'd replied with a shake of her head. "What if I'm rejected?"

Mr. Wirtz had taken off his glasses and given her a patient smile. "Then you try again, my dear. Success in life rarely comes without a measure of failure."

Incredibly, Gwen's work had been accepted; seeing her story in print had been one of the greatest moments of her life. When she'd told her parents about her accomplishment, they had gushed with pride, even if, as their daughter suspected, they couldn't quite understand her love of the written word.

As the years passed, writing had become her passion. Everywhere Gwen went, she saw a story just waiting to be told. It was in the sights, sounds, and even smells of a busy city street. It was in the clink of glasses and silverware in a restaurant. It could be found in the conversations she overheard; that was one of the reasons she'd been so interested in the businessman back in the train station. Writing about events as they actually happened, the type of investigative journalism found in a newspaper, appealed to her every bit as much as spinning tales of make-believe. Words were all around her all the time, ready to be put down on paper. Gwen could no more deny her urge to write than she could ignore the sun in the sky.

The problem was Kent.

When Gwen had first told him of her interest in becoming a writer, she'd hoped he would be supportive, that he might even have some suggestions about how she might make a living doing the thing she loved. At the least, Gwen wished for a reaction not unlike her parents'.

Instead, he had left her speechless.

"Why would you ever want to do that?" he'd asked, putting down his fork and staring at her across their table at the restaurant.

Seeing her fallen face, Kent had apologized for his bluntness, but had proceeded to tell her all the reasons he thought it was a bad idea: that it would be next to impossible to find someone willing to hire her; that the writers he knew worked like dogs, day and night, and brought home little money; and, most importantly, that she was a woman.

For all his many interests, for all his knowledge, Kent could be stubbornly old-fashioned. He expected the woman he married to take on a more traditional role, just as his own mother had done. His wife would stay at home and raise their children while he went off to work and provided for them. In exchange, he would give his spouse whatever her heart desired, be it expensive furniture, a closet full of clothes, vacations to faraway places — all so long as she stayed in her place and upheld her end of the deal.

That night, Gwen had sat in the restaurant and listened to Kent run down her dream. She'd wanted to cry, to scream, to run away, but had instead remained silent, too stunned to react. Later, she'd felt determined to change his mind, to make him understand just how important becoming a writer was to her. But every time she mentioned it, Kent grew dismissive, repeating many of the same arguments. Lately, she'd heard annoyance in his voice, displeasure that she wasn't seeing things his way, that she wasn't letting the matter go.

But she would *never* let it go. She couldn't.

Despite all that, Gwen was in love with him. Kent Brookings was smart, funny, and thoughtful. He worked hard; she had no doubt that he would someday be made a partner at his firm. He was the type of man most women dreamed of meeting. She wanted to build a life with him, to one day marry and have a family, to grow old and gray together. But for that to happen, she knew that something needed to change.

Unfortunately for Gwen, she had no idea what that was.

"Wake up, sweetheart. We're here."

Gwen blinked her eyes, swimming up out of a pleasant dream, the memory of which was already fading. Outside her rain-streaked window, houses slowly drifted past; it took her a moment to recognize that she was in Buckton. Inside the train car, passengers were gathering their things as the engine slowed.

Kent looked at her with a gentle smile.

"How long have I been sleeping?" she asked, then stifled a yawn.

"For a while," he answered. "You drifted off just outside Indianapolis. It looked like you needed some rest, so I tried not to bother you."

Gwen ran a hand through her hair, her head clearing. "Sorry I left you without someone to talk to."

"I was fine. I had plenty to keep me busy."

Though still not fully awake, Gwen understood that Kent was talking about the pile of papers he was now putting back in his briefcase.

She must have frowned because he said, "Now, now, let's not start that argument back up again. I told you I wouldn't work while we were here and I meant it. Nothing's going to get in the way of us enjoying our time with your family."

Kent said it with such honesty that Gwen found herself wanting to believe him. She saw her mother and father so rarely, came back to Buckton so infrequently, that this time, she wanted everything to be perfect.

Silently, she vowed to make the most of this trip. They both would.

"Are you coming?" Kent asked from the aisle, holding out his hand for her.

Gwen took a deep breath. She was ready. She was home.

CHAPTER TWO

"Oh, my dear Gwendolyn . . ."

Meredith Foster hurried across Buckton's small depot, her eyes misty with tears, and pulled her daughter into her arms, embracing her tightly. Gwen returned her mother's hug, her own eyes growing wet as she smiled, overwhelmed with happiness at being with her again.

Five months had passed since Gwen had last seen her parents; they'd come to visit in February for her birthday, taking her to the top of the Chicago Board of Trade Building, the tallest in the city, marveling at the view. Meredith called as often as she could, while Warren wrote letters, but their get-togethers were rare; it took almost all of her parents' money to send Gwen to a prestigious school like Worthington, leaving little for travel.

This was the first time she'd been back to Buckton in years.

Holding Gwen by the hands, Meredith stepped back and, beaming with pride, said, "Let me take a look at you."

Gwen did the same, noticing a few small changes in her mother: wisps of gray streaked her otherwise black hair; a few wrinkles tugged at the corners of her smile, though they did nothing to dampen its intensity; but her green eyes were unchanged and still twinkled like stars. Meredith was dressed simply yet elegantly in a long-sleeved white blouse and a blue skirt. Her favorite opal necklace, a piece that had once belonged to her grandmother, hung around her neck.

To her daughter, she was still the most beautiful woman in the world.

"You've gotten prettier since the last time I saw you," Meredith proclaimed.

"Mother . . ." Gwen replied, a little embarrassed.

"Let me brag!" her mother said with a smile. "Remember, you're the only person I have to gush over."

"What am I, chopped liver?"

At the familiar sound of her father's voice, Gwen left her mother and went to him. Warren Foster stood with his hands pushed deep into his pockets, beaming from ear to ear. He was a short, portly man; his big belly was the product of years spent sampling the breads, rolls, and pastries he made at the bakery, the business he'd run since just after Gwen was born. Even now, he had hand-prints of flour on his trousers and shirt, so when his daughter held out her arms to hug him, he warned, "Careful, sweetheart. I'm still wearin' this afternoon's work."

"I'm used to it," she replied, not caring a whit that her clothes might get dirty.

Holding him tight, Gwen was amazed by how familiar it felt: stretching to get her arms around his neck because of his ample midsection, the scratch of his whiskers on her cheek, and the way he smelled, a mix of all the delicious things he spent his day baking.

"I've missed you, Gwennie," he told her.

Gwen had always liked that her parents each had their own special way of address-ing her, her mother's being more formal, while her father's was as casual as could be. Each said something about the person. Meredith came from money in Pennsylvania and had grown up with maids, cooks, and a chauffeur, her dressers and closets full of fine clothes. Warren's family had struggled to make ends meet, going without food when they had no choice, mending clothes until they practically fell apart, all while living in a home that was little more than a shack.

But somehow, even though they came from very different backgrounds, from what many would consider different worlds, Meredith and Warren had fallen in love. Together, through good times and bad, they'd built themselves a home, a business, a family, a future. Choosing Warren had cost her mother her pampered life. Her parents had been so disappointed in her pick of husband that she'd been disinherited. But Gwen had always known that Meredith had no regrets; it could be seen in the way she smiled at Warren, the way she laughed at his outdated jokes, and how she helped at the bakery, praising the quality of his bread to anyone who walked through the door.

Gwen could only hope her own love would be so strong, so pure.

"It's good to see you again, Mr. Foster," Kent said, choosing the perfect moment to insert himself into the conversation without interrupting their reunion. He stepped over and shook Gwen's father's hand, smiling warmly.

"Glad you could make it, son," Warren replied.

"I hope you'll find Buckton to your liking," Meredith said. Glancing around the small depot, she added, "I know it's a far cry from the big city."

While Gwen and Kent had been in a relationship for more than a year, this was the first time that he'd come home with her to Indiana. They had made plans in the past, had even bought train tickets for Thanksgiving, but something always seemed to come up with his work. So though he had met Gwen's parents when they visited Chicago, charming them both during a long meal he'd paid for at the ritzy Via Lago Café, he'd never seen where she was born, where she grew up, where she had lived before attending Worthington. Much like her mother, Gwen had wondered what his reaction would be.

"It's perfect," Kent answered. Putting his arm around Gwen, pulling her close, he said, "Any place that could produce such a wonderful young woman would have to be."

"Wait'll you see all the hubbub on Main Street," Warren said with a wink. "We better get a move on if we want to beat the traffic."

When her father made to grab their bags, Kent interrupted him.

"Please, let me," he said, snatching them up.

"You sure?" Warren asked.

Kent nodded. "After being cooped up on that train for so long, it will do me good to stretch a bit."

Gwen couldn't help but smile at seeing Kent trying to make a good impression with her parents, though it wasn't all that far from who he was most of the time. From the smile on her father's face, his charm was working.

"Well, come on, then," Warren said with a chuckle, leading the way out of the depot. "Let's give you your first look at Buckton."

". . . and that there's the shoe store Frank Holter's run since his father, Nigel, passed away from influenza during the outbreak in 1919. His cousin, Margaret, is married to Dick Epting, and together they own . . ."

Gwen sat in the backseat of her parents' car listening to her father ramble, explaining the history of what seemed like every other business and building they passed. Warren grew excited as he spoke, his hand darting out the open window to point at one thing or another. Kent sat up front beside him, smiling and nodding along, occasionally asking questions, while Meredith was next to her daughter. During a brief lull in her father's tour, Gwen caught Kent's eye, trying to express her sympathy for his having to listen to such boring talk, but he gave her a quick wink before laughing at one of Warren's infamously stale jokes.

Driving down Main Street, Gwen took a tour of her own, looking at the familiar sights: there was the lamppost in front of Mott's Drug Store where she used to lean her bike before going inside to have a soda at the counter; the tall stone steps of the library, where she would sit whiling away a sunny summer afternoon with an open book on her lap; and the street corner across from the movie theater where, at thirteen, Paul French had given Gwen her first kiss, leaning in unexpectedly to plant a chaste peck on her lips before running away, laughing with his friends.

Surprisingly, seeing these places again made Gwen feel nostalgic, a wave of happiness for something she hadn't even known she missed.

"It's nice to be home, isn't it?" Meredith asked, as if she'd been reading her daughter's mind.

Gwen nodded, still looking out the window. "Everything's the same. It's like all the years I've been gone, nothing's changed."

"Things are more different than you might think."

Meredith pointed out the window as they

drove past Pedersen's Barber Shop, a place Gwen knew well. It was owned by Clark Pedersen, whose daughter, Sandy, had been Gwen's best friend growing up. The two girls had spent countless hours spinning around in the swivel seats, reading on the floor while Sandy's father cut someone's hair, and standing under the awning during thunderstorms, listening to the rain drum against the fabric above their heads.

"You know that Sandy got married."

Gwen nodded. For as long as she could remember, Sandy had been head over heels in love with John Fiderlein, who had loved her right back. Quite frankly, it would've been a shock to the whole town if the two of them *hadn't* ended up together. Gwen had gotten an invitation to their wedding in the mail, along with a three-page letter Sandy had written detailing her excitement. Because of examinations, Gwen hadn't been able to attend, a fact that nearly broke her heart.

"But that's not all," Meredith continued. "She's pregnant."

"Sandy's going to have a baby?!" Gwen shouted; Kent and her father both glanced at the backseat before returning to their conversation.

"Eight months along now," her mother

said. "She's as round as a ball and tired, but excited to bring her and John's child into the world."

Gwen was speechless. On the one hand, it seemed the most natural thing in the world. On the other, it was hard to believe that her friend was about to become a mother. In a way, it made Gwen feel melancholy; it saddened her that she and Sandy, who'd once been as close as sisters, had drifted apart.

"What happened over there?" Kent suddenly asked.

Gwen looked where he was pointing and saw the charred remains of a house; all that was left were a few blackened bits of wood still pointing toward the overcast sky. Debris littered the property. Even most of the grass in the front lawn had been singed away.

"Poor old Stan Nunn's place burned to the ground the night before last," Warren explained. "Stan and his dog made it out, but by the time the fire department showed up, there wasn't much left to save. Heck, with as hard as it was rainin' that night, Mother Nature did most of the work for 'em."

Once they'd driven past the wrecked house, Gwen turned to watch it fade away through the rear window. Something about it spoke to the writer in her. She wanted to put together what had happened, how the fire had started, what Stan Nunn would do now as he began rebuilding his life. In a way, Gwen thought she might understand how Stan now felt; having somewhere to come home to was much better than having no home at all.

As familiar as the rest of Buckton had been, it paled in comparison to how Gwen felt when she saw her parents' house. After Warren pulled into the drive, she got out and stood in the grass, looking up at the gray two-story Queen Anne, largely unchanged in the time she'd been away: the steep shingled roof was broken on one side by the chimney; tall windows opened onto the street, the curtains stirring in the steady breeze; a long porch wrapped around the southwest corner with a couple of wicker chairs set out to enjoy the view; and a pair of viburnum shrubs grew beside the walk, their flowers a brilliant white tinged with purple. While it was less opulent than the estate where her mother had been brought up, it was also much more so than the run-down shack in which her father's family had lived. It was perfect for them, another meeting in the middle.

Once again, Gwen wondered what Kent

thought. His father's mansion had so many rooms that he'd once said he hadn't been in all of them; Gwen hadn't known whether he was joking. But for the second time, he surprised her.

"You have a beautiful home," he said.

"That's kind of you to say," Meredith answered. "We certainly adore it, even if it's a far cry from some of the fancy houses in Chicago."

Kent flashed his warmest, most genuine smile. "Maybe so," he agreed, "but there are plenty of ways in which living in Buckton might be better."

"Now this I gotta hear," Warren said.

"For example," Kent began, "you don't have to fight through crowded sidewalks or elevated platforms just so you can go a couple of blocks."

"That's true," Meredith admitted.

"You also don't have to worry about neighbors, car horns, police sirens, or any number of other things that can keep you awake well into the night," he continued. "This is to say nothing about the smells . . ."

"Maybe we got it better here than I thought." Warren chuckled.

Just then, the deep rumble of thunder shook the late afternoon. The sky, which had grown darker and more menacing since they'd left the depot, finally let loose. Fat droplets of rain began pounding the ground. Laughing, Kent snatched up their bags and they all ran for the porch. They were quick, but not fast enough to keep from getting plenty wet, water dripping from their hair and clothes.

"I'm startin' to wonder if it's ever gonna stop rainin'," Warren said.

Inside the front door was a small foyer; to the left was the living room, to the right the dining room, and down a short hallway was the kitchen. A staircase rose to the second floor. But all Gwen noticed was the little things: the lace doily draped across the fireplace mantel, knitted long ago by her grandmother; the gold picture frame she'd given her mother for Christmas the year she'd turned ten; the end of the banister, the wood worn smooth by countless hands over dozens of years. It was these things that made the house feel like home.

Suddenly, Gwen stifled a yawn.

Her mother noticed. "Why don't you go upstairs and lie down for a while," she said. "There's plenty of time before dinner."

Gwen shook her head. "I'm fine," she answered, though she doubted she would be awake for more than a minute after her head touched the pillow.

"Go on, Gwennie," her father insisted.

She looked at Kent. Gwen assumed that he wouldn't be pleased to be left alone with her parents so soon after arriving in Buckton. But he gently touched her cheek and smiled. "It's fine," he told her. "You should rest."

"But I slept most of the way here."

"By the look of that yawn, you must need a little more. Don't worry," Kent said, glancing at both Meredith and Warren. "We have lots to talk about."

Reluctantly, her fatigue growing by the minute, Gwen gave in. Halfway up the stairs, she glanced back to find Kent laughing at something her father had said. He looked perfectly at ease.

Gwen sighed. She was worried about nothing.

Everything was just right.

Gwen sat up with a start, her heart pounding, a hand rising to her chest as the deep rumble of thunder rolled over the house. Lying in bed, she turned to look out the window in time to see a crooked fork of lightning blaze across the dark sky; seconds later, there was another tremendous boom. A strong gust of wind lashed against the glass, rattling the panes. The storm raged.

Now that she was awake, Gwen stretched before getting up to look at herself in the mirror above her dresser. The young woman who stared back at her appeared more than a little groggy, so she ran a hand through her dark hair. There wasn't a clock in her bedroom, so Gwen couldn't know what time it was, but she was sure she hadn't overslept dinner, convinced that her mother would have come to wake her. She noticed her suitcase lying just inside the door; someone had brought it in without disturbing her.

Back downstairs, Gwen entered the dining room just as her mother left the kitchen, a platter of steaming carrots in her hands.

"There you are," Meredith said. "You're just in time to eat."

"How long did I sleep?" Gwen asked.

"More than an hour. You must've been more tired than you thought."

"Can I help?"

"Put this on the table for me," her mother said, handing her the dish. "I'll be right back with the bread."

The Fosters' large, rectangular table seemed to be overflowing with food; dishes of roast beef, potatoes, and peas were nestled in among her mother's finest china, shining silverware, and crystal glasses. Two long, tapered candles flickered away at either end. As Gwen was finding a place for the carrots, she noticed something. There was a fifth setting. Someone was joining them for dinner.

But then, before Gwen could go ask her mother about their unexpected guest, laughter interrupted her.

"It came outta the oven black as a lump of coal!" Warren said with a snort, clapping Kent's shoulder as if they were old friends. The young lawyer's head was tipped back, and he was laughing like it was the funniest joke he'd ever heard.

Gwen smiled. Things were going better than she could ever have hoped.

Meredith joined them, putting the last dish on the table. "Sit down, everyone," she said. "Let's eat while it's still hot."

Gwen chose the seat across from her mother, beside Kent. He leaned close, put his hand on hers beneath the table, and gave it a squeeze. "Are you feeling better?" he asked, his breath warm against her ear.

"Much," she answered. "Were you all right with my parents?"

"I had a wonderful time," Kent answered. "As a matter of fact, I think you're about to find out just how nicely it went."

"What do you mean?" Gwen asked.

Kent only winked in answer.

Her father said grace, but then, just as Gwen realized that she hadn't asked who was joining them for dinner, Warren rose from his seat, cleared his throat, and lifted his glass. Outside, thunder rumbled.

"I've never been much for talkin', but with all that's happened here today," he began, looking at Kent, his eyes dancing, "I couldn't let this occasion pass without sayin' something."

"Don't you think we should wait a while longer?" Meredith asked, nodding toward the empty setting at the table.

"Nope," Warren replied. "I can't hold it a second longer."

Gwen glanced around the table. Seeing how everyone was smiling, she understood that she was the only one of them who had no idea what her father was talking about.

"Gwennie has always been the apple of my eye," Warren continued. "Since the day she was born, I've only wanted what was best for her. That's why Meredith and I worked so hard to send her to that fancy school. Figured all that learnin' would do her good. I couldn't be more proud of her."

Listening to her father, Gwen wondered where all of this was going. An odd feeling of unease rose inside her.

"Thinkin' 'bout Gwennie growin' up reminds me of the time she was helpin' me make rolls at the bakery. She couldn't have been more than ten, but —"

"Warren . . ." Meredith interrupted, touching his arm and silencing him as only a wife can do to her husband.

"I reckon I've talked enough," he said with a chuckle. "Besides, I'm not the one who's got somethin' important to say."

As if on cue, Kent turned to face Gwen. He took both of her hands in his and flashed his brightest smile.

"What's . . . what's this about?" she asked.

"This," he told her, "is about you and me getting married."

CHAPTER THREE

The car was going fast . . . too fast . . . nearly out of control . . .

The dark road looked like it was swimming before his eyes, racing up and down hills, curving left and then right so sharply that the tires screeched, never straight, never where he thought it would be. His window was down, the spring wind raising gooseflesh on his bare arm, though he didn't notice the cold. High above, a fat, full moon darted among the treetops, as if it was watching, waiting for what was about to happen.

He took a hand off the steering wheel and groped around on the seat beside him, between his legs, and finally down to the floorboard until he found what he was looking for. Bringing the nearly empty bottle of whiskey to his lips, he drank heavily, only vaguely aware that some of it was spilling down his shirt.

On the road ahead, he noticed a pinprick of light. As he watched, it began to slowly spread apart; it took him a moment to understand that he was seeing the headlights of another car. He felt himself drifting toward it, hypnotized, like a moth to a flame and just as dangerous. At the last second, he yanked the steering wheel away, the other vehicle whizzing by just outside his window. He laughed.

A woman sang faintly on the radio, a melody that he knew well, so he mumbled along, slurring his words, messing up the lyrics.

But that wasn't the only sound he could hear . . .

"Stop! Stop the car! You're gonna get us killed!"

Pete sat in the passenger seat. He was seventeen years old. Most days, he was a handsome, confident boy, quick to smile. But not now. Now, he cowered against the door, his eyes wide as saucers, frightened more than half out of his wits.

For an answer, he shouted something at Pete, the words as messed up as his singing. Whatever it was, it worked; Pete shrank farther into the door and closed his eyes, looking like he was trying to convince himself it was all a bad dream.

But it wasn't. It was as real as it got.

Satisfied he wasn't going to hear any more backtalk, he gave the horn a long honk, as if crowing in triumph.

Then, suddenly, unexpectedly, everything spun out of control.

He didn't know what caused it: a deer or some other animal darting into the road, forcing him to reflexively turn the wheel to keep from hitting it; too sharp of a turn; or maybe he fell asleep. But the next thing he knew, Pete was screaming, the whiskey had been ripped out of his hand, and the road had vanished somewhere behind them. The steering wheel bucked like an animal, trying to break free.

At one blink of his watery, bloodshot eyes, there was nothing in front of them; at the next, a tree loomed large.

Amazingly, the next few seconds passed slowly, like they were frozen in time, as if he and Pete were posing for a picture. Then, in a rush, everything sped up. There was a horrific sound, deafening, like the world was cracking open, the last instant punctuated by a scream. Before he could wonder if he was the one making it, pain tore through him, biting down hard, trying to rip him in two.

Then everything went silent. It went black.

Hank Ellis woke with a start, his heart speeding faster than the car in his dream. He was drenched in sweat, his shirt clinging to his skin. Outside the window at the rear of his workroom, a storm raged; lightning flashed and thunder rumbled, a symphony of nature. Angrily, he flung off his thin blanket. He had only lain down for a quick nap, but it had been long enough for his mind to play a familiar trick.

It had happened again.

It was the same dream that had haunted Hank for months. It felt vividly real, so much so that he expected to be covered in cuts and bruises. These dreams were lies mixed with the truth, as much fiction as fact. Details changed, such as the weather and the song playing on the radio, but the end was always the same.

Every time, the car crashed.

As another clap of thunder shook the windows, Hank went to wash up at the workshop's sink. He splashed his face with cold water, trying to clear his head. When he turned on the bare bulb, he winced at the sudden bright light. Glancing at his reflection in the mirror, he barely recognized the man who stared back.

At twenty-three years old, Hank felt like the last year of his life had aged him twenty more. His sandy-blond hair was a bit longer than was the fashion and was mussed from sleep. Eyes the color of an afternoon sky in springtime were hooded in shadow. Stubble peppered his cheeks and the curve of his strong jaw. In the harsh glare of the bulb, he looked drawn, exhausted, as white as a ghost. Once upon a time, he'd turned plenty of pretty girls' heads, but because of all that had happened, with the toll it had taken on him, he couldn't imagine catching someone's fancy. Not now. Frustrated by feelings he would have struggled to explain, Hank peeled off his sweat-soaked shirt, revealing a lean, muscular torso. He grabbed a clean shirt off the back of a nearby chair and slipped it on.

He took one last glance at the mirror.

"You look like hell," he muttered before turning off the light.

Hank's workshop was a converted garage that sat back from the home he shared with his father. Projects in various stages of completion were arranged around the room: tables, a dresser, a child's rocking horse, and a bench that Sarah Enabnit wanted to put near her pond so she could sit and watch the ducks glide down for a swim. Wood was stacked in piles along the far wall: red cedar, black walnut, ash, several types of oak, whatever would be needed for a particular piece. The floor was littered with shavings. Tools hung on the walls: saws, chisels, shaves, files, hammers, planes, rasps, in all different shapes and sizes. His lathe, so old that some might consider it an antique, stood at the ready.

He turned on the radio, hoping he might catch the last few innings of the Reds game, but it had been rained out. Instead, he settled for the station out of Claxton, jazz that sounded scratchy because of the storm.

For weeks, Hank had been trying to finish a project. Now, hoping to quiet the turmoil in his head, he went back to it. He had been hired by a wealthy woman from Mansfield who'd already commissioned three other expensive pieces; she was the type who wanted only the best, no matter what it cost. The chair was to have an intricate design, with small flowers circling the outer spindles, rising to a full bouquet decorating the headboard. He'd done this sort of carving before, but this time, no matter how much Hank worked the wood, something wasn't quite right. Wiping sweat from his brow, he picked up his chisel and mallet and set to it, making a tiny mark here, a small correction there, but it wasn't long before he faltered.

"Damn it," he swore, tossing down his tools in frustration.

Usually, working with his hands allowed his mind to drift, to forget his troubles. Lost in his craft, Hank could spend hours at peace.

But not tonight.

After his dream, he couldn't stop thinking about Pete.

For as long as Hank could remember, Pete had been his shadow. He tagged along to the movies, laughing at the Marx Brothers, marveling at the ray guns in *Flash Gordon,* and squinting through his fingers while watching *Frankenstein.* He followed to the watering hole, shucking off his shirt, pants, and shoes to swing on the old tire, letting go and plunging into the water. He shagged the baseballs that Hank and his friends hit, chasing them into the twilight with only fireflies to light the way.

He was *always* there. That's how little brothers were.

Pete was six years younger than Hank. He idolized his older sibling, wanting to eat every meal across the table from him, demanding to sit next to him at the barbershop so they could have their hair cut at the same time, and often sliding into Hank's bed at night to sleep beside his big brother. For the most part, Hank returned Pete's affection, even if the kid could sometimes be a royal pain in the ass.

The Ellis boys looked a lot alike, both tall and trim with bright blue eyes. They had the same taste in movies, music, and clothes. Both lived and died with the fortunes of the Cincinnati Reds baseball team. Both attended church, held doors open for others, and behaved, for the most part, as gentlemen. But as Pete grew older, Hank noticed that there were differences between them.

Where Hank found comfort in being alone, Pete was at his best around others. When he entered a room, all eyes turned toward him. He could talk to anyone, young or old, learned or uneducated, rich or poor, and make people feel like they were important, like someone was listening to what they had to say. Girls flocked to him, drawn as much to Pete's charm as to his good looks. He had more friends than Hank could keep track of. Before Pete had even entered high school, everyone in Buckton had forecast great things for him. Everything was perfect.

Until the day their mother got sick.

Eleanor Ellis was as bright a presence as her youngest son. She baked cookies and cakes for Buckton's annual Fourth of July picnic, sang in the church choir, hosted a bridge club for a dozen friends, and volunteered at the library. She was loved by one and all, but especially by her sons. To Hank and Pete, Eleanor was an angel. She fed and clothed them, kissed away the pain of their many scrapes, and guided them as they grew toward manhood. It was because of her that they stayed on the straight and narrow. They didn't want to disappoint her.

But then one day, now more than a year back, in the cold of January, Eleanor had collapsed in the kitchen while making dinner. For a week, she'd talked about being tired, worrying that she was coming down with the flu. After a couple of days in bed without improvement, they'd taken her to the doctor.

It was cancer.

Tears were shed. Pills and promises were given, but none of them worked. Four weeks after she fell, their mother was dead.

In Eleanor's sudden, shocking absence, Hank stepped into the void her death had left. He cooked and cleaned. He paid the bills. He helped Pete with his homework;

with the loss of their mother, the brothers grew even closer. Unfortunately, Hank did all these things because his father couldn't.

Without his wife, Myron Ellis fell apart, struggling to find the strength to carry on. A woodworker by trade, he started to let jobs slide, failing to complete the work he'd been hired for. Hank, who had apprenticed to his father for years, managed to keep up, apologizing to their unhappy buyers. As the months passed, Myron grew sullen, quick to let his temper loose. He stopped shaving, grew a patchy beard, and wore the same clothes for a week at a time.

But worst of all was his drinking.

Myron had never been a teetotaler, but the only drinking Hank could remember him doing was having the occasional beer while he listened to a ballgame in the workshop. With Eleanor's death, that changed. Myron began to drink whiskey straight out of the bottle in a misguided attempt to drown his sorrows, not stopping until he passed out in the workshop, the kitchen, wherever he happened to fall. Hank would haul his father to the shower and pour him cups of steaming black coffee to try to sober him up, all while being yelled at, insulted by a downtrodden, broken man whom Hank still loved with all his heart.

Month by month, week by week, even day by day, the stress mounted for Hank, eating away at him. He didn't think it could get worse.

But it did.

Three months ago, on a rainy night not unlike this one, Pete had been killed in a car crash, and as far as everyone in Buckton was concerned, it was Hank's fault.

Because of him, his brother was dead.

Soon after Hank had gone back to working on the chair, his head snapped up at the sound of glass breaking, the noise loud enough to cut through the din of the storm. He looked out the workshop's double doors toward the house. A light was on in the kitchen. He heard shouting but couldn't make out any of the words. Hank knew who was yelling.

It was his father.

For a moment, Hank considered letting Myron be. He'd run out of steam eventually. It wouldn't be the first time.

But Hank wasn't that kind of son. He took a deep breath, put down his tools, and headed into the storm, hurrying against the stiff rain.

Myron was in the kitchen. He sat at the small table, his head on his arm, his mouth

59

smushed against the wood. An empty glass lay on its side, a long trail of whiskey leading over the table's edge to pool on the floor. A half-empty bottle was clutched tightly in his hand. Soup was splattered against the wallpaper on the other side of the room, sliding down into a heap of food and broken dish.

"What happened?" Hank asked.

"Soup was too cold . . ." his father mumbled.

"And that was reason enough to throw it across the room?"

"Felt like it at the time . . ."

Myron stirred, reaching blindly for his glass, but all he managed to do was knock it to the floor with a clatter. Undaunted, he raised his head and took a long swig from the bottle, his Adam's apple bobbing like a cork as he drank.

Back before his wife died, before he allowed himself to slide down a slope slickened by alcohol, Myron Ellis had been a handsome man. He was tall and a bit thin, with his shock of thick black hair and no small amount of charm, he'd had his own share of success while courting Buckton's pretty young ladies. But now, sitting in the dark kitchen, drunk and struggling to stay conscious, he was almost unrecognizable.

His eyes were bloodshot and wet. His skin was pale, with the exception of his cheeks, which were flushed red. His shirt was stained with Lord knows what. Myron looked utterly beaten, and he'd surrendered without much of a fight.

Looking at his father, Hank felt many different emotions all at once. He was angry, sad, and plenty worried.

But most of all, he was disappointed.

Over the last couple of weeks, Hank had allowed himself to hope that his father was finally coming out of his depression. He wasn't drinking every night, and when he was sober, Myron seemed more like his old self. He'd mowed the grass, cooked a stew, and even come out to the workshop to look at his son's craftsmanship, making a suggestion here and there, although he hadn't picked up his own tools for months. They'd shared a laugh about Johnny Temple, the diminutive second baseman for the Reds, wondering whether he'd ever manage to hit another home run.

Now all that hope was gone.

Hank bent down and began to pick up the broken pieces of the dish his father had hurled against the wall.

"Always cleanin' up your old man's messes, ain't ya?"

Hank didn't answer.

"Must be quite the sight . . ."

When his father drank, he became maudlin. His melancholy made him want to drink more, creating a cycle from which Myron never seemed able to escape.

"How about I put on a pot of coffee?" Hank suggested.

"If you've got a hankerin' for it," Myron answered. "As for me, I got my own drink right here, though I'm gonna have to make do without a glass . . ."

When his father lifted his bottle to take another drink, Hank snatched it from his hand. He took it to the sink and began to pour it down the drain.

"Now, wait a minute!" Myron barked, his voice sounding panicked. He made to get out of his chair, his irritation fueling him, but he was too soused to manage it. When he plopped back down, he nearly tipped over and had to steady himself on the edge of the table.

Even as the last of the whiskey disappeared, Hank didn't feel victorious. Every time he found liquor in the house he got rid of it, but his father had proven to be sneakier than expected. He hid bottles everywhere — in the backs of closets, beneath the basement steps, even in the attic, tucking them among the exposed beams. It was a war Hank couldn't win.

"Ah, it's probably for the best," Myron said, surrendering with a shrug. "It wasn't helpin' me forget 'bout Pete anyhow . . ."

Hank stood at the sink with his back to his father. A flash of lightning lit up the sky, illuminating his reflection in the window for a quick second; his face was creased by a deep frown, his lips drawn, his jaw tense. His hands squeezed a dish towel so tightly it was as if he was trying to strangle it.

"The other day . . . I was at the grocery store . . ." his father continued. "There were these two ladies lookin' at me from down the other end of the aisle. They must've thought they were far enough away that I wouldn't hear 'em, but I could . . ." His voice changed, becoming higher, almost theatrical as he tried to imitate the women's conversation. " 'Look at that poor man. Isn't he the one whose oldest boy killed his brother in that car accident a couple months back . . .' "

Hank didn't say a word. He didn't have to.

He'd heard it all before.

Myron chuckled, but it came out a humorless wheeze. "You know, I thought 'bout goin' over and tellin' 'em that they didn't know the half of it, but it wouldn't do a lick a good. People believe what they want to believe. To them, you and me, we're what they call a . . . call a . . ."

But that was as far as Myron got before finally passing out with his head on his arm, leaning hard against the table.

Hank sighed. He slipped an arm around his father's waist and lifted the older man out of his chair. In the living room, Hank laid Myron down on the couch, then pulled a blanket over him, hoping he would sleep it off. Only now, overcome by all the liquor he'd drunk, did his father look at peace.

Deep down, Hank believed that a lesser man would give up, pack his things, and hit the road, leaving his father to face his demons alone. But Hank wouldn't abandon him. He just couldn't. For all Myron's problems, his son loved him fiercely. He wanted him to get better, and still thought that he could.

"Get some rest, Dad."

Back in the kitchen, Hank looked at his workshop through the rain. He knew he should go back and try to finish that chair, but he couldn't bring himself to do it. His head was a mess, full of too many ghosts.

So instead, he snatched up his keys. He'd take his truck for a drive, listen to music,

anything to distract himself. He couldn't stay.

Out he headed into the still-raging storm.

CHAPTER FOUR

This is about you and me getting married . . .

Gwen sat at the dining room table, dumbstruck. It was as if Kent's words hung in the air, taunting her, daring her to respond.

A grin slowly spread across Kent's face, an expression that, she had to admit, made him even more handsome. From the way his eyes danced, Gwen knew he expected her to blush, cry tears of joy, clasp her hands together, and accept his sort-of proposal. In Kent's mind, there could be no other outcome. Rejection wasn't an option.

Glancing across the table, Gwen saw that her parents were equally expectant. Meredith's bright eyes lit up the room while Warren nodded slightly, as if he was giving his approval. Gwen knew that this was what her parents had always wanted for their daughter. They had struggled to send her to Worthington and pushed her to make the right choices, all in the hopes that she would

have a better life than they'd had. And now, right before their eyes, she was on the cusp of succeeding beyond their wildest dreams.

All Gwen had to do was utter one simple word.

Yes . . .

But she couldn't bring herself to say it.

Undeniably, there was a part of Gwen that had always fantasized about becoming Kent's wife, yet another part remained cautious. She loved him, of that there was no doubt, but she knew it wasn't that simple. In the end, it came down to the one obstacle they'd yet to overcome: Kent didn't want her to become a writer. Until the matter was settled, she couldn't possibly accept.

"Kent, I . . . I think that . . ." she managed, unsure what, if anything, she should say.

"I told your father about the Lutheran church on Wheeler Avenue," Kent said, acting as if she'd reacted every bit as emphatically as he'd assumed she would. "I know it's a little Gothic-looking, but it's perfect for the ceremony, large enough to hold all the people who would attend."

"And later we'll have a celebration here in Buckton," Meredith added. "Something for family and friends who can't make the trip to Chicago."

"A lavish party!" Kent said enthusiastically.

"I'll make the best cakes you've ever tasted, Gwennie!" her father chimed in. "Everythin' you loved when you were a kid and more."

"For the honeymoon, I was thinking Niagara Falls," Kent continued, sounding a bit like a traveling salesman using the hard sell to peddle his wares. "I'd prefer somewhere more glamorous, myself. Hawaii, maybe. But with all my work at the firm, I can't be gone for that long. Still, I'm sure it will be wonderful!"

Gwen could only sit and stare, stunned at how everyone was acting. She couldn't believe what she was hearing. What was she supposed to do now? Should she speak up, point out that she hadn't agreed to marry Kent, thereby throwing a bucket of cold water on their good cheer? Or should she just go along with it, smile and nod her head, saying as little as possible, all while waiting for an opportunity to talk with Kent alone and set everything straight?

Or should I just give up my dreams of becoming a writer and be happy to become Mrs. Kent Brookings?

"What kind of flowers would you like, Gwendolyn?" Meredith asked while Warren and Kent began discussing the merits of Champagne. "I know you've always been fond of roses, but lilies would look better with a white dress."

But as Gwen struggled to reply, the front door opened and then closed with a bang, followed by the sound of footsteps coming down the hall. She turned in her seat and finally learned who'd be joining them for dinner.

It was her aunt Samantha.

"Sorry I'm late," she said, breezing into the room, rainwater dripping from her short-cropped hair. Samantha unwound a soaked scarf from her neck and flung it onto a chair by the kitchen door. Half a dozen bracelets around her wrist clattered together as she took off her coat.

"I told you we were eating promptly at six," Meredith scolded.

"You should know by now that if you wanted me here at six, you should have told me we were eating at five thirty," her sister-in-law replied.

"Samantha will be late to her own funeral," Warren said to Kent.

"Probably," she said with a wink.

Other than a few almost unnoticeable wrinkles, her aunt was just as Gwen remembered her. Samantha was only a couple of years younger than Warren, but she carried herself more like she was Gwen's sibling. She dressed in the latest fashions, styled her hair like the stars in the Hollywood gossip magazines, and listened to rock-and-roll music, all in an effort to stay as young as possible. Though she was a beautiful woman, always talking about men who interested her, she had never been married. In fact, she'd never stayed in a relationship for long. Gwen had often thought that it was because her aunt was always on the move. If she settled down, she might miss something exciting.

Finally free from her coat, Samantha came around the table to stand beside Gwen, smiling down at her niece. But then, seeing Gwen's shaken expression, her good cheer faltered. "What's the matter, sweetie?" Samantha asked. "You're as white as a sheet!"

"Well, I . . . I just . . ." Gwen sputtered.

"She's getting married!" her father blurted, bursting with pride.

"She is?" Samantha asked, looking every bit as confused as Gwen felt. She glanced at Kent and said, "And I suppose you're the lucky fellow . . ."

"Kent Brookings," he introduced himself, smiling brightly as he extended his hand. While Samantha shook it, he added, "I've

70

heard a lot about you."

"I just bet," Warren said with a chuckle.

Samantha had always been Gwen's favorite relative, one of her favorite *people,* actually, and she'd spent hours telling Kent about all the scandalous things her aunt had done: wearing a skirt short enough to make Reverend Jordan write her a disparaging letter or driving her brand-new convertible down Main Street with the top down during a rain storm, laughing as she honked the horn. Samantha Foster did as she pleased, no matter what anyone else might think.

"Are you taking good care of my niece?" she asked Kent, her eyebrow arched, looking comically like a movie detective grilling a suspect.

"Of course," Kent answered, his voice honest and his smile bright, all his charms on display. "I love Gwen with all my heart."

His words cut through any skepticism Samantha might have felt; Gwen's aunt was a romantic, through and through. Seconds later, she had joined in the wedding planning, tossing ideas around the table.

"There has to be a band!" she declared. "A big band!"

"Like Tommy Dorsey's?" Warren asked. "I thought you were listening to all that new-

fangled stuff, with all the noise and what-
not."

"Not like with horns, you goof," Samantha replied. "I mean someone with lots of
sound, a band that knows all the latest hits!"

"The music has to be something everyone
will like," Meredith added.

"Who wants that old fuddy-duddy stuff?"
her sister-in-law asked.

While her family began to bicker, Gwen
leaned over and squeezed Kent's arm to get
his attention.

"Isn't this great?" he declared. "Everyone
is so —"

"We need to talk," Gwen said, cutting him
off.

"What about?"

"About us *getting married,*" she told him,
the words sounding strange, almost unbelievable to her own ears. "Right now."

"This instant?" Kent asked, looking across
the table at her parents and aunt still
discussing wedding details. "But we haven't
even had dinner. We —"

"Now!" Gwen hissed, finally putting her
foot down.

Without waiting for a reply, she stood up,
tossed her napkin on her plate, and stalked
out of the room. She didn't look back, but
from the way everyone had fallen silent, she

was sure they were all staring after her.

But Gwen didn't care.

She wanted answers, and she wanted them now.

Out on the porch, Gwen shivered, rubbing her hands up and down her arms to ward off the evening's chill. Rain continued to fall, though not as heavily as before, pitter-pattering on the porch roof, a steady drumming. Water rushed down the gutters, gathered in broad puddles on the sidewalk, and glistened in the grass, reflecting light from the street lamps. The rumble of thunder could still occasionally be heard, but the sound grew fainter, the storm finally moving away.

"Is everything all right?"

Gwen turned as Kent pulled the door shut behind him. Before it closed, she could hear that everyone was already back at it, discussing the wedding.

"What did you tell my family?" she asked.

"That you wanted some air," Kent answered. "I said that I'd offered to keep you company. From the sound of things, they'll be all right without us."

Gwen frowned. "Have you lost your mind? What were you thinking?"

"What are you talking about?" he replied.

From the look on Kent's face, Gwen had to wonder whether he was actually clueless. Then again, as successful an attorney as he was, with every courtroom victory hinging on convincing a jury that he was sincere, Gwen thought he might be trying to snow her, too.

"You announced we were getting married! You never even asked me if that was what I wanted! You never proposed!"

"I just assumed —"

"How could you assume something as important as *that*?!"

"You're right," Kent said, holding his hands up, palms out. "I got ahead of myself. But after spending time with your father, asking him for your hand, I suppose I got caught up in the moment."

Gwen's eyes went wide. "You . . . you asked him for permission . . . ?"

"Of course," he answered with a chuckle. "That's the main reason I agreed to come with you to Buckton. I've had it planned for months. It wasn't like I was going to call him on the telephone or write him a letter."

It was then that Gwen understood why Kent had been so insistent that she go upstairs and take a nap, why he hadn't been the least bit put out to spend time alone with her parents. It had all been part of his plan. While she slept, Kent had asked Warren for his daughter's hand in marriage.

"Did I make a mistake?" Kent prodded. "Should I not have asked?"

Gwen shook her head. "It's not that . . . not exactly . . ."

"Then what is it?"

She didn't know how to answer.

Kent smiled in the faint light. "Maybe I should have done it the old-fashioned way." He stepped closer, then lowered himself down on one knee. He reached up and took her hand in his own. "My dearest Gwen," he began. But before Kent could say more, Gwen yanked herself free and stepped back. She was so shocked by how she had reacted that she started to tremble.

"Don't . . ." she said. "Just don't . . ."

A frown creased Kent's face, and his eyes were touched with concern as he rose back to his feet.

"I don't understand," he said. "Why are you acting like this? I thought you loved me. I thought that you wanted us to get married."

"I do, on both counts," Gwen answered, her gaze finding his, imploring him to believe her. "I want to accept, but I . . . I just . . ." Her voice trailed off.

"Then why don't you?"

For a moment, Gwen considered shaking her head, giving a little self-conscious laugh, and saying that he was right, that she was being silly, that she'd be honored to become his wife. It would undoubtedly be easier. After all, Gwen *did* love him. In almost every way, Kent would be the perfect husband. But deep down, Gwen knew that if she gave in, she'd spend the rest of her life questioning her decision, wondering about what might have been.

So instead, she said, "It's about my writing . . ."

"*That's* why you're so bothered?" Kent replied with a deep exhalation. "What a relief. I thought it was something serious."

Gwen's anger flared. Kent's dismissive reaction was precisely why she hadn't accepted his proposal. That he couldn't understand how important becoming a writer was to her showed that their problems might lie even deeper than she thought.

"How can you say that?" Gwen asked. "Writing is important to me."

Kent's expression softened. He looked as if he was trying to talk to a child, patiently explaining himself to someone who didn't know better.

"We've been over this time and time again, sweetheart," he told her. "Between the money I make at the firm and what I stand to inherit from my father, you don't need to work. I can buy you whatever your heart desires."

"This isn't about the money. It's about me. Becoming a writer is something I want to do."

"What's wrong with being a mother and taking care of a home?"

"I want those things, too," Gwen said with a gentle smile. She stepped closer, reached out, and took his hand, trying hard to convince him. "But they aren't enough. I want to write."

"They were enough for my mother," Kent said, looking away.

Gwen knew she'd struck a nerve. Giving his hand a soft squeeze, she asked, "When did you know that you wanted to be a lawyer?"

Kent's expression brightened. "When I was little. The other kids used to ask me to settle their disputes: who crossed the finish line first, which kite flew the highest, whether someone cheated at jacks, that sort of thing. Most of the time, I was paid in gum balls. Once or twice, I was even enlisted to argue cases before parents." He chuckled. "It was so exciting. I knew there was nothing else I wanted to do."

"That's exactly how I felt when I began to write!" Gwen exclaimed. "We aren't that different."

He frowned. "It's not the same."

"Of course it is."

Kent shook his head. "What I do is important. Every time I step into a courtroom, I perform an essential duty to the community."

"Without writers, how would anyone know what was happening?" she asked, warming to her defense. "Newspapers and magazines expose all that's wrong with the world and champion what's right."

"Gwen, you don't —"

But now that she'd started, Gwen couldn't stop pleading her case, a lawyer in her own right. "What about books, plays, and poems, even the scripts for radio and television? A good writer can make their audience laugh or cry, make them angry or afraid, every emotion imaginable." Giving his hand another squeeze, she said, "*That's* what I want to experience. I want to touch people's lives, make them feel something. I need you to understand this. With you by my side, if you believe in me, I know there's nothing I can't do."

From the way Kent looked at her, his expression softening, Gwen began to hope he was about to agree with her. If he could just accept how important writing was to her, that all she wanted was a chance to prove herself, she would accept his proposal, become his wife, and they could live together in happiness for the rest of their days.

Unfortunately, she couldn't have been more wrong.

"I just don't understand why you'd want to scratch things down on a notepad or tap away on a typewriter if no one is going to read them."

"What's that supposed to mean?" Gwen demanded, her voice rising. From his tone, it sounded like Kent was insinuating she wasn't a good writer.

But it was worse than that.

"Any newspaper or book publisher that would hire a woman to write for them couldn't possibly have much of a circulation."

Bluntly, brutally, Gwen knew the truth. It was because she was a woman. Since she wasn't a man, she couldn't possibly participate in the greater world. Her place was at home, cooking, cleaning, taking care of the children, smiling prettily for her husband, thankful for everything she was given. From the beginning of their courtship, Gwen had known that Kent was old-fashioned, even a bit chauvinistic.

But that didn't mean she had to like it.

One thing was painfully clear to her: if she wanted to keep their relationship from ending, to prevent her love for him from dying, she had to leave.

Immediately.

Letting go of Kent's hand, Gwen brushed past him, went down the stairs into the lightly falling rain, and headed toward the street.

"Wait!" Kent nearly shouted. "Where are you going?"

"For a walk," she answered without looking back.

He chuckled weakly. "You can't be serious."

Gwen didn't so much as slow; she figured that was a good enough reply.

"What am I supposed to tell your parents?" Kent asked.

"You're the one who has all the answers," she said over her shoulder. "You'll think of something."

Kent leaned against the porch railing, watching Gwen pass beneath a streetlight without glancing back, striding purposefully down the sidewalk in the rain. He had given up yelling after her; she'd started to ignore him after a while.

Why does she have to be so darn stubborn?

When she'd first gone down the stairs, Kent had considered following, trying to talk some sense into her. He loved Gwen, dearly, and hated to see her upset. However, with her as worked up as she was, he'd known that the only thing he would've accomplished by going after her was that they would both have ended up wet. In his experience, when a woman got an idea in her head, it was next to impossible to convince her otherwise.

It was one of the reasons they were the weaker sex.

No, what Gwen needed was some time to cool off. Eventually she'd realize that she had been in the wrong, come back, and accept his proposal.

He was sure of it.

Kent knew he needed to go back inside and talk with Gwen's parents, but he lingered on the porch. The Fosters were good people, and their hearts were undoubtedly in the right place, but they were still a far cry from the cultured circles he moved among back in Chicago, although Meredith showed a measure of refinement. He shook his head. He couldn't be too hard on them. After all, they had raised an intelligent and beautiful — if somewhat obstinate — daughter.

Now what am I going to say to explain Gwen's absence?

Kent shrugged. It would be just like standing in front of a jury.

He'd think of something.

CHAPTER FIVE

Gwen stopped abruptly, her feet sliding on the wet sidewalk, and turned toward her parents' house. She was at the far end of the block beneath a street lamp. The porch where she and Kent had just argued was shrouded in shadows, dark save for the faint light coming from inside the home. She couldn't tell if Kent was still there watching her, or if he'd gone back to her parents, spinning some excuse for her absence, talking so convincingly that they had no choice but to believe him.

A gust of wind sent shivers racing across her bare skin. Gwen looked up. Though the sky was clearing and a smattering of stars peeked through the clouds, lightning flashed to the east and rain still fell intermittently. She wished she'd had the sense to grab her coat before going onto the porch, but she hadn't known that she and Kent would argue, that she'd become angry enough to stomp off into the storm. Now it was too late to go back. If she returned, Kent would see it as a victory, that she'd come crawling back to him.

And her pride wouldn't allow that.

So instead, Gwen kept walking. Even in the gloom of night, everything felt familiar: the way Donald Camden's porch sagged on one side; how Louise Detwiler kept every last light in her house turned on; the incessant barking of Eugene Martin's dog following her down the street. Unexpectedly, Gwen took a measure of comfort in her surroundings, as if Buckton was a warm blanket staving off a winter afternoon's chill.

Gwen reached into her pocket and pulled out her notebook. It was worn, the edges frayed and the cover slightly bent, but holding it made her feel better. She flipped through the pages, the scratching of words coming into clearer focus when she passed beneath a lamppost. In the notebook, she had recorded hundreds of observations. It was full of jottings about the brilliant colors of a March sun setting over Lake Michigan, the way a woman's head bobbed as she listened to music, the almost joyful growl a man made when he took his first spoon of soup at a diner counter. It was full of anything and everything that caught her eye.

It held stories, fictional and factual, just waiting to be told.

But if she became a housewife, if she chose to give up her dream, they would remain silent, forever . . .

Gwen walked as if in a trance. When she stepped onto Main Street, deserted because of the weather and the hour, she felt confused and conflicted. Absently, she wandered to her father's storefront, BUCKTON BAKERY painted on the glass. Gwen placed her fingers against the words, just as she'd done countless times before. She remembered the look on her parents' faces at the dinner table, how excited they'd seemed at the idea of her and Kent getting married, then wondered what Meredith and Warren would say if they could see her now. Would they think she was being unreasonable, that she was a fool for not rushing to accept Kent's sort-of proposal? Or would they stand by her, wanting her to chase her dreams?

Unfortunately, Gwen didn't know the answer.

"What am I going to do?" she muttered to her reflection.

Still flipping through her notebook, Gwen left the center of town and headed toward the river. High above, the sky continued to clear; the moon, nearly full, peeked through the fast-moving clouds, then once again disappeared, like a child playing hide-and-seek. Growing up, Gwen had spent countless hours along the banks of the Sawyer River, pulling the sticky, puffy seeds from milkweed pods and tossing them into the water and watching them gently drift away, a parade of white. But tonight, the river was almost unrecognizable. It moved swiftly, swollen with rain, a dark, turbulent rush. Still, like the rest of town, it gave her a sense of solace as she struggled with the dilemma before her.

Suddenly, a strong gust of wind raced along the river, snatched at Gwen's skirt, spun through her hair, and yanked the notebook from her hands. It fluttered before her for an instant, its pages spread open like a butterfly's wings, before landing with a plop in the water.

"Oh, no!" Gwen shouted, running after it.

Fortunately, it hadn't gone far. The notebook lay on the water's surface, a couple of feet from the bank, in a small eddy undisturbed by the current. Gwen knew that she had to act quickly. Even if the river didn't steal it away, the paper would soon be ruined and all her writings lost.

So without hesitation, she stepped into

the shallow water. It was chillier than expected, but Gwen bit down on her lip and inched forward. The water rose from her ankles to her calves, then to her knees. Her every instinct shouted that she was in danger, that she should get out of the river, but she paid them no mind. Her notebook was so tantalizingly close, yet still just out of reach.

But then, unexpectedly, the notebook began to race away from her, as if someone was pulling it on a string. Gwen lunged for it. Immediately, she knew she'd made a terrible mistake. One moment, the river's muddy bottom was beneath her foot; the next, it was gone, leaving behind a dark nothingness for her to fall into. Unable to stop herself, Gwen plunged beneath the water, soaking every inch of her. The powerful, insistent river grabbed her, just as it had the notebook, dragging Gwen away from the bank. Terrified, she fought with all her might, struggling to break free, but she was caught, completely at the river's mercy.

"Help! Somebody help me!"

Even as she shouted, Gwen knew that no one would hear her. All the while she'd been walking, she hadn't seen another person.

No one was coming to her rescue.

She was all alone.

Hank steered down the dark, windswept roads just outside Buckton, his pickup truck's windshield wipers sweeping away what little rain continued to fall. Lightning flashed occasionally, but the storm was moving off. His window was down, his arm draped over the door frame, the breeze tugging at his shirt. Tony Bennett's silky voice sang in the cab.

His hope had been that some time away from his workshop, far from his father and his drinking, would clear his head, but Hank couldn't stop thinking about Pete. Everywhere he went, he was reminded of his brother: the pond tucked among the evergreens off Route 32, where they used to swim in summertime; the steep hill on Caleb Ellroy's land they'd sled down in winter; and the ball diamond Roger Auster's dad cut into an abandoned wheat field so the boys would have a place to play baseball.

There was no escape from his memories.

Hank drove for miles, twisting and turning down the narrow, tree-lined roads. Finally he stopped at an intersection, the way branching in opposite directions. With the engine idling loudly, he peered out the rain-streaked windshield at the hill that rose to his right, a route that led away from Buckton and toward home. Hank's heart thundered like the storm, his mouth as dry as cotton. The accident that had claimed Pete's life happened on that road, on a stormy night a lot like this one, at about the same time . . .

"Damn it," he muttered, squeezing the steering wheel.

Pressing down hard on the accelerator, Hank turned left, his tires skidding as he headed toward the river. He hadn't gone the other way since his brother had died.

"Look at that poor man. Isn't he the one whose oldest boy killed his brother in that car accident a couple months back . . ."

His father's words rolled around in his head. Even though Hank spent plenty of time alone, holed up in his workshop, he knew that to many in Buckton, he was a murderer. Undoubtedly some wished he was behind bars; luckily for him, the county attorney had chosen not to press charges, figuring that living with what had happened was punishment enough. Regardless, Hank was still a prisoner of the past. On his few trips to town, he'd heard plenty, some comments whispered, others spoken right to his face.

". . . don't know why he doesn't leave. Folks will never forget what he done."

"His poor father! First his wife, then his son! It's not fair."

". . . been better if he'd died instead . . ."

Sometimes Hank wanted to scream in frustration and anger, to confront the people talking about him and tell them that they were wrong, that they didn't know what had actually happened. But instead, he held it inside where it festered, a wound slowly turning rotten. Besides, like his father had said, people believed what they *wanted* to believe, and no amount of telling them otherwise would ever change their minds.

Coming down a steep hill, Hank caught sight of a bridge up ahead, spanning the Sawyer River. The moon kept peeking in and out of the dispersing storm clouds; in its soft glow, the bridge's exposed beams looked like bones bleaching in the moonlight. Hank knew this bridge well, had fished off its struts as a kid, so he didn't fight the urge to pull his truck onto it, the tires slapping across its wooden planks, before coming to a stop halfway across.

He got out, leaving the engine on, music drifting from the open window. Facing the water, the breeze was brisk, but Hank paid the chill no mind. He was lost in thought, remembering his mother, worrying about his father's drinking, wondering how different his life would be if Pete were still alive. The only person in the whole world who had stood by him was Skip Young, his friend since they'd been boys. But it wasn't enough.

Hank felt caught in a trap of his own making, with no way out. He desperately wished things were different, but he'd made a fateful decision and there was no going back. This was his lot in life, to be a pariah, all alone.

But then, as Hank struggled against his mounting misery, he heard something, a noise loud enough to cut through the whistling wind and the music playing over the radio.

It sounded like someone was screaming.

I'm going to die!

Caught in the river's grip, Gwen was pulled along by the current. With every passing second, her sense of desperation grew. Again and again swells washed over her, plunging her head beneath the water's surface, pushing her down, and forcing her to fight her way back to air. Her eyes scanned both banks, searching for anyone who might help her, but she was quickly moving away from town and all she saw was darkness.

"Help me!" she shouted anyway.

Gwen was growing weak, too tired to struggle for much longer. Her clothes were soaked through, weighing her down, pulling her like a ship's anchor toward the bottom of the river. She wondered if she would die not from drowning, but from the *fear* of it.

She clawed at the water, hoping for something to grab hold of, a fallen tree branch or some other debris, but there was nothing. Slowly but surely, it was becoming harder for her to stay afloat. How long had she been in the water? How far had she drifted? In the end, Gwen knew it didn't matter. If she didn't get out of the river soon, she was going to drown.

And she would never see her family again . . .

A vision struck her. She imagined her own funeral, her mother weeping uncontrollably, distraught over the loss of her only child, as her father struggled to remain stoic, even though he was devastated on the inside. Her aunt Samantha cried silently, her small shoulders shaking. Kent was there, of course, his eyes bloodshot, underlined by dark circles, while his hands trembled. Seeing him, Gwen realized that one of the reasons he was so overcome with grief was that he blamed himself for her death; she had drowned because he'd forced her away.

Inspired to prevent such a grim future from coming to pass, Gwen made one last attempt to save herself. Fighting hard, she made ready to shout another cry for help, but when she opened her mouth, it was flooded with water. Gagging, her chest burning, she struggled to breathe but found that she couldn't.

Panic grabbed her tight.

But then, briefly, through the swells of water tossing her around, Gwen thought that she saw something up ahead, a building or bridge, a structure looming toward the sky, lit from behind by the moon. She raised her hands, flailing them about, but doing so used all the strength she had left. Completely spent, she closed her eyes, uttered a silent prayer, and surrendered to her fate.

This was the end.

Hank cocked his head and listened. He heard the wind whistling through the bridge's beams, Doris Day singing on the radio, and an owl's hoot from the east bank of the river. But then, just as he was about to chalk it up to a figment of his imagination, Hank heard it again.

It was a shout, the words indistinct.

It sounded like it had come from behind him, upstream. Hank hurried across the bridge, leaned against the railing, peered into the darkness, and searched the river. The Sawyer was running fast, close to overflowing from all the rain. Here and there he saw clumps of leaves, a chair, fallen branches, and even the carcass of a deer, the animal unfortunate to have wandered too close to the river in search of a drink.

Heaven help anyone who fell in . . .

". . . help me!"

Hank's heart quickened when he heard the words, this time clear enough for him to make out. Suddenly he saw a pair of flailing arms coming right at him. He couldn't believe it. Dumbstruck, he was too stunned to do more than stare.

Caught in the powerful current, the person — Hank couldn't tell if it was a man or a woman — came closer in a hurry. Then, just before they reached the bridge, drifting into the darker shadows cast by the moon's glow, their head slipped beneath the water's churning surface, leaving a lone hand raised toward the sky. A split second later, the person was lost from sight beneath the bridge.

Shocked out of his stupor, Hank turned and sprinted for the opposite side. Without any hesitation, he hoisted himself up and over the railing, hurtling into the air, hanging for an instant before plunging down toward the river. He plowed into the water feetfirst, sending up an enormous spray, the rainwater colder than he'd expected. Immediately, he began kicking, forcing his way back to the surface, gulping a lungful of air, his head on a swivel, looking.

Come on, come on! Where are they?

For a long, agonizing moment, Hank feared that the person had gone underwater for good, but then, between swells, he saw the hand again, bobbing in the river ahead of him. He started swimming, his hands knifing through the water, determined to reach them in time.

Hank had reacted without thinking, his instincts telling him to help another, even if it meant putting his own life in danger.

He would save them both, no matter what it took.

Beneath the water's surface, the sounds of the raging river were dull, almost muted. Darkness pressed toward Gwen from every side. Having given up, she was limp, directionless; left was right, back was front, up was down. Somehow, through all the chaos, beauty began to emerge; she felt warm, at peace, and was strangely comforted by the memory of her mother singing her favorite lullaby.

Then someone grabbed her wrist.

The touch was so unexpected that Gwen, as bad off as she was, was frightened. Reflexively, she tried to pull away, but the grip was too strong. Slowly yet insistently, she was pulled upward. When her head broke the water's surface, Gwen began to cough violently.

"I've got you! Don't let go!"

Groggy, still hacking up water, and with all her strength spent, Gwen looked at the person who'd suddenly appeared alongside her in the river. From the voice and what little she could see, Gwen knew it was a man, but she had no idea of the identity of her would-be rescuer.

He pulled her close, wrapping one arm around her waist while the other pushed hard against the current, moving them slowly toward the shore. Exhausted, Gwen struggled to keep her head out of the water, needing to occasionally rest against the stranger's shoulder.

"Hang on," he told her. "This is our chance!"

Ahead of them a dark shape loomed; as they raced ever closer, Gwen realized that it was an enormous rock. The river flowed swiftly around it, the water diverted to either side. The stranger was trying to get them to the inside, closer to shore, but the current was moving so fast that they slammed hard into the stone, a grunt forced from his mouth. Somehow he managed to hold on, stopping their momentum. Gwen clung tight, the bank only fifteen feet away.

"You've got to help me!" the man shouted. "I'll push us off the rock and then you kick with your feet! Use whatever strength you have left!"

Weakly, Gwen nodded.

"On the count of three . . ."

When it was time, Gwen did as he'd asked. From somewhere deep inside, she found the energy needed to scissor her legs and paddle with her free arm. At first she feared that they weren't going to make it, that they would be carried farther downstream, but just as she was about to give up, her foot touched the river's bottom and the man pulled her the rest of the way into the shallows.

Miraculously, the river no longer held them.

Even though Gwen had reached safety,

darkness still pressed down on her. It was a fight to keep her eyes open. The stranger scooped her up in his arms and carried her to the bank, laying her down in the grass. Her chest rose and fell beneath her soaked blouse, her arms limp at her sides.

High above, the clouds had broken up, leaving the moon unblemished in the sky, shining brightly over her rescuer's shoulder. Light encircled his head like a halo, illuminating the beads of water clinging to his hair. Shadows obscured his face. She couldn't make out many details, only that he was looking at her with concern.

"Gwen? Can you hear me?" he asked.

She smiled. He knew her name, though his voice was unfamiliar. Gwen opened her mouth to say something, but that was when exhaustion took her. She slowly tumbled down like an autumn leaf falling from its tree. She blinked once, twice . . .

Then everything went black.

CHAPTER SIX

Gwen . . . It's Gwen Foster . . .

Hank stared down at her face, lit by the moonlight. He tried to wake her, shaking her arm and repeating her name, but she remained unconscious. He had immediately recognized her. Even though he was only a handful of years older than Gwen, he didn't know her personally, not really.

Hadn't he heard that she was living in Chicago?

What was she doing here?

Most importantly, why had she been about to drown in the Sawyer?

Now that his adrenaline was subsiding, Hank felt exhausted. He took deep gulps of air, his heartbeat slowing. Getting them both to shore had been demanding work; his shoulders and legs burned from the effort. He wanted nothing more than to collapse in the cool grass and rest, but he worried that Gwen could be badly hurt. He knew he had to get her to a doctor, fast.

So how in the heck am I going to do that?

They were on a small outcropping, clear of trees, that jutted out into the river. The woods in front of them were thick, the underbrush crowded with bushes and fallen limbs. If Hank wasn't mistaken, they'd drifted half a mile or so downstream from the bridge. Unfortunately, no one lived around these parts. However, if he could get through the woods, there was a little-used road that would take them most of the way back to his truck.

He looked at Gwen. She appeared peaceful, as if she was merely sleeping. A few strands of her dark hair were plastered to the side of her face, her cheeks flushed, her lips slightly parted. The sudden realization that she was prettier than he remembered filled his head. Hank pushed the thought away, chiding himself for thinking such a thing at a time like this.

Even though it would be far faster for him to go back for the truck alone, Hank knew he couldn't leave her behind. If Gwen were to wake while he was gone, disoriented and frightened, she could wander off, and he'd have a devil of a time finding her in the dark.

He didn't have a choice. He had to carry her.

Hank lifted Gwen, one arm hanging limply at her side, water dripping from her clothes, and started for the trees. He moved with determination but also care; if he were to turn an ankle, they'd both be in a world of trouble. Painstakingly, he worked his way through the woods. When the path he'd chosen proved too difficult to navigate, he had to back up and find another route. He turned Gwen one way and then another, weaving among the trees and bushes. Once, they startled something in the undergrowth, probably a rabbit, sending it skittering away. Eventually, and with no shortage of relief, he found the road.

As he trudged toward the bridge, Hank's boots squished with every step, completely soaked through. His arms burned from their burden, but he didn't even consider setting Gwen down for a rest, just gritted his teeth and kept walking. He hoped he'd see headlights coming from either direction, but they were alone, so he continued on, listening to the chirping crickets.

Hank looked at Gwen. Even now, it seemed unbelievable that he would meet her again like this. In all the years they had each lived in Buckton, Hank didn't know if they'd shared more than a couple dozen words, most of them back when they were kids, but Gwen had always been nice, with a bright, friendly smile. Her parents were both well thought of in the community, the same sort of pleasant people as their daughter, but thinking about Warren Foster made Hank frown. In the weeks after Pete's death, one of the most hurtful comments he'd heard had come from the baker's mouth.

I reckon we should be grateful his mother isn't here to see this. If Eleanor was still alive, what that boy did woulda been the death of her . . .

Though the words had stung deeply, Hank supposed he couldn't blame Gwen's father. It wasn't as if he'd been the only person in town to voice such harsh sentiments. Besides, Warren's opinion did nothing to dampen Hank's desire to make sure his daughter was safe.

Eventually, after what felt like an hour and a couple of miles, the bridge came into view. Hank's truck was just as he'd left it; the headlights were on, the driver's-side door was ajar, and the radio was still playing. Pulling Gwen close, he managed to open the other door and place her inside as gently as he could. Making sure she was secure, Hank hurried around the pickup, slid behind the wheel, and put the truck in gear.

Then he stopped, unsure of where he

should go.

Grant Held's house was on the opposite side of Buckton from the bridge; the doctor would surely be able to treat her, but it was a bit of a drive.

The Fosters' home was much closer.

Hank looked over at Gwen. Her head lolled on her shoulder, her hair spilling across her face, her breathing steady but shallow. Even with Hank's recent unpleasant history with her father, the decision was an easy one to make. He would take Gwen to her family. They'd know what to do.

And maybe I'll find out what she was doing in the river in the first place . . .

When Gwen's mother opened the front door, she let out a gasp, then stepped back and placed a hand over her open mouth. Hank didn't wait for an invitation to enter but hurriedly stepped inside carrying Gwen in his arms, still unconscious. Other than some mumbling as he had raced down the darkened streets of Buckton, she'd yet to exhibit any signs of consciousness. He laid her down, still soaking wet, on a divan in the living room. Only now, nearing the end of their ordeal, did Hank begin to feel the price he'd paid for plunging into the Sawyer, swimming against its current, and rescuing

Gwen. His arms and legs burned, the muscles aching, while his ribs were sore from when he'd slammed into the rock. His whole body wanted to rest.

"Get some blankets," he told Meredith, who still stood near the staircase, watching. "She needs to get warm as fast as she can."

All the way to the Fosters' house, Hank had blasted the heater in his truck, but it had done little good. From their time in the water, as well as the long walk in the cool night, his teeth had never stopped chattering. Even with his adrenaline racing, Hank felt chilled to the bone. For Gwen, it was likely worse.

But instead of doing as Hank had suggested, Meredith ran to her daughter. She fell to her knees beside the sofa, pushed away wet strands of Gwen's hair, and slapped her cheek, insistently and with increasing force.

"Gwendolyn, wake up!" she shouted. "Open your eyes and talk to me!"

Before Hank could begin to tell Meredith what had happened, loud footsteps sounded in the hallway. He turned to see three people burst into the room: Warren, Gwen's aunt, and a man Hank didn't recognize. All of them reacted with astonishment at what they saw.

shouted from where she still knelt beside the divan; both Hank and Warren turned to look at her. "I don't care how it happened," she continued. "All that matters now is Gwen. We need to get her upstairs to her room and out of these wet clothes."

Hank knew that Gwen's mother was right. But when he moved to help lift Gwen off the sofa, Warren stepped in front of him, blocking his way. "Give me a hand, Kent."

At the sound of his name, the other man finally stirred, nodding his head. "Right, right," he mumbled, then hurried over, positioning himself at Gwen's shoulders.

"Doc Held needs to be called," Hank suggested.

"I'll do it," Samantha said, and headed for the telephone. As she passed Hank, she touched his arm and whispered, "Thank you," leaving him grateful that not everyone in Gwen's family suspected the worst of him.

Meredith led the way up the staircase. Kent carried Gwen's upper half, his hands beneath her arms, while her father lifted her feet. Hank drifted at the rear of the procession, drawn to follow out of genuine concern. But then, just before they reached the landing, Warren noticed him. He stopped and asked, "What are you still doin' here?"

"I want to make sure she's all right," Hank answered.

The baker shook his head. "This ain't none of your concern," he spat. "You've done more than enough."

"Someone might need to —"

"I want you out of my house!" he barked, his face a dark red.

"But, Warren . . ." Meredith soothed.

Turning his attention from Hank, Gwen's father nodded to Kent. "Let's get her to her room," he said.

Hank watched them leave. From downstairs, he could hear her parents doing all they could to help their daughter. Just then, the memory of Gwen lying in the moonlight on the bank of the swollen river unexpectedly sprang to his mind. This time, Hank didn't chase it away, but instead reveled in it, remembering how surprised he'd been to recognize her, how beautiful she was . . .

Slowly, Hank shook his head. He was a fool. He didn't belong here; Warren had made that clear enough. It was time to leave.

The sooner the better.

Just as Hank turned the knob of the front door, preparing to step back out into the night, a voice called out to him. "Wait!" He turned to see Kent hurrying down the stairs toward him, occasionally looking back over his shoulder as if he was worried about being discovered sneaking away.

"I'm glad I caught you before you left," he said when he reached the foyer, taking another glance up the stairs. "I wanted to thank you for rescuing Gwen."

"I only did what was right," Hank replied modestly.

"You have my gratitude all the same."

Up close, Hank could see that the other man had recovered from his initial shock. He still looked a little harried, his forehead dotted with sweat, his eyes unsettled, though he was trying hard not to show it. His clothes were expensive, cut from rich fabric, every stitch flawless, every button shining; compared to Hank in his soggy attire, he was dressed like a king. The man struck Hank as the sort most comfortable being in control, smiling brightly as he went around a room, enthusiastically pumping every hand. The more Hank looked at him, the more the man reminded him of the attorney he'd met with just after Pete's death.

"I'm Kent Brookings," the man said, extending his hand. When Hank took it, he added, "I'm Gwen's fiancé."

Hank faltered, if only for a moment. Kent's comment had caught him off guard, although Hank had no idea why. It shouldn't have come as much of a surprise that a beautiful young woman like Gwen Foster would attract the attention of someone as clearly successful as Kent. An uncomfortable pang lit across his stomach; realizing that it was jealousy made him feel like an even bigger fool.

"Hank Ellis," he replied halfheartedly, taking the man's offered hand. Kent's grip was far softer than his own. He resisted the urge to squeeze hard.

"I've never seen Warren so out of sorts," Kent said, hazarding yet another backward glance. "What is it about you that set him off like that?"

The last thing Hank wanted was to explain why everyone in Buckton thought he was worth less than the debris floating in the Sawyer River. He especially didn't want to tell this man who rubbed him the wrong way. Besides, Hank knew that as soon as he left, the Fosters would explain every sordid detail.

"It's a misunderstanding," he answered.

Fortunately, Kent let it go. "Whatever the reason, I can't imagine why he wouldn't be grateful to you for saving Gwen's life. I certainly am."

Hank believed Kent's sentiments were

genuine; he seemed legitimately thankful, even relieved that his wife-to-be was safe.

But then he went and ruined it.

"As a matter of fact, I'm so appreciative of what you've done that I'd like to offer you a reward," he explained as he pulled out his wallet; opening it revealed a thick swath of green, more money than Hank had seen in one place in an awfully long time, if ever. Fishing out two twenty-dollar bills, Kent held them out to Hank. "For a job well done."

Working as a woodcarver made Hank money. He was skilled enough to keep his business going and a roof over his head, and to buy food, clothing, gas, all the necessities of life for him and his father. But it wasn't easy. Some months he wondered if he'd make it. Forty dollars would go a long way.

But he wouldn't have taken those two bills from Kent's hand if they were both hundreds, even if there were a fistful of them.

Hank hadn't jumped into the swollen river, risking his own skin to rescue Gwen, for money. He had done it because it was the right thing to do, nothing more, nothing less. Even praise felt uncomfortable. If he accepted the bills Kent was offering, he felt like it would cheapen things, as if he'd lessen himself. No matter what Warren had

111

said, if he could go back to the bridge, Hank wouldn't have changed a thing.

He shook his head. "I can't take that."

Kent seemed as shocked as when he'd first seen Gwen's unconscious body. He looked down at his hand as if wondering whether he held something other than money. Hank suspected he was questioning whether he had offered enough. His eyes narrowed, turning his expression quizzical.

"But you deserve this. You've more than *earned* it."

Hank looked over Kent's shoulder and up the stairs. "Knowing she's all right is more than enough for me."

The other man regarded him for a moment longer, then put the money back in his wallet. "Even if you won't take a reward," Kent said, "I'm sure that everyone in Buckton will want to know what you've done."

Hank's stomach fell. "I'd rather they didn't."

"Whyever not? You're a hero!"

Before Hank could say more, Warren called from Gwen's bedroom, "You can come back now."

"They were changing her clothes," Kent explained, then leaned in, his voice lowering conspiratorially, and said, "The only gentlemanly thing to do was leave, though I wouldn't have minded a peek." For emphasis, he added a wink and a slap on Hank's shoulder, as if the two of them were old friends sharing a laugh.

Hank tamped down the urge to slug the man.

"I'd better get back," Kent said, oblivious to the distasteful feelings he was inspiring. As he'd done before, he stuck out his hand. Hank took it, but a bit more reluctantly than before. "Thanks again."

Watching the man go, Hank understood that he and Kent came from completely different worlds: while one was dressed smartly, his hair combed just so, the other looked exactly like someone who'd just fished himself out of the river; where one was sophisticated, articulate, capable of charming a room full of strangers, the other was shunned, an outcast, someone most others were glad to see leave; and while one had a bright future with a beautiful fiancée, a family to create, the other felt destined to remain alone, paying penance for what he had done.

Stepping onto the porch, Hank paused. Thinking back on the night's events, one thing was painfully clear.

Because of his actions, because of his

brother's death, no matter how heroically he acted, he was always going to be the villain.

Chapter Seven

"Try not to blink and don't move your head."

Gwen stared straight ahead as Grant Held shone a light in each of her eyes, moving it to one side and then the other. The doctor had come when called the previous night, then returned before Gwen had woken to the early afternoon sunlight streaming through the curtains of her bedroom, and performed a series of tests. He checked her pulse, then moved her joints, trying to determine if any damage had been done by her unplanned swim in the swollen, churning river.

"Now open your mouth, my dear," he said.

Surprisingly, given what she had endured, Gwen felt pretty good. Her muscles ached from fighting the Sawyer's current, there was a bruise the size of an apple blossoming on her hip, and she was so tired that she had trouble staying awake, but she knew that it could have been much worse.

She could be dead.

And I would have been, too, if it hadn't been for the stranger . . .

All morning, as she'd drifted in and out of sleep, Gwen had thought about the man who had saved her. She could still faintly hear his voice saying her name, his face undistinguishable, the sky over his shoulder lit by the moon. She had tried to ask her mother about her rescuer, wanting to know who he'd been, but the words never seemed to come out right, a mumbling mishmash that likely made no sense.

"Have you had any headaches?" the doctor asked.

"No, I haven't," Gwen answered, her voice having grown stronger and clearer with every passing minute.

"I'd expect to feel that way for several days."

"She's going to be all right?" Meredith asked from the doorway, where she was wringing her hands nervously.

Dr. Held nodded. "I'd keep her in bed at least through tomorrow, let her have plenty of rest, and call me immediately if she takes a turn for the worse." Patting Gwen's hand, he added, "You were quite lucky, my dear."

While her mother showed the doctor out to his car, Gwen sat up against her headboard, smoothing the soft fabric of her nightgown and thinking about everything that had happened since she'd returned to Buckton. Only the day before, she'd been worried about how Kent would get along with her parents, thinking about old friends and other mundane things. Since then, she'd been blindsided with a proposal of marriage and then had nearly drowned.

Things hadn't gone the way she'd expected they would, not in the least.

When Meredith returned, she crossed the room and began pulling down the blinds, stopping them halfway down the window, reducing the light without eliminating it altogether. "This will help you sleep," her mother said.

"I'm not feeling tired," Gwen lied. The truth was that she would have loved to put her head back down on her pillow and gotten more rest, but now that she was finally alone with her mother, she wanted answers. "I was hoping we could talk about what happened last night, about who pulled me out of the river."

Meredith didn't answer, continuing to fuss with the blinds.

"Mother, did you hear me?" Gwen asked.

"I want to know who rescued me."

Her mother forced a smile and waved her hand in the air. "Oh, that's not really important," she said. "What matters is that you're safe and sound."

"It's important to me. I want to know."

Meredith sighed and almost imperceptibly nodded, seeming to realize that it couldn't be avoided any longer. "It was Hank Ellis."

Gwen thought for a moment, the name swimming through her memory before finally touching ground. "Pete's older brother?" she asked.

Her mother nodded. Her expression looked pained.

Gwen hadn't known the older Ellis boy well. Pete had been closer to her age when they were growing up, but she still had a few memories of Hank: him sitting at the drugstore's soda counter, swiveling back and forth in his seat, drinking a cherry Coke; horsing around with his friends outside the movie theater; throwing a baseball against the back of the post office again and again. Hank Ellis had always been nice to her, though their interactions amounted to little more than a smile or a friendly word here and there. But last night, he'd unexpectedly reentered her life.

"I want to see him," Gwen declared.

Her mother's face soured until she was frowning. "I don't think that's a good idea."

"He saved my life. The least I can do is thank him."

"Hank Ellis isn't the sort of man you want to be spending time with."

"Why not?"

Meredith paused. "Because he killed his brother."

Gwen's jaw fell open in shock. Her heart began to pound. "Pete?" she managed to ask. "What . . . what are you talking about?"

Her mother crossed the room and sat on the edge of the bed beside Gwen, then took her daughter's hand in her own.

"A couple of months ago, back in April, there was an accident . . ." Meredith began.

Late one night, Chief Palmer had been called to the scene of an accident near the Ellis home. When he arrived, he found their family's car smashed into an enormous oak tree, its front end crushed like paper, every window shattered, and two of the wheels blown off. Hank Ellis was pacing back and forth beside the wreck, distraught, screaming at the night sky, his clothing smeared with blood. Hazarding a quick look inside the car, the police chief discovered Peter Ellis. Instantly, he knew that the boy was dead. An empty liquor bottle lay on the floorboard, miraculously unbroken. Hank had reeked of alcohol. It hadn't taken long for the lawman to piece it all together. Hank had been drunk, had gotten behind the wheel with his younger brother in tow, and on the way home had driven straight off the road. There were no skid marks on the pavement, indicating that Hank had never tried to slow down. While the crash had claimed Pete's life, his brother had been spared with no wounds, at least not on the outside.

"Ever since then, the whole town has shunned Hank," Meredith finished. "Peter was such a wonderful boy with a bright future ahead of him, all stolen away because his brother was a fool. I feel so bad for Myron." She paused. "It's a horrible thing to say, but I wish their fates had been reversed."

Gwen couldn't believe that Pete Ellis, a boy she'd known for so long, was gone. They had been friends growing up, their lives following similar paths; sitting in the same classrooms, running down the same streets, watching the same movies. But now she would never see him again. Slowly, Gwen began to understand that death was closer than she'd imagined. While she had managed to survive her time in the river, Pete hadn't been so lucky.

"It was an accident," Gwen said, still reeling from what she'd just heard.

Meredith shook her head. "It happened and it was all Hank's fault. Everyone in town was devastated, including your father," she explained. "Peter had been working for him at the bakery, doing odd jobs after school for a little money. He said he was saving up to go to college. Warren adored him."

Vaguely, Gwen remembered something about this, a snippet of a phone conversation drifting around in her head. Still, she wondered why she was only now hearing about Pete's death. She suspected that her mother had been trying to protect her, or maybe she'd been too upset herself.

"That's why your father acted the way he did last night."

"What are you talking about?"

Again her mother paused. "He shouted at Hank to get out of the house."

Gwen gasped. "But he *saved* me!" she exclaimed. "Hank risked his own life, brought me home, and to show his gratitude Dad threw him back into the storm?!"

"It could have been worse," Meredith said. "At one point, Warren insinuated that Hank might've been responsible for what happened to you."

"It was an accident!" Gwen argued.

"But we didn't know that at the time."

As soon as Gwen had woken, her mother had been at her bedside, asking questions. Still woozy, Gwen had done her best to answer, staying mostly truthful. She explained that her notebook had been blown out of her hands and she'd made an ill-advised trip into the water to retrieve it. Gwen neglected to mention her reason for being out in the stormy night in the first place, that she and Kent had argued, and that she still didn't know whether she wanted to accept his marriage proposal.

"I would have died if Hank hadn't seen me. He's a hero," she argued. "Doesn't that make a difference?"

"Not to your father," Meredith answered, grim-faced.

"What about you? Can't you forgive him?"

Meredith stiffened. "It's different when you have children of your own," she explained. "Whenever I think about Peter, I imagine how horrible Myron must feel. The poor man. First his wife gets sick and then his son is taken from him. Worst of all, he has to spend every day with the person responsible for Peter's death. Someday, when you have a family of your own, I expect that you'll better understand why I

122

can't forgive him."

Without letting Gwen have a chance to argue further, Meredith got up and went to the door. Before leaving, she turned back. "Stay away from him, Gwendolyn," she warned. "Hank Ellis is nothing but trouble."

"You're leaving?"

Kent sat on the edge of Gwen's bed, his legs crossed, a hand on the bedspread beside hers. Brilliant afternoon sunlight filled her bedroom, making it seem as if his blond hair glowed. He smiled at her in a way she found both charming and slightly condescending. Kent was dressed primly in a pin-striped shirt and a dark blue tie, his pants perfectly pressed, looking as if he was about to argue a case — which, in a way, she supposed he was.

"It's only for a couple of days," he explained.

"But . . . but why?" she stammered.

"Because when I called the firm this morning, I was patched through to Morton Wilkinson's office and he told me that they're having trouble preparing the depositions for the Atwood case. He said that they needed me as soon as possible." His smile broadened. "Morton's a partner, Gwen! This is the best thing that could've happened for my career!" Kent rubbed his smoothly shaved chin. "My guess is that Caruthers told the old man how I'd taken over for Burns, to say nothing about the work I did on the Simmons case, where I had to . . ."

Gwen struggled to pay attention as Kent held forth, providing her with more details than she could ever have wanted. She'd learned that once he got going, it was best not to interrupt. So instead, struggling to hold back a yawn, she thought about her new predicament.

Just the day before, Gwen had been worried about bringing Kent with her to Buckton. He was a man of the city, used to the hustle and bustle, the bright lights and thousands of people. She'd fretted about how he would react to being cooped up in the middle of rural Indiana with her parents for company. Gwen had suspected he'd be bored out of his wits and would sneak away to work.

And in a way, that's just what he's doing . . .

A sudden urge filled her. "Take me with you," she blurted, interrupting his discourse.

Kent stared at her. "I don't think that —"

"I'm fine," Gwen insisted, cutting him off again, sensing his coming argument. She was filled with the strong, irrational conviction that if she stayed behind, her life was never going to be the same. "I want to be with you."

She threw back the covers and started to get out of bed, but the sudden movement made the room twist and turn, causing Gwen to fall back down on her pillows, feeling more than a bit nauseous.

Kent slowly shook his head; it looked like he was scolding her, as a parent might a child, which irritated her. "You're not up for it, sweetheart," he said. "Stay here and let your parents look after you." Kent took her hand and gave it a squeeze. "Besides, once I get to Chicago, I'll be working around the clock. If you needed me, I wouldn't be able to leave the office. This is for the best. For both of us."

"When are you leaving?"

"In a little more than an hour," he answered after a quick glance at his watch. "Warren's taking me to the station."

At the mention of her father, Gwen remembered what her mother had told her that afternoon about how Warren had treated Hank. "When I was brought home," she began, "how did my father react?"

"At first, he was shocked witless, just like the rest of us, but when he saw who had come in the door with you, his mood quickly changed."

"In what way?"

"He was angry, far more so than I could've imagined," Kent explained. "Whenever I've been around Warren, which admittedly hasn't been often, he's been easy to talk to, quick to make a joke. But not last night. It was quite the sight."

Gwen felt a twinge of embarrassment, shame for how her father had behaved. She wondered how Hank had felt; he'd done something admirable, risked his life in an act of heroism, and the thanks he got was to be talked down to before being thrown out onto the street.

"I don't understand why he was so upset," Kent continued. "When I talked with the man, he seemed like a good enough sort, even if he looked half-drowned standing there in his soaked clothes."

"You spoke with Hank?" she asked, surprised.

Kent nodded. "I wanted to express my gratitude for what he'd done. After all, he saved the life of the woman I'm going to marry."

Gwen ignored the comment.

"One thing was odd about him, though," he added with a frown.

"What was that?"

"When I tried to thank him properly, as he most certainly deserved, he wouldn't hear of it. He said that he'd simply done the right thing, as if he was some hero out of the comic books. I chuckled about it half the night."

Suddenly, Gwen was forced to wonder what would have happened had it been Kent standing on the bridge, watching as she flailed about in the river. If he'd been in Hank's shoes, would he have dived in? Would Kent have risked his own life to save someone else's? To save hers? Or would he have stood there, helpless, too impotent to act as she drowned? Almost immediately she decided not to give the matter any more thought.

"Later, when Meredith told me what the fellow had done, I could better understand your father's reaction," he explained. Kent shook his head. "Killing his own brother. Can you imagine it?"

Gwen couldn't, but she was exhausted, both mentally and physically, and no longer wanted to talk about Hank and Pete Ellis.

But then, just as she was about to ask Kent what day she might expect him to return to Buckton, he took another glance at his watch, got to his feet, and announced that it was time for him to get going.

"I thought you weren't leaving for an hour," she said.

"I still need to finish packing my things, and then I should say a proper good-bye to your parents. Besides, you need your rest."

Gwen frowned, sulking a bit at how unfair it all was. Her hopes for their vacation had been dashed in less than a day. "Will you miss me?"

"Every second that I'm away," Kent answered with a smile. "As a matter of fact, I need something to tide me over until I return."

He leaned down, tilted Gwen's chin up with his hand, and tenderly placed his lips against hers. Their kiss wasn't particularly passionate, yet it lingered, his touch warm and welcome, a sweet moment that made her heart beat faster. When it ended, Gwen kept her eyes closed, relishing it, knowing she would miss him while he was gone.

When he reached the door, Kent looked back. "I'll call every night."

"You'd better," Gwen warned, though she knew it was unlikely he'd hold to his promise; she worried it'd be like the times he had stood her up outside the theater or restaurants, too absorbed in his work to think of her.

"And when I get back," he added, "we'll

start planning the wedding."

"We still need to talk about —"

But by then Kent was already gone, the door clicking shut behind him, undoubtedly happy that he'd gotten in the last word.

Gwen sighed, feeling more than a little frustrated. Her relationship with Kent was a conundrum, a riddle she couldn't quite solve. She loved him, wanted to marry him, but the question of her becoming a writer remained unresolved. It was a dream she wasn't willing to give up. Maybe now, with some time apart, she could do the thinking she knew she desperately needed.

Fatigue pressed down on her. Gwen yawned, allowed her eyelids to flutter and then close. She'd search for answers later.

First, she would sleep.

When Gwen finally woke, she did so with an itch she had to scratch.

She needed to write.

Unfortunately, the notebook in which she'd scribbled out her ideas, observations, and stray thoughts, almost a year's worth of work, had been the reason for her current condition. She could still see it, floating on the surface of the water, practically begging her to save it, but it had been bait in a trap. It had surely been destroyed, although she fancied the idea that it floated on and on, racing over rapids, around bends, under bridges, and through the other towns farther downstream. Either way, it was gone for good.

Which meant she needed something else to write in.

Gwen got out of bed, steadied herself on the bedpost as her head did a dizzy little dance, then went to her bags and began rummaging in the pockets.

Where is it? I know I packed it before I left . . .

And then she found it. Gwen had another journal in which she doodled from time to time, jotting down names, numbers, and whatever else wasn't quite good enough for the other book. She supposed it would have to do. Snatching up a pencil, she got back in bed and went to work.

Words flowed from her like the water in which she'd nearly drowned. Observations of every sort filled line after line: the chill of the river soaking into her clothes, her skin, down to her bones; how the dark clouds had skidded across the sky, the moon passing in and out of sight; the taste of the brackish water; and how tiny her voice had sounded as she screamed for help that she was sure would never come. For a long while, Gwen lingered on the shadowy form of her rescuer looming over her, saying her name. Her words spoke of her fears, her sadness, and her sudden hope, all the emotions she'd felt. On and on Gwen wrote, like a spigot turned open, wearing down the lead of her pencil until she had no choice but to stop.

Gwen sat back against her pillows. Writing had been invigorating, another way to heal, but deep in her heart she knew there was still something she had to do.

No matter what her father might think, regardless of the warning her mother had given, she had to speak with Hank Ellis.

CHAPTER EIGHT

"He offered you forty bucks and you turned it down? Are you nuts?!"

Hank looked over at Skip Young as they drove down Main Street. His friend was staring back as if he was actually crazy. Two baseball gloves lay in his lap, a bat leaned between his knees, and the ball he'd been tossing was now frozen in his hand. His reaction made sense; Skip was always on the lookout for money.

"It wouldn't have been right," Hank answered.

"Who cares? Do you know how much forty bucks can buy?"

"I didn't jump in the river so I could get a reward."

"Then why *did* you do it?" Skip asked.

"Because I was the only one who could help," he replied. "If I hadn't, she would've drowned."

"So what's wrong with lettin' a guy express his gratitude for savin' his fiancée?"

Hank frowned. "It's not just the money," he said, thinking about his conversation with Kent. "I didn't like the way he was talking to me."

"How so?"

"He made me feel like a bellhop at a hotel getting paid for hauling luggage. It was like I was beneath him, like he was doing me a favor."

"Soakin' wet, I bet you looked like a hobo."

Hank couldn't help but laugh. "You've got a point."

Skip chuckled, too. "Darn right, I do."

They drove past the movie theater, the post office, and the library, all places where Hank had once felt comfortable, even welcome, but that had changed with Pete's death. Everywhere he went, he felt like every eye was on him, watching, judging. His discomfort peaked when they passed the bakery. Hank couldn't keep from looking in the front window. Warren Foster was surely inside, helping his customers with a smile and a good word, a far cry from the man who'd insinuated that Hank had had a hand in his daughter nearly drowning.

I want you out of my house!

"Boy, I wish someone would try to give

133

me forty dollars," Skip said as he stuck his hand out the window, letting the wind turn it this way and that.

"You'd be thrilled if it was a couple of quarters."

"True," his friend replied, nodding. "Which should tell you how bananas I think you are for turning down four sawbucks."

For as long as Hank could remember, Skip had been obsessed with making money. Even as a boy, he'd sold newspapers, collected scrap metal in his wagon, trimmed bushes, whatever it took to make sure there were a few coins rattling around in his pocket. Skip's father was an auto mechanic, a lazy man who was slow to get out of bed in the morning, rarely completed a job on time, and struggled to pay his bills. Hank had always figured that the reason Skip was the exact opposite of his old man was because he was afraid of ending up like him.

"What about Gwen?" Skip asked. "Is she gonna be all right?"

"I reckon so." That morning, Hank had called Grant Held. While the doctor hadn't been forthcoming with details, he'd said that Gwen would be back on her feet in a couple of days.

"So what was she like?"

"Beats me. I didn't really talk to her. She

passed out as soon as I hauled her from the river."

Skip shook his head. "That's not what I mean. I'm askin' if she's still as pretty as she used to be. Gwen was always one heck of a looker."

If Hank could have brought himself to be honest, he would've admitted that Gwen Foster was beautiful. Looking at her as she lay on the riverbank in her drenched clothes, radiant in the moonlight with strands of wet hair splayed across her face, had made his heart pound. Even when she was unconscious, leaning against the door where Skip now sat or lying in her parents' living room, he couldn't take his eyes off her. She'd captivated him. Later, after he had gone home and found his father still snoring on the couch, Hank had lain awake for hours, staring up at his bedroom ceiling, wondering if Gwen was going to be all right, wishing that he'd insisted on staying until the doctor arrived. As the hours slowly drifted past, he began to feel more and more foolish; after all, what was the point of pining for a woman engaged to another man? What sleep he'd had was brief and fitful.

"I didn't really notice," he lied.

"When we were kids, I always wanted to ask her to a school dance."

"Why didn't you?"

Skip shrugged. "I guess I figured she wouldn't be interested."

Though he never would have said it out loud, Hank thought that his friend was probably right. Skip Young was far from the most handsome man that Buckton had to offer. He'd always reminded Hank of Ichabod Crane, the awkward schoolmaster of Sleepy Hollow. He was tall and thin, gangly, all elbows and knees, with a prominent Adam's apple and a nose like a beak. His strawberry-blond hair was so thin that it was only a matter of time before he was bald. Still, Skip's personality more than made up for any of his physical shortcomings. He was smart, funny, driven, and as loyal as a hound dog. The more Hank thought about it, the more he realized that he was selling his friend short. Maybe Gwen would've accepted.

Milt Duesenberg's filling station loomed ahead. Skip rapped his knuckles against the door. "Do me a favor and pull in," he said. "I wanna grab a Coke before the game."

Hank did as his friend asked, stopping short of the gas pumps. The red-and-white Coca-Cola machine sat between the station's two garage doors. Inside one of the garage bays, an Oldsmobile was hoisted up on a jack, but no one was working on it.

"You're buyin', right?" Skip asked when they'd gotten out of the truck.

"How do you figure that?"

"Remember last week when we stopped at that market outside Janesville? You said that if I spotted you a couple bucks for that set of chisels the owner had in that cracked display case, you'd —"

Hank interrupted. "All right, all right," he said. "I believe you." When it came to money, Skip's memory was encyclopedic.

He fished a couple of nickels out of his pocket and dropped the first into the soda machine's coin slot. It clinked around a bit before hitting bottom. Hank opened the door, grabbed a bottle, and pulled it free. Popping the cap on the opener, he handed the drink to Skip, who took a healthy pull.

"Boy, that sure hits the spot," he said.

But then, when Hank stuck the other nickel into the machine, it sounded as if it traveled only half as far as the first. He grabbed a bottle, hoping that he'd misheard, but the soda wouldn't budge.

"You've got to be kidding me," he grumbled.

"The coin got stuck," Skip observed. "Give it a good whack."

Hank slapped the side of the machine with

the palm of his hand, once, twice, a third time, each harder than the last, until the nickel at last came free, falling to the bottom. He'd grabbed his drink, opened it, and started to swig the sweet beverage when he heard footsteps approaching from behind.

"What in the heck's goin' on out here?"

Milt Duesenberg strode purposefully toward him. The filling station owner held a large wrench in his hand. Smudges of grease darkened his hands, chin, and overalls. At first, he didn't seem particularly angry, but then he took a good long look at Hank. There was a flicker of recognition and his mood instantly went south; his brow furrowed and his eyes narrowed.

"What're you up to, troublemaker?" he snarled, pointing the wrench at Hank. "You tryin' to bust into that machine? Steal from me?"

Before Hank could respond, Skip was between them playing the peacemaker, a broad, soothing smile on his face. "It's not like that at all, Mr. Duesenberg," he explained. "His nickel got stuck on the way down. I told him to smack it. If there's anyone you should be sore at, it's me."

Milt's glare softened, if only a bit. "I reckon that makes sense . . ." he said. "Does that to me, too, from time to time."

But even as the man backed down, he kept looking over Skip's shoulder at Hank, as if he was reluctant to let it go.

"We'll be off as soon as we're done with our Cokes," Skip added.

Milt nodded, then began slowly backing toward the pumps and his office beyond. Even at the doorway, he lingered, still watching Hank.

Hank stared right back.

"Don't let him get to you," Skip said, still trying to smooth things over. "He's havin' a bad day, that's all."

While Hank wished he could do as his friend suggested, just let the accusatory words fall away like water off a duck's back, he couldn't. No matter what he did, folks assumed the worst about him. He was a murderer. Nothing but trouble. Bad news. Someone to steer clear of. This was the way it was always going to be, and nothing he could ever do would change that. The only person who didn't judge him was Skip.

But even he didn't know the truth. Not all of it . . .

Skip chugged the rest of his Coke. "Come on," he said, playfully slapping Hank on the shoulder. "We're gonna be late."

Hank hesitated, still staring at the door to the filling station's office, practically daring

Milt to come back and have it out, but he didn't.

"Get the lead out," Skip hollered from the truck's cab.

Hank took a deep breath.

It isn't worth it . . .

Someday, he hoped, he would actually believe that.

Hank pulled into a gravel lot, the truck's tires skidding a bit on the loose stones. In front of them, a rough baseball diamond had been hewn out of an abandoned pasture; makeshift bases had been found and laid out, dirt had been piled high for a pitcher's mound, and the outfield came to an abrupt end where it met the encroaching woods. About a dozen men tossed balls back and forth, laughing and carrying on beneath the afternoon sun.

"Are you sure this is a good idea?" Hank asked.

"Of course I am," Skip answered. "You love playin' ball, don't you dare say otherwise. Now get your glove and come on."

For as long as Hank could remember, he'd been smitten with baseball. The heft of a bat in his hands, the deep sound the ball made when it thudded into a leather mitt, the smell of the dirt and grass . . . everything about the game spoke to him. He listened to it on the radio and once, one memorable July three years ago, had traveled to Crosley Field in Cincinnati with Pete to see a game in person, both brothers yelling themselves hoarse cheering the Reds on to victory.

Still, it had been a long time since he'd played.

Like he had with almost everything else in his life, Hank had walked away from baseball in the weeks and months after Pete's death. It had been easier that way, to isolate himself, to stay away from others, who didn't want him around anyway. His woodworking was his comfort, his way to take his mind off everything he'd lost. But then Skip had shown up with a bat, glove, and ball. When his friend had asked him to play, Hank felt a stirring in his chest and had surprised himself by accepting the offer.

When he and Skip approached the other players, Hank saw plenty of familiar faces: Rusty Pals, Tad White, Matt Glidden, all guys he'd grown up with in Buckton. Most of them offered a nod or wave in greeting, though no one said much or came over to shake his hand. It seemed that not everyone was as keen as Skip to have him join in their fun.

"What in the hell is *he* doin' here?"

Hank turned to see Jed Ringer coming toward them with a baseball bat slung over his shoulder like a gun. Two years older than Hank, Jed was considered to be one of the biggest troublemakers in town. Wherever he went, his mouth never stopped running, cracking wise and picking fights; tall and broad-shouldered, with thick, muscular arms, Jed was more than capable of backing up whatever trouble he talked himself into. When they were kids, Hank and Jed had scrapped plenty of times, playground brawls that left noses bloodied and chins bruised. They had *never* been friends. Hank counted a half dozen or so other men walking behind Jed. These toughs hung on the braggart's every word, reveling in the excitement that traveling in his wake brought.

"Who do you mean?" Skip asked, playing dumb.

"Like you gotta ask," Jed answered with a sneer. Grabbing his bat, he pointed it at Hank. "The killer."

Hank stiffened. This was why he'd been reluctant to come. His hands bunched into fists. If Jed was looking for a fight . . .

But Skip cut through the rising tension. "The only killin' that's gonna happen here today is what I do with my bat." While some guys started laughing, including a couple who'd arrived with Jed, Skip tossed the bruiser a baseball. "Enough jawin'. Let's play."

Jed angrily snatched the ball out of the air and dismissively answered, "Whatever." But even as his team started to make their way to the other side of the field, his gaze lingered on Hank, just like Milt Duesenberg's back at the filling station.

Once again, Skip interrupted, putting his arm around his friend's shoulder and steering him away. "Don't pay him no mind. Jed's the sort who'll keep yappin' even if no one's listenin'. To tell you the truth, with the way he's always runnin' that mouth of his, I'm hopin' one day it'll break."

Hank chuckled.

"That's the spirit," Skip said. "Now let's kick their asses!"

When they took the field, Hank played shortstop while Skip pitched. At first it was hard for him to concentrate, his mind still struggling to let go of the things Jed had said. But with every pitch, he began to get more into the game. When a ground ball was sent rocketing toward him, Hank bent to scoop it but it skipped on a stone and hit him right in the chest. Fast as lightning, he picked it up and hurled it to first base, just beating the runner, who loudly protested —

but from the beginning it was obvious his heart wasn't in it, that he knew he was out.

"That's the stuff!" Skip shouted in encouragement.

At the plate, Hank also started slow, his timing off, rusty, the ball arriving faster than he expected. Jed pitched for his team, throwing gas. Hank looked blankly at the first strike, quickly past him and into the catcher's mitt with a crack. Somehow, he managed to foul off the second pitch, but then completely whiffed on the third, swinging far too late and eliciting a string of triumphant curse words from Jed that followed him all the way back to the makeshift dugout.

The next time, Hank stayed patient, more relaxed, wanting to atone for his earlier failure, and lashed a hit into the outfield gap. Running hard, he ended up with a double, causing Jed to let loose with more swearing, though this time there wasn't any humor in it.

The game went back and forth, one team scoring a couple of runs but then the other answering. After making another tough defensive play, Hank realized that for an hour or so, he hadn't thought about his father, Pete, or what Warren Foster had said to him. He was simply playing the game he loved, sweat dripping from his brow, shouting encouragement to his teammates, desperately wanting to win.

But then, in the top of the ninth inning, things began to unravel. With the score tied and two outs, the other team strung together a couple of hits, pushing across a run and taking the lead. With runners on second and third, and with Jed, their best hitter, coming to the plate, Skip walked off the mound.

"You're gonna have to get him," he said, plopping the ball in Hank's glove.

"There's only one out to go. You can do it."

His friend shook his head. "My arm feels like it's about to fall off. If I keep goin', he's gonna put us even farther behind. It's up to you."

Hank took the mound and started tossing a few warm-up throws to his catcher. The first was off target but he soon began to feel more comfortable, the ball leaving his hand and quickly meeting leather at the other end of its journey. Hank did his best to ignore Jed as he stood off to the side, smirking.

"Let's see what you got," Jed snarled when he stepped into the batter's box.

The first pitch was wide for a ball, but the second caught the edge of the plate. Jed kept right on grinning. The third toss felt good leaving Hank's hand, but it appeared to be just what the other man had been waiting for. Jed crushed it, the crack of the ball meeting his bat sounding explosive, and it sailed off into the afternoon sky. Hank whipped around, staring at it, willing it to go foul; by a miracle it did, drifting too far left and disappearing into the woods beyond.

"Another one just like that," Jed told him. "I'll straighten it out."

Hank rubbed his new baseball hard, feeling its raised stitches, trying to calm his nerves.

"Blow it by him," Skip said; he'd taken Hank's place at shortstop. "Strike that loudmouthed asshole out!"

Hank toed the pitching rubber, staring at the catcher's mitt. He took a deep breath, went into his short wind-up, and let loose of the baseball, sending it whistling toward the plate. Jed's muscles tensed as he swung with all of his considerable might, his arms fully extended. For a moment, it felt to Hank as if time stood still, but then it raced forward, the ball arriving where it was supposed to, safely in the catcher's mitt, Jed's bat hitting nothing but air.

He'd struck him out.

Now Hank's team had one last chance to

tie the score, maybe even go for the win. Things started poorly with two quick outs while Hank was still several batters away from getting his chance. Then their fortunes turned. A bloop single dropped in front of an outfielder. A wild pitch advanced the runner. Skip was up next and lashed a hard hit past the diving third baseman, allowing his teammate to race around the bags and just beat the throw home, kicking up a cloud of dust. They had tied it up. Yet another hit moved Skip around to third, ninety feet away from scoring the winning run. A walk followed, loading the bases.

And Hank was up to bat.

It was obvious to him that Jed was gassed, his arm tired from all the pitches it had thrown, but unlike Skip, he showed no sign of giving up the baseball; it wasn't like any of his flunkies was going to ask for it. Instead, he furiously kicked at the mound as if it had insulted him. Climbing up on the pitching rubber, he scowled toward the plate, not wanting to back down.

Just toss it up here and I'll do the rest . . .

"Knock it outta here!" Skip shouted from down the line.

Hank knew that this was his big chance. He could win the game. No matter what Skip said, he wasn't looking to hit a homer.

All he had to do was make solid contact with the ball, and he felt certain that something good would happen. Keeping his hands loose on the bat, he watched as Jed went into his windup, came toward the plate, let loose, and —

The ball hit him in the ribs.

"Take that, you no-good son of a bitch!" Jed yelled.

Hank stood there, staring, as hot pain began shooting across his side. They'd won the game, the winning run scored because he had been hit, but he didn't give a damn. Anger flooded him and Hank made no effort to hold it back. Instead, he embraced it. He was dimly aware of Skip shouting, still trying to play peacemaker, but Hank wasn't listening. Next thing he knew, he was at the mound, his fists flying, hitting Jed Ringer as hard as he could. A punch landed on his chin, then someone slammed into his back. Fortunately for Hank, not everyone who was rushing to join in the fight was there to hurt him. He kept brawling, so angry that he hardly felt anything. Incredibly, in the midst of the brawl, Hank was reminded of what had happened with Gwen.

Even when he won the game, he somehow ended up losing.

CHAPTER NINE

Gwen lifted her face to the afternoon sun, reveling in its warmth. Three days had passed since she'd nearly drowned in the river, and every single one of them had been spent cooped up in her parents' house. It had been comforting having her mother close by, bringing her meals and anything else she might need, but it'd been a little suffocating, too. Finally, when she'd regained much of her strength, the urge to go outside and stretch her legs, to breathe fresh air, to be well and truly alone had become too powerful for Gwen to ignore.

"Are you sure you're feeling up to it?" Meredith had asked.

If I stay here one minute longer, I'm going to burst! Gwen had wanted to scream, but instead she had kissed her mother's cheek and headed out the door.

Oddly enough, Gwen found herself retracing the steps she'd taken the night of her accident. In the daylight, she noticed things that hadn't been visible during the storm, like the Levitts' new garage and that Yvonne Walker had repainted her house, going from white to green.

Standing at the intersection of Maple and Roosevelt, she once again looked at the burned-down house she'd seen just after arriving back in town. Stan Nunn's home remained nothing but charred wreckage. Even after the downpour, the smell of burnt wood continued to cling to the air. Gwen thought about taking out her new notebook to write down a few observations, but in the end she decided against it. She didn't want to stay still for long.

Still, even as she continued on her way, her thoughts were slowly but steadily drawn away from her surroundings.

Gwen couldn't stop thinking about Kent.

Just as Kent had promised, he had called once he'd arrived back in Chicago and continued to keep his word the following night. He had rambled on and on, his voice rising with excitement as he overwhelmed her with the details of his court case. It was only at the very end of their conversation that he'd bothered to ask how she was feeling. But then last night, at the appointed time, the phone had stayed silent. At first

Gwen had brushed it off, figuring that Kent was running late, that he would still call. Even her mother had joined in making excuses for him, declaring that whatever it was that was keeping him had to be important. Gwen wasn't so sure. In the end, the clock had kept ticking, the hour hand relentlessly moving forward, until she'd finally given up and gone to bed. When she'd woken this morning, Gwen hadn't been angry, not really, more disappointed. *This* was why she hadn't accepted Kent's proposal. *This* was why she worried about ever becoming a writer. *This* was why she sometimes wondered whether she would be the most important part of his life.

And then there was Hank Ellis . . .

Ever since her mother had told her to forget about him, Gwen couldn't help but do the opposite. She had plenty of questions and no answers. Why had Hank jumped into the raging river, risking his own life to save hers? How had he felt when her father ordered him out of their house? Had he really been responsible for his brother's death? Gwen even wondered what Hank looked like. In those hazy moments after he'd pulled her from the water, she hadn't gotten a good look at him before falling unconscious. She had continued to try to talk with her parents about him, but every question she asked was met with a frown or a short answer. Gwen could see that her father, in particular, was growing increasingly annoyed that she wasn't letting the matter drop.

"No daughter of mine needs to bother herself with a man like that!" he'd loudly declared before returning to his newspaper.

But for Gwen, it wasn't that simple. Her parents' evasiveness only made Hank *more* interesting, like a mystery she needed to solve. The writer inside her grew curious. She wanted to ask questions, to learn truths or, at the very least, to have a face to go with his name. Deep down, though, Gwen knew that she couldn't let go so easily.

She strolled down Main Street, glancing in store windows, waving to people she knew, genuinely enjoying her day. Gwen was just wondering whether she should stop in the diner for a bite of lunch when the door to the drugstore opened and revealed a very familiar face.

"Sandy!" she shouted with joy.

Sandy Pedersen was her oldest, dearest friend. She hadn't changed much since the last time Gwen had seen her. Sandy was short, with expressive green eyes, auburn hair that barely touched her shoulders, and a smile bright enough to rival the sun. But there *was* something incredibly different about her, a detail far too obvious to miss.

She was very, very pregnant.

Sandy's large belly strained so hard against the buttons of her blouse that it looked as if they might pop off at any moment. Even though her mother had told her that Sandy was expecting, Gwen was still surprised. But Sandy's bulging stomach didn't deter her from excitedly wrapping her arms around her old friend.

"Gwen!" Sandy exclaimed. "I heard you were back! I'm sorry I haven't come over or called, but . . ." she said, then stepped back to show off her belly. "I have a lot on my plate these days."

"I can see that," Gwen agreed, unable to look away.

Seeing her interest, Sandy said, "You can touch it if you want."

"Are you sure?"

Sandy laughed. "Don't worry. I won't crack like an egg!"

Not quite able to believe Sandy's claim, Gwen gently placed her hand on her friend's swollen belly. It was harder than she expected, almost like stone. Imagining that there was a baby in there made Gwen smile.

"Pretty crazy, isn't it?" Sandy asked.

Gwen could only nod.

Just then, something pushed against her fingers. From the inside. Stunned, Gwen yanked her hand away. "What . . . what was that?" she asked in amazement.

"A kick or a punch," Sandy answered matter-of-factly.

"Does that happen often?"

"All the time. When I'm trying to sleep, when I eat, even walking down the sidewalk." Sandy rubbed her stomach with affection. "He's a feisty little bugger."

"It's a boy?" Gwen exclaimed.

"Well, there's no way to know for certain," her friend admitted. "But John's convinced. Every time he talks to the baby, he calls it 'Junior.' He's bought baseballs, army men, popguns, every last thing a little boy could dream of playing with." Sandy smiled mischievously. "Imagine his surprise if it's a girl."

The mention of her husband made Gwen realize one other thing that had changed. Her friend was no longer Sandy Pedersen; her last name was now Fiderlein. When Gwen had left for school at Worthington, when she'd begun to make a life for herself in Chicago, it wasn't as if time had stood still back in Buckton. Sandy had gotten married, started a family, done all the things she'd talked about doing when they were girls.

But while Sandy's dreams had come true, Gwen doubted that either of them had expected their friendship to drift apart. When Gwen had originally left town, they'd sworn through tears that nothing would change, that they would write and call every chance they had, and, for a while, that's just what they did. But with time, the letters and telephone visits grew less and less frequent. Learning of Sandy's pregnancy from her mother had been another sign that they were no longer as close. But now, seeing her old friend again, Gwen felt as if all the distance between them had vanished, disappearing like so much smoke. For that, she couldn't have been happier.

They moved to the bench in front of Al Lemon's shoe repair shop so that Sandy could get off her feet and sit in the shade of the awning. There, Gwen pressed for details about her pregnancy: if she'd had any unusual food cravings, how she had decorated the baby's nursery, whether they'd chosen a name, and if she was nervous about giving birth. Sandy answered honestly, her responses peppered with laughter. It was obvious she was excited about becoming a mother.

"Enough about me," Sandy finally said. "I want to know what it's like living in Chicago! Is it like the movies and magazines make it out to be?"

Gwen shrugged. "Maybe not *that* exciting."

She talked about her time at Worthington, what it was like to live among so many people, how she'd eventually gotten used to the noise. She spoke of meals eaten at fancy restaurants, the bright lights up and down Michigan Avenue, and even what it was like to push her way onto a crowded train car. She talked about her apartment in the city, rented after she had graduated, small but cozy, a home of its own. Finally she talked about Kent, about how they had met, his important job, and that her parents adored him.

Sandy leaned closer, her voice lowering. "Is he handsome?"

Gwen nodded, a little embarrassed; she didn't want her friend to think she was bragging. "So is John," she added.

The truth was, John Fiderlein and Kent Brookings couldn't have looked more different. Unlike Kent, who was prim, proper, and always impeccably dressed, Sandy's husband was big and boisterous, with broad, muscular shoulders, a man who didn't mind getting his hands dirty.

Sandy laughed. "I don't think you'll see John's face on any movie posters," she said, "but he managed to steal my heart all the same."

"He'll make a wonderful father."

"He most definitely will," her friend said, beaming as she rubbed her swollen belly. "Do you think you and Kent will get married?"

This was the very question Gwen had been struggling to answer. She considered opening up to Sandy, telling her about Kent's proposal, about how she wanted to become a writer, even about how she was willing to give up a man as wonderful as Kent if that's what it took to achieve her dream. But she couldn't do it. Instead, she smiled and nodded. "We'll see."

"I'll be praying for you," Sandy said.

Just then, as Gwen forced herself to match her friend's smile, a thought struck her, one she was unable to keep from voicing.

"What do you know about Hank Ellis?" she asked.

Sandy's expression soured, much like Gwen's mother's had. "Why are you asking about *him*?"

Gwen took a deep breath. "Because the other night, I had an accident . . ."

Starting from when her notebook had been blown out of her hand, she spoke of her harrowing time in the river. As Sandy listened, Gwen recounted how she'd been terrified, certain she was about to die, only to be miraculously pulled from the raging water.

"It wasn't until the next morning that I learned who had rescued me," she finished. "It was Hank."

"Are . . . are you all right?" Sandy managed.

"I am now," Gwen answered. "But if it hadn't been for Hank, I have no doubt that I would've drowned. He saved my life."

"I believe you, of course I do," her friend said, "but it sure flies in the face of what everyone in town says about Hank."

"Because of what happened to his brother?"

Sandy nodded somberly. "Before the accident, most folks in town likely didn't pay Hank much mind. He was always nice enough, but more quiet, something of a loner. But Pete was special," she explained. "Everyone adored him. For him to die like that, especially after what happened to his mother, it caused people to turn on Hank. Now, most can't stand the sight of him. After all, it was his fault Pete died."

"That would explain my father's reaction."

Her pregnant friend's eyes narrowed. "What did he do?"

Gwen related what her mother had told her — that Warren had insinuated Hank might have been responsible for her misfortune, and that her father had eventually thrown him out of the house.

"That's terrible!" Sandy exclaimed. "Even with what happened to his brother, that doesn't mean Hank isn't capable of doing good. Saving your life is nothing short of heroic!"

Gwen was relieved to discover that she wasn't the only person who thought so. "I just wish I'd had the chance to thank him."

"What's stopping you?" Sandy asked.

"My parents would be furious," Gwen replied. "They made it perfectly clear that they don't want me to have anything to do with Hank."

"It's not like you're going to marry the guy! He saved your life! The least you can do is tell him that you're grateful."

"Do you really think I should?" Gwen asked, thinking about how angry her father got at the mere mention of Hank's name.

But Sandy didn't seem concerned. She nodded enthusiastically. "Absolutely," she said. "It would only be polite."

Her friend's certainty began to grow on Gwen. "I suppose I could look up his address in the telephone directory."

"He and his father live off Miller's Road," Sandy added helpfully.

Gwen could see how it would happen. It was simple, really. She would go out to Hank's home, thank him for what he'd done, offer her condolences for Pete's death, and tell him that she was sorry for her father's rude behavior.

That would be that. There was only one problem.

Somehow, she had to convince her father to let her borrow the car.

When Gwen pushed open the door to the Buckton Bakery, she felt like a little girl again. Everything was just as she remembered, as if she'd been there only yesterday. Three glass display cases were lined up side by side, showing off the day's delicacies. On the wall behind, loaves of bread were arranged to catch a customer's eye. A brass cash register sat at one end, its keys worn smooth from decades of being pressed.

But the most familiar thing of all was the smell.

She recognized the richness of butter, the sweetness of sugar, the unmistakable hint of chocolate, a whiff of spices, all wrapped in the warmth of the ovens. Everything mixed together, creating an aroma that made her mouth water.

"Gwennie!" her father shouted as he stepped out of the back room. Flour dusted his hair and clothes. A smudge of chocolate darkened the corner of his mouth, evidence that he'd been sampling his work, trying to get the recipe just right. Even though Warren was messy, Gwen happily embraced him when he came to her with his arms wide. "Now ain't this a surprise! I didn't expect to see you up and about so soon," he said. "You sure you're feelin' up to it?"

"I couldn't take being cooped up in the house anymore," she answered. "I needed to get some fresh air and stretch my legs."

"So you came to see me," her father declared proudly.

"Of course," Gwen said with a laugh. She looked around the bakery. "Everything's just the way I remember it."

"I'm thinkin' of makin' some changes. Maybe add a few —" he began, but abruptly stopped as he glanced at the clock on the wall. "Shoot! I've got somethin' in the oven and don't want it to burn. I'll be right back."

Once her father had left, Gwen bent down in front of the nearest display case for a

161

closer look. Cookies were lined up in rows: chocolate chip, oatmeal, and peanut butter. Sugar doughnuts, cream-filled éclairs, and long johns topped with a maple glaze were arranged on another shelf. She knew from experience that everything tasted as good as it looked. But then, when Gwen glanced at the adjacent case, she frowned; it held a two-tiered wedding cake complete with a miniature bride and groom perched on top, decorated with flowers made of frosting.

Gwen couldn't help but think of Kent.

If she accepted his proposal, in a matter of months she would be wearing a white wedding dress, while he'd don a tuxedo. They would look just like the plastic couple before her. There'd be a big party in celebration, and there would undoubtedly be cake, although Gwen suspected that Kent would probably want something fancier than one of her father's creations.

Once again, she was filled with doubt. Should she marry him?

"Fresh out of the oven," Warren announced, interrupting her troubling thoughts. In his hand was something golden, flaky, and steaming.

Gwen took it and popped it in her mouth. Instantly, she was flooded with amazing flavors. It was so delicious that she closed her eyes, enjoying it.

"I love it!" she gushed with a smile. "This is going to sell like crazy."

"I hope so," her father answered.

"While I'm more than happy to eat such a delicious treat, I have to admit that I stopped by for a reason," Gwen explained. "I wanted to ask you for a favor."

"Name it, sweetie."

"I was wondering if I could borrow the car tomorrow."

"Got something planned?"

"I thought I'd go for a drive, maybe head out of town a ways," she answered, the half-truth uncomfortable. "Go visit some people . . ."

Convinced that her father would see through her weak attempt at concealing her true intentions, that he'd know she wanted to talk to Hank, Gwen steeled herself for another outburst.

Instead, he said, "Sounds good to me. If you're out and about, you really oughta go see Sandy. You can tell her all 'bout the weddin'."

Even as Gwen struggled to smile, she was filled with guilt for misleading her father. She considered coming clean and telling him the truth, explaining that despite his contempt for Hank, she needed to thank him for saving her.

Before she could, Warren added, "Just be careful. You never know if that damned Hank Ellis is out on the roads. He's already bothered you once, which is too often in my book."

"Dad, that isn't —"

But as she started to defend Hank, Gwen was interrupted by a woman entering the bakery.

"Mrs. Spencer!" Warren welcomed his customer. "I made more of those dinner rolls you liked so much. Let me get you some."

Listening to her father, Gwen knew that her intuition had been right; it would've been a huge mistake to tell him the truth. He couldn't understand why she needed to do this, so it would have to stay a secret. Tomorrow, she would drive to Hank's house and thank him, and no one in her family would be any the wiser.

And maybe then I can start figuring out what I'm going to do about Kent . . .

CHAPTER TEN

Hank carried the chair out of the workshop and placed it in the back of his truck, then he leaped up into the bed, securing it in place with rope. Though he doubted it would shift during the drive, he still draped wool blankets over the chair for added protection. After all the work he'd put into it, it'd be a hell of a shame if it got nicked now. He straightened up and looked to the sky. The early-afternoon sun was hot, so Hank pulled out a handkerchief and wiped the sweat from his face.

"Damn it!" he swore with a wince. Lost in thought, he'd absent-mindedly touched his painful bruise.

He hopped down out of the truck and looked at his reflection in its side mirror. The skin around his cheekbone was mottled an ugly mix of purple and brown where Jed Ringer had landed a clean blow. While Hank had managed a few punches of his own, bruising his knuckles and hopefully making the loudmouth's mug even uglier, it was little consolation.

You're a damn fool for letting him get to you . . .

The whole drive home, Skip had talked a mile a minute, laughing about what had happened. He reveled in their winning the game and even seemed to have enjoyed the brawl, bloody nose and all. Hank had let him talk, nodding occasionally, but on the inside he had been embarrassed. By reacting the way he had, letting his fists do the talking, he'd reinforced the stereotype people had about him. If anything, he'd made things worse.

Hank Ellis is a hothead.

Acting like that, it's no wonder he got his brother killed.

It's best to stay far away from him.

Once Skip left, Hank had gone to his workshop and tried to use his tools to take his mind off his troubles. Early this morning, before the sun had begun coloring the horizon, he'd finished the chair. A couple of hours later, he had telephoned the customer and made plans to drop it off in the afternoon.

Hank stretched in the sun. Usually work gave him peace of mind, but last night, even as he chiseled in the final details on the chair's headpiece, a persistent thought kept intruding. No matter how hard he tried pushing it away, he hadn't succeeded for long.

He could not stop thinking about Gwen Foster.

Maybe it was because he'd talked about her with Skip. Maybe it was because every time he closed his eyes, he saw her lying on the bank of the Sawyer, lit by the moon, her hair wet against her face. Or maybe it was because rescuing her had been the first good thing he'd done in a long time. Whatever the reason, he couldn't help but wonder what Gwen would've thought of his fight with Jed. Sadly, he suspected he knew the answer.

She'd think her father was right about me. She'd think I was dangerous, someone to stay far *away from.*

Hank shook his head. He was a fool for thinking about her. It was pointless anyway. He was never going to see Gwen Foster again.

Back in his workshop, Hank looked at the clock. He still had an hour before he needed to be in Mansfield to deliver the chair. If he left now, he'd arrive too early, so instead he flipped on the radio, grabbed his broom, and started sweeping up wood shavings, bent nails, and other debris from his work. He was humming along to "You Belong to Me" by Jo Stafford when he heard tires crunch the gravel of his drive.

Hank turned, a curious look on his face. He wasn't expecting anyone. Skip hadn't said anything about coming over and his father was still inside, sleeping off the previous night's drinking.

So who was it?

Outside, he didn't recognize the car, a black sedan, and couldn't see in the windshield because of the sun's glare. So when the door opened and the driver stepped out, Hank was stunned to see that it was the very person he couldn't stop thinking about.

It was Gwen.

This is crazy, this is crazy, this is crazy . . .

Half a mile from Hank Ellis's home, Gwen considered turning around. It was the same thought she'd had five minutes earlier, and five minutes before that, all the way back to when she'd turned the key in the ignition of her parents' car. She felt nervous, as if she was doing something she shouldn't, and was afraid of getting caught. She supposed that it had a lot to do with the fact that she'd outright lied to her father about why she

168

wanted to borrow the car. It made her feel guilty.

To make matters worse, Kent still hadn't called. Last night, sitting in the living room while her mother read and her father listened to a radio program, Gwen had had to fight the urge to pace the floor. She looked at the telephone intently, as if she was willing it to ring. So much between them remained unresolved that it was becoming a burdensome weight to bear. She'd tried to smile, to act as if it hadn't bothered her, but from the looks Meredith kept giving her, she supposed she hadn't done a very good job of it. The more time that had passed, the angrier Gwen had grown, mostly with herself, but also at Kent. He had put her into a position where she'd lied to her parents. Because of him, she had to pretend everything was fine, that she was excited to get married. It frustrated her that while Kent seemed to have no trouble forgetting about her, she couldn't return his disinterest.

Gwen rounded a curve and saw Hank's place ahead, right where Sandy had said it would be. She lifted her foot off the gas pedal and the car began to slow, though she wondered if she shouldn't put it back and zoom on down the road.

The only thing crazier than coming all the way out here would be to drive past without stopping.

She had to speak with Hank, to thank him for what he'd done. It wouldn't take long, a few minutes at most. Then she could get back to trying to make sense of her frustrating, confusing life.

Gwen turned down the gravel drive, passed the main house, and stopped in front of an old truck. There was another building at the rear of the property. She squinted through the windshield and saw a man standing between a pair of open doors, watching her, but the afternoon sun was too bright for her to see his face clearly. With her heart speeding, Gwen took a deep breath and got out of the car.

She walked toward the man as he remained in the doorway, the sun hot on her skin, her blouse sticking to her back with sweat, and offered him a smile. It wasn't returned. She felt reasonably sure that she knew who he was, but when she said his name, it came out sounding like a question. "Hank?"

"Afternoon, Gwen," he answered, friendly enough.

Hank Ellis wasn't what Gwen had expected. Not at all. Where Pete had been tall

170

and thin, handsome enough in a lanky sort of way, Hank was broad across the shoulders and chest, his muscular arms obvious in his short-sleeved shirt. While she'd always thought of Pete as a boy, his older brother's features were undoubtedly those of a man: piercing blue eyes regarded her closely, so intent that she couldn't look away; his sandy-blond hair was a bit long and stubble peppered his cheeks; his voice, deep yet unthreatening, had caught her off guard. Even the bruising on his cheek, likely the result of his daring plunge into the Sawyer, made him look rugged, as if he was a hero in some Hollywood picture. Hank was rough around the edges, even a bit unkempt, and nothing like Kent, but there was no denying that she found him handsome. For as quick as her heart had pounded before, it now beat even faster.

"I . . . I hope you don't mind my dropping by like this," Gwen began, trying to keep her voice steady and her intrigue in him hidden.

He answered with a short shake of his head.

All morning Gwen had practiced the things she'd wanted to say, wondering just how you thanked someone for saving your life, but now, standing in front of him, looking into Hank's eyes, she struggled to find the words.

Aware of the silence growing between them, Gwen willed herself to speak, hesitantly at first, but then with more confidence. "I wanted to thank you," she told him. "You saved my life."

"I did what had to be done," he answered simply.

"But not everyone would have," Gwen said. "Diving into the Sawyer River isn't the smartest thing on the best of days. With the water as high as it was, you could've drowned right along with me."

Hank nodded once, looking like he wasn't too comfortable with her praise. "I'm just glad you're all right."

"I also wanted to apologize for the way my father treated you," she told him, the words sincere. "He was wrong to speak to you the way he did."

"It didn't bother me any," Hank said, but he frowned slightly, making Gwen wonder if he wasn't being a bit dishonest with her.

"He should've thanked you from the bottom of his heart."

"Your father's no different from everyone else in town. When they look at me, all they see is the guy who killed his brother. Even if I *had* died pulling you out of the river, it wouldn't have changed a thing. I'll always be the bad guy."

"Not to me, you aren't," she disagreed defiantly, unable to believe that *anyone* wouldn't think him a hero.

Surprisingly, her declaration seemed to break through Hank's cool exterior. A hint of a smile played at the corners of his mouth and his eyes softened as he looked at her.

Another silence settled over them, but Gwen didn't find this one uncomfortable. Truth was, Hank Ellis was becoming more and more interesting with time. She was convinced that there was more to him than he was letting on. It was like he was a locked door; all she needed to do was find the right key. The writer in her wanted to know his story, all of it, the good and the bad.

For the first time since she'd arrived, Hank's eyes left her. Gwen followed his gaze and saw that he was looking at a clock on the wall.

"Are you sure I'm not interrupting?" she asked.

Hank shook his head. "You're fine. I've got something I need to drop off in Mansfield, but I don't have to leave just yet."

"All the way in Mansfield?"

He nodded over her shoulder at the truck. "I just finished carving a chair for a customer and made plans to drop it off this afternoon."

Gwen looked around, only now taking in her surroundings. They stood in the doorway of a large workroom full of tables; many of them were littered with tools, pieces of wood, paintbrushes, and projects in various stages of completion. A pile of wood shavings had been swept up near their feet. Gwen was surprised to be noticing it only now; it made her realize that she had been so intent on Hank, so captivated by his voice and very presence, that she'd been oblivious to everything else around her.

"Is this where you work?"

"Most days, and more nights than I'd like," he said.

A memory stirred inside Gwen of a long-ago fair in Buckton's city park. "Wasn't your father a woodcarver, too?"

Hank stiffened. He bit the inside of his lip and didn't immediately answer. "You're right. He was," he finally said, "but it's been a while since he's picked up his tools. Fortunately, I was at his elbow for as long as I can remember, watching, learning how to carve, so I've been able to follow along after him."

"You were his apprentice?" Gwen asked, thinking about all the tricks of the trade she'd learned from years spent at her father's bakery.

"Something like that."

"Are you as good as he was?"

He chuckled, a warm, easy sound. "In some ways, sure, I'd say I'm his equal, but in others I still have work to do."

Gwen looked back at Hank's truck. "You can make a chair?"

"Indeed, I can."

"That sounds plenty hard to me."

"Putting it together was easy. The tough part is carving in the details on the headpiece. One mistake and you'll likely have to start over."

Curiosity got the better of Gwen. "Can I see it?" she asked.

"Sure," Hank replied.

He led the way to the truck and pulled a pair of wool blankets off the chair. Its finish gleamed in the sunlight. Gwen leaned close, marveling at what Hank had done. The chair's back was practically alive in flowered vines, twisting this way and that, each end culminating in a bloom. Looking at his craftsmanship, she was struck by the realization that it was a work of art.

"It's beautiful," she said a little breathlessly.

Her compliment changed him. He smiled

at her, showing just a hint of teeth, and Gwen saw shallow dimples beneath his whiskers. Staring at Hank, his hair glowing as brightly as the chair in the afternoon sun, Gwen felt herself being taken in by him, unable to look away even if she'd wanted to, which she most certainly did not. At that moment, she found him so good-looking that it almost seemed dangerous.

"Thank you," Hank said, the sound of his voice breaking the powerful spell he'd cast on her.

Gwen looked back at the chair, her thoughts racing. She could feel her heart begin to beat faster and faster. She wondered if she might be blushing, then silently prayed that she wasn't.

"Would you like to come with me?"

She turned, surprised. "Come with you where?"

"To Mansfield," Hank answered, leaning leisurely against the side of the truck, his hand only inches from hers. "I just thought that if there wasn't somewhere else you needed to be, you might like to ride along. It won't take too long, a couple of hours." He paused. "But if you've got other plans, then —"

"I'd love to come," Gwen said quickly, cutting him off. Her boldness surprised no one more than herself.

"All right, then," Hank said, clearly pleased that she'd accepted. "Let me grab a couple of things and then we can go."

Gwen watched him return to the workshop, disappearing when he passed from sunlight to shadow, leaving her alone with her turbulent thoughts.

What am I doing?! I came here to thank him for saving my life and now I'm going with him all the way to Mansfield!

The more Gwen considered it, the more conflicted she became. On the one hand, she was shocked that she'd agreed to be alone with him, more or less a complete stranger. She was already supposed to be heading for home. But she didn't want to leave his company, not yet. Maybe she would feel differently after their trip. Maybe she'd even come to regret wasting the time. Maybe she was getting nervous and excited for nothing. But there was no way to know for certain unless she went. Still, in the back of her head, she heard a familiar refrain, one she'd been thinking on the drive over.

This is crazy, this is crazy, this is crazy . . .

CHAPTER ELEVEN

This is crazy, this is crazy, this is crazy . . .

Hank drove toward Mansfield, just as he'd done dozens of times before. He crossed the covered bridge over Milton's Creek. He passed through Sunnyside, a wisp of a town made up of a couple of houses and a makeshift post office. He looked up at Eunice Weber's weathervane, still in the breezeless afternoon, although it was covered in so much rust that it would scarcely have moved in a thunderstorm. In almost every way, this trip was the same as all those others. But this one had one huge difference.

Gwen Foster was sitting beside him.

Every once in a while, he stole a glance at her. Gwen leaned against the door, her dark hair caught by the breeze from the open window, forcing her to occasionally tuck a few unruly strands behind her ear. She seemed content to sit quietly, watching the countryside zip past. She was as beautiful a woman as he'd ever laid eyes on.

When Gwen had arrived, Hank had been taken aback, unsure what to say or do. He hadn't considered that she might want to see him, to thank him for what he'd done. Watching her walk toward him, his heart racing, he had wondered whether she'd told her parents where she was but had quickly dismissed the thought. In the end, it didn't matter. All he cared about was that she was here, with him. Still, at first it had been awkward. But as they talked, he'd found himself more at ease, enjoying her company. By the time Gwen had complimented his chair, the smile she flashed making his heart pound, he'd known that he didn't want their time together to end, not so soon. The boldness of asking her to go with him to Mansfield had surprised even him, but once he'd spoken the words, he couldn't have taken them back. Fortunately, she'd accepted.

And now here they were . . .

"So what's it like living in Chicago?" Hank asked, wanting to hear her voice again, to know more about her.

"Busier than I could ever have imagined," she answered. "I still don't understand how there can be so many people in one place. Most days it feels like I can't turn around without bumping into someone. It was a little overwhelming at first, but over time, I suppose I got used to it."

"The biggest city I've ever been to is Cincinnati, and that was plenty large enough for me. All the buildings, the cars honking. I couldn't wait to leave. Give me open country any day."

"It's not *all* bad there."

"How so?"

"There's always something to do," Gwen explained. "If I want to go to a movie, a play, or a concert, I have plenty to choose from. If I have a hankering for some particular food, odds are I can find a restaurant that serves it. There are museums, an aquarium, libraries, and boat rides on Lake Michigan. I even went to a baseball game last year."

"Which team?" Hank asked, curious.

Gwen thought about it. "I don't really remember."

"Where was it at?"

"What was the name . . . oh yeah, it was Wrigley Stadium."

"Wrigley *Field,*" he corrected her.

"That's it! It was a nice enough day and the people around me were awfully excited, but I thought the grass growing on the walls was kind of ridiculous."

"It's not grass, it's ivy!"

The sound of their laughter filled the truck's cab. Hank might have *hated* the Chicago Cubs, but the fact that Gwen had been to see one of their games impressed him. It even made him feel a little envious.

"Does your fiancé like baseball?" he asked.

For days, Hank's conversation with Kent Brookings had been roaming around in his head. He'd disliked the man almost instantly, though there was clearly something about him that Gwen found attractive; after all, she'd agreed to marry him. Hank still remembered how Kent had initially been incapable of helping, frozen with shock. He recalled how the expensively dressed man had offered money for rescuing his fiancée. Worst of all, he could still hear the almost bragging way Kent had commented on wanting to see Gwen without her clothes. It made Hank sick to his stomach.

Still, his disgust didn't change a thing. Gwen and Kent would be married. Knowing that, accepting it, made his attraction to her seem pointless. Nothing would come of it. At least, that's what he'd been telling himself.

And that was why her reaction to what he'd said was so surprising.

Immediately, Gwen's smile vanished. She looked away, her gaze shifting out her window. When she finally spoke, her voice was so soft that he could barely hear her. "I'm not engaged."

Hank looked at her, at the road, and then back again. "Wait . . ." he began, not understanding, "then who did I talk to that night?"

"Kent," she answered.

"I thought he was your fiancé."

"He isn't."

"Does he know that?"

Finally Gwen turned to him, her expression serious. "Kent sort of proposed without proposing . . ."

"That doesn't make sense," Hank admitted.

"I agree," Gwen replied. "But Kent doesn't see any problem with it. Even though I never actually answered, even if he didn't really ask, he just assumed that I'd accepted." She paused. "So did my parents."

"Hang on. Does that mean you're going to marry him or not?"

"I don't know."

Hank shook his head. He was more confused than ever. "Pardon me for saying so, but isn't that something you ought to be sure of?"

"There are plenty of reasons why I should marry Kent," Gwen began. "He's kind, smart, and well-spoken. My family adores him. He's already an accomplished lawyer. Someday he might even be made a partner at his firm. Everything he does, he succeeds at." But then she sighed. "Unfortunately, there are reasons, a few in particular, for me to turn him down . . ."

Hank waited, thinking that Gwen might explain, but she remained silent. Though it was hard, he chose to do the same. Clearly this was a personal matter, one that was still unsettled, and he didn't want to pry.

But he'd learned something, too. Gwen's relationship with Kent wasn't as rosy as he'd thought. Maybe her agreeing to come along with him wasn't such an odd decision after all. An unexpected feeling coursed through him.

He recognized it right away. It was hope.

Gwen thought that Mansfield looked a lot like Buckton. As they drove down its long Main Street, she saw a diner, a bank, the police station, a post office, and a movie theater. There was even a bakery, a small storefront nestled between a hardware store and a shoe repair shop; seeing it caused her another pang of guilt for having deceived her parents.

But it was too late to turn back now.

"We're almost there," Hank told her. "Just a couple more blocks."

He drove into a neighborhood, the street lined with tall elms whose branches provided plenty of shade from the afternoon sun. Children raced down the sidewalk playing a game, shouting and laughing; Gwen waved to them when they drove past. Hank eventually pulled into the driveway of an enormous Victorian and turned off the engine.

"Before we get out, there's something I need to tell you," he said.

"What's that?" Gwen asked curiously.

"The woman I made the chair for, well, she's . . . she's a little . . ." Hank faltered. "Let's just say that she can take some getting used to."

"In what way?"

He gave her a mischievous smile. "You'll see."

While Hank lifted the chair from the back of the truck, Gwen stretched her legs and thought about their conversation during the drive. Hank had been surprisingly easy to talk to. Still, she hadn't expected to be so forthcoming, especially about her relationship with Kent, but hearing him referred to as her fiancé had made her angry. Fortunately, when she'd stopped talking, Hank

184

had respected her silence and hadn't pried.

"There you are!" a voice suddenly shouted.

Gwen looked up to see an old woman emerge from the house and hurry as quickly as she could down the steps toward them. She was thin and quite frail-looking, her shoulders stooped, her skin a mess of wrinkles. She was dressed in a bright-pink blouse and white slacks, with lipstick that matched her shirt. Her curly hair had been dyed midnight black, in great contrast to the white of her eyebrows. Bracelets jangled at her wrists and every finger on either hand was festooned with rings. Hank met her and the woman flung her tiny arms around his muscular neck, hugging him tightly.

"You're right on time!" the woman declared.

"I wouldn't think of being late," Hank answered. "Come here, there's someone I'd like you to meet."

He brought the older woman over. "Gwen," he began, "this is Mrs. Winnifred Holland. She's probably my best customer."

"I'd better be!" the woman said with a chuckle. Taking Gwen gently by the hand, she added, "Please, my dear, call me Freddie."

Gwen introduced herself. "It's a pleasure

185

to meet you."

"So," Freddie began, smiling brightly as she looked up at Gwen, "I take it that you're his sweetheart."

"No!" she exclaimed, louder than intended, which made her feel so uncomfortable that she was sure her face was the same color as Freddie's blouse.

But Hank didn't seem the least bit put out. "It's not like that," he told the older woman. "Gwen went to school with Pete."

For a moment, Gwen wondered if that was indeed how he saw her, if all she was to him was a figure from his past, tied to his dead brother.

"That's too bad," Freddie said with a frown, looking a bit disappointed, before leaning closer to Gwen and lowering her voice. "I think you should reconsider. He's a rascal but he'd be a fine catch."

"Do you want to see your chair?" Hank interrupted, oblivious to what was being said about him.

"I do!" the old woman exclaimed, clasping her hands together in glee.

Gwen followed them in a daze, her thoughts spinning.

Freddie's face lost twenty years as she inspected her new piece of furniture. She walked around the chair, occasionally touching it, marveling at all the details. Hank watched with obvious pride in his craftsmanship, his muscular arms folded across his chest.

"It's exactly how I had imagined it! Better, even!" Freddie exclaimed. She took Hank by the hand, her small fingers practically disappearing in his. "This is the fourth thing I've hired him to make and each makes me happier than the last. There's more to him than meets the eye."

"How about I take it inside so you can see how it looks with the others," Hank offered. Freddie agreed, so he lifted it and headed for the stairs.

"Then we can talk about the next thing I have in mind," the old woman said. "I want a chest of drawers for my napkins and tablecloths. I have more lying around than I know what to do with! Oh, and I made lemonade!"

Watching the two of them together, Gwen could see the dutiful way Hank spoke to Freddie, as well as how much she cared for him in return. She then thought about the horrible things she'd heard about Hank, from the hateful words of her father to the warnings of her mother, and even Sandy's gossip. What she was seeing simply didn't match. *This* was the dangerous man she was supposed to stay away from? *This* was the drunkard whose irresponsibility had gotten his poor brother killed and earned him the disgust of everyone in Buckton?

Right then, Gwen realized that Freddie was right.

There was *far* more to Hank Ellis than she could ever have imagined.

They left Mansfield with the sun beginning its slow fall toward the horizon. Freddie had filled them with cookies and lemonade. Hank had sketched out a rough drawing of the chest she wanted, this one to be decorated with a flock of birds soaring across the front of each drawer. When it had been time to go, the old woman had hugged them both tightly, then waved from the porch as they drove off.

"Freddie is wonderful," Gwen said.

"She's a heck of a lady, all right," Hank agreed. "Now do you understand what I meant when I said she was a little different?"

"She's eccentric, that's all. She reminds me of my aunt Samantha."

"Really?"

Gwen nodded. "She's the same kind of colorful soul, walking to the beat of her own drummer, not caring what anyone else thinks."

He shrugged. "That sounds an awful lot like Freddie."

"How did you meet her?"

Before answering, Hank turned onto the main road headed back to Buckton, his arm lying lazily along the open window, a hand loosely gripping the wheel. Through a break in the trees, sunlight flooded the cab, coloring his skin such a bright yellow that Gwen had to look away.

"It was at an art fair a while back," he explained. "I go around to towns in the area, Vicksburg, Thornton, Quinn, and the like, and set up a few pieces of furniture — a table, some chairs, or a dresser, whatever I've been working on. Freddie came by and liked what she saw. We started talking, she wanted a bookcase, and the next thing I know I'm making regular trips to Mansfield."

"She sounds like a good customer."

"The best. I just wish I had a dozen more like her."

It was faint, but Gwen thought she heard a touch of dissatisfaction in his voice. Tentatively, she asked, "Is it hard making a living this way?"

Hank shrugged. "Some times are better

189

than others, but what's the hardest is that I have to look so far and wide for a sale." He paused. "Most folks in Buckton would rather spit on me than give me a dime. I understand, but that doesn't make it any easier."

Gwen was quiet for a moment, weighing whether she should voice the words in her head. Finally she plunged ahead. "I'm sorry about Pete."

Ever since she'd made up her mind to thank Hank for saving her, Gwen had wondered whether she should mention his brother. She worried that he might get upset or ask her to leave. Undoubtedly it was a sore subject. Still, ignoring Pete's death felt wrong. In the end, she decided that even if Hank was responsible for what had happened, that didn't mean she couldn't be sorry, for the both of them. She'd gotten the chance, and taken it.

In answer, Hank nodded, then fell silent.

Gwen thought back to the first leg of their journey. When talking about Kent had grown uncomfortable, Hank had respected her silence and hadn't pried, so now she did the same for him.

But even though she chose not to ask more about Pete, that didn't mean she wanted to stop talking altogether.

"What's it like to work with your hands?" she asked.

Just like that, the chill that had descended over Hank thawed. "It's peaceful," he told her, flashing a wisp of a smile. "I usually start with an idea, then lay out the tools I'll need, all in preparation to carve that first notch in the wood." By now, he was gesturing with his free hand, excited to talk about his profession and passion. "It's funny, but most jobs, I still make plenty of mistakes. I cut up my hands or find out that what I want to do isn't possible. But when I'm done, when I see someone's face light up like Freddie's did, it makes all the troubles worth it." Hank paused. "Still, days like today are hard."

"What do you mean?"

"I have a tough time letting pieces go," Hank explained. "I always see more that I could have done, another knock of the chisel, another detail." He chuckled. "You probably think I sound completely nuts."

But Gwen understood all too well. She thought about her writing, about how she agonized over each word, frowning as she took one out, adding another in its place, all in an attempt to make it perfect, working and working until she was finally satisfied. "I know *exactly* what you mean."

"You do?" Hank asked curiously.

Gwen wondered if she was revealing too much of herself to someone she hardly knew. She considered lying, making up some story to cover her misstep, but somewhere, deep inside, she felt that there was something about Hank she trusted, a part of her that understood she could tell him the truth.

"I want to be a writer," she said simply.

In the brief interlude before he answered, Gwen realized that she was holding her breath, waiting for his reaction.

"Even though I've always worked with my hands, they've never been much good for writing," Hank explained. "But because of that, I've got nothing but respect for those who can. Are you any good?"

She nodded. "I think so." She told him about submitting her article to a magazine and the joy of seeing it published. She talked of how everything she saw held a story, no detail too small to ignore. Once she started talking, it was as if the gates had been thrown open and all that she'd been holding back came pouring out. She even spoke of her journals, of how one being blown from her hands had ultimately led to his rescuing her from the river.

"Did you manage to grab it?" Hank asked.

Gwen shook her head. "I'm afraid it's gone for good."

"So what happens next? Do you want to write a novel, work at a newspaper, teach, what?"

"I'm not sure," she admitted. "All I know for certain is that when I have a pencil and a piece of paper in front of me, I'm happy."

"Kent must be awfully proud of you."

In for a penny, in for a pound . . .

"No, he isn't," Gwen said with a frown. "Kent's old-fashioned. He thinks that a woman's place is at home, raising children, taking care of the house, and supporting her husband. He doesn't think that I should have a career."

"Is this why you haven't agreed to marry him?"

"Yes," she replied truthfully.

Hank was silent for a while, the only sound coming from the countryside rushing by outside their windows.

"Kent's got it wrong," he finally said. "My folks didn't agree on everything. They argued from time to time, just like any husband and wife, especially with two boys underfoot, but they always supported each other, no matter what. I reckon your parents are the same way." Hank looked over at her, his eyes strong yet gentle. "If you want to be a writer, you need someone by your side who will help you succeed, not hold you back." He paused. "This is just me talking, but if I was you, I'd have some serious thinking to do."

Gwen didn't answer. She didn't have to. She knew that Hank was right. In a way, she'd known since the moment Kent "announced" their engagement. Watching the tall grass that filled the ditch blur by, she understood that she had to do something, though she wasn't exactly sure what. A decision felt just out of reach yet tantalizingly close. Gwen hazarded a glance at Hank, but his attention had returned to the road. He'd been honest, telling her things he had to know she might not want to hear. But she hadn't been angry. She was grateful.

It was true. Hank Ellis was full of surprises.

Gwen sat behind the wheel of her parents' car, the engine idling softly, her hands on the steering wheel, but she made no move to put it in gear. Hank leaned against her door, an arm draped across the roof, flashing an easy smile. Outside the windshield, the sun was brushing the treetops, painting the sky a darker shade with every passing minute. Odds were it would be dark by the time she finally got home.

"I had a nice time this afternoon," she told him.

"Me, too," he replied. "I enjoyed the company. It's a lot more fun making that drive with someone along for the ride. Talking to myself gets boring."

Hank laughed easily, a sound Gwen was starting to like. She thought back to how nervous she'd been on the drive over, how she had even considered turning around and going home. She was glad she'd seen it through.

She smiled. "Thanks again for saving my life."

"Any time." Hank made like he was going to step away, but then stopped and leaned closer. "Would it be all right if I saw you again? I know you'll be going back to Chicago soon, but I thought that if you were still here in a day or so, we could get a cup of coffee and talk some more."

Gwen's heart sped up. She nodded. "I'd like that."

Another moment of silence stretched between them. Finally Hank pushed himself away from the car. "I'll be seeing you."

With a slightly shaking hand, Gwen put the car in gear and began backing down the drive. Hank watched her go. Starting for home, she realized that there at the end, before he'd stepped away, she had expected something else to happen.

She thought he'd been about to kiss her.

Gwen wondered what it meant that she wouldn't have minded if he had.

CHAPTER TWELVE

When Gwen entered the kitchen through the side door off the driveway, both of her parents were waiting for her. Her mother looked up from the small table where she'd been flipping through the pages of a magazine. Her father froze in midstride, turning at the sound of the door's hinges. It looked as if he'd been pacing.

"There she is!" Warren declared. "Where have you been?"

"You were gone an awfully long time, Gwendolyn," her mother added.

Gwen didn't need to look at the clock on the wall to know that they were right. It *was* late. When she'd first gone to see Hank, she had assumed that her visit would be short. But that was before he'd invited her to Mansfield, before she'd accepted, before they had talked . . . Now the sun had gone to sleep for the night, leaving thousands of stars to fill the cloudless sky in its place.

Gwen had been forced to drive the last couple of blocks with the car's headlights on.

"I'm sorry," she answered sheepishly. "I must have lost track of time."

"That's one heck of an understatement," her father huffed with a frown. "We ate without you. By now, yours is likely cold as ice."

"I can heat it up," Meredith said, getting up from the table to turn on the oven. As she passed her daughter, she gave Gwen a kiss on the forehead. "We were worried, that's all. Isn't that right, Warren?"

Her husband gave a grunt and a nod.

"He's just mad because he had to walk home from the bakery."

Gwen's stomach fell. When she'd borrowed the car, her father had had only one condition, that she be back in time to pick him up from work. Somewhere during her drive with Hank, it had slipped her mind.

"I spend all day on my feet, bakin' or helpin' customers," Warren explained, sounding a little put out. "When it's quittin' time, all I want is to sit on my duff and drive home. I've earned it!"

"Oh, Dad," Gwen said, slipping her arms around his ample waist to give him a hug. "I'm so sorry. I forgot."

Warren Foster had a gruff exterior and could talk a blue streak, as Hank well knew, but the one person who had always been able to cut through his bluster was his daughter. Fortunately, this time proved to be no exception.

"It's all right, Gwennie," her father replied, giving her a gentle squeeze. "It's like your mother said, I was just startin' to worry. All that matters is that you're home. So tell me, did you have a good time?"

"I did," she answered truthfully.

"Where all did you go? Who all did you see?"

"I . . . I just drove around . . ."

Her father frowned. "For all the time you were gone, I was hopin' for more details than that."

Flustered, Gwen said, "I drove through some neighborhoods, down Main Street, across the river, up into the countryside, all over, really."

I went to see Hank Ellis.

He asked me to go with him to Mansfield, so I did.

I had a great time talking to him and didn't really want it to end.

Gwen had already lied to her parents enough. She didn't want to fib further, but she couldn't be completely honest with them, either.

Fortunately, her mother chose that moment to place a plate of food on the table, giving her a bit of time to collect herself. She took a seat and her parents sat down opposite her.

"Did you have a chance to visit Sandy?" Meredith asked.

Gwen shook her head. "Not since yesterday."

"Well if you didn't go see Sandy, then what the heck were you up to?" her father prodded, sounding a bit suspicious.

"I told you, I went for a drive."

"One that lasted the whole day?"

"Stop it, Warren," her mother said. "I know *exactly* what she was doing."

"You do?" Gwen asked, a forkful of food hovering before her open mouth.

"Of course. I did the same thing the first time I went home to Pennsylvania after being away. I visited all the places I remembered. I went to my old schoolhouse, drove by the homes where my friends used to live. I even visited the cemetery, looking at the tombstones of people I'd once known. It felt like another memory was waiting around every corner. All I had to do was find it."

Her father grumbled. "It's a shame you went and got involved with a crumb bum like me and got taken away from all that."

Meredith reached over and picked a bit of bread off her husband's shirt. "You got the crumb part right."

As her parents laughed, Gwen couldn't help but wonder how they would react if she were to admit the truth: that she'd spent the day with Hank, and that it was likely she would see him again. In a way, her father perplexed her. He was an outcast from her mother's family, rejected for being too far beneath them in standing and station, too poor to measure up, too uneducated to be worthy of their daughter. So why was it so hard for him to understand what Hank was going through? It wasn't the same — her father wasn't responsible for someone's death — but it wasn't so different, either. Couldn't he sympathize, even a little?

In the other room, the phone rang. "I'll get it," Meredith said, rising from the table and leaving Gwen alone with her father.

"I had a customer at the store today who made me think of you," he told her.

"Who was it?"

"Myron Ellis," Warren answered. "He looked like hell, his clothes all rumpled, his eyes as red as a fire hydrant." Her father shook his head in pity. "The way I see it, what that son of his did ruined him."

Gwen was about to rise to Hank's defense, to try to convince her father that he was wrong, when her mother stuck her head in the kitchen.

"The phone's for you, Gwendolyn," she said, sounding excited. "It's Kent."

Just like that, what little appetite she had vanished.

Out of the frying pan and into the fire . . .

". . . and Hutchinson still hasn't interviewed the woman at the cosmetics counter like I wanted. If I've told him once, I've told him a dozen times that I need that testimony, but he keeps saying 'I'll get it, I'll get it.' I swear, if he doesn't come through, I'll go to Smithers and he'll be out on his ear!"

Gwen struggled to pay attention as Kent went on about work. From the moment she had picked up the phone, he'd been talking a mile a minute, scarcely pausing for breath. She wasn't even sure if she'd said "hello" before he had started in. He hadn't asked a single question, not about whether she was feeling better, nothing about what she'd been up to, and not a word about how she was holding up alone with her parents in Buckton. Everything was about him.

Just like always.

"Then yesterday, out of nowhere, old man

Pritchard shows up and right there in front of everyone invites me to his office for a drink. He poured me a cognac from the most ornate crystal decanter I've ever seen and said . . ."

Lifting the telephone from its stand, Gwen walked down the short hallway that led to the bathroom, trailing the cord behind her. She sat beneath an open window, the night air cool on her skin. Even though Gwen didn't think that her mother or father would eavesdrop, she wanted to be alone.

". . . practically see my name on the letterhead now! If even half of what Pritchard told me is true — and I have no reason to doubt him, he's a partner after all — then by Christmas at the latest, I figure they'll have . . ."

Even as Kent's one-sided conversation continued, Gwen recalled what her father had said about Myron Ellis. She couldn't imagine what the man had experienced, having lost both his wife and his youngest son. No wonder he was so distraught. Slowly, a shred of doubt crept into her thoughts. Maybe she was wrong about Hank. While he'd been charming, incredibly kind to Freddie Holland, and even supportive of her becoming a writer, none of that changed the fact that he had gotten drunk, crashed his car, and killed his brother. Maybe instead of agreeing to see him again, she should've —

"I've missed you."

Kent's simple, soft-spoken words surprised her.

"You have?" she asked.

"Of course," he said with a chuckle. "Even though I'm working from dawn to dusk, and most days later than that, I'm always thinking about you. I know I haven't called like I promised I would, that's entirely my fault, but you're right here with me in my heart."

Gwen knew that Kent was a smooth talker. Many a jury had fallen under the spell his tongue could cast. But what he'd said had touched her, so much so that the anger she had been feeling toward him began to fade.

"Do you remember the picture I have on my desk?" he asked.

She most certainly did. Gwen had framed it and given it to him on his birthday. The photograph was of the two of them standing in front of Lake Michigan, her arm around his waist, his across her shoulders, smiling brightly for the camera. Back then, she couldn't have imagined the troubles that now threatened to pull them apart.

Gwen nodded, then realized that he

couldn't see her. "Yes," she said.

"Every time this case starts to get to me, whenever Hutchinson doesn't get me what I asked for," Kent said, throwing one more insult toward his harried assistant, "I just look at that picture, think about you, and things get better."

Just then, as she was about to answer, Gwen was distracted by a sharp smell, like something was burning.

"Oh!" Kent declared. "I almost forgot to tell you the best news of all."

"What's that?"

"Well, I don't know for certain, but there have been a lot of whispers around the office that as soon as you get back to Chicago, the firm is going to throw us an engagement party! Isn't that wonderful?"

Faster than a struck match bursting into flame, Gwen's anger returned, magnified tenfold. "You . . . you've been telling people that we're getting married?"

"Why wouldn't I?" he asked innocently.

"Because I haven't accepted your proposal yet!" she hissed, the words louder than she would have liked in the narrow hallway. She cupped the receiver, trying to muffle her voice. "Kent, no matter what you think, we aren't engaged!"

He was silent for a long moment; Gwen

imagined that he was leaning back in his chair, his feet propped on his desk, thinking hard. "Why are you being so stubborn?" he finally asked. "I thought that we —"

"Don't you remember our argument?" she interrupted. "I went storming off into the rain. I nearly drowned in the river! All because you can't accept that I want to be a writer! Tell me you haven't forgotten that."

"Okay, okay, so I may have jumped the gun a bit," he admitted, sounding as if he was trying to placate her. "But the reason I started to talk about it around the office was because I know that you're eventually going to come around. You know it, your parents know it. I mean, what, are you *really* not going to marry me?"

Gwen was too stunned to answer. For the very first time, she seriously considered what it would mean if she didn't accept his proposal. Even on the night she'd left him on the porch, she had thought that they would talk like adults, that there would eventually be a compromise, and that, in the end, she would become Mrs. Kent Brookings. But now, listening to the dismissive way he spoke, understanding that he hadn't taken a single thing she'd said seriously, she started to think that this was the end for them.

But even as Gwen struggled with how to tell Kent what she was feeling, the burning smell she'd noticed earlier grew stronger. She was sure it was coming in through the window. Stretching the phone's cord, Gwen peered into the night. What she saw made her pulse race.

A house was on fire.

Even in the darkness, she could see it clearly. It was close, a couple of houses farther up the block but behind her parents', facing the next street over. Orange, yellow, and red flames licked hungrily up its sides, devouring it and sending smoke billowing up toward the stars. Faintly, she heard voices, shouts for help.

Gwen knew what she had to do. Every instinct she had, the part of her that wanted to be a writer, was screaming to go to the blaze, to record everything she saw. She needed to be there.

"I've got to go," she told Kent.

"Wait a second, Gwen, don't you think that we should —"

But whatever else he had intended to say was lost when she put the receiver back in its cradle, hanging up on him.

Even as Gwen started running, she shouted, "There's a fire!"

Her mother appeared in the kitchen's

entryway, her expression concerned, a hand rising to her collar. "Where?"

"Look out the window!" Gwen yelled as she rounded the banister and raced up the staircase. In her room, she snatched up her new notebook and a handful of pencils. Back downstairs, she found her parents gawking at the blaze.

"We should call the fire department," her father said.

Once again, the phone rang; it had to be Kent, calling back to resume their conversation. But even as her mother answered, Gwen was already gone, bounding down the steps and into the night, running toward the fire.

Outside, the smell of smoke was strong, nearly overpowering. It burned her nose, covering the neighborhood like a blanket. Gwen raced down the sidewalk, running as fast as she could. All around her, people stepped onto their porches, drawn to the fire just as she had been. In the distance, she heard the rise and fall of a siren.

Hurry, hurry, hurry!

Gwen cut through John Gabrielson's yard, skirted a garden, vaulted over a low fence, and narrowly avoided colliding with a birdbath. Finally she plunged between some bushes, their branches clawing at her hair, her clothes, even her notebook and pencils, before bursting out a hundred feet from the raging fire. Shielding her face, Gwen gasped.

It was David and Elise Morgan's house. Years ago, she had spent many an evening inside, babysitting the couple's two children. Gwen had made cookies in the kitchen, hung tinsel on the Christmas tree in the living room, and read dozens of stories in the upstairs bedrooms. Now it was being destroyed before her very eyes.

In the short time since Gwen had first noticed the fire, it had grown in intensity. Flames poured from the broken windows and leaped out of a hole that had been eaten through the roof. Smoke climbed high into the sky, blotting out the moon and stars. A wall of heat pushed against her, keeping her from coming closer.

So Gwen stayed where she was. Though it was likely dangerous for her to be so close to the blaze, she felt no fear, but rather a twinge of excitement, even a swelling sense of duty. It wasn't until the earsplitting sound of the fire engine's siren drew near that she went to the front of the house.

The crowd that had gathered parted, allowing the fire truck through. Firefighters began to run in every direction, many carrying ladders, axes, and seemingly endless lengths of hose. Gwen recognized a lot of their faces, men from the community, volunteers who had been rousted from their homes — some surely just sitting down to dinner — and into the night. A few were still buttoning up their coats or putting on their hats. Their shouts were loud, even over the fire.

"— check 'round the back of the house!"

"Once we're hooked up to the main line, turn the spigot!"

". . . out of the house? Is there anyone still inside?"

In unspoken answer to the last question, Gwen searched for the Morgans and was relieved to find them. The whole family was huddled together on the front lawn, the parents clutching their children tight; Gwen was surprised to see how much the kids had grown in the time she'd been away. Neighbors gathered around them, offering their support, some pointing, many crying, as David and Elise's home was destroyed.

Gwen sat on the curb opposite the house, out of the way but still close enough to see all that was happening. She pulled out her notebook and began to write down everything she saw. She wrote about the firemen's shouted instructions, the sharp smell of the fire burning the back of her throat, the thunderous noise the Morgans' porch made when it collapsed, Elise's sobs as she fell into her husband's arms, and the constant hiss of water spraying from the hoses as the fire was slowly brought under control, though far too late to save much. As she wrote, page after page was filled with her observations. Her hand moved fast, though it struggled to keep up with her frenzied thoughts, producing a flood of words. She was still scribbling notes, working on her fourth pencil, when a blanket was unexpectedly draped across her shoulders. She looked up to find her mother standing beside her.

Meredith took a seat on the curb. Looking at the house, she said, "What a shame."

Gwen nodded. In the crowd, she saw her father talking with David Morgan, a sympathetic hand on the grieving man's shoulder. She was too far away to hear what was being said, but she was certain that Warren was offering whatever help the now homeless family might need.

"What are you doing?" Meredith asked, pointing at Gwen's notebook.

"Writing down what I see."

"Why?"

Gwen turned to stare at her mother.

"I didn't mean to upset you," Meredith replied soothingly. "I just don't understand what would draw you to something like this."

"Someone needs to record this."

"But why you? To what end?" She nodded at the open pages, filled to overflowing with words. "Who is all that writing for?"

Her mother's questions were simple, yet they profoundly shook Gwen. In some ways, they reminded her of the criticisms and dismissive things that Kent had said. If he could see her now, would he shake his head, smile at her condescendingly, and ask why she had run off to sit before a raging fire? She suspected he would. But Gwen wondered if he wasn't partially right to doubt her. If writing was truly her passion, then who was she filling all these pages for? Was it just for herself?

Or could it be something more?

Sitting beside her mother, Gwen thought she might finally have an answer.

Chapter Thirteen

Gwen stifled a yawn and pushed herself away from her father's desk. Early-morning sunlight streamed through the window of the office, washed over the rug at her feet, and was slowly making its way up her leg. Songbirds called to each other, signaling the beginning of a new day, although Gwen's old one had yet to end. Stretching her arms above her head, her body sore from sitting for so long, she glanced at the clock; it wasn't quite seven.

She'd been up all night.

When Gwen had finally left the Morgans' house, the wreckage still smoldering as the fire department sifted through what remained, she couldn't stop hearing her mother's words repeating over and over in her head.

Who is all that writing for?

Back in her bedroom, smoke clinging to her clothes, Gwen had begun transcribing her notes, organizing them, deciding what was important enough to keep and throwing away all that failed to meet that standard. Once she was satisfied that she had what she needed, Gwen had gone downstairs. Though it was late, already well past midnight, she'd sat down at her father's typewriter.

And so, with a deep breath, she had started to write, hoping she wouldn't make too much noise as she struck the keys. She kept telling herself to follow the advice Mr. Wirtz had given her back at Worthington.

"If you can make your reader believe in what you're writing," he'd said, "there's nothing you can't achieve."

Because she was a perfectionist, Gwen agonized over each word, every sentence, and even the punctuation marks. She wanted nothing to be out of place. The balls of crumpled paper that soon filled the wastebasket, then overflowed onto the floor, were a testament to how difficult that struggle had been.

But now, finally, she was done.

Gwen picked up the two sheets of paper and read through them for what felt like the hundredth time. Absently chewing at one of her nails, she used a critical eye as she looked for mistakes. When she finished,

Gwen smiled. There was nothing more she could do.

Now she just had to follow through with her plan.

Gwen paced back and forth in front of the *Buckton Bulletin,* her account of the fire clutched in her hand. Once she had finished writing, she'd sat down to breakfast with her parents; with a wrinkled-up nose, her father had commented that Gwen smelled like she'd been fighting the blaze, not writing about it. After a much-needed shower, Gwen had hurried to the newspaper office, anxious yet hopeful, only to find that it hadn't opened yet. She glanced at the clock above the bank. It was almost nine. Where was everyone?

As if in answer, a voice spoke behind her on the sidewalk. "Now there's someone I never would've expected to see this fine morning."

Gwen turned to find Sid Keaton, the publisher of the *Bulletin,* walking toward her. Sid was a handful of years older than her father, but where Warren had grown plump sampling his wares, Sid was rail thin; she supposed it made sense, since words couldn't make you fat. The newspaperman was nearly bald, with what little graying hair he had left hopefully combed over the top of his head. He held keys in one hand, a coffee cup in the other.

"Good morning, Mr. Keaton," she said.

"Hello, Gwen," he replied, flashing a friendly smile.

They had known each other for as long as she could remember. Sid Keaton and his wife, Marlys, were regular customers at her family's bakery. Thinking back, she recalled that Sid was an avid fisherman. Most every visit, he would regale her father with tales of the latest lure he was using, something he'd cooked up with bobs, feathers, weights, and whatever else he thought might attract a fish.

"Have you had much luck fishing this spring?" she asked.

"The best in years," Sid answered. "With all the rain we've had, to say nothing of the new lures I cooked up, they're practically jumping into my basket. Why, just the other day . . ." But then he trailed off, looking at her suspiciously. "Odds are, fishing isn't the reason for this unexpected visit, unless you've started a new hobby, in which case I'm all ears."

"That's not why I came by," she admitted.

"So what can I do for you?"

Gwen took a deep breath. This was the moment she'd come here for.

"Did you hear about the fire last night?" she asked. "The one at the Morgans' place?"

Sid nodded. "I did."

"I was there," Gwen told him. "I wrote about what happened and wondered if you might want to publish it." She stuck out her hand, which trembled slightly, presenting her pages.

Gwen wasn't sure what sort of reaction she'd expected: for Sid to throw her work on the ground in disgust, to jump for joy as he enthusiastically accepted it, or, more likely, something in between. At the very least, she thought he would look it over. Instead, the publisher stuck the pages beneath his arm, turned his key in the lock, and said, "Why don't we go inside."

Many years had passed since Gwen had last been to the *Bulletin* offices. Rows of desks were spread across the room, the typewriters and telephones all silent. There was a door at the rear, the glass stenciled with Sid's name, which led to his office. It was so quiet that Gwen thought it resembled a funeral parlor more than a newspaper. At this hour, she imagined that the *Chicago Tribune* or the *Daily News* was a hive of activity, with reporters and photographers racing to get their stories submitted.

"Buckton isn't like the big city," Sid explained, as if he knew what Gwen had been thinking. "There isn't a lot that happens in these parts, and since we publish only once a week, there usually isn't any reason for someone to be here so early. When we get closer to going to press, things pick up."

Sid led the way to his office, flipped on the light, and offered Gwen a seat. He tossed her pages down on his blotter, dropped into the chair behind his desk, and sipped at his coffee before asking, "How was school?"

"Good," she answered.

"Where was it you went again?"

"Worthington."

"That's right," Sid said. "For as much as your dad talked about you, you'd think I'd remember. What was it you studied?"

"Lots of things, but I was especially interested in writing." Gwen paused. "A story I wrote was accepted by a magazine," she added, feeling a bit self-conscious, afraid it would sound like she was bragging.

Sid nodded, but his expression didn't change.

So Gwen set out to alter it.

She opened up, talking about how much

she loved to write, how she often felt compelled to jot down everything she saw, that she thought she was improving, and that all she wanted was a chance to show what she could do.

"And that's why you wrote this?" the publisher asked, pointing at her pages, still sitting on his desk.

"Yes," she told him.

Sid leaned forward and picked up Gwen's work. He opened a drawer, pulled out a pair of glasses, and put them on. He tipped back in his chair, causing the springs to protest, and began to read.

Gwen tried not to fidget, listening to the steady tick of a clock in the outer room. She'd written only a couple of pages, but it felt like it was taking Sid forever to review them. She kept glancing at him, trying to read his face for any reaction, unable to shake the nagging suspicion that the only reason the newspaperman was doing this was as a favor to her father.

So what happens if he doesn't like it?

She wasn't sure of the answer. Would one failure be enough to make her give up her dream? Would she admit that Kent was right, that she had been acting foolishly, and agree to become his wife? Or would a rejection just make her try harder?

Then Gwen thought of Hank. When she'd admitted to him that she wanted to be a writer, he had listened, and even been supportive. He was passionate about his own work, which showed in his craftsmanship, and he understood why she wanted it so badly.

Kent might not believe in her, but someone else did.

Finally Sid put her pages down and nodded. "It needs a bit of work." Gwen's face must have soured slightly, because he quickly added, "Relax. No one submits something that I don't make changes to."

"Did you like it?" she asked tentatively.

"Sure," Sid told her. "Don't take this the wrong way, but it was better than I thought it would be. Much better."

Gwen swelled with pride, struggling to hold back a smile.

"There's one bit of it that gives me pause, though."

"What part is that?"

"Toward the end, where you suggest that the fire might be arson."

Even as she had been watching the fire, it had struck Gwen as odd that there had been two blazes in Buckton within such a short time. As the night, or more accurately the early morning, had crawled along, that feeling had grown stronger. Trying to explain it, she had ventured the idea that foul play had been involved and inserted the conjecture into her article.

"It's just a thought," she explained.

"Do you have any proof?"

"Well . . . no . . ."

"When reporting the news, I expect my employees to keep their opinions out of their writing as much as possible," Sid explained, leaning back in his chair and lacing his hands behind his head. "To insinuate something like arson without any facts to back it up is irresponsible. The last thing I'd want is to start a rumor. Buckton has enough of those already."

"I'm sorry," Gwen said, feeling quite chastened.

"You don't have anything to apologize for. This is how one learns."

She nodded, believing that he would know best.

"So tell me," Sid said. "Does this mean you want to become a reporter?"

"I don't know yet," Gwen answered honestly. "But I liked it. Sitting there, watching the fire and all the people, the commotion, writing everything down, it was exciting. I felt like I was doing something important."

The newspaper publisher was silent for a

moment, watching her. Then he got up from his chair, went over to the wall, and removed a framed photograph. He handed it to Gwen before sitting on the edge of his desk. "Believe it or not, that's me," Sid said, tapping the glass. "The third from the right."

In the black-and-white picture, a row of young men, all with their collars unbuttoned and their ties hanging loosely around their necks, stood in front of an enormous printing press. Each held up a newspaper, smiling brightly.

"Did you know that I used to work in Chicago?" Sid asked.

"No, I didn't."

"It was a long time ago, around the year you were born, I suspect. Longer than I'd like to admit," he explained with a wry smile. "I was hired by Harry Romanoff, the man who ran the *American.*" Pointing at the picture, he said, "That there is the edition in which I had my first byline. I was so damned proud. Bragged about it to everyone I knew." Sid chuckled. "But in the end, I couldn't hack it. I lasted three years before I came home."

Gwen handed him the picture. "Were you disappointed?"

"At the time, sure," he explained as he hung the photo back on the wall, "but it didn't take long for me to realize that failing in the big city was probably the best thing that ever happened to me."

"How so?"

Sid spread his arms to the room. "Because I found this," he explained. "Back when I was first brought on by the *Bulletin,* it was my job to write the obituaries. I threw myself into it, trying to make every person who died in Buckton seem as important as the king or queen of England. The years went by and I moved from one task to another, and before I knew it, I was running the place." Smiling, he added, "And I've never regretted it. Not for a minute."

Gwen could only hope that her own career would be as satisfying.

"Maybe you'll be different," Sid continued. "Maybe you'll go back to Chicago and take the city by its . . . well, you won't let it get the best of you like it did me." He shrugged. "Or you could always . . ." he began, but his voice trailed off.

"I could what?" she asked.

The publisher shook his head. "Never mind. It's nothing. In the end, whatever road you go down, it'll be your choice to make."

Sid went back behind his desk. He pulled a ledger out of the bottom drawer and said,

"Let me write you a check."

"For what?" Gwen asked.

The publisher laughed long and loud. "For your article," he told her. "You weren't doing it for free, were you?"

He scribbled out a check and then handed it to her. Gwen stared at it, hardly able to believe that it was real. It wasn't much, only a couple of dollars, but she wouldn't have cared if it had been made out for a few cents. All that mattered was that she'd been paid for writing. It was even better than when her story had been accepted by the magazine. Having something in the *Bulletin* felt *real.*

As Sid walked her back to the front door, Gwen saw that the newspaper was coming to life. A few employees had arrived, lights had been turned on, coffee was brewing, and typewriters were in use, the keys clacking as fast as gunfire. A telephone began to ring. Maybe it wasn't so different from what she'd expected after all . . .

"Thank you," she told Sid, holding up the check.

"If you write anything else while you're home, let me take a look at it." Then, just as Gwen was going out the door, he added, "You have real talent. Keep at it and you might have yourself something."

Out on the sidewalk, Gwen could hardly contain her joy. She wanted to jump up and down and scream at the sky to celebrate all that she'd accomplished. She could have called Sandy, or gone to see her father at the bakery, or rushed home to share the good news with her mother. She could even have telephoned Kent. But when Gwen thought about who she wanted to talk to first, the answer surprised her.

She wanted to tell Hank.

At first, Gwen wasn't sure how to get in touch with Hank. After all, it wasn't as if she could go home or to the bakery to call, not with her mother and father around. In the end, she thought it best to use the telephone booth on the corner opposite the drugstore. She stepped inside the cramped space, hot from the summer sun, and closed the partition behind her. Then she looked up Hank's number in the directory, dropped a coin in the slot, and dialed. Seconds later, it began to ring.

And ring and ring and ring . . .

But then, just as Gwen was about to give up, someone answered.

"Hello," a man said, sounding slightly out of breath.

"Hank?" she asked tentatively, not sure if

she recognized his voice, wondering if she might be talking to his father.

"Yeah," he said a bit brusquely. "Who is this?"

"It's Gwen."

Instantly, his demeanor changed. "Hey! This is a surprise. I wasn't expecting you to call," Hank said, sounding genuinely pleased that it was her. "Sorry that it took me a while to answer, but I was working in the shop and there isn't a line out there. I heard it ringing in the house and had to run to get it."

"Are you busy?"

"Nothing that can't wait."

"I want to celebrate something. Would you be interested in joining me?"

"Sure. What's the occasion?"

Gwen smiled. She knew it was cheeky to keep it from him, but she wanted to hold on to her secret for a little while longer. "I can't tell you," she explained. "It's a surprise. Let's just say that I have some good news to share."

"I don't get a hint?" Hank asked.

"And ruin the suspense?" she teased with a soft laugh.

"Okay, okay. I get it," he said. "Where do you want to go?"

"How about I treat us to ice cream at

Mercer's Malt Shop?"

Gwen had thought Hank would argue with her, insisting that he be the one to pay, but instead he was silent; the pause lasted so long she began to wonder if their connection hadn't been lost. But finally he asked, "You want to stay in Buckton?"

"Is that all right?"

Another pause. "Sure . . . yeah, that's fine . . ." he said, by the end sounding more like himself. "Give me twenty minutes to get cleaned up and I'll meet you in front of the movie theater."

"I'll be waiting," Gwen said, then hung up.

Back outside the phone booth, she raised her face to the sun. Today was wonderful. She had taken a chance writing about the Morgans' fire and submitting her piece to the newspaper, but it had paid off. She was going to be published. On top of that, she'd been paid for it.

Things were definitely looking up.

And now she was going to see Hank again . . .

Just then, Gwen realized she was taking a chance that someone in town would see the two of them together. Word could get back to her parents. There was no reason to think they wouldn't be upset with her. But she didn't care.

This was a time for celebration.

And who knows what other surprises might lie ahead . . .

CHAPTER FOURTEEN

Hank absently drummed his fingers across the top of the truck's steering wheel as he looked over at the malt shop for what felt like the twentieth time. Even though Buckton's streets were mostly empty, he felt conspicuous, like he was parked beneath a billboard or up on a stage.

He didn't want to be in town. He wanted to drive away, fast.

But he stayed for Gwen.

Hearing her voice on the telephone had sent a charge racing through him. Ever since Hank had watched her drive away after their afternoon together, all he'd thought about was her: the curve of her smile, the smell of her perfume, the sweet sound of her voice. Being unable to focus made it hard to work. That very morning, he had flubbed the same piece of wood so many times that he'd finally thrown it away. His father had been sleeping off another night of drinking, so her call had been a welcome surprise. That Gwen had wanted to get together had been even better. Hank had figured he'd pick her up and take her for a drive in the countryside, somewhere they could be alone and talk.

He hadn't expected her to want to stay in Buckton.

Ever since Pete's death, whenever he'd come to town, it had been uncomfortable. Everyone stared. A few pointed. The boldest walked up and gave him a piece of their mind. Once, in the grocery store, Hank had been slapped; Grace Gesell had done it, an older woman he knew from church. He reckoned that he deserved it, though not in the way most folks believed, and so he took their abuse without complaint. But that didn't mean he liked it. After a while, it became easier to stay away, to do his business in places like Mansfield. Hank couldn't remember how long it had been since he'd last driven downtown.

What's taking her so long?

Having Gwen at his side made it worse. It was one thing for him to take abuse for what happened to his brother, but the last thing he wanted was for her to see it. That burden was his alone. Besides, it would ruin her good mood.

When Hank had pulled up outside the movie theater, Gwen had been a bundle of excitement. He'd tried to match her happiness, but he doubted that he'd been very convincing.

"This is my treat," Gwen had said once he'd parked in front of Mercer's Malt Shop.

Hank had wanted to argue, to insist on buying, but he also hadn't wanted to get out of the truck. He'd been trying to protect her.

Gwen had opened her door, then looked back at him in surprise when she'd realized he wasn't joining her. "Aren't you coming?"

"Just get me a chocolate."

She had paused, a frown on her otherwise beautiful face, but then gone inside.

Now, sitting behind the wheel, Hank felt like a fool. His growing attraction to Gwen didn't change the fact that she was involved with, if not actually engaged to, another man. While he was thrilled to spend more time with her, it was pointless to get his hopes up. Even *if* Kent Brookings didn't exist, *if* Hank could somehow start a relationship with Gwen, then he would have no choice but to tell her the truth about himself. He would have to confess a secret he'd sworn to take to the grave.

Could I do that? Could I be completely hon-

231

est with her?

The sudden honk of a horn startled him.

Hank turned to look out his window and found Jed Ringer staring at him, sitting in his own car as it idled in the middle of the street. He had two of his flunkies with him, men Hank recognized from the baseball game.

As if I didn't feel uneasy enough being in town . . .

"What in the hell are you doin' here?" Jed asked with a sneer. It pleased Hank to see that the troublemaker's face was still bruised and battered from their brawl, one of his eyes swollen and purple. It made him look uglier than ever.

"None of your damn business," Hank answered.

"Don't you talk to him that way," the goon closest to the passenger-side door snapped. A thin, wiry man, he reminded Hank of a yippy little dog snarling behind a fence, thinking that he was far bigger and tougher than he was.

"Shut up, Clint," the middle crony said. "Jed don't need your help."

"You ain't the boss a me, Sam! Don't go thinkin' that —"

"Quiet, the both of you!" Jed barked, instantly silencing his fawning menagerie.

232

Turning his attention back to Hank, he said, "You ain't wanted 'round here, murderer."

Even though Hank had been uncomfortable about being in Buckton from the moment Gwen had suggested he join her for ice cream, the last thing he would have done was leave because Jed Ringer wanted him to.

"You man enough to make me go on your own," Hank began, unable to resist baiting the other man, "or do you need your girlfriends' help?"

Jed's face flushed an angry crimson. "No," he said as he popped open his door, pushing it wider. "I'm gonna enjoy this by myself."

But before he could set foot on the pavement, another horn sounded. All four men looked to see a police car in the street behind Jed's sedan; the officer wanted him to get moving. None of them had a good reputation, including Hank, so if there was trouble now, they'd likely all be hauled off to jail.

Hank didn't want to cause a scene, especially in front of Gwen; too late, he realized that it had been stupid to antagonize Jed.

So he was plenty relieved when Jed eased back behind the wheel.

Putting his car in gear, the tough stared

daggers at Hank. "The next time you see me, there's gonna be trouble," he said, then drove away.

Seconds later, Gwen finally came out of the malt shop holding two ice cream cones, none the wiser about what had just happened.

Even as he put the truck in gear, Hank was grateful for that.

"So are you ever going to tell me what your big surprise is?"

Gwen looked at Hank. He was turned in his seat, away from the sidewalk and toward her, licking at his ice cream cone. Ever since he'd picked her up in front of the movie theater, he had seemed a bit out of sorts, distracted. She'd been surprised he hadn't argued about her offering to pay, and then when he'd chosen to stay in the truck rather than go inside the malt shop. He hadn't said much as he'd driven them to a more secluded spot, away from Main Street, parking in the shade on the east side of the park. She was sure it was nothing, convinced that she was imagining it, but before she told Hank what had happened, she was determined to make him smile.

"Isn't it obvious?" she teased.

Hank shrugged.

234

"You're eating it," Gwen said, nodding toward his ice cream.

He smiled, just a little, causing her heart to beat faster. "Most days, ice cream would be more than enough to get me out of my workshop, but I got the impression that you were talking about something bigger."

Gwen laughed, the sound filling the truck's cab and spilling out the open windows. "You're right," she said. "And it's amazing!"

She told him everything, beginning with the fire that had destroyed the Morgans' house. She struggled to explain how horrible it had been to sit helplessly and watch people she genuinely cared for lose everything they owned, even as she scribbled down the details of what she saw. Then how she'd stayed up all night writing, submitted her article to Sid Keaton, and ended with it being purchased for publication in the *Bulletin.* Occasionally she had to pause to keep from getting melted ice cream all over herself. Gwen admitted to Hank that she'd been nervous, worried that she wasn't good enough, but that in the end her hard work had paid off. The only thing she didn't tell him about was her disastrous phone call with Kent.

"That's great, Gwen!" Hank told her

235

when she'd finished. From the tone of his voice, she knew that he meant it. "I'm really happy for you."

"Thanks. I knew you'd understand."

"So are you going to do it?"

"Do what?"

"Sid said that if you wrote something else he'd take a look at it," Hank explained. "You should take him up on the offer."

"I don't know," she said. "What would I write about?"

"Didn't you tell me on the way back from Mansfield that everything around you is a story waiting to be told? If that's true, it shouldn't be all that hard."

"Maybe you're right," Gwen said, momentarily warming to the idea before a sliver of doubt crept in. "But what if he doesn't like *that* one?"

Hank shrugged. "Then you write another. If this is what you really want to do, then failure's going to be a part of it every bit as often as success. Maybe more. It sure is in woodworking. But if you can handle getting knocked down from time to time, if it makes you want to get back up and try again, you'll earn your success."

Gwen found Hank's confidence infectious. Listening to him erased her doubts. To Hank, the only way she could fail would be if she quit trying. She wasn't used to someone having that kind of faith in her.

"You make it sound easy," she told him.

"I know it isn't," Hank replied. "Far from it. But if you've come this far, it'd be a shame not to see how far the road goes."

"I just worry that I'm not good enough," she admitted.

"Who doesn't?"

"I doubt you do."

"Then you'd be wrong," Hank answered. "No matter how many times someone like Freddie tells me they love my work, there's always the fear lurking in the back of my mind that the next piece I make will be a failure, that it will sit unsold." He nodded at her. "Most artists I know feel the same."

"I don't see myself that way," Gwen insisted.

"You should. As a matter of fact, if I was a betting man, I'd be willing to wager that you'll end up being a lot more famous than I ever will."

Gwen smiled. She wasn't happy because Hank believed she would one day be a well-known and respected writer. She was grinning because he had once again been kind and considerate, had complimented her and offered encouragement, far different from how she'd expected him to be. She thought about taking his hand, a touch to express how she was feeling, but then thought better of it. She wasn't sure of herself and worried she might send the wrong message, even if she had no idea what the *right* message would be.

So instead she asked, "Would you like to play a game?"

"Sure," he answered, not quite sure where she was going.

Gwen pointed out the windshield at the few people walking Buckton's sidewalks. "All you have to do is pick someone out and invent a story about them," she explained. "It can be about whatever you want. What they do for a living, where they went on vacation last year, the kind of movies they like to watch. Anything you can think of. The most creative story wins."

"You mean make something up?" Hank asked hesitantly.

"Exactly. I'll go first so you can see how it works."

Farther up the street, a man made to cross, looking both ways for traffic before stepping off the curb. He was dressed smartly, his hat pushed back a bit on his head and a newspaper folded under his arm. From where Gwen sat, it looked like he was whistling.

She pointed and said, "His name is Lou Morris and he —"

"That's Phil Mounts," Hank interrupted. "He moved to town three years ago to practice law. He and his family bought the Palmers' old place up on Sycamore. His wife teaches at the —"

"Shush!" Gwen cut him off. "The less I know about him the better. Otherwise it interferes with the story." She'd had an elaborate tale beginning to form in which the man was off to visit his mistress after having just embezzled thousands from the bank. But now it would remain untold. "Let's try again."

"Gwen, I don't —"

"There," she said, pointing at an older woman just coming out of the five-and-dime carrying so many packages that she could barely see over them. Gwen thought it might be Carol Starks, a longtime fixture behind the counter of Buckton's post office, but her view was obscured. Besides, as she'd told Hank, she didn't want to know anything about her subject.

"That's Marjorie Blanchard," she began. "She married her husband, Jeffrey, because he was the wealthy heir to a manufacturing business, but now, after fourteen years of loveless marriage —"

239

"C'mon, this isn't —"

"— she has a surprise for her whole family. You see, each one of those packages contains a gift that she purchased especially —"

"— funny. I don't think that we should —"

Gwen was faintly aware of Hank saying something but she was so focused on creating a fictional history for the older woman that she wasn't paying close attention. So when he finally made himself heard, she was shocked.

"Stop it, Gwen!" he snapped, his voice loud and angry.

She immediately fell silent, her heart hammering. Gwen looked at Hank, wondering what she'd done to make him so upset. He stared silently ahead, his eyes narrow slits, his jaw tight. When he tossed the last bit of his ice cream cone out his window, he no longer looked angry, but almost a little sad.

"What's wrong?" she asked tentatively.

He didn't answer.

"Hank, what did I do?"

For a while longer, he still wouldn't reply. Finally he said, "I just didn't want to play, that's all . . ."

Gwen didn't believe a word of it. Whatever had upset him, it wasn't something he was going to reveal easily. It would've been easy to accept his answer, to drop the matter, but she couldn't.

She needed to know the truth.

"Tell me," she insisted.

Stubbornly, Hank kept staring out the window.

"Please," Gwen pressed, overcoming her earlier reluctance and gently placing her hand on his arm. Hank made no move to pull away. Her touch proved enough to lift his gaze to her. Trying to read his expression wasn't easy; she saw pain and confusion, but she also recognized indecision, as if he was weighing telling her what she wanted to know.

"After Pete died, I mostly kept to myself . . ." Hank began, his words slowly unspooling. "That was because whenever I came to town, someone would always be looking at me. It didn't matter if I was walking down the street, in line at the bank, or in my truck; I'd see them watching, whispering. It made me so angry."

Gwen listened breathlessly. Ever since she'd learned about the car accident that had claimed Pete's life, she'd wanted to know more, but she'd been afraid to pry into Hank's past, to upset him. She had hoped that he would eventually reveal it himself. Now it seemed as if her patience was about to be rewarded.

"Everyone was judging me for something they knew nothing about," he continued. "There's only one person who knows exactly what happened that night, and that's me." Hank turned to her, staring hard, his eyes pleading, as if he desperately wanted her to believe him. He shook his head. "But that sure as hell didn't stop damn near the whole town from inventing their own version. There were more rumors floating around than stars in the sky."

Gwen thought about her parents. She was certain Warren and Meredith had heard all the wild speculation about the night Pete died. She was also convinced that they'd done their part to make things worse. Gwen could easily imagine her father leaning against the bakery's counter, spreading the latest gossip, loudly declaring Hank's guilt. Samantha, Sandy, everyone in Buckton had likely done it.

Slowly, she began to understand why Hank had gotten so upset.

"You didn't like me making things up about people," Gwen said.

Hank nodded. "I imagine folks sitting in cars, just like we're doing now, watching me go by and saying terrible things. That I'm a drunk, a murderer, that if it weren't for me, my brother would still be alive, that they wish I was dead." He took a deep breath. "Those people don't know the truth. They think they do, but they're *wrong!*" Hank grabbed the steering wheel, squeezing hard. "I just want to whip open their doors and scream that they're fools, that they don't understand, but I . . . I . . . just . . ." Though Gwen desperately wanted more, Hank stopped talking.

Voices drifted in through the open windows, a few people on the sidewalks braving the summer sun, but inside the truck's cab there was silence. Gwen's thoughts raced. There was something Hank wasn't telling her, that much was certain, a secret about the night of the accident. Sitting there watching him, Gwen understood that Hank had become important to her, maybe more than she was willing to admit. He'd saved her life, but her feelings for him weren't made up only of gratitude. She had been surprised by how much she enjoyed their drive to Mansfield. When her article had been accepted at the *Bulletin,* Hank was the first person she'd wanted to tell. Even now, under the circumstances, she was happy to be in his company. She wanted to know his secret, not because of the curiosity that drove her as a writer, but because if he told her, if he could bring himself to trust her, it would strengthen the bond growing between them.

"If you ever wanted to talk about that night . . . about what happened to Pete . . . I would listen . . ." Gwen tentatively told him.

Hank looked at her with such intensity that she had trouble holding his gaze. His mouth opened, then closed. He seemed unsure of what to do, as if he was weighing her suggestion. But then he shook his head.

"Gwen . . . I, I can't . . ."

She fought back a feeling of disappointment, then again reached out and put her hand on his arm, more purposefully than before. "It doesn't have to be now."

He nodded, then surprised her by placing his hand on top of hers. His touch was rough yet warm. Gwen wondered how Kent or her parents would react to seeing her and Hank like this. Undoubtedly there would be questions, hurt feelings, even anger. But she had no desire to move away. This was right where she wanted to be. As the seconds slowly ticked past, as their touch lingered, Gwen pleasantly realized that even though Hank hadn't told her what she'd hoped to hear, somehow they had still managed to grow closer.

"I didn't mean to upset you," she said, wanting to make things right, worried that she'd pushed him too far.

"I know," Hank replied, his voice empty of annoyance. "It just caught me off guard, is all. If anything, I should apologize for reacting the way I did."

"How about we just call it even?"

"Fair enough."

But then, before she could suggest that they go for a drive so that Hank didn't feel like he was being watched, he turned the key in the ignition and the truck's engine grumbled to life. "I've got an idea," he said.

"What is it?"

Hank flashed a thin smile. "Our first go-around at playing a game might not have gone so well," he explained, "but maybe the second time will be better."

"What do you have in mind?" Gwen asked.

"I'm not telling you that easily," he told her with a warm chuckle. "Now it's my turn to have a surprise."

"Oh, really?"

"I even have everything we'll need," he said, thumbing out the rear window into the back of the truck. "You want to give it a shot?"

Resisting the urge to look in the truck's bed for some clue as to what Hank was planning, Gwen nodded. As they pulled away from the curb, quickly accelerating down the street, she was filled with anticipation.

So far, from the fateful night in the Sawyer River until now, their time together had been one heck of an adventure.

CHAPTER FIFTEEN

Gwen listened as Hank sang along softly to a Tony Bennett tune on the radio, a ballad that she and her friends had played again and again back at Worthington. He drove from the center of town through quiet neighborhoods, toward the river. She leaned against her door, still wondering where he was taking her, trying to imagine what sort of game he had in mind. Gwen considered asking more questions but chose to let him keep his secret a little while longer.

Though in many ways Hank was still a stranger, Gwen was surprised by how comfortable she felt around him. With some people, there was a constant pressure to say something, an awkward need to keep the conversation going. But with Hank, she found that even the silences felt right, as if they'd known each other forever, which in an odd way they had. Just sharing his company was enough. So while he could have been taking her anywhere, a fact that would surely have unnerved her father, Gwen wasn't worried. She trusted him.

A mile or so outside of town, Hank turned down a short gravel drive and stopped the truck. Looking out the window, all Gwen could see was an empty pasture ringed by trees. There wasn't a house in sight.

"We're here," he said.

"For what?" Gwen asked without the faintest idea of the answer.

"You'll see."

When they got out, the sound of their doors shutting echoed faintly off the distant trees. Hank began rummaging around in the truck's bed. "Are you right-handed or a lefty?" he asked.

"Right," she answered.

He tossed something at her. Reflexively, Gwen raised her hands to catch it, but she still almost managed to let it fall to the ground. Turning it over in her hands, she took in the dark leather and heavy stitching, but couldn't make head nor tail of it. "What is this?"

"Seriously?" Hank blurted in amazement. "It's a baseball mitt. You told me you went to a Cubs game, right?"

"Well, I wasn't in uniform or out on the court."

"The diamond," he corrected her.

"Whatever."

Looking closely, Gwen could see that there were spaces in the mitt for her fingers, but when she tried to stick her right hand in it, everything felt wrong.

"It goes on your left," Hank explained. "You use it to catch the ball and then you throw it with your good hand."

Embarrassed, Gwen did as he instructed. It felt strange.

Hank led the way from the truck into the field. "Stand right there," he told her before walking a couple dozen paces away. When he turned around and looked at her, he frowned, then moved closer. "Are you ready?"

"For what?" she asked.

"To catch this," Hank answered, holding up a baseball.

Gwen's eyes went wide. "Wait a second! You're going to *throw* that at me?"

He chuckled. "Well, yeah. That's how you play catch."

"But . . . but what do I do?"

Hank jogged back and stood behind Gwen. Holding her left arm, he raised her gloved hand. "Keep it steady," he explained. "Palm up. When I throw the baseball, all you have to do is move the glove and try to catch the ball in the webbing. When it hits, just squeeze your hand shut and that's that."

While he talked, Gwen struggled to pay attention. All she was aware of was Hank's free hand on her waist and his chest brushing against her shoulder.

Back in place, Hank held up the baseball. "Ready?"

Even though she wasn't, Gwen nodded.

The ball left his hand and began a gentle arc toward her, floating across the few clouds in the sky. Tracking it, Gwen took a couple of tentative, awkward steps forward. She stuck out her hand as Hank had shown her and then, just as she was sure the ball was about to strike the glove, she closed her eyes.

But nothing happened.

She heard the baseball land with a thud in the grass behind her. She looked at Hank. "Was I close?" she asked.

He smiled and generously offered, "Kind of. Now throw it back."

Gwen picked up the baseball and took a closer look. She rubbed her thumb across its surface, liking the way the red stitches felt. It was much lighter than she had expected. She couldn't remember the last time she'd thrown something — probably a rock down at the river when she'd been a girl — but she was too embarrassed to ask Hank for help.

Here goes nothing . . .

From the moment the baseball left her hand, Gwen knew that she'd done something wrong. She had no idea where it was going to go, but was certain it wasn't going to end up as intended in Hank's glove. "Whoops!" he shouted, racing to his left, stretching futilely as the ball dropped at his feet.

"Sorry!" Gwen apologized.

"You did fine for your first time," he told her. "But when you throw, step forward on your left leg, then bring your arm up and over, only letting go of the ball when your hand is at the top." He demonstrated in slow motion.

"Got it," Gwen said, hoping she sounded more confident than she felt.

"Let's give it another try."

And so they did, but with only the slightest improvement in results. A couple of times later, Gwen was able to touch the baseball with her glove, but she never managed to actually catch it. Hank began to regularly snag her errant throws, but only because he quickly understood that he needed to start running just as soon as the baseball left her hand.

"Let's try something else," he finally said, heading for the truck.

Gwen thought he meant that they were giving up on playing, but Hank reached into the bed and pulled out a long, tapered piece of wood. Ignorant as she was, even Gwen knew that it was a baseball bat.

"You want to give this a shot?"

Gwen shook her head. "With as bad as I throw, there's no way you could ever hope to hit the ball."

Once again, Hank laughed. "You're probably right. That's why I'm going to pitch and you'll be the batter."

Hank showed her how to position her hands on the bat and watched as she took a couple of practice swings. Unlike the baseball, the bat was much heavier than Gwen had anticipated. The first time she swung, she nearly fell over.

After Hank had backed up a bit, he held up the baseball. "Here it comes," he said. "Give it a good whack."

But in the end, Gwen had just about as much luck hitting the elusive ball as she'd had trying to catch it. Time after time she swung, and time after time she missed. Once, she managed to nick it, sending the baseball squibbing off to the side and into the grass, the impact causing stinging tremors to race up her arms. It didn't take long for sweat to dot her brow.

"This is your idea of fun?" she eventually asked.

"It sure is," Hank declared proudly. "I've loved baseball for as long as I can remember. What's not to like?"

Gwen had an answer on the tip of her tongue, one she suspected he wouldn't want to hear, but she became distracted by a memory of Hank's brother running down the sidewalk, a baseball bat slung over his shoulder. "Pete loved it, too, didn't he?"

"Yeah, he sure did," Hank answered, smiling as he stared off into the distance. "Some summers, we would play from sunup to sundown, until we could barely see the ball. We'd listen to games on the radio, read box scores in the newspaper, and buy packs of bubblegum cards down at the five-and-dime. Even in the winter, we'd while away the days thinking about spring, about the season to be played. There's nothing we loved more than baseball."

"You must be pretty good at it, then."

"I'm not half-bad," he answered modestly.

It was obvious to Gwen how much happiness Hank got out of the game. Still, her own experience with it — short, sweaty, and filled with plenty of failure and frustration

— wasn't anywhere near as much fun. "Even when you were seven, I bet you were better than I am now," she groused. "I'm never going to hit that ball."

Hank frowned. "Not with that attitude, you won't."

"What's that supposed to mean?" Gwen asked, a little fire in her voice.

He stared at her, tossing the ball into the air and effortlessly catching it without even looking at it. "Do you remember the first thing you wrote?"

"Sure . . ." she answered, wondering what he was getting at.

"Was it any good?"

"Not really," Gwen answered. "It was all over the place, mostly because I had no idea what I was doing."

"I bet it was hard to write," Hank said.

She nodded. "What does this have to do with me hitting a baseball?"

"In some ways, nothing," he answered. "In others, everything."

"That doesn't make sense."

"Sure it does," Hank explained. "Whenever we try something new — it doesn't matter if it's writing, woodworking, or even baseball — odds are that we aren't all that good at it. Most times we struggle. We think about quitting, complaining that it's too hard. But if we stick at it, if we learn from our mistakes, we get better." He smiled brightly. "Heck, look at you. Think of how far you've come from that first attempt at writing to now, about to be published in the *Bulletin*. All because you never gave up."

Gwen knew that Hank was right. It would've been easy to quit writing after her first few failed efforts. It was hard, frustrating work, and if she were a different person, she might have put down her pen. Instead, she'd persevered, and today had been one of the best days of her life because of it.

Hank held up the baseball. "Compared to that, what's hitting this thing?"

Gwen lifted the bat and put it on her shoulder, feeling more determined than ever to smack the ball. Hard.

"One more time, then," she said confidently.

Hank smiled, clearly pleased with himself for needling her enough that she'd give it another try. He went into his windup and the ball left his hand the same as the dozen times before. Gwen watched it come closer, clutching the bat tightly, her body coiled with anticipation. Once again, she swung as hard as she could, hoping to make contact. But this time, unlike before, she was rewarded. With a sharp crack, the ball rocketed off the thickest part of the barrel, shooting forward as if it had been launched out of a cannon.

And right at Hank.

He moved as quickly as he could, raising his glove to protect himself, but he wasn't fast enough. The baseball slammed into his shoulder, spinning him sideways before it flew off into the grass. Hank shouted, surely as much from surprise as from pain, and immediately grabbed where it had hit him.

"Hank!" Gwen shouted, running to him.

"Dang, that smarts," he said through gritted teeth.

"I'm so sorry! It's all my fault!"

"You didn't do anything wrong," he told her. "I should've known that when you finally got ahold of one, you'd whack it like Hank Greenberg."

"Who?"

"Never mind," Hank said with a chuckle.

"Let me take a look at it."

He shook his head. "I'm fine. It's not like I'm bleeding or anything."

"I don't care," she insisted.

Finally Hank relented, moving his hand away. Gwen tried to peer down the collar of his T-shirt, but when she still couldn't see, he pulled an arm free and exposed his chest and side. She was momentarily distracted by the pronounced musculature of his body, unlike any she had seen before, but Gwen quickly turned her attention to the ugly redness spreading across his shoulder. It looked extremely painful.

"Does it hurt?" Gwen asked, gingerly putting her fingers to the tender spot, causing Hank to hiss and pull away from her.

"Only when you touch it," he said, offering a teasing smile.

Gwen found herself drawn forward, unable to resist the feel of his skin beneath her fingers. Trying to steady her racing heart, she stepped close and tenderly placed a hand on his chest, far enough from his bruise so as not to cause him any more pain. This time, Hank didn't move, his flesh warm to the touch.

"So which did you like better?" he asked, his mouth only inches from her ear.

She looked up into his eyes. Even after touching him, Gwen had continued to move closer, so near that had he been someone else, it would've felt uncomfortable.

But not him. Not now.

"Which what?"

"Well, the first game we played wasn't much of a success," Hank said. "And up until you hit that ball, this one didn't seem all that great, either. I was just wondering which one you liked better."

"This one," she told him. "It was much better."

"I'm not so sure," he answered.

Gwen felt a heaviness in the air, like something inevitable was about to happen. When she spoke, her voice sounded distant to her ears, as if she'd begun to float away, watching herself from afar. "You aren't?"

Hank shook his head and flashed a mischievous smile. "It's close. But something's still missing."

"What's that?" she asked, butterflies in her stomach.

"This," he answered, then leaned down and placed his lips against hers. Even though Gwen had been looking right at him, had seen it coming, his boldness surprised her all the same. But only for a moment. Faster than a few frenzied beats of her heart, she found herself letting go, welcoming it, hungry for what he was offering. She closed her eyes, opened her mouth, and surrendered to their kiss. Without thinking about what she was doing, Gwen eased into Hank's embrace and was enveloped by his strong arms. Her hands roamed across his bare skin, over the taut muscles of his stomach, to the soft hair covering his chest, and onto the broad expanse of his back. Kissing Hank Ellis was unexpected. It was completely out of character for her. She couldn't believe it was happening.

But it was also so very, very wonderful.

She didn't think about how her parents would react. She didn't consider what her aunt or Sandy might say. She didn't even think of Kent.

At that moment, Gwen thought only of herself, of Hank, and especially of the passionate kiss they were sharing, one she didn't want to end.

And that was just fine with her.

Walking down the sidewalk toward her parents' home, Gwen felt like she was floating on air. As familiar as her surroundings were, everything seemed different. The moon looked brighter. The calls of the swallows as they swooped through the dusk, filling their bellies with bugs, sounded louder. The smell of Jane Oliver's flowers, neatly arranged in their beds, was stronger than Gwen remembered. Nothing was the same. Not after what had happened.

Not after that kiss . . .

Hank had dropped her off a couple of blocks away, not wanting Warren or Meredith to see them together. Sitting in the cab, they'd shared one last kiss. It had been less passionate than the first, only a soft, tender touch of their lips, but still more than enough to cause Gwen's head to spin. She didn't regret what she'd done, not in the least, but it raised far more questions than it answered.

Am I falling for Hank Ellis?

If she was, what sort of future could there be between them, especially given how everyone in town, including her family, felt about him?

Have I been unfaithful to Kent?

But even as Gwen bounded up the steps to home, she knew that none of these issues would be easily resolved. It would take time. Maybe after dinner, she'd enjoy a long soak in the bathtub and turn things over in her head. It couldn't hurt. Maybe she could call Sandy and confide what had happened, just like she'd done when they were younger. Opening the front door, she hoped that she could soon find a —

"What the hell were you thinkin'?"

Gwen recoiled, nearly stepping back out the door. Her father had been waiting for her in the foyer and was irate. His face was an angry shade of red, sweat dotted his forehead and cheeks, and his hands were clenched at his sides. Her mother stood behind him at the foot of the staircase, frowning.

"Dad . . . what . . . what are you talking about?" she stammered.

"Don't act like you don't know," Warren snapped. "Let me guess: if I asked, you spent the day walkin' 'round town, sight-seein' and talkin' with old friends."

Gwen heard her father's sarcasm and understood that something had happened to make him doubt her earlier story. Think-ing quickly, she decided to opt for an abridged version of the truth, omitting her afternoon with Hank. "I went to see Sid Keaton down at the *Bulletin*," she explained, hoping that her accomplishment might defuse the tense situation. "You won't believe it, but he's going to —"

"Don't lie to me!" her father shouted. He wasn't in the mood to listen. "You were out with that bastard Hank Ellis! Maggie Cav-anaugh saw you in his truck with her own two eyes, so there ain't no use denyin' it!"

Gwen's stomach dropped. It was like Hank had told her: whenever he went to town, someone was watching. In this case, that someone had seen them together and thought that the only responsible thing to do was tell her father. She'd even considered this possibility herself, just after calling Hank, but had dismissed it. Now it had come back to bite her.

She was caught.

"You're right. I spent the afternoon with him," she admitted, her tone defiant; she wanted it to be clear that she felt no guilt.

"Oh, Gwendolyn," Meredith said, finally finding her voice. "Didn't I tell you to stay away from him? Why didn't you listen?"

Before Gwen could answer, her father interjected. "Use your head, Gwennie," Warren told her. "You keep messin' around, you're gonna ruin things between you and Kent. I can guarantee you he ain't gonna be happy 'bout his bride-to-be goin' out with some other fella."

"We only want what's best for you, sweetheart," her mother added. "That's why we sent you to Worthington. That's why we were overjoyed when you met a successful young man like Kent. You're better than Buckton now. Don't allow some meaningless dalliance to ruin all you've worked for."

"The last thing you need is to be spendin' time with a piece of trash!" her father declared, folding his arms across his chest, acting as if he'd settled the matter.

Anger flared inside Gwen. At that moment, she wanted to defend both herself and Hank, to tell her parents that they didn't know the first thing about him, to argue that they had completely misjudged him. But deep down, Gwen knew that it was pointless. Her parents had already made up their minds. To them, Hank could never redeem himself. He would always be to blame for what happened to Pete, and not even saving their daughter's life could change that. There was no use in saying another word.

So instead, she turned and headed out the door.

"Where do you think you're goin'?" her father asked incredulously.

Gwen turned and stared first at him, then at her mother. It was already too late to go back.

"Anywhere but here." Then she left.

CHAPTER SIXTEEN

Out on the sidewalk, Gwen stopped. The sun had sunk beneath the treetops, speeding toward the horizon. She heard the sound of kids laughing as they enjoyed their last play of the day before it was off to supper, a bath, and finally to bed. Ahead, an approaching car turned on its headlights, staving off the approaching dark. Everything was just as it should be.

But for Gwen, all was in turmoil.

She wondered what was happening back at the house. Likely her mother wanted to come after her, to try to talk some sense into her daughter, to make things right. But Gwen was just as certain that her father wouldn't allow it. Warren would insist on making a point. He would want his stubborn child to realize she was wrong and come home with her tail between her legs. The more Gwen thought about it, the more he resembled Kent, always convinced that he was right.

So where was she going to go?

Her first instinct was to call Hank. The thought of being with him again, especially after what they'd just shared, was enticing. Yet deep down, Gwen knew that it was the wrong decision. Like it or not, many of her newfound problems revolved around Hank. If she was going to sort out her feelings for him, he couldn't be around.

Next, Gwen considered Sandy. The two of them had always been there for each other, through thick and thin. Gwen had no doubt that Sandy would listen. Her friend would be honest, and based on what she had said the last time they'd talked, she was willing to give Hank a fair shake. But then Gwen thought about her friend's pregnancy. She couldn't barge in on Sandy and her husband now. They had more important things to deal with.

But if I can't go to Hank or Sandy, then who else is left?

Gwen looked back up the sidewalk in the direction she'd come. Darkness was falling fast. She had to make a decision.

I can't go home! I just can't!

That's when the solution struck her. There *was* somewhere else to go. Somewhere she wouldn't be turned away. Somewhere there would be a sympathetic ear. Somewhere she might even find an answer or two.

Gwen walked quickly.

The sooner she got there, the better.

By the time Gwen neared her destination, it was almost dark. While the sun continued to shine from beneath the horizon, leaving only a faint smudge of color in the western sky, the streetlights had already come on, illuminating the sidewalks under her feet. Finally, rounding one last corner, she was there.

Her aunt Samantha's house was built in a newer, bungalow style. In almost every way, it resembled her neighbors', just another in a row, as if they'd all been made with a cookie cutter. But Samantha wasn't the type of person who liked to conform. She stood out, and so did her house.

For one thing, it was lit up like a Christmas tree. Colorful strings of lights had been wrapped around each porch column and most of the windows. From where Gwen stood, it looked as if every inside bulb was on, too. Plastic animals were arranged around the yard, and a flock of pink flamingos gathered at the base of the walk. There was an antique record player up on the porch, so old that it had a hand crank; Samantha liked to lounge in a chair, listening to music. She did this loudly, causing no small number of complaints to the police. When she was a girl, every visit Gwen had made to her aunt's had been an adventure. No two had seemed the same. Samantha had always been the most confident, strongest woman her niece had ever known.

If there was ever a time I needed her advice, this would be it . . .

Before Gwen had finished knocking, the front door was whipped open and her aunt stood there, smiling. Oddly enough, Samantha was wearing an elaborate black dress. She had chosen to accessorize it with a floppy yellow summer hat and a necklace of fake red pearls. She was also barefoot.

"Just who I was expecting," Samantha announced.

Gwen was taken aback. "You were?"

"Of course! What kind of aunt would I be if I didn't know when my favorite — if only — niece was about to drop by for a visit?" With a sheepish grin, Samantha added, "Or maybe I knew you were coming because your father called and asked if I'd seen you lately."

"He called you?" Gwen asked, her eyes wide. "What did he say?"

Her aunt shrugged. "Not much, really. But

I didn't spend all those years as his little sister without learning how to read him like a book. I'd have had to be deaf not to understand he was angry with you."

"He is," Gwen admitted, remembering the look on her father's face when she'd opened the front door. "Are you going to tell him that I'm here?"

Samantha laughed loudly, as if her niece had told a hilarious joke. "Absolutely not! If he can't keep better track of his only child, that's his problem," she declared with a wink. "Now, come inside. No need to gossip out on the porch. We can do that from the comfort of the couch."

The interior of Samantha's house was just as bright and eclectic as the outside. Towers of books were stacked here and there, some of them precariously close to toppling. Shoes spilled out of a closet, some plain while others were outrageously colored, a few with ridiculously high heels. A portrait of an old woman, someone Gwen didn't recognize, hung upside down on the wall. Pushing aside a feathered boa, Gwen made a place for herself on the sofa.

"Do you want something to drink?" her aunt asked.

Gwen shook her head. "No, thank you."

Samantha shrugged. "Your loss." After

pouring herself a glass of what looked like bourbon, she took a seat opposite her niece, throwing her legs over the chair's arm, and said, "All right, then. Spill it."

And that's exactly what Gwen did.

She started all the way back at the afternoon she and Kent had arrived in Buckton, touched on her surprise at the announcement of their engagement, and then related every important thing that had happened since, including her and Hank's kiss. Feeling the need to be honest, she left nothing out.

"And now I'm here," she finished.

The whole time Gwen had talked, her aunt hadn't said a word, steadily drinking from her glass until it was now nearly empty. "Let me get this straight," Samantha finally said. "You're going to throw away everything you've got going with Kent for some small-town fling?"

Gwen's jaw dropped and her heart sank. She never would've imagined that her aunt could speak to her in such a way. "It's not like that," she argued, defending herself, a touch of anger in her voice. "Whatever Hank and I have together, it most certainly is more than you're making it out to be."

Samantha shrugged. "Kent's got plenty of money," she observed. "Heck, that getup he had on for dinner the other night probably costs more than my whole wardrobe. A fella like that could make a gal's life mighty easy. You're gonna give that up for a guy who makes chairs?"

"I'm not with Kent because of his bank account," Gwen answered. "All I want is someone I can love and who will love me back. I don't give a damn about clothes, jewelry, or whatever other luxuries people think are important." Still rattled by the way her aunt had spoken to her, she added, "I thought you knew me better than that."

Samantha paused, draining the last of her whiskey. "You've been gone so long that I just assumed you were a city girl now," she said. "After all, how could Buckton hold a candle to Chicago? I figured you'd changed."

Gwen stared at her aunt, her heart pounding, incredulous. She'd been a fool to think she would find comfort here. Somehow, it was even worse than with her parents. She was going to have to go elsewhere for a solution to her problems, because she definitely wasn't going to find one here.

But when Gwen stood, intending to march out the door, Samantha rose with her. Her aunt smiled sweetly and asked, "What are you doing, kiddo?"

"I'm leaving," she answered curtly. "I am not going to sit here and listen to you talk to me this way. It's not fair! It's not —"

"I was lying," Samantha interrupted her.

Flabbergasted, Gwen didn't know how to answer. Her knees felt weak; for a moment she worried she was going to fall back onto the couch. "You were what?"

"I wasn't telling the truth," her aunt answered. "I suppose I could've found a better way of going about it, but I wanted to know if you were serious about this. About Hank. If I said things I figured you wouldn't want to hear, I thought you might show me your true colors." Samantha placed her hands on her niece's shoulders and added, "And that you most certainly did. In spades."

If it had been anybody else, Gwen would have found such behavior inappropriate, even a bit cruel. But her aunt was unconventional, to say the least. She came at problems from directions most people wouldn't ever consider. That wasn't to say that Gwen enjoyed having been manipulated. Far from it. But while she was no longer angry, she was still plenty confused.

"But why did you . . . oh, this is making my head hurt . . ."

"Then let me tell you a story," Samantha

said. "Believe it or not, I know *exactly* how you feel about this."

Once both of them had sat, Samantha looked at her empty glass and frowned. "Maybe I better pour myself another before I get started."

"Get me one while you're at it."

Fortunately, her aunt gave her only a third of what she poured for herself. Sipping at it, Gwen winced as the liquor burned its way down her throat. Within seconds, she could feel it in her head.

With everything that's happened today, maybe getting a little drunk wouldn't be such a bad thing.

"Have you ever heard me mention Brent Irving?" Samantha asked.

Gwen shook her head.

Her aunt took a deep swig before she continued. "Brent used to work down at the courthouse. It was an easy enough job for him to get, after all his father had been a sitting judge for years. This was all back in the thirties," Samantha explained. "I can still remember the first time I met Brent. I swear I saw stars. He was *so* handsome, charming, everything I'd been looking for. It was like something out of a Hollywood fairy tale, all that sappy, lovey-dovey stuff, only this time it was real. We had one of those whirlwind courtships, which was fine with me, since after three weeks it felt like I'd known him all my life. Every morning, I'd get up and think today was going to be the day when he'd get down on one knee and ask me to marry him . . ." Her voice trailed off. She took another drink.

"What happened?" Gwen prodded.

After a pause, her aunt answered, "For the longest time, I had no idea."

"I don't understand."

"One day, Brent and I were like two peas in a pod, up to our eyeballs in love, and the next he wouldn't give me the time of day," Samantha said, her expression pained. "No phone calls. No letters. He wouldn't even look at me when I showed up at the courthouse and demanded to know what I'd done wrong. It just ended. I cried and cried and cried some more. Months went by and I was still a wreck, moping around the house, feeling sorry for myself. It was the worst time of my life."

"Did you ever find out why he did it?" Gwen asked.

Samantha nodded. "About a year later, he wrote me a letter. I found it slid under the front door. In it, he told me that his parents had objected to him marrying me. They'd told him I wasn't good enough, that I was someone he shouldn't associate with. He couldn't find the strength to stand up to them, I suppose. And so, because of what others wanted, he threw what we had away and broke my heart."

For as long as Gwen could remember, her aunt had been searching for a man to share her life. One after another had been proven unworthy. It was shocking to learn that decades ago Samantha had been so close to having what she'd always wanted. It made Gwen see the older woman in an entirely new light.

"Do you understand why I'm telling you this?"

"I think so," Gwen answered.

"I don't want you to make the same mistake Brent made," Samantha told her. "Or even me, for that matter."

"You didn't do anything wrong."

"Sure, I did," her aunt disagreed. "What if I'd stood up for myself? What if I had marched across town to his parents' house and pleaded my case, like I was in his father's courtroom? Maybe I could've convinced them that I wasn't the terrible person they imagined me to be. What would've happened if I'd fought for our love instead of lying in bed, crying my eyes out?" At that, a tear ran down Samantha's cheek;

she wiped it away with a sad smile, smearing her mascara. "If I hadn't been such a coward, then maybe I wouldn't have to pretend everything's fine when I see Brent and his beautiful, surely upstanding wife walking down the sidewalk."

Gwen didn't know what to say, struggling to hold back tears of her own.

"If you learn anything from me," her aunt continued, "it's that when it comes to the things in life that really matter — and that most definitely includes finding someone to love — you have to fight. If you listen to your heart, you have to be deaf to everything else. Who cares if other people are angry or sad or even disappointed?" Samantha looked hard at her niece. "When it comes to Hank Ellis, no one else gets the final say; not your parents, not me, not even Kent. If all of Buckton thinks you're wrong but you believe you're right, then to hell with them. It's your choice to make. Being happy is worth everything. You need to ask yourself, 'Do I love Hank? Is he the man I want to be with? Is loving him, no matter what other hardships that might cause, worth it?' "

Listening to Samantha, Gwen knew that she'd been wise to come here. While her aunt may not have given her any answers, at least not directly, she had pointed her in the right direction and given her plenty to think about. What mattered now was what Gwen did with her newfound wisdom.

She had one heck of a decision to make.

CHAPTER SEVENTEEN

"And then I kissed her."

Hank watched Coca-Cola spray from the bottle Skip had pressed to his lips, dribble down his chin, stain his shirt, and begin to splatter at his feet. Skip's mouth moved like he wanted to say something, though no words came out. His friend tried to put his soda on the workbench beside him, but he was so out of sorts that he set it down with a wobble, nearly causing it to fall onto the concrete floor.

Skip had come over in the morning, full of excitement for his newest money-making scheme. Hank had been out in his workshop, bright sunlight streaming through the doors. Talking a mile a minute, Skip had laid out his plan, something that involved old newspapers, while Hank applied varnish to an end table. Hank nodded occasionally, knowing that there wasn't much point in trying to talk once Skip had built up a head of steam. Once he'd finally finished, Skip had asked Hank what he'd been up to the last couple of days. Hank had put down his brush.

Then he'd told Skip what had happened with Gwen and achieved the impossible, rendering Skip Young speechless, if only for a moment.

"Wait, wait, wait," his friend stammered, the words coming out in a rush, making up for lost time. "She actually let you *kiss* her?"

"As opposed to what? It's not like I forced her to do it."

"I didn't mean it like that," Skip explained. "It's just that Gwen's one heck of a looker. She's about as fine a catch as a fella could ever hope to land. Whoever's lucky enough to make her his . . ." His voice trailed off, his face scrunched up in thought. "Hang on, didn't you tell me you met her fiancé?"

Hank nodded. "The night I pulled her from the river."

"Don't take this personal, but if she's supposed to be marrying some other guy, then what's she doin' swappin' spit with you?"

This was the question that had been bothering Hank ever since he'd dropped Gwen off near her home. What *were* they doing? While she had gone to great lengths to make it clear she wasn't engaged to Kent, they were most definitely in a relationship. Why else would she have brought him to Buckton? Still, Hank had reason to be optimistic; wrapping his arms around a woman as beautiful as Gwen, both inside and out, and then kissing her had a way of doing that. But doubt continued to nag at him. He worried that he wasn't good enough for her, that he never would be. Worse, he'd considered that he might be nothing more than a fling.

"That's why I'm trying not to get my hopes up," he answered truthfully. "More than likely, nothing will come of it."

With that, Hank picked up his brush and went back to work. It wasn't until he'd made a couple of strokes that he realized Skip still hadn't spoken. He looked up to find Skip glaring at him.

"Are you out of your freakin' mind?" his friend nearly shouted. "A girl like *Gwen Foster* shows an interest in you and you're tellin' me you're not gonna go after her with everything you got?" Looking disappointed, he shook his head. "I can't believe you're that dumb."

"What's that supposed to mean?"

Skip drained the last of his Coke, then stared hard at Hank. "Ever since your brother died, I've been keepin' a close eye on you, praying that something would come along and pull you outta your funk," he explained. "That's why I'm always tryin' to get you to play ball or grab a bite to eat. I get that you feel guilty about what happened — hell, who wouldn't — but wallowin' in it ain't right." Skip looked around the workshop. "It's like you crawled from that car to here, locked the door, and every once in a while you crack it open and let me in to visit. Now Gwen's knockin', too. She's smart, funny, and plenty gorgeous. What more do you want? An invitation?" Skip sighed. "Mark my words, if you don't do whatever it takes to make her yours, you'll regret it every bit as much as your brother's death."

Hank could only stare. In all the years they'd known each other, Skip had never spoken to him that way. He hadn't known that his friend had been watching so closely, worrying about how he was dealing with Pete's death. Skip was right, though. Hank had walled himself off, keeping everyone at arm's length. But now Gwen had come along, forcing him to make a difficult choice. He could take a chance or play it safe. Hank wished he felt as confident as Skip seemed to be.

"What if it doesn't work out?" he finally asked. "What happens if Gwen decides to stay with that other guy?"

"Then you get up, dust yourself off, and go on with your life," Skip answered. "You've got to take a, what is that, you know, a jump . . ."

"A leap of faith," Hank finished.

Skip snapped his fingers. "That's it! That's what you've got to do. It ain't all that different from when you jumped into the Sawyer. You reacted without thinkin', and look what came of it."

"It's not the same," Hank said. "I only did it because Gwen needed saving."

"So do you," Skip replied.

Hank didn't know what to say. Maybe Skip was right. Maybe he was drowning, too. Maybe he needed to be rescued from his past, from himself. And maybe it was also true that Gwen was his salvation, that meeting her after so many years, falling for her, was the first step toward making things right again.

"Is she worth fighting for?" Skip asked.

He nodded. "Yeah, she is."

"Then what in the hell are you waitin' for? Go get her."

"Right now?"

Skip chuckled. "Still waitin' for that

281

invitation, huh? I tell you one thing: if it was me that Gwen Foster was sweet on, I'd have been there yesterday, poundin' on her door, doin' whatever it took to squeeze in one more date, hell, one more minute of time together."

Hank shook his head. "You make it sound easy."

"That's 'cause it is."

"No, it isn't," he disagreed.

"Why not?"

"For starters, her parents hate my guts. If I just show up at their door, the first thing I see won't be Gwen, but her father's shotgun pointed at my chest," he explained. "Then there's the rich Chicago attorney who thinks he and Gwen are engaged to be married."

Skip hopped down off the workbench. "You can stand here and make excuses till you're blue in the face, but the way I see it, you owe it to yourself to try. It's called a leap of faith, remember?"

With everything that's already happened, with all the troubles trying to pull me under, I've proven to be a hell of a swimmer . . .

"Besides, if she turns you down, you'll always have me," Skip joked.

"That's not much of a consolation."

His friend shrugged. "Beggars can't be choosers." He put his hand on Hank's

282

shoulder and added, "Get goin'."

So Hank put down his brush, grabbed his keys, and did just that.

Hank took a deep breath, then rang the doorbell.

Standing on the Fosters' porch, shaded from the late-morning sun, he felt conspicuous. The whole drive across town, he'd talked himself through what he wanted to do and say, slowly gaining confidence. But by the time he'd parked his truck against the curb, the ticking engine sounding far too loud on the otherwise quiet street, that confidence had vanished. Walking to the porch, Hank had felt as if every eye in the neighborhood was on him. He kept expecting Warren to burst out the front door, shotgun in hand. After taking a moment to steady his nerves, remembering how Gwen's lips had felt pressed against his, he'd rung the bell.

It was too late to turn back now.

Seconds crawled past like minutes, but no one answered. Hank rang the bell again; he could hear the chime sound inside.

But still nothing.

He rapped his knuckles against the door's frame, trying not to hit it too hard, worried that it might sound like he was pounding, as if he was demanding entry. He raised his hand, but before he could knock again, a voice spoke behind him.

"Hank? What are you doing here?"

He turned to find Gwen standing on the walk. Sunlight shone off her hair. Her smile was every bit as radiant, although Hank was surprised that she was wearing the same outfit as yesterday.

"I wanted to see you again," Hank told her truthfully, even if he left out the part about Skip prodding him out of his workshop.

It was clear that his words affected her; Hank saw it in the way a smile spread across her face, how her eyes lit up before looking away, unable to hold his gaze, but then just as quickly returned.

"You wanted to see me that badly?" she asked.

"I did."

"I suppose I should be flattered."

"Maybe so." Hank chuckled. He raised his thumb toward the door. "I knocked, but no one answered."

"That's strange," Gwen said with a frown. "My father's been at the bakery for hours, but my mother should be home. Maybe she went to the grocery store." She paused. "You were willing to come here, to face them, even after what happened the last time they saw you?"

Hank came down the stairs to stand before her. "It doesn't matter," he answered. "Not enough, anyway."

"Now I'm *definitely* flattered," she replied with a laugh.

As much as he wanted to, Hank couldn't return her good cheer. Her outfit kept distracting him, nagging at his thoughts. Something had happened, he was sure of it. "Is everything all right?"

"Why do you ask?"

He nodded at her. "You're wearing the same clothes as the last time I saw you. I'm no Dick Tracy, but it makes me wonder."

"I spent last night at my aunt's," she told him.

"Why not here?"

Gwen sighed. "My parents and I had an argument."

"Let me guess," Hank said, running a hand through his light hair. "They heard that we'd spent the day together."

She didn't answer, her eyes falling to her feet. He knew he was right.

"I'm sorry," he offered.

When Gwen looked back up, her expression was serious. "Don't apologize," she said. "They're the ones at fault. My parents might choose to believe the worst about you, but they're wrong. They don't know you like I do."

Even though a part of Hank was happy to hear Gwen standing up for him, he still felt guilty that he'd caused her so much trouble.

"I don't want to come between you and your folks," he said.

"You're not."

Hank chuckled. "Sure seems that way to me."

"All right, some of it is about you," Gwen admitted. "I just can't understand why they won't recognize what you did for me, or why they aren't willing to give you a chance." She paused. "But a lot of what's happening is because of me."

"How do you figure?"

"The problem is that they still think of me as a little girl. They want to be able to tell me where I can go, what I can do, and especially who I can do it with." Gwen tenderly slipped her hand into his. "They don't realize that I'm a woman now, and that these decisions are mine to make." She smiled, causing his heart to skip a beat. "And right now, what I want most of all is for you to take me out for lunch."

"Downtown?" Hank asked, the thought of being seen on the streets of Buckton as unsettling as ever.

Gwen noticed his discomfort. "We don't have to," she said quickly. "Let me fill a picnic basket instead, then we can drive into the countryside."

Hank knew that Gwen was just trying to make things easier, but it embarrassed him. "Let's go to the diner."

"Are you sure?" she asked.

He thought back to his conversation with Skip. Hank wondered if his friend wasn't right, if he hadn't been making excuses for hiding himself away after Pete's death. Sure, whenever he was in town people stared or made hurtful comments, but why did he let it get to him? He knew the truth about what had happened that night. That's what really mattered. Right then and there, Hank resolved not to let any of that keep him from spending time with Gwen.

"Yeah, I am," he answered.

He had taken a leap of faith, all right.

Now he hoped he didn't end up dashed on the rocks.

When Hank pushed open the door of the diner, its bell chimed. Gwen stepped inside. Lafferty's Diner was a Buckton institution. A countertop ran most of its length, with swivel seats to sit on, a cash register at one end, and the kitchen behind. Booths lined the other side of the restaurant. Large windows filled the room with light. The pleasant aromas of burgers, bacon, coffee, and other smells mingled. At nearly noon, the diner was busy, full of customers.

And every one was staring at them.

Gwen saw many faces she recognized. Alice Merkel, one of her mother's bridge partners, paused midbite. She noticed Nils Crabtree, whose son she had sat behind almost all the way through middle school, gawking over his companion's shoulder. She even saw Eleanor Burch, the organist at the Methodist church, a woman who had babysat Gwen long ago, turn toward her sister, Violet, and start whispering in hushed tones. No one smiled or waved. Most of them frowned, their disapproval obvious.

And Gwen knew why.

It was because of who she was with. It was because of Hank.

"There's a booth in the back," he said pleasantly enough, so used to the stares that he either no longer noticed, or, more likely, chose to ignore them.

Walking across the diner, Gwen felt as if she was being judged with every step. But by the time she slid into her side of the booth, the one that faced toward the en-

288

trance, she had resolved to follow Hank's example, determined not to let the unwanted scrutiny get to her.

"Are you all right?" she asked.

"Oddly enough, yes. It probably doesn't hurt that I'm hungry enough to eat a horse," Hank said, picking up the menu.

Gwen stared at him. She still couldn't believe that he had been at her house, willing to knock on the door and face her parents' disapproval, all because he'd wanted to see her again. The whole walk home from her aunt's, Gwen had thought about him, wondering what he was doing at that moment. Nearing home, recognizing his truck parked against the curb, and then seeing him on the porch, she had gotten her answer. While being with Hank brought its share of troubles, it was worth it. No matter what anyone else thought, he made her happy.

"Do you know what you want?" he asked, closing the menu.

She shook her head. "I can't remember what I used to order."

"Get the meat loaf," he said. "That was always Pete's favorite."

Just then, the waitress appeared. She set a couple of glasses of water down so roughly that some sloshed onto the table, but she made no move to wipe it up. Silverware, fortunately wrapped in a napkin, was tossed down as well.

"What can I get for ya," she said curtly, chewing a piece of gum so hard it seemed as if she was angry at it.

While they ordered — Gwen took Hank's suggestion — the waitress didn't offer more than an occasional grunt. She didn't tell them about the lunch specials, comment on the weather, or make any other idle chitchat. She walked away still scratching what they'd wanted on her notepad.

All of which made Gwen plenty annoyed.

But before she could talk to Hank about it, he said, "Excuse me for a second. I'm going to use the restroom," then got up and left.

Sitting in the booth, Gwen could see the disgust, even outright hostility on the faces of the other diners as Hank moved among them. A few looked back at her, appearing shocked, even a bit disappointed that she was with him. Gwen had always been one of Buckton's favorite daughters, but now she realized that she was being judged guilty for sharing Hank's company. When they had eaten ice cream in his truck, someone had seen them together and decided to tell her father. There was no way Warren wouldn't hear about *this.* When Gwen had first suggested to Hank that they get a bite to eat, she'd believed that it no longer mattered.

Now she wasn't so sure.

Shortly after Hank entered the restroom, their waitress returned to the table. She surprised Gwen by leaning close. When she spoke, her voice was low, barely more than a whisper. "This might be hard for you to hear," she began, pausing to look back over her shoulder, "but that fella you're with is a murderer."

Gwen felt as if someone had slugged her in the stomach. She wanted to argue, to shout how wrong the woman was, to demand that she apologize to Hank, but no words would come out of her open mouth.

"He got drunk and drove his car off the road, killin' his brother," the waitress continued. "When the cops found him, he was walkin' 'round in the road, screamin' at the stars, covered in blood and stinkin' of booze."

Looking at the woman, Gwen realized that she didn't recognize her. She must be new to Buckton, or at least she'd arrived after Gwen had left for Worthington. The waitress believed that she was acting out of kindness, warning a stranger away from someone she thought to be dangerous. But to Gwen, she was spreading rumors about a good man, albeit one who had made a sad, terrible mistake, and dragging what was left of his reputation through the mud.

"He's not like that," Gwen began, her voice rising. "You don't —"

"Is everything all right?"

Gwen glanced up to see Hank looking at her with a concerned expression; while they'd been talking, he had returned from the restroom. His sudden arrival spooked the waitress, who quickly hurried away without another word. Hank shook his head as he slid back into the booth.

"What was that all about?" he asked.

Gwen knew that she couldn't tell him the truth. Though it pained her to realize that he was right, that many in Buckton considered him to be nothing more than a criminal, a killer, she knew what a big step it had been for him to take her out to lunch, to show his face in public. She wouldn't kick his legs out from under him now, not when he'd only just managed to stand.

"Nothing," she lied. "She had a question about our order."

"I hope they get it straightened out quick," he said with a wink, "otherwise I'll go back there and start cooking it myself."

Gwen forced herself to smile, even though,

after what had just happened, she'd completely lost her appetite.

Once they'd finished lunch, and after Gwen had somehow managed to hold her tongue as Hank left the tip for their waitress, they headed for home. Between the contentedness that came from eating a good meal and the refreshing breeze that blew in through her window, to say nothing of Hank's company, Gwen was happy. Still, she knew that this was the calm before the storm. While neither of her parents had been home when Hank had first come calling, her mother would surely have returned by now.

Out of the frying pan and into the fire . . .

"Do you want to drop me off at the end of the block?" Gwen asked, suggesting the same, safer choice they'd made the night before.

But Hank shook his head. "I'm tired of hiding," he said, then chuckled. "We survived the diner, didn't we?"

"Yes," she answered, though it had been harder than he knew.

As the distance to her parents' house grew smaller and smaller, Gwen slipped a hand into Hank's. No matter what was about to happen, Gwen wanted him to know that she wouldn't abandon him, that because of the way he made her feel, they would face their troubles together. As if he'd read her thoughts, Hank looked at her, smiled, and gave her hand a soft squeeze.

The next thing Gwen knew, they had pulled up to the curb.

She took a deep breath. "Are you ready?"

"Not really," he admitted. "But if I sit here too long, I'll talk myself into driving away, and to hell with that." Hank turned to her, a grin spreading across his handsome face. "I'm a lot of things, but a coward isn't one of them."

Stepping out of the truck, Gwen felt buoyed by Hank's strength. She was beginning to believe that together they could convince her parents to see him in a different light, to give him an honest chance to prove their assumptions wrong. But by the time her door swung shut behind her, all of that confidence had vanished. That was because three people were headed down the walk toward them.

Her mother. Her father.

And Kent.

CHAPTER EIGHTEEN

The first time Gwen saw Kent had been at one of her Worthington girlfriends' parties. Crossing the dance floor, coming toward her with a drink in hand, he'd been nothing but smiles. Once, when they sailed on Lake Michigan, she'd told him that his eyes sparkled like the summer sun; though Kent had laughed, he hadn't contradicted her. In a courtroom, he always presented a friendly face to the jury, cracking the occasional joke, acting as if he'd known them for years. A huge part of Kent's incredible success was that he charmed everyone he met.

But now he looked far from friendly. Kent was frightening.

"What is the meaning of this?" he demanded. "Why are you with *him*?"

Normally prim, proper, and so composed that many of his fellow attorneys thought he had ice water running in his veins, Kent was a disheveled mess. His face was twisted into an ugly scowl, his complexion red. His tie was unknotted, his expensive clothes wrinkled, as if he had slept in them. Sweat soaked his brow, ran down his cheeks, and darkened the collar of his shirt.

Gwen had never seen him in such a state.

"I've been worried sick!" he said. "And it seems for good reason!"

" 'Cause she's been runnin' around with this troublemaker," her father added, shooting a withering look Hank's way.

"Here I was, working day and night back in Chicago, trying to build a future for the two of us, thinking you wanted the same thing. Was I wrong?"

Back and forth the two of them went, as if they were a duo, like actors on a stage. They were relentless, not giving Gwen a chance to protest, verbally assaulting her with their accusations. She hazarded a glance at her mother; while Meredith had yet to join in the badgering, she hadn't spoken in her daughter's defense, either.

"The last time we talked you hung up on me!" Kent continued.

"There was a fire and I wanted —" was all she managed before he interrupted.

"I was willing to give you the benefit of the doubt. I assumed there must have been a reason that you never called back, likely that you were having a good time with your friends and family." He looked hard at her, his expression darkening. "But then your father telephoned and told me what you'd been doing. I knew I had no choice but to get on the first train back to Buckton and show you what a terrible mistake you're making."

Gwen realized that the reason her parents hadn't been home when Hank knocked was because they'd been at the depot picking up Kent. It hurt her that they had gone behind her back, acting as if she'd behaved badly, as if she had been out of control.

"I haven't done anything wrong," she answered, her voice defiant.

"He's a murderer!" Kent insisted, waving a hand at Hank, who, with his muscular arms folded across his chest, still hadn't said a word.

"You don't know the first thing about him!"

"He might not," her father interjected, "but I sure as heck do." Warren put his hands on his daughter's shoulders. "I know I must sound like a scratched record, but he ain't good for you, Gwennie. You got some mixed-up thoughts runnin' around in your head. You're confused and he's takin' advantage."

Gwen shook herself free, clearly surprising her father. "He saved my life!" she argued. "Have you forgotten that?"

"The rottenest of apples rises to the top of the bushel from time to time. But no one's ignorin' what he did. He got his share of thanks for it."

"All he got from you were ridiculous accusations that he'd had something to do with what had happened to me," Gwen argued, unable to believe what she was hearing. "Then you threw him out of the house!"

"She's right," Meredith agreed, finally speaking. "We were all scared out of our wits, but Hank wasn't treated right."

"And as for you," Gwen said, turning her ire toward Kent. "You thanked Hank for rescuing me by offering him money?!"

Kent's reaction wasn't to deny her accusation, or even to reluctantly acknowledge that it was true, but rather to turn and glare at Hank for ratting him out, like he'd violated some rule, as if they were members of a club.

Hank remained silent, responding with a stare.

"How else was I supposed to express my gratitude?" Kent asked Gwen.

"Not by pulling out your billfold," she argued. "You may find this hard to believe,

298

but there are people who do things out of a genuine desire to help, not because they want a pile of money stacked in their hand."

Gwen could see that she was irritating Kent, but she didn't regret any of her words. He needed to understand that what he and her father had done, treating Hank so poorly, was wrong.

But Kent wouldn't, or possibly couldn't, understand.

"Let's go inside and talk about this," he said.

"No," she answered with a shake of her head. Gwen knew that Kent wanted to get her away from Hank. If she accepted his offer, Hank wouldn't be allowed to follow. Once again, he'd be left outside.

This time, she wasn't going to allow that to happen.

"Come on, Gwen," Kent persisted, reaching for her arm.

"If there's something you want to say to me," she replied, stepping back to avoid his touch, "then say it right here, right now."

Kent leaned close and lowered his voice. "Come on, honey," he said sweetly, obviously hoping that the sugar in his voice would help make her see reason. "This isn't any way to act. A woman who's engaged to be married shouldn't —"

"Stop it!" Gwen shouted at him, her frustration finally boiling over. "I've told you again and again, ever since you announced that we were engaged, that I never agreed to it. You didn't even propose! Don't you dare act otherwise!"

"Gwennie, you're bein' ridiculous," her father said. "Your mother and I have always wanted what was best for you. Trust me, that's marryin' Kent. Why would you risk all you've got for some two-bit woodcarver?"

"Hey, now," Hank said, finally roused to speak.

"Shut your mouth!" Warren barked, not letting him say more. "Ever since you butted into her life, all you've done is mess it up!"

"Stop blaming him!" Gwen shouted, surprising herself by so blatantly standing up to her father. "Hank isn't forcing me to do anything. It's my choice to spend time with him!"

To Gwen's ears, her words sounded innocent enough, but from the way Kent reacted, it was as if she'd admitted to kissing Hank.

"How *dare* you?" he demanded. "Have you no respect? No decency?"

Gwen stepped back. Kent was irate, his eyes wild, nothing like the man who up until then had been sharing her life.

But he wasn't irate with her. He was yelling at Hank.

"What kind of man are you?" Kent continued. He stepped toward Hank and began to jab a finger into Hank's chest, over and over, as hard as he could. "Too ignorant to know better? Is that your excuse for meddling with another's girl?"

Once again, Hank stayed silent, letting Kent vent his rage. His hands were balled into fists, but they never left his sides. He watched the other man with flat, almost impassive eyes, refusing to let any of Kent's insults get to him.

But his indifference only fueled Kent's anger. "Are you the kind of man who gets his kicks from manipulating innocent girls?"

Hank shook his head. "Gwen's a woman. She can think for herself."

Kent replied with a humorless chuckle. Then, without warning, he shoved his hands into the bigger man's chest, forcing Hank to stumble backward, though he remained on his feet. "Stay away from her."

"Stop it, Kent!" Gwen shouted, but he wasn't listening.

What happened next felt as if it occurred in slow motion, and even though Gwen saw it coming, she was helpless to stop it.

Without another hateful word, Kent

punched Hank in the face. Though Kent was hardly an experienced brawler, Hank's head snapped to the side. The blow sounded powerful, bone hitting bone. The shock of it was enough to make Gwen gasp. Her parents were equally dumbfounded, watching in disbelief.

Hank put his fingers against his mouth; when he drew them back, they were red with blood.

"I understand why you're mad," he said, lifting his gaze from his crimson-stained fingers to Kent, "but that's the last time you put your hands on me. Try it again and I won't be the one bleeding."

Though Hank's threat was meant to dissuade Kent from more violence, he reacted like he'd been laughed at, as if his manhood had been questioned or he'd been outright challenged to throw another punch.

"We'll just see about that," Kent spat as he reared back, his fist cocked.

But before he could throw it, Gwen stepped between the two men, her hands raised. "That's enough!" she shouted.

Kent didn't seem dissuaded. "Get out of the way, Gwen," he said, moving steadily forward, as if he meant to walk right through her.

Thankfully, in the end, her father proved

to be the voice of reason. Calmly but firmly, he grabbed Kent by the arm and pulled him away. The lawyer struggled to break free of the baker's grip, but Warren was too strong. "Take a stool, Joe Louis," he said. "I agree with what you're aimin' to do, but fightin' ain't the way to go about it."

Gwen's heart raced. She could hardly believe what had happened. Kent had come back from Chicago. He'd punched Hank. Everything was a mess.

"I should go," Hank told her out of ear-shot of the others.

She looked and saw blood smeared across his chin, as well as a bruise already flower-ing where Kent's blow had landed.

"Don't let him chase you away," Gwen told him.

Hank chuckled, low and short. "It isn't on account of him," he said, nodding toward Kent. "If it came to a fight, it wouldn't take long to show Mr. Fancy-Pants the error of his ways." He paused. "But I shouldn't be here, for your sake."

"Me? But why? I don't understand."

"Your father's right. No good will come from causing a scene. If this goes on much longer, someone's going to call the police," he explained. "With my reputation being what it is, there's no telling what might happen. But if I leave, maybe things can get sorted out."

What Hank was suggesting made sense. With him gone, Kent and her parents would likely calm down. They *might* even be willing to listen. But she was tired of fighting for every inch. Deep down inside, she knew it was too late. Too much had happened already for her to put things back the way they were. Regardless of whether she could, she didn't *want* that.

It was time to take a different path.

"If you leave," she told Hank, "then I'm going with you."

Hank stared at her for a moment, then nodded. "Are you sure?"

"With all of my heart."

But when Hank rounded the front of the truck, Gwen didn't follow. She had something else she had to do first.

She went straight to Kent, who was still trying to free himself from her father's grip. "We're finished," she told him matter-of-factly.

Gwen had expected her self-declared fiancé's face to fill with anger, his eyes to widen with shock, but instead he seemed confused. "What are you talking about?" he asked.

"You and I, we're done. I can't be with

you anymore," she explained; with every word, Gwen felt liberated, as if a huge weight was being lifted from her shoulders. She wasn't frightened or nervous, her hands weren't shaking, and she wasn't plagued by doubt. In fact, she couldn't remember the last time she'd been so certain. "I'm sorry," she said, "but this is the way it has to be."

Slowly but surely, Kent understood. "What . . . what are you saying?" he sputtered. "You can't be serious . . ."

"Good-bye, Kent," she replied, then turned to leave.

"Hang on there, Gwennie," her father began, causing her to pause. "Don't you think you oughta —"

"Hush, Warren," Meredith said, silencing her husband. Through all the arguing, her mother had said little, though she'd appeared concerned. Looking at her daughter, she asked, "Are you sure about this, Gwendolyn?"

"I am," Gwen answered.

Meredith nodded. "Then do what you have to." Buoyed by her mother's words, Gwen opened the passenger door and got in beside Hank.

Kent's anger grew by the second. "Don't you dare drive away from me!" he shouted, finally managing to shrug free of Warren's grip and come closer to the truck. "We aren't finished! Not yet!"

In answer, Hank pulled away from the curb.

"If you leave, you'll regret it!" Kent kept on, his voice rising. He'd drawn near enough to bang his fist on the truck's rear panel; inside the cab, it sounded as loud as a gunshot. "This isn't over! I won't let you get —"

Whatever else he said was lost behind them as they drove away.

Gwen never once looked back.

Ever since they'd driven away from her parents' house, the only voices heard inside the truck's cab had come from the radio. Gwen stared out her window, absently listening to Doris Day. Her head was a stormy sea. She couldn't stop thinking about what had just happened. Snippets replayed themselves over and over again. The anger written across Kent's face. How her mother had unexpectedly stood up for her. The sharp sound of Hank being struck. Her words as she ended her relationship with Kent. Gwen felt as if her life had spun out of control the moment she had arrived back in Buckton, picking up speed as it went.

But she didn't regret what she had done. Not at all.

Hank didn't speak, either. He didn't complain about the terrible things that had been said about him. He didn't regret not fighting back. He didn't ask questions about her breakup. And he never told her where they were going.

Still, Gwen wasn't the least bit surprised when they pulled into his drive.

He parked in front of his workshop and shut off the truck's engine. By now, the sun had started to set; if they'd arrived five minutes later, it would have been right in their eyes. Dark, ominous clouds were looming to the west. Gwen suspected it would soon rain. Looking over at Hank, one of his hands still on the steering wheel, Gwen found him undeniably handsome; even under the circumstances, he was still capable of taking her breath away. No wonder Kent had been so jealous.

Without the radio playing, the silence between them became more noticeable. "I'm sorry about what happened," Gwen said.

Hank shook his head. "Don't be. We've got no more control over what other people say than we do over when the sun rises each morning. If anyone's to blame, it's me."

"How could it be your fault?"

"Because I knew that by showing up at your folks' place, we were asking for trouble. Kent being there made it that much worse."

Gwen didn't know how to respond. He was right. They should've known what they were getting into. After all, it wasn't as if her parents had kept their feelings for Hank a secret. But she hadn't anticipated that her father would call Kent. It was like adding gasoline to a fire.

"Are you hungry?" Hank asked.

"A bit," Gwen admitted, thinking back to how she'd only nibbled at her lunch, rattled by what their waitress had said.

"Come on. I'll whip something up."

Gwen followed Hank inside. When they entered the kitchen, he said, "I'm not too bad of a cook, you know. My omelets are nothing to —"

When Hank abruptly fell silent, he also stopped moving; Gwen was so close that she couldn't avoid bumping into his back. But then, even as she wondered what had happened, she saw the answer.

Someone was lying on the floor.

The curtains had been drawn and the lights were all off, shrouding the room in dark shadows. A man lay facedown with one arm outstretched. He wasn't moving. A broken plate and the remains of a meal were scattered across the floor. A pair of nearly empty bottles added to the mess. A chair was tangled up with his legs, making it appear as if he'd been sitting at the small table before falling.

She smelled alcohol.

Then Gwen noticed the dark puddle near the man's head. At first she assumed that something had spilled. But when Hank flipped on a light and she saw how big it was, how *red* it was, she gasped from fright and surprise.

"Dad!" Hank shouted as he ran over and began to shake the man's shoulder. There was no response. "Can you hear me?!"

Gwen moved as if in a trance. Her foot crunched on a broken piece of plate. She reached Hank just as he rolled his father over. Myron Ellis was hard to recognize. Gone was the cheerful man she'd once greeted at the bakery, someone who always had a joke ready for her father. Looking down at him, Gwen saw a face that was both gaunt and pale, his cheeks covered with an unkempt beard. His nose, a maze of ruptured blood vessels, looked as if it had been broken, twisted awkwardly to one side. But what she couldn't tear her eyes away from was the deep gash just above one eyebrow, still oozing blood.

Over and over, Hank shouted his father's name, but Myron's eyes didn't flutter, his limbs remained motionless, and no words escaped his lips. To Gwen, he looked dead.

"Call an ambulance! We need to get him some help!"

It took Gwen a moment to realize that Hank was shouting at *her.* Tearing her eyes from Myron, she looked at his son and saw fear written on his face. She ran into the living room, searching for the telephone.

Even as she found it, Gwen feared that they were already too late.

Hank stood at the sink, washing his father's dried blood from his hands. Again and again he scrubbed them beneath the scalding-hot water, staining it crimson before it swirled down the drain. It was under his nails, deep in the nooks and crevices of his skin, between his fingers. In a way, it also coursed through his veins.

Even over the hiss of the faucet, Hank could hear Gwen offering thanks to the last remaining police officer. Ever since they had discovered Myron unconscious on the floor, she'd been a godsend. Without her help, especially in dealing with the authorities, Myron wouldn't already be at the hospital.

When they'd first found his father on the kitchen floor, Hank had thought he was dead. Myron had gotten drunk and then fallen, hitting his head on the edge of the table, the blow powerful enough to kill him. Cradling him, Hank had silently said goodbye. But then, before the ambulance arrived, his father had sputtered awake, sitting up as if nothing had happened, reaching for an overturned bottle before he'd even said a word. When Myron had noticed Gwen standing in the doorway, wide-eyed with disbelief, he'd demanded to know who she was and what she was doing in his house; even as Hank explained, his father had looked at *him* like he was a stranger. Myron had initially argued against any medical attention, but had eventually realized that his cut was more than a simple bandage could heal, so he'd agreed to stitches and a night's observation at the hospital, leaving Hank to clean up his mess.

Again.

"Everyone's gone."

Hank looked up and saw Gwen's reflection in the window. Beyond, night had fallen, the stars obscured by clouds. A storm was rolling in.

"Thanks. For everything," he told her.

He saw her shake her head. "You don't

have to thank me," she said. "I'm just glad I was here."

"Me too."

Hank shut off the faucet but didn't turn around. Silence descended. He took a deep breath. Ever since they'd found his father, Hank had understood that things between him and Gwen would be different. She would have questions she wanted to ask, questions that deserved answers. He owed her the truth.

Ever since Pete had died, he'd kept himself locked away, trapped by fate as well as by a snare of his own making. But then, in the aftermath of a storm, entirely by chance, he had found Gwen and everything changed. Accepting how he felt for her, allowing their relationship to grow, meant that he would have to unburden himself.

He had to take another leap.

She'd stood up to her parents, to Kent, defending him when almost no one else in Buckton would. She had jeopardized all she'd built back in Chicago.

For him.

How can I not risk something in return?

"Gwen . . . there's something I need to tell you . . ." he began, gripping the edge of the counter. "Something that's going to be hard to hear. Something you might not believe, though I swear that it's true." He paused, gathering himself. "It's about Pete. About the night he died . . ."

Hank's heart pounded. This was the furthest he'd ever come in talking about what happened to his brother. No one knew, not even Skip.

"What is it?" Gwen asked innocently.

He turned around, ready to answer, but her beauty stopped him short. Every time he looked at Gwen, Hank wondered how he was lucky enough to have her be a part of his life. Skip was right; she *was* a knockout. He wanted their time together to go on and on. Forever. To make that happen, he couldn't falter. Not now. He had to trust in her.

"Everyone thinks that I'm responsible for Pete's death. The police. Your parents. The whole town. But it isn't true." Hank shook his head. "I didn't kill my brother."

CHAPTER NINETEEN

The last twenty-four hours of Gwen's life had been full of surprises. The argument with her parents that had led her to spend the night with Samantha. Coming home to find Hank standing on her porch. The terrible things their waitress had said at the diner. Discovering that Kent had come from Chicago to confront her. Finding Myron Ellis unconscious in a pool of his own blood.

But none of them compared to what she'd just heard.

"What . . . what did you say?" Gwen asked, thinking that she must have misheard, that she hadn't understood.

"Pete didn't die because of me," Hank repeated. "I wasn't driving."

It made no more sense the second time she heard it. Gwen's thoughts twisted and turned, as if the ground had fallen out beneath her feet; it was like being back in the raging river. All she had heard since she'd been back in Buckton was that Hank Ellis was a murderer, that he had gotten drunk and killed his brother in a car accident. Now he was telling her that it wasn't true.

A sudden, painful thought occurred to her. Maybe Hank was telling her this in order to overcome the many obstacles their relationship faced. If everyone, especially her parents and Kent, was mistaken, then they could be together more easily. Maybe he wanted to be with her so badly that he was willing to lie.

"You don't believe me, do you?" Hank asked, as if he'd read her mind.

"It's . . . I just . . ." Gwen stumbled.

"It's all right," he said. "I understand why you wouldn't." Hank pushed himself away from the sink and came a couple of steps closer. "I bet if you asked every last person in Buckton who was responsible for Pete's death, they'd all say the same thing. That I did it."

Gwen nodded. She was sure he was right.

He reached out and gently took her hand. "But I swear it isn't true," he said emphatically. "I'm *not* responsible for Pete's death."

She searched Hank's face, looking for something, anything that might prove his sincerity false, but she found nothing. As crazy as it seemed, Gwen believed him, which only raised more questions.

"If it wasn't you, then why does everyone think otherwise?" she asked.

Hank was silent for a moment, staring intently at her. Through the window over his shoulder, lightning flashed.

"Because that's what I want them to think," he answered.

Gwen was stunned. "You *want* them to think you killed your brother? Why? It doesn't make any sense!"

"I did it to protect someone I love," Hank explained. "I had no choice. There was nothing else I could do. So I lied to the police. I lied to all of my friends. I've lied to everyone since that night." He raised a hand and tenderly placed it against her cheek. His skin was warm to the touch. "Until now."

Looking into Hank's eyes, Gwen thought that she might know the truth. It was Pete. His brother had been the one driving, had lost control of the car and crashed, costing him his life. Maybe they'd both been drinking. Maybe there was another reason for the accident. But in the end, Hank had chosen to protect Pete's reputation at the cost of his own.

The low rumble of thunder rolled over

the house. "It was Pete, wasn't it?" she asked, voicing her suspicion.

Surprisingly, Hank shook his head. "No," he answered. "Pete died just like everyone believes, right there in the passenger seat."

"I don't understand. If it wasn't you or Pete driving, then who?"

A profound sadness filled his eyes. "It was my father."

The night that Pete died began like many others in the months after their mother's passing, with the two brothers out in the workshop while Myron was off somewhere getting drunk. The sounds of a baseball game echoed around the room, interrupted by the occasional scrape of a lathe or knock of hammer and chisel.

"Come on, already! Get a hit!" Pete shouted at the radio. He sat on a bench, legs dangling, nervously picking at his thumbnail.

"They can't hear you, you know," Hank teased before blowing away shavings in order to get a better look at the chair he was working on.

"You don't know that. If every Reds fan started yelling at the same time, I bet they could hear it all the way at Crosley Field."

Hank laughed. "You're nuts."

Just then, the unmistakable sound of a bat hitting a ball came over the radio, followed by the announcer's call. "There's a looping liner over the head of the second baseman and the lead runner moves over to third!"

"See?" Pete said, as if he'd been proven right.

Even as he was enjoying it, Hank already missed this time with his brother. Pete would be graduating from high school in a couple of months before heading off to college, the first in their family to do so. Though Pete was too modest to admit it, he was too smart to stick around Buckton. Hank knew it wouldn't be the same without him, but he was happy for his brother, too. Pete was going to be successful enough for the both of them. Hank was certain that their mother was watching up in heaven, proud of the men her boys were becoming.

"The Reds are gonna win the pennant this year, for sure," Pete proclaimed.

"You say that every year."

"Yeah, well this time I mean it."

As much as Hank loved baseball, his passion for the game paled in comparison to his brother's. Every Cincy win was cause for celebration, every loss an occasion for despair. When Pete had been younger, he'd refused to go to bed unless he could sleep with his glove.

"I hope they're as confident as you," Hank said. "If so, then —"

He was interrupted by the sound of the phone ringing in the house. Hank went to answer it; there was no way Pete was going to budge from the game. Halfway across the yard, he heard cheering. The Reds had scored.

"Hello?" he said as he picked up the receiver.

"Hank?" a man's voice asked.

"Yeah."

"Hey, it's Rex McChesney down at the bar. I hate to call you like this, but we just tossed your old man outta here for bein' ornery. He was threatenin' to bust up the joint if he didn't get another drink, but I'd already cut him off. Shoulda done it an hour earlier. He stumbled off, but from the way he was actin', I'm pretty sure he's gonna cause more trouble. I figured you'd wanna know."

"Thanks for the warning."

Hank ran a hand through his hair. Ever since their mother had died, Myron had been in a downward spiral. In the beginning, the drinking had been understandable, a way to cope with the pain of his loss. He missed Eleanor. Everyone did. But where his sons fought through their grief, refusing to let it define them, Myron wallowed in it. They kept expecting their father to snap out of his malaise, but he never did. It only got worse. Every time Hank saw Myron nowadays, there was sadness in his eyes, a wound so raw that his son wondered if it would ever heal.

"We scored three that inning!" Pete exclaimed when Hank returned to the workshop. "The Reds got this one in the bag!" But then, seeing his brother's sour expression, he asked, "What's wrong?"

"I just got a call from the bar," Hank began, then recounted what he'd heard.

Pete pointed at the car in the drive. "How'd he get there?"

Hank shrugged. "Walked or hitchhiked. As bad as Dad's gotten, he's not going to let a couple miles keep him from a drink."

"I thought he was inside, asleep."

"All I know is that I've got to pick him up before he causes a ruckus and ends up in jail."

"I'll go," Pete offered, hopping down from the bench. "You keep working on your chair."

"Are you sure? You know how he can get."

Normally Myron was an easy, if slightly melancholic, drunk. But every once in a while, when he'd had way too much, he could get feisty. Just last week, he'd tried to shove Hank but had lost his balance and fallen on his face.

"I'll be fine. A Coke says he falls asleep as soon as he gets in the car."

"What about your game?"

"Aw, the Reds are gonna win easy. Besides, I can listen to it in the car," Pete said, flashing an easy smile. "You got the keys?"

Hank tossed them across the workshop and Pete effortlessly snagged them like the good outfielder he'd always been.

"Be right back," he said over his shoulder, walking to the car.

Hank had no way of knowing it, but that would be the last time he ever saw his brother alive.

Once Pete had gone, Hank returned to his chair. As he worked his hammer and chisel, he listened to the end of the baseball game; just as Pete had predicted, the Reds won. He carved a notch, then another, and another and so on, each bringing him one step closer to his vision of the piece. As was often the case when Hank worked, he lost track of time; he didn't know whether a minute had passed or an hour or two. He was cleaning off his tools when he heard it, a sound nearby. It was faint, yet unmistakable. The screeching of tires. A second later, a crash. Then silence. Hank's heart lurched.

Right then, just like that, he knew. It was as clear to him as if it had happened right in front of him. His tools hit the floor with a clatter.

Hank ran. In seconds, he was past the house, had burst through a copse of trees, and was sprinting toward the sound. His hands and legs pumped hard, his chest heaved, but he still cursed himself for not moving faster. It was dark, the half-moon obscured by patchy clouds, and he stumbled but refused to go down. A quarter mile from home, Hank found what he'd feared he would.

The car had dropped down an incline before smashing into a towering oak. The front end was crumpled, folded in on itself like an accordion. Tires were missing, probably shot off into the trees. Gouges had been dug into the soft earth, showing the path the vehicle had taken. While one headlight was out, the other continued to shine, illuminating the woods with an eerie glow. Even wrecked, he immediately recognized the car.

"No, no, no, no, no," Hank kept repeating, as if by wishing for it he could make the crash not have happened.

He ran to the driver's side and yanked hard on the door. It protested, but opened. Hank had expected to find Pete, so he was stunned when his father fell onto the ground. Myron landed on his back, then moaned. High above, the cloud cover parted; enough moonlight shone down for Hank to see blood on his father's face and staining his clothes. The smell of alcohol was strong.

When Hank looked in the car, it felt as if his heart stopped.

Pete was as broken and motionless as the car, but that didn't keep Hank from crawling inside, through the blood, booze, and broken glass, to touch him. He shouted Pete's name over and over again, then cursed what had been taken from him while tears streamed down his face. He bargained and bartered, offering his own life in exchange for the ability to wind back time, to insist on being the one to drive into town, to make this wrong right, but nothing changed.

His brother was still dead.

"Wha . . . what in the hell's goin' on . . . ?"

Hearing his father's voice filled Hank with rage. In a flash, he was out of the wrecked car and lifting Myron off the ground by two fistfuls of his bloody shirt, not giving a damn if the man was hurt.

"What have you done?" Hank demanded, his voice echoing off the trees and down the empty road.

"What . . . what're you talkin' 'bout?" his father slurred, his head lolling around on his shoulders, his eyes unfocused and distant.

"Why were you driving?" Hank roared, giving the drunken man a rough shake. "Why was it you and not Pete?"

"I . . . I ain't done nothin' wrong . . ." Myron managed. "Where's my . . . Wait . . . I think I . . . think I dropped my drink . . ."

As Hank listened to his father, who was either unaware or uncaring of the damage he'd caused, his fury threatened to consume him. He wanted to take his fists and beat the man, to end his life as the crash had somehow failed to do, to take a measure of revenge for his having caused Pete's death. But before Hank could act on his murderous impulse, Myron fell unconscious, his head slumping onto his son's chest.

Looking down at his father's bleeding face, Hank felt his anger drain away. In its place was a mixture of sadness and pity. He was flooded by memories of better times: Myron showing his oldest son how to hold a hammer, teaching him the intricacies of throwing a baseball, taking him and Pete sledding at Christmastime. So much had been taken from Myron with the death of his beloved wife that he hadn't been able to cope. Now that failure had cost him even more.

Hank began to sob. He no longer wanted to hurt his father. He wanted to heal him. Myron was now all the family he had left.

During the walk back to the house, carrying Myron in his arms, Hank formulated a plan. It was risky, dangerous even, but with every step he took, he felt as if he had no other choice. And so, after laying his father on the couch, checking his wounds, and taking a deep breath, Hank picked up the phone.

"I'd like to report an accident," he began.

Back at the site of the crash, Hank struggled to cope with the enormity of his loss. Disbelief tried to coax him into taking another look inside the car, but he fought off the urge. He knew all too well the sight that waited for him. Hank doubted that he'd ever be able to forget it. So instead, he raged. Covered in blood and liquor, he clenched his fists and struck his chest, his eyes overflowing with tears as he shouted at the sky, demanding answers he knew he would never receive.

When the first police car arrived, its siren loud, its blue and red lights bouncing off the trees, Hank was screaming at the top of his lungs.

". . . and that's when I saw the police car."

Listening to Hank's story, Gwen had been spellbound. Everything she'd been told about the night Pete Ellis had died was wrong. Hank wasn't responsible. He hadn't killed his brother, no matter what he'd led everyone in Buckton to believe.

"You told the police that you did it," she said, putting the final pieces of the puzzle together. "You said that you were driving."

Hank nodded. Outside, another bolt of lightning flashed.

"You could have gone to jail."

"I did, for a while." Thunder grumbled. The storm was coming closer.

"It could have been forever."

"I know."

Gwen's head spun. There were details that nagged at her, that made the writer in her sit up and take notice.

"What about the bartender?" she asked.

"Rex? What about him?"

"He talked to you on the phone. Wouldn't he have known you hadn't been drinking?"

"Maybe, but I only said a couple of words

326

to him," Hank explained. "For all he knew, I was every bit as sloshed as my old man. After I hung up with Rex, I got in the car, dragged Pete along, and headed for town, just like he'd suggested, but we never made it. I was too drunk to drive and got in an accident."

"That still doesn't explain how Myron got home. If you didn't pick him up, then how did he get here?"

"The same way he made it to the bar in the first place," he answered. "He either walked or hitched a ride."

"What about when you reported the accident?" Gwen continued. "Who did the police think made the call?"

Hank shook his head. "You're acting like there were questions about who caused the accident, but there weren't. I was standing there in the road, covered in blood and alcohol, and I never once claimed that I didn't do it. As far as the police and everyone else in Buckton was concerned, I was as guilty as sin."

"Didn't the police want to know what happened?"

"Of course they did. I told them I had no idea. I also said that I'd been drinking."

"You lied."

"What choice did I have?" Hank asked. "I

couldn't tell them the truth."

"You took the blame so your father wouldn't have to."

Hank nodded. "I had to make a quick decision," he explained. "Maybe if I'd had more time, I would've done things differently, but once I picked up the phone and reported the accident, there was no turning back." He sighed deeply. "All I wanted was to protect my dad. After everything he'd already lost, I was convinced that if he had to accept responsibility for Pete's death, it would've been too much for him. I was afraid that he'd grab his gun and take his own life. I reckoned he couldn't live with what he'd done."

"Does he know what happened?"

"At first, I wasn't sure. Once in a while, when he'd get good and drunk, he'd black out and wouldn't remember anything. For a time after the accident, he didn't speak to me. I thought he was just angry, blaming me for Pete's death. But then, about a week after the funeral, and right after the judge had decided not to charge me with anything, he came up behind me in the workshop . . ."

When Hank fell silent, Gwen wanted to press, but didn't.

"He told me that even though I hadn't been driving that night," Hank eventually said, "it was still my fault that Pete was dead."

CHAPTER TWENTY

Outside, the storm had let loose its fury. Wind gusted, swinging tree branches back and forth, some to their breaking point. Thunder followed lightning, one after the other in their heavenly dance. Rain lashed against the windows and drummed on the roof in a frenzied cadence, though it couldn't keep up with the furious beating of Hank's heart.

Telling Gwen the truth had been, in some ways, easier than he had anticipated. Letting go of his secret, especially to someone he genuinely cared for, eased much of the burden he'd been carrying. But now, remembering all the terrible words his father had spoken brought the pain rushing back.

"Myron said . . . he said that *you* were to blame?" Gwen asked in stunned disbelief. "*He* was driving! It was *his* fault!"

Hank shook his head. "That's not what my father meant."

"What else could he mean?"

"Pete's death was on me because I let my brother go get him that night. My father said that if I'd been the one to pick him up, he never would've been able to take the keys from me. He told me that Pete wasn't as strong as I was, physically or otherwise, and I could have stopped him." Hank paused, listening to another clap of thunder. "In some ways, he's right."

Tears filled Gwen's eyes. "You couldn't have known."

But I should've . . .

Hank didn't give his thought voice. He didn't confess that he'd turned that night over again and again ever since: tossing his keys across the workshop, Pete saying that he'd be fine, watching him walk toward the car . . .

"Even if your father truly believed that," Gwen told him, "why would he say it to you? It's so cruel."

"He only said it because he was drunk," Hank explained, then sighed deeply. "The worst part about that night, about deciding to take the blame for what happened to Pete, was that I did it in the hopes that it would straighten my father out. I figured that even if he thought I had been the one driving, that I was drunk, it would scare him into giving up the booze. But it only made things worse. He drank more than ever. Each time I found a bottle around the house, I'd throw it away or hide it, but he always managed to get his hands on more. My becoming the most hated man in Buckton didn't heal my father. It ripped his wound open that much wider. He might be alive and out of jail, but I've lost him all the same."

Lightning flashed, another fork shooting toward the ground.

"Do you want to hear something crazy?" Hank asked.

"What?"

"I dream about that night."

Gwen nodded. "That's perfectly understandable."

"No, not like that," he said. "In my dreams, I'm behind the wheel, drunk as a skunk, screaming at my terrified brother. Pete's scared out of his wits, but nothing he says makes me slow down. Sometimes I even hit him." Hank clenched his fists, shaking, fighting his demons. "I wake up right as the car crashes, drenched in sweat, shouting, convinced that that's how it actually happened. Maybe it's because of the guilt my father made me feel. Or maybe I actually blame myself."

Hank felt the familiar anger welling up inside him. Talking about Pete's death hadn't completely rid him of the months of hurtful, bitter frustration. But then, just as he feared he might boil over, Gwen reached out and took his hand in her own. Though her palm was much smaller than his, it felt as if she was enveloping him, her warm, soft touch the perfect antidote for his rage. Just having her near, listening without judging, made all the difference. She soothed him.

"You can choose to believe the nonsense your father said," Gwen told him, tenderly rubbing her thumb over the back of his hand. "You can beat yourself up, wondering whether you should've done something differently. Or you can consider what Pete would say." Hank had been looking away from her, but at the mention of his brother's name, his eyes found hers. She gave him a gentle smile. "He wouldn't blame you for what happened. Not a chance."

Tears began to well in Hank's eyes, but he held them back. "I miss him so much."

"I know you do."

"He was just such a damned great guy."

"Yeah, he was."

"Some brothers and sisters can be jealous of each other."

"So I've heard," Gwen said.

"In Pete and my case, it would've been easy to hold his success against him. He was so smart. So funny. Everything I struggled to do was a piece of cake for him. But I never held it against him. I was always so damned proud. Everyone he met might have loved him, but no one more than me."

Gwen moved closer, her body brushing against his. "Pete's not the only one who lost something that night," she told him. "So did you. You just need to understand that it will take time to heal."

"I wish it was that easy," he answered.

"It isn't," she agreed. "But that doesn't mean it's impossible, either."

Hank stared into Gwen's eyes, mesmerized by her beauty. That she was even a part of his life was miraculous, but he never would've imagined that she'd touch him the way she had, making him feel things he'd thought lost for good. She was a lighthouse, he a ship lost at sea. Because of her, he'd made his way safely to shore.

He may have let Kent and her father rant and rave. He'd even allowed himself to be struck. But for Gwen Foster, he would fight like hell.

This time, when the thunder rumbled, it made the house shake.

"There's something I want to ask you,"

she said.

"What is it?"

Gwen paused, as if weighing whether to voice her request. "You told me the truth about what happened," she said softly. "Why? Why me?"

Hank smiled. The answer to her question was simple. It welled up inside him, something that had been steadily building from the moment he had recognized her on the bank of the river. It was there in the sound of her voice. The tender touch of her lips. The curve of her smile. He supposed that he'd known it for a while but hadn't yet been able to put it into words. But now, after finally unburdening his deepest secret, he had his chance. Thinking about telling her didn't make him nervous but filled him with happiness.

"Because I love you."

Gwen's head spun. Hearing what had really happened the night Pete died had been a lot like being back in the swollen river. She'd been tossed this way and that, helpless to choose where she was going. Every twist and turn threatened to pull her under. But in the end, Hank came through again. Gwen *believed* him. She believed that he hadn't been driving. She believed that he'd been willing to take responsibility for his brother's death in order to protect his father. Without question, she knew that he was telling the truth.

Just like when he told her he loved her.

It wasn't the first time Gwen had heard those three simple yet powerful words. Kent had said them many times, but the way she'd reacted then was a far cry from the feelings Hank elicited. Her eyes grew wide. Her mouth fell open. Her pulse quickened. She felt as if she was floating on air and weak in the knees, both at the same time. Gwen realized that she'd been waiting and hoping for this moment, the seeds of which stretched all the way back to their ride to Mansfield. All that had happened since, including ice cream, baseball, kisses, and even the obstacles placed in their way, was part of a journey she was happy to have traveled.

With him.

And that was why she had to put a stop to the lie his life had become.

"You have to tell people the truth," Gwen said.

Hank shook his head. "I can't."

"You'd rather let everyone in Buckton continue to think that you're to blame for Pete's death?" she asked incredulously.

"I have to protect my father. Nothing's changed."

"But you said it yourself. It hasn't worked." Her hand swept over the floor where they'd found Myron only hours before. "He's still drinking."

"It's too late," Hank insisted. "I made my choice."

"But what about —"

"Stop it, Gwen," he interrupted. "Even if I agreed with you, it's pointless to consider it because no one would believe me. Not now. Too much time has passed. Everyone would think I was lying. Would your parents look at me any differently if I claimed that what happened to Pete wasn't my fault?" He laughed a humorless chuckle. "If anything, it would make it that much worse."

Gwen suspected that Hank was probably right. Her mother and father would likely make the same assumption she had, that he was trying to make it easier for them to be together.

"Besides," Hank continued, "how would I do it? Go door-to-door and tell people that I'm innocent? Put an ad on the radio? No, this is the hand fate dealt me. Heck, I pulled these cards out of the deck myself. Hard as it is to accept, I can't change this."

She shook her head. "I don't like people

thinking the worst of you."

"Not everyone does," he said, stepping closer. "There's Skip," he explained, placing his hand against her cheek. "And there's you . . ."

And there's me . . .

It hadn't taken Gwen long to realize that Hank wasn't the person everyone in town made him out to be. Every moment they spent together revealed something new. Hank was charming, kind, and funny. He was considerate and hardworking. He was even supportive of her dream to become a writer. And just then, staring up into his eyes in the dimly lit kitchen, as the storm's fury continued to rise outside, she found him to be incredibly handsome.

Hank was everything she'd ever wanted in a man.

So when he leaned down to kiss her, Gwen willingly surrendered to him and his touch.

At first, their kiss resembled those they'd shared before; soft yet full of emotion, restrained yet holding the promise of more. But then something changed. Their lips parted to allow their tongues to touch, igniting a hunger inside Gwen that demanded to be sated. With every passing second, she found herself wanting more, needing it. She didn't know whether this new desire came from herself, Hank, or the both of them, but she quickly decided it didn't matter. Whatever its origin, she didn't resist.

Their lips weren't the only parts of their bodies that wanted more. Gwen's hands slid up his arms, crossed the muscular peaks of his shoulders, and became entwined around his neck, pulling him close. Hank's found her waist before starting to slowly slide up the front of her blouse. Gwen understood that he was going to touch her breasts, but she made no move to stop him. She nearly trembled with anticipation as he inched upward . . .

But then Mother Nature interrupted.

Lightning lit up the stormy sky, almost immediately followed by a deafening boom. A second later, the lights went out, plunging them into total darkness. Gwen was so startled that she yelped.

"That knocked out the power," Hank said, flipping a light switch to no effect, "but there's a generator in the workshop."

Gwen looked at the pouring rain. "We aren't going out in that, are we?" she asked. "Why don't we just stay here, where it's dry?"

And dark, so we can get back to kissing . . .

Hank looked around the room. "Ever

since my mom died, there's something about being in this house that's bothered me. Maybe it's because it's where my father does most of his drinking. Whatever the reason, it makes me uncomfortable. I'm more at ease in the workshop."

As if on cue, the rain intensified. "We'll get soaked," Gwen said.

"Then I guess we'll have to change out of our wet clothes."

Gwen knew exactly what Hank was intimating. But he was giving her a chance to say no, and she had no doubt that he'd respect her decision.

"Let's go turn on that generator," she said, her heart racing.

Hank led the way from the house and into the storm. It wasn't far to the workshop, but as she ran across the wet grass, dodging puddles and trying not to slip in the mud, Gwen was battered by the rain. Flashes of lightning lit the way. By the time Hank threw open the double doors, they were both drenched from head to foot. As rainwater pooled on the floor beneath them, Gwen couldn't stop laughing.

"What's so funny?" Hank asked.

"We're quite the pair," she told him as water dripped from her hair. "I bet this is exactly what we looked like when you pulled

340

me out of the river."

Now it was Hank's turn to laugh. "The spitting image," he agreed before disappearing into the black depths of the workshop. Moments later, Gwen heard machinery sputter to life, then a bulb was switched on.

"That'll keep the lights on for a while, but I don't know how much gas is in the tank," Hank said. He walked over and placed his hands on Gwen's arms; she was trembling slightly. His brow furrowed. "Are you sure you want to do this?" he asked.

Gwen nodded. It was just like when she'd ended her relationship with Kent; she had no doubt. "I wouldn't be here if I wasn't."

Hank led the way out of the shop's larger workspace to a small room at the back. It wasn't much; a cot, a nightstand, and a rickety chair piled high with old newspapers. A sink stood in the far corner.

"I wish it was nicer," he said. "Give me a second and I can —"

"It's perfect," Gwen told him.

Hank didn't turn on any switches as they moved toward the cot; the only light was what filtered in from the outer room, though it was enough to see by. For a moment, they were content to look at each other, their hands entwined. When Gwen shivered, Hank pulled her close, his skin warm even after the rain.

"Thank you," she said, her cheek pressed softly against his chest.

"For what?" he asked.

"Saving my life," Gwen answered, though she was talking about far more than just his diving into the Sawyer River. Because of him, because of the risk Hank had taken for her, the road she'd been traveling on had unexpectedly forked, and Gwen had chosen to take a different route, one she believed would lead to a far happier future. *This* was where she was meant to be.

"Any time," Hank answered, then tilted her face toward his, his eyes dancing in the meager light, and kissed her.

Though thunder continued to crash all around them, the storm was no longer capable of interrupting their passion. Gwen pressed into Hank and shut her eyes, giving herself over to his touch. When his hand rose from her waist to gently caress her breast, Gwen gasped into his open mouth, the pleasure she felt too undeniable to hold back.

Wanting to feel his bare skin, Gwen started to undo the buttons of his shirt. What followed was a flurry of undressing, as items of wet clothing were removed, one after the other, and strewn into a pile on the floor until there wasn't anything left to take off. Another flash of lightning revealed the full length of their naked bodies, a sight that fueled both of their desires.

When they slid beneath the cot's woolen blanket, Gwen allowed her hands to roam across Hank's muscular flesh. She touched his arms, his broad chest, and his washboard stomach until she finally decided to go lower. She took him into her palm, pleasantly surprised by his size, the ardor of his passion, and the heat that his body radiated. She stroked him gently, from base to tip, causing his breath to catch and a deep, thunder-like moan to escape his lips.

But while Gwen had been busy exploring Hank, he'd been doing the same to her. Although his touch was insistent, his skin rough on account of his work, Gwen yearned for more. She encouraged him with a gasp, a tremor shooting through her body, or by whispering his name into his ear. Hank cupped the heft of her breast before teasing her nipple. He ran his fingers down the length of her rib cage as masterfully as a classical pianist at the keys. His lips and tongue caressed her neck, an earlobe, the curve of her jaw before once again finding her mouth. But it was when his hand moved between her legs, gently yet insistently spreading them farther apart, allowing him to truly touch her, discovering just how excited his advances had made her, that she began to shake with pleasure.

"Hank . . ." she managed as she arched her back, the storm inside her body rivaling the one continuing to rage outside the window.

"I want you," he said, nearly breathless.

In answer, Gwen spread her legs wider, encouraging him to come between them, his body raised above her, held in place by his strong arms.

She placed her hands on his cheeks and stared into his eyes. "I love you," she told him, the words coming from somewhere deep inside, made of far more than physical desire, as heartfelt as they could possibly be. She wasn't thinking about her parents. She wasn't thinking about Kent. Gwen was thinking only about Hank Ellis, the man who had stolen her heart.

With a tenderness in stark contrast to the passion burning between them, Hank entered her. Inch by inch, he lowered himself, so that when their hips were finally pressed together, Gwen was nearly overcome with pleasure.

"Gwen, I —" Hank began, but she kissed him before he could say more.

He started to move in and out, slowly at first, but their excitement quickly escalated, causing Hank to thrust faster. For Gwen, it felt as if she was climbing a musical scale, each note higher than the last. It was so pleasurable as to be nearly painful, but she had no desire to stop. Rather, she wanted it to last forever.

"Oh . . . oh, Hank . . ." was all she could manage to say.

Events spooled out before her like a film missing some of its frames. One image came into focus but then was gone, replaced by another: her hands sliding up and down his body, incapable of staying still; beads of sweat dotting Hank's face; another tongue of lightning illuminating the night sky. Over it all, she heard the rhythmic sound of their skin colliding, a melody of lovemaking.

"I can't . . . I can't last much longer . . ." Hank gasped.

Gwen couldn't answer. As his movements reached a fever pitch, it felt as if she'd reached the top of an oceanside cliff and then jumped off, plunging toward the water; when she struck its surface, her whole body trembled and shook. One of her hands grabbed Hank's arm so tightly that she feared drawing blood, while the other crimped a fistful of the blanket. An instant later, Hank shuddered, his hips coming to a hard and sudden stop, and Gwen was filled with warmth.

Though he had to be exhausted, Hank didn't collapse on top of her but carefully lowered himself to the side, their bodies sliding apart. Gwen rolled toward him and snuggled close, both of them slick with sweat but fulfilled in every way. As each of their chests rose and fell, sleep beckoned. Gwen surrendered to its sweet embrace knowing that this was what she'd spent her whole life looking for but had never managed to find.

This was love.

CHAPTER TWENTY-ONE

Gwen woke to the sound of birds singing. She opened her eyes, but the sunlight was too bright so she shut them again. For a moment, she wondered if last night had been a dream, nothing more than a figment of her imagination, but then she felt someone move, warm skin brushing against her own. She turned her head and looked again. Hank slept at her side.

Last night *had* been a dream, but very, very real.

Making love to Hank had been more than Gwen could ever have hoped for. She remembered every touch, every breathless word, every moment of pleasure. Amazingly, she hadn't once thought of Kent. Even though she'd only just ended things between them, the break felt clean, final. The truth was, she had been with the wrong man. So while one relationship had ended, another beckoned, holding out the promise of happier times, of a chance to live the life she'd always wanted.

But that didn't mean there weren't problems, too.

Over and over, like a record needle skipping on a scratch, Gwen thought about what Hank had told her of the night Pete had died. She understood why he'd initially lied; protecting his father was noble, but she couldn't accept that Hank would willingly ruin his own reputation to do it. It was too high of a cost.

Gwen knew that she could always choose to let the matter lie; she wanted to be with Hank regardless of whether people knew the truth about Pete's death. But she wouldn't do it. It wasn't right. Something had to change.

So it was then, lying beside Hank in the cot, looking up at the ceiling of the workshop, that Gwen made a decision of her own.

As carefully and quietly as she could, Gwen slid out of the cot and padded across the floor to her clothes. Fortunately, they'd mostly dried during the night, though they were badly wrinkled. She dressed quickly, her eyes rarely leaving Hank, watching for any sign that he might be waking.

Once she was fully clothed, Gwen dug in

Hank's pants pocket, quickly finding what she was looking for: the keys to his truck.

". . . gonna try to hit it in the . . ." he suddenly muttered, an arm flopping out from under the blanket.

Gwen froze, holding her breath, her heart pounding, convinced that he was about to wake. She could only imagine what Hank would think, wondering what she was doing, why she was sneaking away like a burglar. Inevitably, he'd have questions that she would struggle to answer.

But then, just as abruptly as Hank had stirred, he settled, his breathing steady, and returned to sleep, allowing her to steal out the door.

The morning sky was a brilliant blue, though the air was cool, making her shiver in her damp clothes. Gwen opened the truck's door as quietly as she could, cringing when the hinges gave a squeak. She got inside, not bothering to shut the door behind her, and put the key in the ignition. This was the moment of truth. Gwen knew that the second she started the engine, Hank would wake. If she couldn't manage to get the truck moving fast enough, if it sputtered and stalled or she wasn't able to put it in gear, he'd reach her before she could drive away.

What Gwen was going to do was *for* Hank, but he couldn't be a part of it. Not yet. She was convinced that he wouldn't understand.

"So here goes everything," she whispered.

Turning the key, she heard the engine shudder to life, the sudden noise deafening to Gwen's ears. She pumped the gas pedal, silently praying that it would catch; when it did, she nearly shouted with joy. Grabbing the gearshift, she put the truck in reverse and sped back down the drive so fast that the tires sprayed gravel. Reaching the road, she tromped on the brakes, pointed the truck toward town, ground the gears in her impatience to get moving, and then once again pressed the accelerator. Out of the corner of her eye, she saw Hank stumble groggily out of the workshop, the wool blanket wrapped around his waist, wondering what in the heck was going on. Seconds later, he was lost from view.

Gwen gripped the steering wheel tight. She wouldn't allow herself to look back. She was determined to keep going, to do what she had to.

Their future depended on it.

The unexpected sound of the truck rumbling to life was like a buzz saw cutting through Hank's peaceful sleep. He shot wide awake and sat up in the cot, so disoriented that he had trouble telling up from down. The bright sunlight hurt his eyes, but he looked around anyway, trying to get his bearings. He leaped out of bed, clear-headed enough to snatch up the blanket so that he wasn't running around naked, and hurried for the door. Stepping outside, his feet wet in the dewy grass, he saw his truck back out of the driveway and onto the road before speeding away. There was a familiar face behind the wheel.

"Gwen!" he shouted, waving his arm. "Gwen, wait!"

But it did no good. Seconds later, the truck was out of sight, leaving Hank alone and more than a little confused.

He went back into the workshop, leaving wet footprints on the floor, retreating to the rear room as he tried to make some sense of what had just happened. He noticed that Gwen was no longer curled up in bed and that her clothes weren't piled on the floor; even though Hank had just seen her drive away, in his addled state, these facts seemed firmer confirmation that she was no longer there. He ran a hand through his hair, took a deep breath, and started to think things through.

Why didn't she wake me?

Where's she going?

What did I do to make her leave like that?

Hank didn't know the answers to any of these questions, but he imagined that none of them were good. Maybe last night Gwen had been vulnerable, still reeling from the confrontation with Kent and her parents, and had allowed herself to get caught up in the moment. In such a state, she'd willingly made love to him, but the next morning, her head finally clear, she had realized what a terrible mistake she'd made. Wanting nothing more than to get away from him, Gwen had dressed silently, snuck out to his truck, and raced away, too ashamed of herself to face him, to even ask if he'd drive her back to town.

Maybe their relationship was over before it had really even begun.

Leaving his still-wet clothes on the floor, Hank headed for the house. Inside, he took a quick shower, hoping it would chase away the clouds in his head while he figured out what to do next. Dressed, he paced the kitchen, trying to come up with another explanation for Gwen's behavior but failing.

"Think, damn it, think!" he exhorted himself.

In the end, Hank knew he had to speak

with her. If Gwen was actually rejecting him, he wanted to hear it from her lips. Even if he had to endure more insults, or take another punch, he had to know what he'd done. He would ask for forgiveness and ultimately accept her decision, no matter whether it was good or bad.

Hank picked up the telephone receiver, then dialed. After about a dozen rings, the other end of the line was answered.

There was a deep sigh. "Yeah . . ." a sleepy voice said.

"Skip, it's Hank."

A long pause. "What time is it?"

"I need you to come pick me up," he said, ignoring the question. "Now."

"Somethin' . . . somethin' wrong with your truck?"

"Just get over here!"

"Okay, okay," Skip said. "No need to get bent outta shape. Gimme fifteen minutes to get it together and I'll be there."

After they'd hung up, Hank resumed his pacing. He felt guilty for barking at his best friend, but this was urgent. Silently, he vowed to fix what was broken between him and Gwen. Whatever it was that had caused her to drive away, he would make it right. He wouldn't let it end, not like this.

He loved Gwen Foster like he'd never

loved before.

He wouldn't give her up without a fight.

Buckton's hospital was a two-story brick building on the north end of Main Street. The doctors' offices were located on the lower floor, while the patient rooms were on the upper. An American flag flapped in the breeze. When Gwen pulled Hank's truck into the parking lot, there were few cars and fewer people; an old man inched slowly along with the help of a walker, while a young mother practically dragged her reluctant son toward the front door, the boy far more interested in kicking rocks than whatever awaited him inside. Gwen shut off the engine but made no move to get out.

You're here. So now what?

There was a small part of her that wanted to drive back to Hank, to come up with an excuse for why she'd left, to act as if nothing had happened.

But she couldn't do it.

Too much was at stake. Even though Gwen had no idea what sort of reception she would receive, she had to face it.

For Hank. For me. For us.

Stepping inside, Gwen was greeted by the receptionist. When she inquired what room Myron Ellis was in, the woman asked whether Gwen was a member of his family; Gwen said that she was, the lie coming so easily that it might as well have been the truth. She was given the room number and climbed the stairs. Standing in front of Myron's door, she took a deep breath and went inside.

Myron lay in the bed, his face tilted toward the window. Sunlight streamed through the narrow slats of the blinds, painting dark lines across his already discolored face. A large bandage covered the cut he'd sustained to his forehead the night before; the smallest drop of red blood seeped through to stain the white material. Dark bruises, a mottled mix of browns and purples, spread out from the wound, another sign of his fall. He looked much older than his years, his cheeks sunken, his hair a disheveled mess, his skin a canvas of wrinkles. There was enough of a resemblance between him and Hank to send a shiver running down Gwen's spine. Myron's eyes were closed as his chest rose and fell beneath his thin blanket.

Gwen had hoped that they might talk, and was therefore disappointed he was asleep. Still, she knew Myron needed his rest. She could wait, go outside for some air, or maybe find some breakfast. That or —

"Issit time for my pills . . ."

Myron blinked awake. When he yawned, he winced as if in pain.

"I'm not the nurse," Gwen replied.

He looked her over. "No, you're a hell of a lot prettier than that battle-axe who kept tryin' to jam pills down my throat all night."

"I don't know if you remember me, Mr. Ellis," she said, then stepped closer, thinking that it might help if he could see her more clearly. "I'm Gwen Foster."

Myron ran a hand across his whiskered chin, then nodded. "You're Warren's girl, ain't ya," he said. "You used to help down at the bakery."

"That's right."

"Don't go takin' this the wrong way, but you're 'bout the last person I would've expected to see this mornin'."

"I hope you don't mind my dropping by like this, but I was hoping we might talk," Gwen explained with a measured smile, not too bright but still friendly, hoping she might get their conversation off on the right foot.

Myron eyed her suspiciously, " 'Bout what?"

"About your son."

There was a long pause before he asked, "Which one?"

"Both of them, actually."

This time, Myron's silence stretched longer. He looked toward the window. Gwen worried. Only a couple of minutes in the door and she was losing him.

So she pressed ahead. "A week ago, Hank saved my life."

"He what?" Myron exclaimed, turning back to her, his expression one of genuine surprise; he clearly knew nothing about it.

"Your son dove into the Sawyer River to keep me from drowning. Since then, over the time we've spent together, I've fallen in love with him," she explained, acknowledging her feelings for Hank. "Last night, after we found you . . ." Gwen started, then faltered, pausing to steel herself, "he told me what happened the night Pete died. He told me that he hadn't been driving."

Myron stared hard at her. "And that it was *me* who done it . . ."

Gwen nodded.

Once again, Hank's father turned from her, gazing into the distance. She wondered whether she'd said too much too soon, worrying that Myron would now clam up. But then he cleared his throat. "Damn, if my mouth ain't dry as a ball of cotton. You think you could find me somethin' to drink? If I'm gonna talk 'bout this, I reckon I should wet my whistle first."

Gwen thought he was asking her to get him some booze. Myron must've seen it written on her face.

"Just water, darlin'," he said with a sad frown. "You must think me a hell of a sight. A good-for-nothin' drunk."

She shook her head. "No, I don't."

"Wait till you hear my story, then." He chuckled humorlessly. "I might end up changin' your mind."

Gwen filled a glass with water from the cooler out in the hall. Myron gulped it thirstily, a little running down his chin. When he was finished, he twirled the empty glass in his hands.

"When my wife died," he began, sounding a little clearer, "everythin' went to hell. It was like turnin' off a light switch, my whole life goin' dark. I was in so much damn pain that the only way I could make it stop was by numbin' it with a drink. The inside of a whiskey bottle was my church, the only place I could find comfort. I stopped workin'. I spent all my money on booze. I turned my back on my boys when they needed me most. I was a coward who couldn't face the truth of things, so I laid down and quit." Myron gave a short snort. "It's funny in a way, but right here, right now, startin' with when I fell face-first on the kitchen floor, is probably the longest I've gone without a drink since Eleanor passed."

Though Gwen was well aware that Hank's father had brought much of his misery on himself, she couldn't help but feel a measure of pity for him, too. Here was a man who had lost someone dear to him, the woman he loved, and was unable to cope with his grief. That weakness had caused him to lose even more.

"What happened the night of the accident?" she asked.

Myron shook his head. "A lot of it's a haze," he told her. "I've spent months now tryin' to piece it together, but all I got are snippets."

"Tell me what you can," Gwen pressed.

Myron nodded, then took a deep breath. "I remember bein' down at the bar, like plenty of times before, and gettin' into an argument, maybe a fight. I think Rex tossed me out, which, odds are, I deserved. The next thing I know, there's Pete helpin' me up off the sidewalk, wantin' to put me in the car so he can take me home. Then it goes black again, time lost that can't never be found, but I must've wrangled the keys from him 'cause next thing I know I'm behind the wheel, drivin' us home."

Again he stopped. In the morning light, Gwen saw that his eyes were filling with tears. She didn't say a word, hardly felt like she was breathing, as she waited for him to continue. Her only worry was that a doctor or nurse would walk through the door and interrupt.

"I can still hear him, you know."

"Pete?" Gwen asked.

Myron nodded. "He was sittin' next to me in the car, beggin' me to stop, but I wouldn't listen," he explained as a lone tear slid down his cheek. "What kind of man does that to his own son?"

"You'd been drinking," she told him. "You weren't thinking clearly."

He shook his head. "That might explain it, but it ain't an excuse, not a good one, anyway. It don't make what I done right. It don't change a damn thing."

Gwen understood that this was why Myron tried to numb his pain with drink. It was ironic to think that the very thing that had taken his beloved son from him was the same one he misguidedly used to try to drown his sorrows.

"I don't even remember the crash," Myron continued. "One minute I'm weavin' all over the road, the next I'm flat on my back,

360

lookin' up at the stars, my whole body hurtin'. My head was ringin' loud, too, but I could still hear Hank yellin' at me, demandin' answers I couldn't give. Then everythin' went black again, so when I come to on the couch back home, I had no idea how I'd got there. I stripped off my clothes, not even noticin' they was covered in blood, stumbled into the shower, and started soberin' up. When the police pounded on the door, I answered wearin' nothin' but a towel."

"They told you that there'd been an accident," Gwen said, not a question but rather just the next part of the sad story. "They told you that Pete was dead and Hank was responsible."

Myron's expression soured. "I coulda put a stop to all that nonsense right then and there," he said. "I coulda told them police that there'd been a mistake, that I done it, but I didn't say a word. I was still so messed up that I started wonderin' if I wasn't imaginin' it, if it was all a bad dream. I couldn't figure out why Hank woulda taken the blame for somethin' he didn't do."

"He was trying to protect you."

"I know that now, but back then I couldn't make it add up. So I went along with it. The worst part came later. First time I went into town after the crash, I saw how folks were lookin' at me. They pitied me and hated my son." He paused, struggling to continue. "By then, I knew it shoulda been the other way 'round."

"Why didn't you say something?"

There was a long pause. Myron's expression was one of shame. " 'Cause I reckon it was easier to crawl back into my bottle. When you're hurtin', booze makes the wrongs into rights. It wasn't ever my fault when I was drunk."

"Hank said he wasn't sure if you knew what had actually happened," Gwen pressed. "He told me that you didn't say anything to him for days, but then when you did . . ." Her voice trailed off, remembering the terrible words.

But Myron looked at her expectantly, as if he had no idea what she was talking about.

"You don't remember what you said, do you?" she asked.

"Did he say if I'd been drinkin'?"

Gwen nodded.

"Then odds are I wouldn't. What was it?"

Gwen didn't know how to answer. If she told Myron the truth, it would only cause him more pain. Still, both he and Hank had been forthcoming about that terrible night. There was no point in holding back now.

"You told Hank that even if you'd been the one behind the wheel, he was responsible for his brother's death. You told him that he should've known better than to let Pete go. That he should've come instead."

Myron's expression was one of utter disgust. Looking at him, Gwen understood that a man was truly capable of hating himself. A wet sob forced its way out of his mouth, but he squelched it, refusing to let it become something more.

"Every goddamn day since then, I've wished that I'd been the one who died," he told her. "Without me around, my sons coulda been happy. Instead, 'cause I lived and I'm a coward, Hank's gotta bear my burden." Myron sighed as he wiped away a tear. "The few times I manage to sober up, I want to make things right, apologize to him, tell him I know it ain't fair, but then the guilt hits me and I go crawlin' back to the booze. When I'm drunk, I can convince myself it ain't my fault. I can numb myself to the pain." He paused. " 'Sides, it's too late. There's no changin' things now. What's done is done."

"Maybe not," Gwen told him.

Myron stared at her, his eyes narrowing. "What are you talkin' 'bout?"

"What if I told you that it wasn't too late?

363

What if there was still time for you to turn a wrong into a right?"

"How could I do that?"

This was the reason Gwen had snuck out of Hank's bed and driven to the hospital. Myron was the solution to their problems. If she could convince him to take the risk, it could change all of their lives.

"I have an idea," she said.

Chapter Twenty-Two

When Gwen left the hospital, she headed for home. Though the last time she'd gone there had been a disaster — watching in disbelief as Kent struck Hank; ending her relationship with the young lawyer — Gwen knew that she couldn't avoid it forever. Running away, even for a little while longer, wouldn't help anyone. Besides, Kent had surely headed back to Chicago, likely cursing her with every mile the train traveled. With her father at the bakery, that left only her mother to deal with.

As she drove, Gwen thought of all that had changed.

Last night, as a storm raged all around her, she had willingly and happily given herself to another man. She was in love with Hank. Whatever future lay before her, she wanted to discover it alongside the handsome woodcarver. By breaking things off with Kent, she'd opened the door to a new life.

Gwen parked along the curb in front of her parents' house. She had thought she might have a moment alone to compose herself, to take a deep breath and consider what she was going to say to her mother, but it wasn't to be. Out the passenger window, she was startled to see Kent rise from a chair on the porch to stare at her. A suitcase stood at his feet. Surprised, she considered driving away but instead shut off the engine and got out.

"You're alone," Kent said as she made her way up the walk; his tone suggested that he wasn't sure if that was a good or a bad thing.

"I am," Gwen answered.

"What did you do?" he asked, nodding toward the street. "Steal his truck?"

She didn't answer, not because Kent had come surprisingly close to the truth, but because she felt he was trying to goad her into an argument.

"You spent the night with him." It wasn't a question.

Gwen thought it must be obvious. Not only had she failed to come home since driving away with Hank, but she was still wearing the same clothes from the day before yesterday. She didn't need a mirror to know she was a mess.

For his part, Kent didn't look a whole lot better. He was dressed expensively, if not quite in what he'd wear to court, but his face betrayed him. Gwen suspected that he'd had a rough night. She had expected her rejection to drive him away, make him leave Buckton far behind, but he had chosen to stay, to wait so that he could have another word with her. His eyes were thin and red, underlined with dark bags. Gwen wondered if he had gotten any sleep, or if he'd been awake all night, relentlessly pacing the floor, talking with her parents, all the while wondering whether she would return. With every passing hour, Kent had surely grown angrier and angrier. Other men would have eventually been overcome by their jealousy and driven across town, pounding on Hank's door, wanting to fight for her hand. But not Kent. He would want her to come crawling back, to apologize. Likely that's what he thought was happening now.

It was up to Gwen to show him just how wrong he was.

"I stayed with Hank last night," she admitted, choosing to be honest and expecting him to be furious, to erupt with anger.

But instead, Kent offered a thin smile as he shrugged his shoulders, then came down off the porch to wrap his arms around her, holding her tight. Gwen was so surprised that she couldn't even speak. Reflexively, she returned his affection, sliding her hands behind his back.

"It's all right," he said, then stepped back. "I forgive you."

Gwen's anger flared as hot as the sun, though she remained too out of sorts to lash out at him, to tell him just how insulting his words were.

"I understand why you did it," Kent continued, his expression serious. "You had something you wanted to get out of your system, an itch that needed to be scratched before we got married. I don't like it, but I can live with it."

"But I broke up with you!"

"You weren't serious," Kent replied dismissively.

"Yes, I was!" she insisted.

His smile and conviction didn't falter. "You were angry; we both were," he said. "But we all make mistakes from time to time. Even me."

"*You're* admitting to a mistake?" Gwen asked, her tone skeptical.

"Of course," he answered, briefly flashing his famous smile. "Obviously I was wrong to go back to Chicago, even though we both know I had no choice, not if I wanted to someday make partner," Kent explained, the last bit making Gwen question the sincerity of his words. "You'd been hurt, maybe you were still a little scared, and you wanted me by your side, so when I left, you started running around with this small-town yokel with a bad reputation." He held up his hands, palms out. "Believe me when I say that I've learned my lesson."

The truth was, Gwen didn't think Kent had learned a thing. To her, he sounded just like he did in court, arguing a case, trying to sway a jury. He was presenting evidence, accepting some culpability but also trying to shift blame. Looking into his eyes, Gwen was struck by the sudden, almost sickening realization that she might never have known Kent at all, that everything he'd ever said to her, every smile he had given, might be nothing but an act, a performance from behind a mask, all to get the verdict he wanted.

"You make it sound like my spending time with Hank was meant to punish you," she told him.

"What else would it have been?"

"It isn't like that at all," Gwen answered defiantly. "After you left, I wanted to thank Hank for saving my life. But the more time we spent together, the more I got to know him, and the more I realized that . . ."

Her voice trailed off. Gwen knew what came next was an admission that would hurt Kent. Even though his rude assumptions and slightly condescending tone had made her angry, even though she'd ended their relationship, she still retained enough good feelings toward him, memories they'd shared, to not want to purposefully cause him pain.

Once she finished that sentence, there would be no going back.

"You realized what?" Kent pressed, not realizing that she was trying to protect him.

Gwen took a deep breath. "That I'm in love with Hank."

Kent's reaction ran a range of emotions. Within seconds, he went from shock, his mouth falling open; to anger, his expression darkening; before ending at disbelief by shaking his head. "You're joking, right?" he asked, then let out a burst of nervous laughter.

Gwen didn't answer, certain that her silence would tell him everything.

It did.

"You're serious . . . You really *did* mean it before, when you . . . when you . . ." he said, hardly louder than a whisper.

"I'm sorry," she told him. A part of her was relieved that the truth was out, but she braced herself for what she knew came next.

"You'd rather be with *him* than *me*?!" Kent asked, his voice back with a vengeance, the words he spat incredulous. "You're choosing some bumpkin woodcarver," he said, pointing at Hank's truck, "who doesn't look like he has two nickels to rub together, who your parents despise, over *me*?"

Gwen wasn't surprised by his outburst. Everything in Kent's life was measured in prestige and wealth. If a man didn't have an important job, the respect of his peers, and a bank account stuffed with money, then he was nothing, a failure. She supposed that she couldn't blame him for being this way, not entirely. He'd been raised in opulence and was expected to carry on the family tradition, just like his father before him. Kent didn't know how else to live.

But Gwen wanted more than money could buy.

What mattered to her was the love of someone who would support her, who wished for nothing more than to be by her side.

And that man was Hank.

"What can he possibly give you that I can't?" Kent pressed, struggling to accept what she had told him, some of it said the day before.

"Hank wants to walk next to me, not tower above me."

Kent threw his hands up. "What are you talking about?"

"The night you announced to my parents that we were getting married without bothering to ask me first," Gwen explained, "I made it perfectly clear to you how I felt. I told you I had my heart set on becoming a writer, and that because you couldn't support that, I wasn't ready to accept your proposal."

"*That's* what this is about?" Kent asked, using almost the same words and dismissive tone as he had on the night of the storm.

Gwen wanted to answer "yes," but she realized that what had led to the end of their relationship was about so much more. It wasn't just that Kent didn't want her to pursue her dream of becoming a writer, it was that he didn't want her doing *anything* that might contradict the image he had of their life.

"Give me another chance," he said, bartering.

"Kent, I don't —"

"With time, maybe I can see things differently. Maybe I can figure out a way to live

372

with you doing this."

"You shouldn't have to force yourself," Gwen said, exasperated. She shook her head. "It's too late. I've made up my mind."

Once again, Kent's expression changed. Where an instant before he'd appeared hopeful, his cheer collapsed, leaving behind a frightful scowl beneath flat eyes. "You never loved me," he said with a sneer.

"Kent, you know that I —"

"Save me your fake pity," he snarled, stepping closer, a finger jabbing the air inches from her face. "The only reason you were ever with me was that you liked riding my coattails, enjoying the fruits of my success. Oh, you might insist otherwise, but you ate every one of those fancy meals I bought, you wore each dress I brought home from Wieboldt's, and you attended every play or party my name got us into." Kent was smiling again, but this one was cruel. "I was your ticket out of this backwater nowhere into the upper crust of Chicago! You took it all in like Cinderella at the ball, but without me, your life will turn back into a pumpkin!"

Gwen quickly saw that Kent's argument made no sense. If she was so obsessed with his status, if she was only with him because of what his money could buy, then why was she leaving? Wouldn't she have fallen all over herself accepting his proposal in order to live a life of luxury? And why would she stop their relationship to be with someone who struggled to make ends meet? Kent's anger had blinded him. He was so upset at being rejected that he was lashing out, saying anything and everything he could think of to hurt her, to render the time they'd been together meaningless. But she wouldn't take the bait.

"I'm sorry," she told him again, meaning it but knowing that it could never be enough, that it would likely enrage him further.

"Stop saying that!" Kent snapped, stepping close and grabbing her arm; even though her heart raced, Gwen held her ground. "I bet deep down you're gloating. You really took me for a ride, didn't you?" he continued, his words dripping with both rage and sarcasm. "And to think, I was going to marry you. What a mistake that would have been! You're nothing but a conniving —"

But before Kent could finish his insult, the front door opened and her mother stepped onto the porch.

"Is everything all right out here?" Meredith asked.

From the expression on her mother's face,

Gwen understood that she'd been listening to their conversation from inside the house. Gwen didn't know how much she'd overheard, but it'd been enough to make Meredith decide to intervene.

Faster than a snap of his fingers, Kent's angry, almost frightening frown disappeared, replaced by his more familiar charming smile. "Everything's fine," he cheerfully told Gwen's mother, addressing her as deferentially as he would a judge in the courtroom, which made sense, since Meredith was someone whose favor he coveted. "Your daughter and I were just having a little disagreement, that's all. It's nothing to worry about."

While Kent was distracted, Gwen yanked her arm free from his grip. "I want you to leave," she told him.

When he turned back to her, his smile slipped, revealing his simmering anger. "Now, Gwen, why don't we go and —"

"Now," she hissed, cutting him off.

"I think you should listen to her," Meredith added, folding her arms across her chest.

Kent's eyes smoldered. He looked like he wanted to argue more but knew it wouldn't be wise to defy the judge's decision. He stepped close. "Is this the way things are going to be?" he asked.

"I've made my decision," Gwen answered.

He leaned even closer. "Then promise me something," Kent said, lowering his voice. "When you're struggling to make ends meet, when you're living in a run-down shack and are exhausted from taking care of a couple of bawling brats, when your sad little dream of becoming a writer has failed, I want you to think of me. Think about the life I could've given you, one of luxury, of privilege. Then have yourself a good cry when you realize you were stupid enough to throw it all away."

Without missing a beat, Kent turned to her mother, his smile again at full wattage. "Thank you for your hospitality, Mrs. Foster."

Then he retrieved his luggage and started off down the sidewalk under the summer sun, headed for the train depot and ultimately Chicago.

Though Gwen had been hurt by the terrible things Kent had said, it wasn't enough to make her shout back at him or burst into tears. If anything, his spiteful words had only proven that her concerns about their relationship had been well-founded. Not that long ago, Gwen had believed she loved him. Now she understood that until she met

Hank, she hadn't known what true love was. So while they'd made memories together that she hoped never to forget, there was no doubt in Gwen's mind that Kent Brookings was *not* the man she was meant to marry. All she could do now was watch him walk away.

Kent never looked back.

"Are you all right, sweetheart?" Meredith asked as her daughter climbed the steps, heading for the front door.

She knew that her mother was concerned, that she wanted to talk, but Gwen wouldn't allow herself to be distracted from what was really important. Right now, she needed to go inside, take off her two-day-old clothes, shower, and get to work.

"I'll be fine," she answered.

Meredith sighed softly. "He wasn't right for you anyway," she said. "What you need is a man who will walk by your side, not tower over you."

To Gwen's ears, her mother's words sounded more than a little familiar, given that she'd spoken something similar herself only a few moments before. She knew that Kent was the type who would always want to dominate the spotlight, that her career and success would always take a backseat to his. But Hank was different, a partner upon whom she could depend.

"Maybe you should lie down for a while," Meredith suggested. "Things might look better when you wake up."

Her conversation with Kent *had* exhausted her, but Gwen didn't dare take her mother's advice. If she closed her eyes, she was certain she'd sleep for days.

"I can't," she said, offering a weak smile. "I need to be strong. I just have to keep going."

The older woman's lower lip trembled and her eyes filled with tears. Meredith reached out and pulled her daughter into an embrace. Even as Gwen returned the affection, she knew that her mother had misunderstood what she'd said. Meredith had thought she was talking about breaking up with Kent.

But that wasn't it. Not by a mile.

What happened next would determine her future with Hank. Talking with Myron had brought her a step closer, but there was still a long way to go. She couldn't stop now. Maybe she'd do the right thing and bring herself and Hank closer together. Or maybe she would fail and ruin what they'd only just started to build. Gwen didn't know what the future held.

Either way, it was time for her to do her

part to make it come to pass.

"Oh, man," Skip said. "I'm pretty sure *that* ain't what you wanted to see."

Hank didn't answer. He was too busy grinding his teeth.

After being rousted from bed, Skip had picked Hank up in his car and the two of them had driven into Buckton to look for Gwen. After searching aimlessly for a while, they'd finally spotted Hank's truck headed toward her parents' house and had followed at a distance, curious as to what she would do. At the corner before her block, Skip had pulled over, the engine idling, leaving them a good view down her street. Gwen had parked, gotten out, and started talking with someone on the porch. Hank hadn't known who it was but hoped it was her mother. His heart had skipped a beat when Kent came sauntering down the stairs.

It felt like it'd stopped altogether when the big-city lawyer pulled Gwen into his arms.

"Drive," Hank said.

Skip looked at him, then back at the couple down the street. "You sure? Maybe you oughta do somethin'."

"There's been enough fighting in front of that house."

"Yeah, but —"

"Just get going!" Hank snapped.

Skip stopped arguing. "All right, all right," he said, pulling away from the curb and racing down the street. "You're the boss."

As fast as his friend drove, Hank's thoughts raced faster.

What did I just see?

Even after what happened last night, am I not enough for her?

Has Gwen gone back to Kent?

"I can't believe you're just gonna turn your back on that," Skip said, unable to hold his tongue. "If I stumbled across the girl I was sweet on in some other guy's arms, she wouldn't get off that easy."

"What was I supposed to do?" Hank asked, his head starting to hurt.

"Confront 'em! Give her a piece of your mind! It ain't right for Gwen to be treatin' you like that!"

Skip didn't know the half of it.

Hank hadn't told his friend the whole story of what had happened between him and Gwen the night before. Skip knew that they had found Myron unconscious on the floor and that Gwen had spent the night at the house, but he didn't know that they'd made love. Hank could only imagine Skip's reaction if he did.

Right now, the only thing Hank could think to do was give Gwen space. Clearly she was confused about her feelings, both for him and for Kent. As hard as it would be, he'd go home, try to lose himself in his work, and wait for her to come back with his truck. Then they would talk.

Hank could only hope that he'd like what she had to say.

CHAPTER TWENTY-THREE

Gwen stood with her back to the shower's spigot, her eyes closed. Hot water pounded her neck and shoulders. Soap slid down her skin as it rushed toward her feet before finally swirling down the drain. Steam billowed, clouding the windowpanes. All the while, her mind raced, weaving the tapestry of a story.

By the time Gwen shut off the water, she was ready to write.

She quickly toweled her hair and dressed, then sat down in front of the typewriter. Gwen fed in a clean sheet of paper and took a deep breath before getting to work. Words poured out of her as fast as she could type them, her fingers practically dancing across the keys. Before she knew it, she was finished.

And now let's see what I have . . .

Whatever optimism she'd had was soon dashed. Nothing was as she'd wanted it.

Gwen wadded up the pages and threw them in the trash. She put more paper into the typewriter and tried again.

Her second go-around was better, but she still wasn't satisfied.

So she did it again.

And again.

And again, until the rejected pages overflowed the wastebasket and were strewn across the floor, like an odd arrangement of flowers.

Somewhere between the fifth and sixth drafts, Meredith brought her lunch; Gwen was thankful that her mother didn't ask what she was doing.

Finally, after so much typing that her fingers hurt, she read a version that she was happy with. Gwen got out of her chair and paced the room. Early-afternoon sunlight spilled across the floor as she went over what she had written, weighing every word.

On those two pages, Gwen laid out the truth about the night Pete Ellis died, just as Hank had told it. She'd added quotes from Myron, who had agreed to her proposal and confessed from his hospital bed. Her article also explained the motivation for Hank's lie: that he'd taken the blame for the accident in order to protect his father. What she held in her hands was a bombshell.

All she had to do to make it explode was take it to Sid Keaton.

For the first time since she'd woken up that morning, Gwen's resolve faltered. A sliver of doubt crept into her mind. Was she doing the right thing in revealing Hank's family's deepest, darkest secret? Would it help Hank as she intended, or would it make matters worse? How would he react? Would he be angry with her? She'd been all set to march her pages over to the *Bulletin* in the hopes that they would be published, but now she wasn't quite so sure.

Downstairs, the phone rang. Moments later, her mother answered.

"Gwendolyn, dear," she called from below. "It's for you."

Descending the staircase, Gwen's first thought was that it was Hank, wondering why she'd left the way she had, driving off in his truck and not bothering to tell him she was going. She'd meant to call him before taking a shower, but with so much swimming around in her head, she had forgotten. She knew that they needed to talk, that she had to tell him what she was doing, but she feared his reaction. Whatever they would say to each other needed to wait a while longer. Her second guess, more of a worry, was that it was Kent calling from the depot. Maybe he was making one last attempt at reconciling. That, or he wasn't done cursing her name.

But she was wrong on both counts.

"Gwen!" a man shouted when she picked up the phone. "It's me! I mean, it's John Fiderlein! You know, Sandy's husband!"

"What's wrong?" Gwen asked, certain from the frantic tone of his deep voice that something bad had happened.

"Sandy's in labor! She's gonna have the baby!"

"Now?!" she cried.

"It came on real sudden," John explained. "One second she was in the kitchen finishin' lunch, and the next she could hardly stand, she was crampin' so bad. I drove her to the hospital just as fast as I could, but I started to worry she was gonna have the baby right there in the backseat!"

Sandy's husband's love for his wife was so obvious that it brought tears to Gwen's eyes. "I'm so happy for you both!"

"Then get over here."

"Wait, what? Me? You want me to be at the hospital?"

"Sandy sure does!" he said with a loud laugh. "Right before they took her into the delivery room, she made me promise to call you. She said that you're like a sister to her and she wants you to be here when the baby's born. It's like Sandy's always sayin',", he added, "the more the merrier!"

"I'll be right there," she said, her thoughts about Hank, Kent, even her newspaper article all momentarily forgotten.

As quickly as she could, Gwen told her mother what was happening. Then she flew up the stairs to gather everything she'd need. Within minutes, she was out the front door, running toward Hank's truck.

Sandy is having her baby!

For the second time that day, Gwen entered Buckton's hospital. Unlike her first visit, when she'd taken Myron Ellis's incredible confession about the death of his son, this trip was one of celebration. She raced up the stairs two at a time before breathlessly bursting into the waiting room.

"Gwen!" a deep voice boomed.

John Fiderlein embraced her. He was a big man, broad across the chest and shoulders, seemingly three times the size of his wife. Even as a boy, John had been a head taller than his peers. He was always the first chosen for sports, the last anyone would ever want to fight. But inside, he was as gentle as a lamb, kind, considerate, and quick to laugh. He had taken one look at

Sandy from across the playground and been instantaneously smitten. Since then, he'd never left her side, loving her unconditionally, wanting nothing more than to build a family with the girl of his dreams.

Today, with the birth of their child, it would happen.

Many of the other seats in the waiting room were filled with faces Gwen recognized, including Sandy's parents and John's younger brother. They were all people she'd once known well but hadn't seen for years. She briefly spoke to each of them, offering her congratulations, before returning her attention to John.

"How are you holding up?" she asked.

"Just fine," he answered. "Sandy's the one doin' all the work."

"Are you nervous?"

John chuckled. "Not in the least," he told her, while pulling a handkerchief from his back pocket to wipe sweat from his brow.

Just then, a door opened and a nurse stepped out. John practically leaped at her, hoping for a bit of news, looking like a dog that'd been waiting all day for its master to come home, but the woman shook her head.

"Nothing yet," she said, then set off on her rounds.

John's brother laughed. "He's been like

that since he got here. It's like he's got a blister on his backside and can't stand to sit down!"

"Well, maybe I am a *little* nervous," John admitted.

"You're just excited to become a dad," Gwen told him.

"You don't know the half of it," he replied. "I've been dreamin' about this day for as long as I can remember. Think of all the fun we can have! Throwin' the baseball, goin' fishin' down at the river, trompin' through mud puddles — all the stuff I liked doin' when I was a kid."

Gwen thought back to the conversation she'd had with Sandy in front of the drugstore. Her friend had said then that her husband was sure they were having a boy; from the way John was talking, describing activities that weren't ideally suited for a young lady, he was still convinced.

"What if Sandy has a girl?" she asked.

John snorted and shook his head. "Won't happen," he answered.

"But what *if*?" Gwen insisted. "It's just a flip of a coin either way, you know. One side you have a boy, but if it's the other . . ."

"Then she'll be the biggest tomboy Buckton's ever seen!" he announced enthusiastically, but then grew serious. "Truth is, for

388

as much as I go on about havin' a boy, I won't be disappointed if it goes the other way. All that matters is that Sandy and the baby are healthy."

John's heartfelt declaration of love for his wife and as-yet-unborn child moved Gwen. Here was a man for whom family truly mattered. It made her think about the relationship growing between her and Hank. Could they have a similar future? Was it possible that one day she'd be in the delivery room, while Hank nervously paced outside, waiting for their baby to be born? The thought made her pulse race, but in a good way.

"So did you ever talk to Hank Ellis?" John asked out of the blue.

Gwen was caught off guard and couldn't answer.

"Sandy told me what happened," he explained, seeing her confusion. "She said he dove into the Sawyer after you."

"He saved my life."

John nodded. "You know, I always liked Hank. Unlike most folks in town, I've never been angry at him for Pete's death. I just pity him, I reckon," he explained. "Who can't feel for a fella who lost someone like that?"

My father, for one.

"I think Hank's a little misunderstood,"

Sandy's husband added.

"More than you know."

The pages Gwen had written were now folded up in her handbag. She still had plenty of doubts about what to do with them, but John's opinion of Hank gave her hope. Maybe there were more people in Buckton who felt the same way. If they knew the truth about the accident, would they look at Hank differently? Would they be able to understand why he'd lied? Would they be willing to give him another chance?

Just then, the delivery room door opened. Once again, John jumped at the sound. A different nurse walked out, smiling broadly.

"Congratulations, Mr. Fiderlein," she said. "You're now the father of a baby girl."

Without hesitation, John began to whoop and holler, running from person to person, unable to stay still as he was overcome by happiness. He acted like it was his birthday, Christmas morning, and the moment his favorite sports team won the championship all rolled into one. One moment he was bear-hugging his brother, the next he was spinning his mother-in-law around the room, tears of joy streaming down his face.

There wasn't a dry eye in the room, Gwen's included.

■ ■ ■ ■

"She's the most beautiful baby I've ever seen."

Gwen stood beside Sandy's bed, holding her friend's brand-new daughter. Kelly Fiderlein slept soundly, swaddled tight in a blanket. She weighed next to nothing, but Gwen cradled her close, as if she was the most precious jewel in the whole world. Everything about her was small and delicate, from her button nose to her pursed mouth and squeezed-shut eyes, but especially her fingers; they opened and closed in no discernable rhythm, as if they were being manipulated by a puppeteer. Deep inside, Gwen felt something stir, a desire for a child of her own, a chance to be a mother, to build a family of her own with Hank Ellis. Looking down at Kelly, rocking her gently, Gwen couldn't stop smiling.

"Do you like her name?" Sandy asked.

"I love it."

"I know John had his heart set on a boy he could call Junior. I hope he wasn't *too* disappointed."

Gwen shook her head. "There's no chance of that," she said as Kelly's eyes fluttered open, sparkling a brilliant blue, then quickly shut. "You should've seen him out in the waiting room. No one has *ever* been that happy."

Her friend laughed. "That sounds like when he first came in here. He couldn't stop bouncing around the room or lifting the nurses up off the ground," Sandy explained. "He didn't stop until one of the doctors got after him. I think he was afraid that John would be too rough with the baby. But when they brought Kelly in, he held her like she was a china plate, like he was afraid he'd break her. Here was this bear of a man and his itty-bitty daughter. It was quite the sight."

"So how are you feeling?" Gwen asked.

"Like I got run over by a truck," Sandy answered. "Twice."

Though Gwen still thought her friend was beautiful, glowing in the aftermath of childbirth, she had to admit that Sandy looked exhausted, too. Her hair was mussed up, a few strands sticking to her forehead with sweat, and she'd stifled a couple of yawns since Gwen had entered the room. In short, she looked exactly like one would expect, given that she'd just delivered a baby.

Sandy frowned. "I'm sorry. I shouldn't have said that."

"Why not?" Gwen asked.

"Because I don't want to scare you," she answered. "You might want to do this yourself one day."

"Don't worry. I've already heard all the horror stories."

Her friend's eyes narrowed. "You have?"

Gwen nodded. "My mother," she explained. "She used to say that giving birth to me is the reason I don't have any siblings."

"It *does* hurt," Sandy acknowledged. "But it's worth it." She looked at the bundle of joy in her old friend's arms. "You know, it's kind of strange," she admitted. "I thought I was prepared to see my baby for the first time, but when the doctor held her up, my whole life changed. It was both scary and exciting. Just like that, I realized that I wasn't living only for myself and John, but for that little girl, too."

There was a knock on the door. A nurse entered to take the baby for a while so that Sandy could get some rest. Gwen very reluctantly handed Kelly over, missing her before she was even gone. "I should go, too," she offered.

"Wait, Gwen," Sandy said. "What's wrong?"

"I'm fine," she lied, not wanting to burden

393

her friend with her troubles, especially at a time like this.

Sandy smiled. "I may not have seen you much the last couple of years, but I know you better than almost anybody. I can tell when something's bothering you. Spill it."

"It can wait," Gwen said. "The nurse is right. You need to rest."

"We both know that if you don't tell me now, I'm going to lie here and think about it. I won't be able to sleep a wink! Unless you want that on your conscience, I suggest you start talking."

Gwen sighed. Sandy was right; she wouldn't be able to let it go.

So she told her friend everything, starting at the beginning. She laid out all that she'd learned about the night Pete died. It sounded almost as unbelievable coming from her own lips as it had coming from Hank's. Sandy listened, wide-eyed and silent; Gwen imagined that she herself had looked much the same when Hank had told her the truth.

"Wow . . . just . . ." Sandy stammered once Gwen had finished. "Wow . . ."

"But I don't know what to do now," Gwen continued. She pulled the folded pages from her pocket. "Should I take what I wrote to the *Bulletin*? Surely Sid Keaton would publish it. I mean, if this isn't news, I don't know what is."

"So what's stopping you?" Sandy asked.

"Hank," she answered. "He lied about what happened because he wanted to protect his father. If what I wrote is published, then his sacrifice becomes worthless."

Sandy was silent for a moment, thinking. "How did Myron react when you saw him?" she finally asked. "Was he reluctant to talk?"

Gwen shook her head. "Just the opposite. He told me that this has weighed on him ever since the night of the accident. He hates himself for not being brave enough to admit to what he did. Myron knows it isn't fair that Hank assumed the blame for Pete's death. He wants to make it right."

"Then there's your answer."

"I don't understand."

"What happened that night is as much Myron's story as it is Hank's. Probably more so," her friend explained. "Hank loved his father enough to take the blame for something he didn't do, but that doesn't mean Myron has to go along with it. Not forever. If he wants to confess, who can stop him?"

Gwen understood that Sandy was right. It obviously bothered Myron that Hank was hated by most everyone in town, especially when that anger should've been directed at him. Maybe it was guilt that fueled his drinking. Regardless, Myron had been clear when they'd talked in his hospital room. He wanted the truth known, no matter what it might cost him. Still, she couldn't stop worrying about how Hank would react.

"I don't want to make Hank angry," she said. "I'm afraid that by doing this, I'm going to end up ruining what we have."

"He might be mad," Sandy conceded. "At least for a little while. But it won't last long. I'd bet that both Hank and his dad will feel better quick. Carrying around all that guilt can't have been good for either of them."

For the second time since Gwen had come back to Buckton, it'd been her dearest friend who had pushed her in the right direction.

Toward Hank.

Nothing about making her decision had been easy. Standing in Sandy's hospital room, taking in all that had been said, Gwen understood that now that she had put her plan in motion, she had to see it through to the end.

"I think I know what to do," she said. "Thank you."

"I'm just glad I could help. Maybe you could —" Sandy began but then yawned, too tired to hold it back.

"That's my cue to go," Gwen said, leaning over the bed to kiss the new mother's forehead. "Get some rest."

Sandy was asleep before Gwen reached the door. Out in the hallway, she looked at the pages she'd typed.

It was time to take them where they needed to go.

CHAPTER TWENTY-FOUR

"Are you telling me *this* is what really happened?"

Sid Keaton leaned back in his chair, his feet on his desk, the pages Gwen had written in his hands. When she'd first arrived at the *Bulletin,* the publisher had been hurriedly putting the final touches on the latest edition, double-checking with his reporters, making edits, and laying out advertisements. The issue was scheduled to go to the printer in less than an hour. While Sid had been friendly, asking if she was excited to see her article in print, it was clear he had little time to talk.

Until Gwen had told him the reason for her visit.

They'd gone into his office. Sid had shut the door and even lowered the blinds, making it clear to his employees that they weren't to be disturbed. Before Gwen had even taken a seat, he'd bombarded her with questions, wanting to know where she'd gotten her information. In answer, Gwen had handed him what she'd typed up. He had sat down and begun to read, his eyes racing across the pages.

"I gotta say, at first glance, it's hard to believe," he said.

"It's the truth," she told him.

"So let me get this straight. Myron was driving, but Hank took the blame for his brother's death to protect his old man."

Gwen nodded.

"He could've gone to jail," Sid observed.

"I don't think he cared. With his mother and Pete dead, most everyone he loved was gone. His father was all he had left. Besides, he wasn't thinking clearly just after the accident. He did what he thought was right."

"There's a lot of quotes from Myron in here," Sid said, tapping the pages. "Did he know what you planned on doing with what he told you?"

"When we talked, he made it perfectly clear that he wanted people to know what he'd done," she explained. "Myron's tired of hiding it. He knows that I was writing something to bring to you."

"What's Hank's take on all this?"

"He doesn't know," Gwen answered honestly.

Sid stared at her for a moment, then tossed the pages on his desk. "You're awfully close to this story, aren't you?" he asked. "I can see it in your writing."

Gwen frowned. She'd taken great pains to try to remove her personal involvement with Hank from her work. As she'd rewritten the pages over and over, Gwen had strived to make it about the facts of the accident and the quotes that revealed the truth, leaving out any opinions or conjecture. Obviously she hadn't done as good of a job as she'd thought.

"Don't worry. It isn't *that* obvious," Sid told her, as if he'd once again read her mind. "But I'd be willing to bet I'm right."

"You are," Gwen admitted.

"How so?"

She took a deep breath. "I'm in love with Hank."

The room went silent. Outside the closed door, Gwen could hear the hustle and bustle of the newspaper. People called out to each other. Telephones rang. But inside Sid's office, neither of them made a sound.

"Have you thought about the possible consequences of this being published?" he finally asked. "It could be ugly."

"I have," Gwen answered, remembering her conversation with Sandy.

But she and Sid weren't thinking about the same sorts of consequences.

"You might want to think again," he said. "Hank dodged a bullet before, but when word of this gets out, he could end up behind bars."

"What?!" Gwen blurted. "How?"

"I've never met a police officer who took kindly to being lied to," Sid explained, "and that's just what Hank did. Now, the fact that they didn't press charges after the accident makes it likely they wouldn't do it now, but there's no guarantee. There could be trouble for publishing this. For Hank *and* Myron."

Gwen felt foolish for never considering that Hank could get in trouble for lying. Maybe Sid was right and nothing would happen. After all, punishing Hank or his father now wouldn't bring Pete back. Was it worth the risk?

"Let me make a phone call," Sid said.

He dialed, and after a couple of seconds greeted the person who answered. "Margaret! Hey, it's Sid over at the *Bulletin*," he said, as friendly as could be. "Say, is Bruce in? I've got something I want to run by him." A pause as he listened to her reply. "Sure, I'll wait."

Gwen knew that Sid was talking about

Bruce Palmer, Buckton's chief of police. Her nerves started to get the better of her; she had such a hard time keeping her hands still that she considered sitting on them.

But she needn't have worried.

When the policeman got on the line, Sid went to work. Gwen marveled at how he maneuvered their conversation. He never came out and said that he had evidence Hank wasn't responsible for his brother's death, but instead beat around the edges of it. He suggested things rather than stating them. He hinted rather than declared. Listening to him gave Gwen an idea of what being a professional journalist was all about. By the time Sid hung up, he was smiling.

"I think Hank will be in the clear," he said.

"Are you sure?" Gwen asked, unable to shake her worry.

"I've known Bruce since we were kids," Sid explained. "We might not agree on everything, but I don't think he'd steer me wrong."

"Does that mean you want to publish what I wrote?"

"Absolutely. But the final decision is yours to make."

But it wasn't, not completely.

Gwen remembered what Sandy had said. What happened that fateful night was

Myron's story to tell. While it had been her idea to put the truth in the newspaper, Hank's father had *agreed* with her, had *wanted* his guilt and responsibility for his son's death known. While Hank might end up angry at the both of them, Gwen still believed that the only way for him and her to be together, to start building a future, was to stop living a lie.

In the end, her choice was easy.

"It should be published," she said.

Sid smiled broadly. "In that case, I've got another call to make."

This time, the conversation wasn't as friendly.

"Yeah, Gary, I'm gonna need you to hold the paper," he began, then immediately frowned. "I know. I know what time it is. I can read a damn watch, but look, something's come up." She could hear shouting through the receiver. "Yeah, but . . . no, I don't know how long it's gonna take, but we have to wait."

Listening to the back-and-forth, Gwen realized that a newspaper publisher wore many different hats. While Sid had had to tread delicately when talking to Buckton's police chief, a friendly tone wasn't always going to get the job done.

Sometimes, you had to raise your voice.

"I don't care if you don't want to wait! Do it!" Sid shouted, then hung up. Turning to Gwen, he said, "Sorry you had to hear that, but folks start to get grumpy when we're close to printing. Nine times out of ten, it all goes like clockwork." With a wink, he added, "Unfortunately for Gary, this is that one."

Sid stuck his head out the door and called for someone to come take Gwen's article so that it could be edited and typeset.

"I know I said it the last time you were here," he told her once he was back behind his desk, "but I think you've got a future in this. If you'd ever want a recommendation for one of those fancy papers back in Chicago, I'd be happy to write you one." Sid chuckled. "I don't know how much it'd help, but I don't think I burned enough bridges when I left for it to hurt."

"What if I wanted to work *here*?" Gwen asked, the suddenness of her question surprising even her.

Sid nodded, mulling over what he'd heard. "You're thinking of staying?"

"I am," she admitted.

"What about Chicago? I thought you were happy there."

Gwen gave a thin smile. "I thought so, too," she said. "But since I've been home,

I've started to realize that things aren't always what they seem."

"Falling in love has a way of doing that."

She couldn't have agreed more.

Just last week, Gwen had come back to Buckton in the company of another man, thinking that it was only for a short visit. But since then, her whole world had been turned upside down. Now, there was nowhere else she wanted to be, no man other than Hank with whom she wanted to share her life.

"If you work here," Sid explained, "you'll have to start at the bottom. I know you've already had two headlines, but that's not the way I do things. Whatever you get, you'll earn, same as everyone else. In the beginning, that might mean answering phones or soliciting advertising. Can you do that?"

"I can. I *will*," she answered enthusiastically, stunned that her dream of becoming a writer was one step closer to reality. "I accept!"

"Hold on a second," Sid replied, tempering her happiness. "You should think it over for a day or two. The last thing I want is for you to realize you jumped the gun and quit on me after two weeks. Nobody wins if that happens. Once you're sure this is what you want to do, then we'll sit down and talk again, get all the details ironed out."

"All right," Gwen agreed, although she knew nothing would change her mind. She couldn't wait to tell Hank the good news.

Just as she was about to leave, mindful that Sid still had a newspaper to put out, he said, "By the way, it looks like you were right about the fires."

"What do you mean?"

"There was another one last night," Sid explained. "Carl Tate's auto garage went up in flames. Fortunately it didn't spread to any nearby buildings, largely thanks to the storm. Still, Carl lost a couple cars and his livelihood. That's three fires in not quite two weeks. If someone isn't setting them deliberately, I'll eat my hat."

"Do you need something written up about it?" Gwen asked.

Sid chuckled. "You don't ever quit, do you?" he said. "Don't worry, I've got it covered. Besides, you've got plenty on your plate. Remember, when people read the paper in the morning, things in Buckton are going to be different. Tongues will wag and phones will ring off the hook. My advice would be to talk to Hank, right now. He deserves to know what's comin'."

Gwen nodded. Sid was right.

It was time for her and Hank to have a

long talk.

Hank paced his workshop as restlessly as a caged animal, a paintbrush in his hand. So far he'd tried finishing the detail work on a table, taken his axe and chopped a dozen pieces of oak for a project he'd been meaning to start, and then begun applying varnish to a bench. He had done all these things to try to quiet the storm raging in his head, but nothing had worked.

He couldn't stop thinking about Gwen.

His hands busy or still, his eyes open or shut, Hank couldn't erase the sight of her in Kent's arms. He wanted to believe that there was an explanation, that it hadn't been what it seemed, but the image wouldn't go away, taunting him. Doubt gnawed at his guts.

Angry at himself, Hank whipped the paintbrush across the room and stalked outside, turning his face up to the late-afternoon sun.

After speeding away from the Fosters' house, he and Skip had gone to the hospital. Hank had been reluctant to visit his father, struggling to come to grips with what he'd just witnessed, but his friend had insisted. Seeing Myron hadn't helped Hank's mood. His father had been sleeping, his head heavily bandaged. To his son, he looked frail, older than his years, yet surprisingly peaceful. No matter how many indignities Hank had suffered since his mother's death, regardless of the sacrifices he'd made in claiming responsibility for the accident that took Pete, Hank loved his father. He just wished it had been enough, that it would've fixed what was broken.

"He's gonna be all right," Skip had said. "You'll see."

When watching his father became too much to bear, Hank had gone in search of a doctor. Reading from a chart, the physician had explained that Myron's cut was deep but it would heal, though it would likely leave a scar. The real warning had been reserved for his father's drinking.

"If he doesn't stop soon," the doctor had said, "it will kill him."

Hank had nodded, silently praying that this time, the lesson would be learned.

The whole drive home, Hank kept hoping that when they pulled into the drive, Gwen would be there waiting for him. But she wasn't. Skip had stuck around for a while, making small talk, suggesting that they go get some lunch or throw the baseball, but Hank hadn't been interested. Eventually

Skip had left his friend to battle his worries alone.

And so here he was, confused, annoyed, and heartsick.

It was then, lost in thought, that Hank heard the sound of a vehicle approaching. He walked up the drive, convinced that it was Gwen, excited to see her again yet dreading the difficult conversation that was sure to follow.

But it wasn't her.

A red Plymouth turned onto the gravel and headed slowly toward him. Hank instantly recognized the car. It belonged to someone he never would have expected to see. Someone whose arrival heralded bad things.

It was Jed Ringer.

To make matters worse, he wasn't alone. The two goons who'd been with him outside the malt shop popped out of the passenger door. "Thought you said he wasn't gonna be home," one of them said, a baseball bat slung over his shoulder, before his boss silenced him with a raised hand.

Looking at the three men, Hank realized that fighting with Jed at the baseball game and goading him outside the malt shop had been playing with fire. A tough like Jed had likely been stewing about things ever since.

Now he was searching for revenge. No doubt, there was about to be trouble.

"What the hell are you doing here?" Hank asked as he bunched his hands, preparing to fight. He was trapped in a sort of no-man's-land, too far from both the house and his workshop; he wondered if he'd have time to reach either and grab something heavy before his unwanted visitors were on top of him.

"Is that any way to talk to an old friend?" Jed replied.

"We aren't friends."

"No, we sure as shit aren't," he said with a humorless chuckle. "But that don't mean I haven't been thinkin' a lot about you. Lately, seems like everywhere I go, there you are. One day, you're messin' up my baseball game; the next, I find you parked downtown, showin' your face where it don't belong."

While Jed talked, Hank noticed that his two companions — he faintly remembered that their names were Clint and Sam — were slowly inching off to the sides, as if they were trying to flank him. Clint, the scrawnier one, shook the bat in his hand, testing its weight.

"People don't wanna see you," Jed continued. "It makes 'em sick."

"I've got as much right to be there as everyone else."

"See, that's where you're wrong," he said, smiling menacingly, coming closer, walking Hank down. "A murderer ain't got no rights."

Even as he listened to Jed while trying to keep an eye on his flunkies, Hank worried about Gwen. What would happen if she suddenly showed up? She'd have no idea of the danger she was getting herself into. Was Jed sadistic enough to hurt her? Could Hank protect her if the bastard tried?

"So what happened to your old man?" Jed asked. "Word around town is that he had himself an accident. Let me guess," he added with a smirk, "you tied one on for old times' sake and tried to do him like you did your brother."

Skip had been right; Jed loved to hear himself talk. But right now, Hank didn't mind. He hoped it would be the man's downfall.

Hank knew he had only one chance to gain the upper hand. While Jed was busy listening to the sound of his own voice, he'd strike, take the most dangerous thug out of the fight, then move on to his cronies before they even knew what had happened. It was risky, but Hank didn't have a choice.

411

"What were you drinkin'?" Jed asked. "Whiskey? Or was it —"

Before he could finish, Hank closed the distance between them and threw as hard a punch as he could. Things worked just like he'd planned; his fist cracked into Jed's jaw, snapping his head sideways, dropping him to his knees in the gravel.

Hank spun, knowing that his plan rested on taking advantage of the others before they could react. He'd hoped that the suddenness of his attack would catch them off guard, that they wouldn't be ready for what came next.

But he was wrong.

The first blow caught him in the ribs. The second clipped his nose. But he was really done in when the baseball bat knocked him upside the head. Everything went topsy-turvy. One minute, Hank was on his feet, preparing to fight, and the next he was facedown in the rocks. Stars swam before his eyes. He struggled to keep from throwing up.

"Home run!" Clint crowed.

Groggy, Hank saw a blurry version of Jed get back to his feet, wipe blood from the corner of his mouth, and then spit into the yard. "Now why in the hell did you have to go and do that?" he asked, sarcastically offended. "Boys, I think this stupid son of a bitch wants us to make an example outta him."

Hank heard more than saw Jed walk away, back toward his car. In the man's absence, he tried to clear his head, to get back on his feet, but as soon as he rose to his hands and knees, one of the others kicked him in the ribs.

"Stay down, dummy! You got a surprise comin'."

Jed returned and knelt beside Hank, who was still holding his aching side. He placed a large metal can on the rocky drive. The smell of gasoline was powerful enough to cut through the fog clouding Hank's head.

"Now," Jed told him, "you burn."

CHAPTER TWENTY-FIVE

The gas can. Jed's history of causing trouble. The recent fires that had plagued Buckton, including the one Gwen had written about for the newspaper. Even with a muddled head, Hank easily put it all together, though if he hadn't been able, Jed would've been happy to do it for him.

"That's right," the thug said as he removed the lid from the canister. "I'm the one who's been burnin' places to the ground. I tell you, seein' those flames, feelin' their heat, watchin' from the shadows as folks cry about losin' everythin' they got, it's powerful stuff. Once you get a taste for it, it's hard to let go. Like you and drinkin', I suppose."

Jed started to splash gasoline on the walls of Hank's shop, sloshing it over his work, his livelihood, spilling what was left onto the floor.

"Up till today, I've been real quiet about it," he continued, flinging the now-empty can toward his car, apparently not wanting to leave it as evidence. "I like to case a place for a while, figure out when folks are home, when they sit down for dinner, that sort of thing. That's what I was doin' with you," Jed explained, nudging Hank with his foot. "I figured you'd be at the hospital, visitin' your old man. Because believe it or not, I ain't out to hurt nobody. I just enjoy seein' things burn. I was gonna do the same to your place, but you bein' home, sluggin' me, that done changed things for the worse."

"Hey, wait a second," Sam said, starting to see where things were headed, as if a lightbulb had suddenly gone on over his head. "He's seen us. He knows what we've been doin'. He knows!"

"Don't worry about it," Jed replied. "He ain't gonna tell no one."

Sam shook his head. "We can't just take him at his word," he said, a touch of worry in his voice. "Soon as we leave, he'll call the cops!"

Clint chuckled, the smarter of the pair.

Jed walked over, his shoes crunching in the gravel, and knelt beside Hank. "Remember how I said I ain't out to hurt nobody?" he said. "For this piece of shit, I'm gonna make an exception."

Hank knew exactly what that meant.

They were going to kill him, then throw his body into the fire to try to make it look like an accident.

The slower of the two flunkies was still adding it up, slowly realizing that he was about to have blood on his hands. "You never said nothin' 'bout hurtin' him," Sam protested. "I ain't sure I wanna do this."

"Quit bein' such a damned sissy!" Clint snapped, clearly having no reservations about using the baseball bat clutched in his hands.

"Like I said, don't worry about it," Jed said, sounding surprisingly calm for someone planning to commit murder. "Ain't no one gonna miss him. Hell, if folks knew what we done, they'd throw us a parade down Main Street."

For emphasis, he kicked Hank in the shoulder, a glancing blow, but enough to put him down on his face.

"What say we get this show on the road?" Jed asked, then pulled a book of matches from his pocket. He scratched one to life and tossed it into a puddle of gasoline, where it instantly caught, sending flames running up the side of the building.

The workshop was on fire.

Gwen drove out of Buckton with the radio playing and a soft summer breeze blowing through the open window. She kept thinking about little Kelly Fiderlein, not even an hour old; what an absolutely beautiful day to be born. She chuckled. As strange as it might seem, Gwen realized that she had something in common with Sandy's baby daughter.

Her life was at a new beginning, too.

The truck's tires passed noisily over the planks of the bridge spanning the Sawyer River. Not long before, Hank had noticed her flailing about in the turbulent water, then had leaped in to save her. From that moment, their lives had become intertwined. What blossomed between them had been as wonderful as it was unexpected.

She had found love, *real love,* for the first time.

Now she just had to make it last.

Gwen had no way of knowing how people would react when they read tomorrow's edition of the *Bulletin.* Many would undoubtedly be shocked, others skeptical, and a few might even be angry to learn they'd been lied to.

But the only reaction that mattered to Gwen was Hank's. Would he be mad at her? Relieved? Whatever it was, she silently prayed that it wouldn't ruin what they had, that he wouldn't walk away from her. Not now. Not when they were just getting started.

As she drove up a steep hill, the truck protested, and Gwen had to force the gears into place. She was less than a mile from Hank's house. The first time she had driven this way, she'd been a bundle of nerves, anxious to talk to her mysterious rescuer. Now, she felt more apprehensive than nervous. Still, Gwen was determined to be honest with him, to tell Hank the truth about what she'd done.

Then the cards would have to fall where they may.

Rounding a gentle bend in the road, Gwen saw something up ahead that made her pulse race. A plume of smoke rose above the treetops, marring an otherwise clear sky. With every frenzied beat of her heart, it seemed to be growing bigger, darker. She couldn't be certain, but it looked to be coming from near Hank's home. Deep in her gut, she knew something was wrong.

Gwen pushed the gas pedal to the floor.

Flames rose up the workshop's walls. They raced across the floor. They leaped onto worktables and began to consume chairs, bookcases, dressers, and even tools, anything and everything they touched. Red, orange, and yellow, the fire was a kaleidoscope of destruction. Heat radiated in waves, soon growing unbearably hot. Dark smoke billowed out of the open doors and rose toward the sky.

And there wasn't a damned thing Hank could do about it.

"We gotta get movin'," Sam said nervously, still unsettled. "Somebody's gonna see the smoke."

"There's time," Clint disagreed. "Ain't nobody comes out this way."

Jed pointed at Hank. "Lift him up."

Each flunky grabbed an arm and hauled Hank to his feet; Clint never let go of the baseball bat. Slowly but surely, Hank's head continued to clear. He understood that he had to act fast. He was running out of time.

Jed grinned, enjoying the carnage he'd wrought. "I'd tell you to say hi to your brother for me," he snarled over the crackling fire, "but he ain't gonna be where you're goin'." With that, Jed punched Hank in the stomach hard enough to lift him from the ground before he fell back into the gravel.

But unbeknownst to Jed, Hank wasn't as hurt as he appeared. He'd known that the bully wouldn't be able to resist inflicting more pain, and so before the blow landed, he'd tightened the muscles of his stomach. The punch stung, but not nearly as much as it could have.

"Finish him," Jed said.

"My pleasure," Clint replied, raising the baseball bat.

And that was when Hank struck.

He grabbed a fistful of rocks and hurled them in Jed's face, distracting him. Before the stones had fallen back to the ground, Hank drove his elbow into Clint's groin. The flunky screamed in agony. He dropped the baseball bat as he collapsed into a heap, both hands cradling his smashed privates. Hank snatched up the bat, turned, and swung. Though Sam had shown reluctance to join in the more grisly aspects of Jed's plan, he remained dangerous. Hank couldn't afford to show mercy. The thickest part of the wood barrel hit the man flush in the ribs, breaking at least one, and down he went. Spinning, Hank landed another blow on Clint, strong enough to silence the goon's shouting.

Hank rose on unsteady feet. Now it was just him and Jed.

"Well, looky here," Jed said, still wiping dirt from his eyes. "Seems you had more stones than I gave you credit for."

"You're about to see how much fight I've got left," Hank snarled.

Behind him, the blaze raged out of control. Heat singed his back, burning the exposed skin on his arms and neck. Glass cracked and wood creaked, a symphony of destruction. It wouldn't be much longer before there'd be nothing left to save. But Hank didn't dare look; he couldn't risk taking his eyes off Jed.

As if to demonstrate how true that was, the man pulled a knife from his pocket. When he popped open the blade, it glinted in the sun.

"Show me," Jed said.

Hank held the bat cocked, ready to swing, watching for the slightest movement. Jed stepped to his side, forcing Hank to do the same, the two men moving in a circle. Occasionally, Jed would feint, coming forward, testing his opponent, but he never fully committed himself. Not yet. Smiling wide, showing plenty of teeth, he looked like he was having fun.

"What're you waitin' for?" Jed asked. "Come get me."

Rather than respond, Hank readjusted his grip on the bat.

But then, like a flash, Jed went for blood. He jab-stepped to the left, then quickly changed direction, slashing with the knife. The blade cut an arc through the smoky air. The tip pierced the skin of Hank's forearm, leaving a painful, bloody gash several inches long.

"Little slow there," Jed crowed. "You don't move faster than that, next time, my knife's gonna end up in your heart."

Little as Hank wanted to admit it, the bastard was right. The bat was a powerful weapon, but he couldn't swing as fast as Jed could strike with the knife. If he was going to survive this, if there was to be any chance to save his workshop, Hank had to be smarter. He had to guess where Jed was going to be before the man even moved. Then he would make him pay.

He'll come straight at me this time . . . he'll be looking for the kill . . .

Hank was right. And he was ready.

Jed reversed his strategy from before, lunging forward with his first move and dropping his outside shoulder, making it look like he was going to step away, but he never hesitated, going right at Hank. The bat found him first. Before Jed reached his intended target, the heavy barrel smashed into his hand, sending the knife flying and crushing fragile bones.

"Damn it!" he hollered in pain.

Unfortunately for Jed, Hank wasn't done with him yet. The next blow hammered his shoulder. Another clipped his knee, dropping him to the ground. A final swing slammed into his ribs. In a matter of seconds, the tough had been transformed from a bloodthirsty braggart into a whimpering mess.

But then, as Hank was trying to figure out what to do with his defeated opponent, something in his workshop exploded.

The loud blast sent flames and broken glass shooting out the open doors. Debris rained across the yard. Immediately, Hank knew what had happened. In his work, he used all kinds of paints, stains, and varnishes. Most of them were strong, noxious stuff. The fire must have reached them, and at least one had blown up. There would likely be more.

Jed's two flunkies still lay on the ground, moaning and nursing their injuries. Both men were close enough to the workshop that another explosion could endanger their lives. Hank knew what he had to do.

Shielding his face, he dragged each man away, dumping them farther back in the yard where he thought they'd be safe. Briefly, he wondered whether they would've done the same for him — he supposed Sam's conscience might have gotten the better of him — but in the end he knew it didn't matter.

As Hank wiped plenty of sweat from his brow, something moved out of the corner of his eye. It was Jed. He was crawling across the gravel, heading for his car. At the same time, Hank heard a noise, distinct over the din of the fire. He knew it as well as a child knows his mother's lullaby.

It was his truck's engine.

Gwen was back.

Beyond the windshield, Gwen watched as the cloud of smoke grew larger. A black spire stretched upward; when it was caught by the wind, it smeared across the sky like dark paint on a light canvas. She knew this wasn't a harmless brush fire. This was a blaze raging out of control.

And she was convinced that it was coming from Hank's house.

Fear gripped her, squeezing harder and

harder by the second. Was Hank hurt? Had there been an accident? Her mind worked furiously to create an explanation for what she was seeing, but nothing she came up with put her mind at ease.

Though the truck wasn't built for speed, Gwen pushed it as fast as it would go, stepping on the accelerator, forcing the speedometer's needle to climb, making the vehicle shudder from the effort. She couldn't get there fast enough. Gwen was so intent on the billowing smoke that she had to periodically remind herself to keep her eyes on the road.

When Hank's place finally came into sight, it put her heart in her throat. Gwen jammed on the brakes, causing the truck's tires to skid, then turned into the drive, still moving quickly.

The first thing she saw was Hank's workshop. It was a raging inferno. Flames raced up the walls, charring the wood. They had burst out the windows and burned through a corner of the roof, hungry for more, insatiable until there was nothing left to destroy. All Gwen could think about was the exquisite pieces Hank had built by hand, like the one that had made Freddie Holland so happy. They would all be lost.

Gwen was so dumbstruck by what she was

seeing that she didn't immediately notice the car parked ahead of her in the drive. She hadn't expected it to be there and had to swerve to avoid hitting it; she failed, clipping its rear bumper with her own, filling the air with the screech of metal against metal.

But there would be no missing the man who suddenly loomed before her.

Gwen screamed as she slammed on the brakes, but it was far too late to stop. With a sickening thud, she sent him flying like a rag doll, arms and legs pinwheeling through the air. One second he was there and the next he'd disappeared from sight. She wasn't even sure who it had been.

Hank! Oh no, oh no, oh no, oh no . . .

Throwing the truck into park, Gwen was out of the cab like a shot, running toward the fallen man. He lay in a twisted heap, one arm bent at an unnatural angle, clearly broken, as blood spilled from a cut on his forehead. He wasn't moving. Though she was terrified she might have killed someone, Gwen was relieved to see that it wasn't Hank she'd hit, but a man whose face looked vaguely familiar . . .

"Gwen!"

She turned and saw Hank. Gwen ran to him, but just as she was about to throw her arms around him, to hold Hank close and thank the heavens that he was all right, she stopped. Bruises marred his face and blood dripped from a cut on his arm. "You're hurt!" she exclaimed.

"Compared to them, I got off easy," he said with a weak smile, then pointed.

Gwen looked to see two other men sprawled in the yard. Both were rolling around, but neither looked like he had any fight left in him.

"I hit someone with the truck," she said as her hands started to shake, realizing what she'd done.

"It's all right," Hank told her, pulling her into his arms, quieting the tears that threatened to fall. "There was nothing you could have done."

As Gwen tried to take comfort in Hank's soothing words, a pair of explosions ripped through the burning building, shaking the air and making her jump with fright. Hank calmly walked them farther away and closer to the house.

"Your workshop!" she cried, her attention drawn back to what had sent her speeding to his side. "Your things! Call the fire department! We can still —"

"It's too late," Hank interrupted. He sighed, his eyes wet as he looked over the damage the fire was still causing, the broken glass, the sagging beams, the destruction of all he'd worked so hard to build. "It's gone."

By the time Hank's workshop had been completely consumed by the fire, the sun had nearly set. The moon was already high in the still-blue sky, as if it had become impatient waiting for its celestial opposite to leave. The firemen had come and gone, spraying more water on the grass and nearby trees than on the burning building, trying to keep the blaze from spreading. One policeman remained, taking a statement from Hank.

Jed Ringer had been placed in an ambulance, his two flunkies stuffed into the back of a squad car. Gwen had been relieved that she hadn't accidentally killed Jed with the truck, but from the way he howled in agony when he was lifted onto a gurney, she figured he had an awfully long mend ahead of him. By the time he healed, he'd likely be in a jail cell.

"They're gonna figure it out," Sam had been overheard saying to Clint almost as soon as the cops had arrived.

"Shut up, stupid!" his fellow goon had hissed back.

Sam had been right. When a policeman

opened Jed's trunk, he'd found a couple of canisters of gasoline, rags that could have been used for lighting fires, and a collection of knickknacks that at first seemed innocent, but ended up being the most damning evidence of all. Apparently, before Jed and his gang torched a place, they took a memento; Gwen recognized a birdhouse that used to hang from a hook on the Morgans' porch.

Even though Hank was little liked around town, Gwen could see that the police officers and firemen were still sympathetic. She wondered how they'd feel in the coming days, after her article had been published in the newspaper and they learned that their disdain for him had been misguided.

Finally the last police car backed down the drive, leaving Gwen and Hank alone.

He stood with his back to her, staring at the wreckage of his workshop, ruined tools mixed with the ashes of his labor. Absently, he toed a still-smoldering piece of wood. If he heard her approach, he didn't react.

"I'm sorry," she told him, knowing it did nothing to fill the void of his loss.

"No reason to be," he replied flatly.

"I feel bad all the same."

When Hank didn't respond or even look at her, Gwen frowned. Ever since she'd gone to call the authorities, he had been distant with her. At first, Gwen chalked it up to the trauma of being attacked, of having his livelihood stolen, to his being in shock, but now she wondered if it wasn't something more.

"I also wanted to apologize for leaving so early this morning," she said, knowing that this was as good of a time as any to broach the subject of her speaking with his father. She needed to tell him what she'd written. "I had some important things to do."

Hank nodded but still didn't speak.

Growing a bit frustrated, Gwen touched his arm. When he looked down at her, she saw that his bruises were getting darker and that soot stained his cheeks. It didn't matter. She found him as handsome as ever. But almost as soon as his gaze found hers, Hank turned away.

"What is it?" she insisted. "What's wrong?"

Hank took a deep breath, his broad chest rising and falling. "I saw you today," he told her; it sounded like an accusation.

"You what?" she asked, confused. "Where?"

"At your folks' place," Hank answered. "Skip picked me up and we went looking for you. We saw you pull up to the house."

Thinking back on it, Gwen couldn't understand what Hank had seen that so bothered him. Had he not liked watching her argue with Kent?

"Then why are you acting like this?" she pressed.

When he turned back to her, his eyes were flat, piercing. This time he didn't look away. "I saw you with Kent," he said. "I saw you in his arms."

CHAPTER TWENTY-SIX

Even since he and Skip had driven away from the Fosters' house, his heart hammering, his hands balled into fists, Hank had wondered how Gwen would react to being confronted. He couldn't imagine she would deny being in Kent's arms; after all, he'd *seen* her. Would she be embarrassed, start crying, or admit that she couldn't let go of the successful lawyer and the exciting life they had back in Chicago? Would Gwen say that making love to him had been a mistake?

The one thing he hadn't expected her to do was laugh.

It started as a chuckle but steadily grew until her eyes were wet with tears. Completely taken aback, Hank had to ask, "What's so funny?"

"You said that you saw me drive up to the house, right?" Gwen replied.

Hank nodded.

"Then I got out of the truck, went up the

walk, and eventually Kent came down the stairs," she said, laying out events just as they had occurred.

"And that's when you hugged him," he said.

"No, I didn't," Gwen disagreed.

"I *saw* it," he snapped. The sight was burned into Hank's mind; he wondered if he'd ever be able to forget it. Just thinking about them, Gwen's head against Kent's chest, his arms pulling her close, made him mad all over again.

But then she threw a glass of cold water on his anger.

"What you saw was *Kent* embracing *me,* not the other way around," she explained. "Tell me what happened next."

"I don't know," he admitted. "I told Skip to drive off. I couldn't stand the sight of you in another man's arms."

Gwen smiled, a beautiful, delicate gesture that disarmed him further. "I wish you would've stuck around a while longer."

"Why?" Hank asked, confused.

"What you saw may have been a nightmare," she said, "but you missed the happy ending."

Gwen told him that she'd pushed Kent away, that she had admitted to falling for another man, and that their relationship was over. She seemed genuinely hurt by the mean, spiteful things Kent had said once he'd understood she was serious. Gwen hadn't wanted to hurt him, but there'd been no other way.

"I ended things with Kent because I'm in love with *you,*" she said. "This is where I want to be, by your side, forever."

She rose on her tiptoes and placed her lips against his, kissing him gently. Even as Hank returned her affection, his head swam.

He felt like a damned fool.

How could he have doubted her? If he'd only followed Skip's advice and talked to her, everything would've been out in the open and he wouldn't have spent the rest of the day sick with worry. Hank supposed that part of the reason he'd been willing to jump to conclusions was because love was so unfamiliar to him. It was a lot like the smoke still rising from his workshop, impossible to grab hold of. But somehow, despite himself, that's just what he had done.

"I thought that the way you left this morning," he explained, "along with what I saw, meant that you regretted what we'd done."

"Never," Gwen said. "But looking back, I shouldn't have driven off the way I did."

"Where did you go?" he asked. "What was so important it couldn't wait?"

Now it was her turn to take a deep breath.

"You didn't need to worry about Kent," she said, "but that doesn't mean there isn't reason for you to be mad at me."

Hank had a sinking feeling in his stomach. "Why is that?"

Then she told him.

When Gwen explained to Hank that she'd visited his father in the hospital, he looked shocked; his eyes widened, his jaw fell open, and he seemed to momentarily hold his breath. But when she told him the reason she had wanted to talk to Myron, that surprise quickly changed to anger; his gaze narrowed, his mouth clamped shut, he breathed raggedly through his nose, and the muscles of his neck and shoulders grew tense. However, it wasn't until she said that she'd written an article detailing the truth about the accident that claimed Pete's life, as well as the fact that it would be published in tomorrow's newspaper, that he finally spoke.

"How could you do this?" he shouted, as mad as she'd ever seen him.

"I had to," she said simply.

Hank began to pace back and forth in front of the wreckage of the workshop, too angry to remain still. He ran a hand through his hair, showing the bandaged cut on his forearm. "Everything I've done was to protect my father," he told her. "But now you've ruined it all."

"You had the best of intentions, but it hasn't worked," Gwen said. "Look at the state your father is in. Do you really believe that getting drunk, falling down, and hurting himself means that he's handling his guilt well?"

"If people find out what he did, it'll kill him!"

"I think Myron's doing a good job of that on his own."

Hank stopped and stared hard at her.

"It's the truth," she continued, desperate to make him understand. "When I talked to him, he didn't hold anything back. He admitted to everything. He's ashamed for what he did, for what he continues to do, and is tired of running from it. He doesn't want you to carry this burden anymore. I don't think he ever did."

Hank shook his head. "You still should've told me what you were planning to do."

"Why? You would have tried to talk me out of it," Gwen said. "You told me that you made your decision on the spur of the moment, right after you found out Pete was dead. You weren't thinking clearly. Surely you must see that." She took a tentative step toward him, wanting to be closer. "But for you to cling to that choice now, months later, knowing that it hasn't made a difference in anyone's life, that it's actually made things worse, means you're just being stubborn. This has to stop, Hank. It has to."

"I suppose you think you know what's best for me," he said, his words tinged with a hint of sarcasm.

"In this case, absolutely," Gwen answered, refusing to back down, wanting him to understand, to agree with her. "Look at my parents. Think about all the terrible things they've said about you. When you risked your life to save mine, when you brought me home to them, my father ended up throwing you out of the house, all because of what he believed to be true! How many other people in town wrongly feel the same? None of them know you like I do, but until you fight to clear your name, until you declare your innocence, nothing will change."

For the first time, Gwen thought she might be reaching Hank. There was something in his eyes, a glimmer of hope, maybe, but he refused to let go of his pessimism. "People won't believe what you've written."

"Some won't," she agreed, "but others

will. It will take time, a lot longer than you've spent living this lie. But in the months and years to come, I bet most people will look at you the way Freddie Holland does."

Hank paused. "I'm still mad at you."

"I can understand why."

"This is that important to you?" he asked, his eyes searching her face, his tone softening.

"Yes, it is," Gwen replied.

"Why?"

She smiled. "You really don't know?"

Hank shook his head.

"Can I make a confession to you?" she asked.

"Sure."

"I didn't go see your father just for you," she admitted. "I also went for me."

"What do you mean?"

"I want to build a life with you, so I started to wonder whether I wouldn't be judged guilty by association," Gwen explained. "What if when I went to the department store I had to listen to people whispering about me, saying things like 'There goes that woman whose husband killed his brother'? What about our children? Would they be burdened by your decision, too?" In a way, it was hard to tell him about her hopes for their future, to confess to what she wanted, but she pushed forward. "You may not like it, but I had to do something. I respect you wanting to protect your father. A part of me admires you for it. But you aren't responsible for Pete's death. It's past time the truth came out."

Gwen had spoken with Hank's father, had written her article and presented it to Sid Keaton for publication, all because she loved him. She wanted a future with him, wanted it badly, but in order for it to come to pass, Hank's slate needed to be wiped clean. His well-intentioned lie had to be destroyed and the foundation of his life rebuilt. It reminded her of his workshop; sure, it was wrecked now, but something would rise from the ashes, better than ever.

For a long while, Hank was silent, mulling over what she'd told him. Finally he said, "You're right. I wouldn't want you or the family we might one day have to be punished for what I've done." Hearing him talk about a future together, the same things she had, made Gwen's heart beat faster. "But I don't want my father to be hurt, either. Even though he and his drinking have caused all sorts of trouble, I still love him. I don't like the idea of people treating him badly, even if it's deserved."

"Myron knows what he's doing," she said. "Trust me."

Hank nodded and the matter was settled. Suddenly, even though darkness had fallen, the future looked brighter than ever.

"Why don't we go see your dad?" Gwen suggested. "The two of you should talk before tomorrow's paper is published."

"Okay," Hank said, "but there's something I want to do first."

He took her by the elbow and pulled her close. Gwen felt as if she had floated into his embrace. Heat radiated from the smoldering fire, insects called out in the darkness, and the moon shone brightly above, surrounded by thousands of twinkling stars, but the only thing she was aware of was Hank. She knew what he wanted because she wanted it, too. As he lowered his mouth to hers, Gwen closed her eyes and surrendered to the moment. Seconds later, she found that it was everything she'd hoped it would be.

They went to the hospital. Visiting hours had long since ended and the two of them looked quite the sight — sweaty, bandaged, and bruised — but no one was around, so they let themselves in. Hank sat on the edge of his father's bed and asked questions.

Some were about how Myron was feeling, but he mostly wanted to know whether his father was really fine with everyone in Buckton knowing the truth about Pete's death.

"I'm tired of hidin' it," Myron answered. "Lyin' ain't doin' either of us any good nohow. This way, you can get on with your life."

"I don't like the idea of people thinking you're a murderer," Hank said.

"But that's what I am," he said, placing his hand over his son's. "If folks want to hate, let it be aimed at me, where it belongs. Not you."

"All I wanted was to protect you."

"I know," Myron replied with a weak smile. "No father, not even a bum like me, could ever wish for more."

Listening to them talk, Gwen noticed a change in Myron. He seemed more alert than when they'd spoken that morning, as if his head had cleared. Maybe it had something to do with not having anything to drink. She wondered whether he was capable of breaking the hold liquor had on him, or if it would drag him back down. For all of their sakes, but especially Hank's, she hoped that Myron would find the strength to stop.

Before they left, Hank's father looked at

Gwen and said, "Thank you for what you done. I reckon the next couple of days are gonna be a mess, but sometimes you gotta break things to put 'em right again." He turned to Hank and added, "Hold on to her, son, and don't let go."

Outside, few cars drove Buckton's streets beneath the starry sky. Gwen didn't need to look at a clock to know it was late. She could only imagine what her parents were thinking. After the unpleasant scene she'd caused that morning with Kent, as well as their disapproval of her spending time with Hank, they were probably beside themselves with worry. Tomorrow, once they'd read her article, things would hopefully get better.

But that still left tonight.

"I should get you home," Hank said.

When they pulled up to the curb, every light in the house was on. Gwen frowned; it wasn't a good sign. She wondered if Hank would stay or if he'd want to get some much-needed rest. She would have understood. After all he'd just been through, the last thing he'd want was another confrontation with her folks. But he pleasantly surprised her by getting out and walking with her toward the porch.

She took his hand and gave it a gentle squeeze.

Before they reached the stairs, her mother stepped out the front door. Meredith must have heard the truck. She looked harried, a bit out of sorts from her normal reserved self. Gwen braced for a barrage of questions, but instead her mother rushed down the steps and pulled her into a tight embrace. "Oh, Gwendolyn! You're all right!"

"I'm fine," she said, confused by her mother's tone of relief. "Why wouldn't I be?"

"You'd been gone so long that we grew worried," Meredith explained. "Especially your father."

Gwen remembered how Warren had reacted the first time she'd gone to visit Hank, ambushing her just inside the front door when she'd returned, peppering her with questions.

"This time he got so worked up that he called the police department," her mother continued. "One of the officers said that he'd seen you out at Hank's. He also told us about the fire and the arrests that had been made. The next thing I knew, Warren left to pick up Samantha and the two of them went looking for you. I stayed behind in case you returned."

Likely, when she and Hank had gone to visit Myron at the hospital, they'd passed her father and aunt somewhere along the way.

"Let me take a look at you."

Meredith's words weren't directed at her daughter, but at Hank. Gently, she placed her hands on either side of his face, turning it one way and then the other, examining his wounds in the sparse light. Her expression showed concern; Gwen wondered if her mother wasn't looking deeper than Hank's cuts and bruises and reevaluating the man on the inside.

"You should see the other guys," Hank joked.

"Let's go inside," Meredith said. "I'll get you properly cleaned up."

But before they'd gone far, Warren and Samantha returned. The car zipped into the drive, then skidded to a stop. Gwen's father hurried across the yard, his sister right behind him. He hugged his daughter tightly, just as his wife had done. "Thank the stars above, Gwennie!" he exclaimed. "I about worried myself sick."

"When you weren't at Hank's, we went to the hospital," Samantha explained. "Myron told us that we'd just missed you."

Gwen glanced at Hank. Where before he had willingly allowed her mother to inspect his injuries, now that Warren was here, he'd stepped back, not standing too close, as if he was anxious about what might happen. She turned to her father; he was eyeing Hank in return, his expression hard to read.

Then Gwen noticed something in his hand.

"What are those?" she asked, pointing to several formerly crumpled pieces of paper, though she thought she recognized them.

"I found these and a bunch more like 'em in the trash basket in my office," Warren answered. "I smoothed a couple out and read 'em."

Even though the pages were ones Gwen had rejected for her article, they contained much of the same information as those she'd submitted to Sid Keaton. If her father had indeed read them as he had said, then he knew that Hank wasn't responsible for his brother's death. He knew the truth.

Looking at Hank, Warren said, "When we were at the hospital, I asked your father 'bout what's in these pages. Myron said you didn't have nothin' to do with what happened to Pete. He said you were lookin' out for him."

Hank nodded. "That's right."

Warren walked over and stood before the other man, his expression grim. As much as she was hopeful, Gwen couldn't help but be nervous.

"My father wasn't the smartest fella in the world," Warren began. "He struggled to make ends meet, scroungin' and savin' for all he had. He never opened a bank account in his life 'cause he never had anythin' to put in it. But one thing he taught me when I was growin' up is worth more than its weight in gold. He said that whenever a man knows he's wrong, the best thing he can do is admit to it, no beatin' 'round the bush." Warren stuck out his hand. "I was wrong 'bout you. For that, and especially for how I reacted when you brought my daughter back to me safe and sound, I'm mighty sorry."

Gwen held her breath as Hank stared at Warren. She wondered if he would refuse her father's apology, leaving his offered hand unshaken. She could understand why he might; after all, Warren had said many hurtful things to him. Forgiving such insults would likely be easier said than done.

But in the end, that's just what Hank did.

"Apology accepted," he said, soundly shaking Warren's hand.

Gwen's eyes filled with tears. This was what she'd wanted, for Hank to be given a second chance. She knew it wouldn't take long for her family to see the same things she had, for them to realize that the wood-carver was someone to love and cherish, not despise. She was also aware that it had been her words that brought about this change.

She might be a writer after all.

"Let's go inside so I can tend to Hank's injuries," Meredith said.

"I'm gonna fix up the couch," Warren offered. "With the fire and all, it makes sense for him to sleep here tonight. In the mornin', we'll drive out, look over the damage, and decide what comes next."

"I'll make something to eat," Samantha added, not wanting to be left out. "After all they've been through, they must be hungry."

Gwen and Hank watched as her family hurried into the house and left them alone, which was likely their intent.

"Am I dreaming?" Hank asked, touching her cheek.

"Maybe we both are," she replied. "Maybe we're still asleep on the cot in the workshop."

"If that were the case, at least all my things wouldn't have burned to a crisp."

They both laughed, finding some humor in it after all.

"I can't believe all that's happened since this morning," Hank said. "You saw my dad at the hospital, wrote an article about Pete's death for the paper, and broke things off with Kent."

"Even though you thought I was leaving you to go back to him."

Hank smiled sheepishly. "I'd like to forget that part."

"I bet," she told him.

"As for me," he continued, "I got in a brawl with Jed Ringer, had my workshop and most of my belongings destroyed, and then your father apologized to me." Hank shook his head. "I still can't believe that last one."

"But that's not all!" Gwen suddenly exclaimed.

"Oh, yeah?"

"Sandy Pedersen, I mean Fiderlein, had her baby! A little girl named Kelly! Oh, and I got hired down at the *Bulletin*!" she added. "I can't believe it, but in all the excitement, I guess I forgot."

"How about tomorrow we take it easy?" Hank suggested.

"No promises," Gwen replied.

Hank pulled her close. She looked up into his eyes, hardly noticing the stars beyond, and knew happiness. "This might sound strange," he said, "but I'm glad you fell in the river."

"You are?" Gwen replied, raising her

eyebrows. "I could have drowned."

He shook his head. "But you didn't."

"Only because you were there to save me."

"In the end," Hank said, leaning close, "we saved each other." Then he kissed her, the perfect exclamation point.

As a writer, Gwen was always searching for a story. They were everywhere she looked: in train depots and burning buildings; in Chicago and Buckton; in selfish acts that claimed lives and selfless acts that saved them; in the relationships that ended and the ones that added a new member to the family; in the past and the present.

Hers and Hank's was only just beginning.

EPILOGUE

"This is pretty good."

Gwen smiled. Her desk in the *Bulletin*'s office was neat, with everything just the way she wanted it: a small box to hold her pens and pencils; a stapler; the lamp she'd brought from home to use when she worked late; a pile of notebooks; a framed photograph of her and Hank standing beside the Sawyer River, smiling at both the camera and the irony; a potted plant; and of course, her typewriter. Sid Keaton sat on one corner, reading the pages she had written.

"Myrna collected oil lamps?" the publisher asked.

"She had dozens of them, in almost every room," Gwen explained. "If they were all lit, her house would've been the brightest in town."

"With her bad eyesight, it's a miracle she

never caught the place on fire."

"I thought the same thing myself."

Just as Sid had told her, when Gwen accepted his job offer she'd started at the bottom of the ladder. For the first couple of months, her days had consisted of editing the other reporters' articles, making phone calls and going door-to-door drumming up advertising, and generally learning the ropes of the business. But whatever it was that she'd been asked to do, Gwen threw herself at it with enthusiasm. Eventually there'd been more and more responsibility given, until she landed her current position, writing obituaries.

Gwen hadn't shied from this slightly morbid task, but had embraced it. With most obituaries she'd read, the writeup in the newspaper was little more than basic information: where the deceased was born, the names of family members, and what he or she had done for a living. But to Gwen, that didn't seem enough. So when she heard that someone had passed, she visited their home and talked with those who had known them, all in an attempt to learn who that person had actually been. She wanted each obituary to be personal. For Myrna Portnoy, she'd included the fact that the old woman had a collection of lamps. Sid often praised her work, appreciating the details she added; the job had been his a long time ago.

Her dream of becoming a writer was coming true, one obituary at a time.

Gwen knew there would be more opportunities as time passed. She was patient. Maybe someday she'd even end up replacing Sid as the *Bulletin*'s publisher.

Who knew what the future held?

"You'd better get a move on or you're gonna be late for your lunch date," Sid said, nodding at the clock. "Don't want to keep him waiting."

Outside, the day was perfect, one of those late-spring afternoons without a cloud in the sky. A gentle breeze carried the scent of flowers, and the sun was warm on her skin. As she started down the sidewalk, Gwen couldn't believe that not even a year ago, she'd still been living in Chicago, daydreaming about becoming a writer, imagining a future with Kent.

The last time she had seen the successful lawyer had been when he'd walked away from her toward the depot. Since then, Kent hadn't called. He'd never written any letters. When Gwen and her parents had traveled to Chicago to gather her things from her apartment, she had found a box just inside the door. Kent must've passed it to the building supervisor. In it were all the Christmas and birthday presents Gwen had given him, their love letters, and even some clothes she'd left at his place. At the bottom of the box she had found the photograph she'd framed for him, the one that had sat on his desk at the law firm. Kent had smashed the glass, causing cracks to radiate in every direction, as broken as their relationship had become. Gwen threw it all away.

There would be no looking back for either of them.

As she walked, Gwen waved to people she knew and glanced in the store windows she passed. The baby carriage on display at the department store reminded her that she wasn't the only one in Buckton whose life had been dramatically changed in the last year.

Sandy and John had taken to being parents like ducks to water. While Kelly hadn't been the best sleeper at first, making for some long nights in the Fiderlein house, she was still the sweetest baby Gwen had ever laid eyes on. Whenever Gwen stopped by for a visit, which was as often as she could, the girl instantly brightened at the sight of her "aunt," full of gurgles and smiles. Sandy returned the favor, dropping in at the *Bulletin,* pushing a stroller up and down Buckton's streets, showing her daughter her hometown. For his part, John was as dutiful a dad as there had ever been. Having a girl instead of a boy had done nothing to diminish his enthusiasm. Sandy playfully complained that her husband was spoiling Kelly, bringing home so many toys they might as well open up a shop.

For Gwen, Sandy's growing family was an inspiration.

The sweet and savory smells of her father's bakery reached her nose from more than a block away. Customers came out carrying loaves of bread and other delicious treats. Even though she was running late, Gwen poked her head in the door, as she did every time she went past.

"Gwennie!" her father shouted from behind the counter. "Come on in! You gotta try this new pastry I whipped up. I swear it's my best yet!"

"I can't, Dad," she replied. "I'm on my way to pick up Hank for lunch. I don't want to spoil my appetite."

"You're missin' out," Warren said with a wink, trying to tempt her. "The two of you are still comin' for dinner tonight, right?"

"Of course."

"Should be fun. Your mom's makin' meat loaf, so you know I'll be bellyin' up to the table plenty early!"

Her father was still laughing as the door closed behind her.

What a difference a year makes . . .

In the weeks and months after Gwen's article about Pete's death had appeared in the newspaper, no one's attitude toward Hank had changed more than her father's. Warren had admitted that he'd been wrong, apologized for his behavior, and played a different tune from that day forward. He and Hank fished in the Sawyer, worked on projects around the house, and even drank beers as they listened to baseball games out in the garage. Gwen suspected that her father had also worked to influence others from behind his bakery counter, talking to those who were reluctant to give the former pariah another chance.

Meredith had also mended her ways, much as she'd tended to Hank's wounds the night his workshop had been burned. Gwen suspected that one reason her mother had forgiven Hank so quickly was because his sacrifice had been for family; having been rejected by her own over her choice of husband, Meredith was particularly protective of familial bonds and appreciative of

455

those who felt the same. It didn't hurt that she'd also proven to be a huge fan of Hank's woodworking craftsmanship, ordering a number of pieces for her home.

As for Samantha, little had changed. Along with Sandy, she'd been one of the only people who had encouraged Gwen's interest in Hank. Still a regular presence around her brother's dinner table, she seemed genuinely happy for her niece, jokingly asking when she should expect a wedding announcement. Even though Samantha was still searching for Mr. Right, she didn't let that keep her from enjoying all that life had to offer. Still, whenever Gwen saw Brent Irving, the judge's son her aunt had once hoped to marry, her heart felt a little heavy.

Hurrying down the sidewalk, Gwen nearly bumped into a man as he stepped out of the post office. "Good afternoon, Mr. Tate," she said.

"Right back atcha, Gwen," the auto mechanic replied. "Say, when you see Sid, let him know I've got some new ads I wanna try out."

"I will," she said before hurrying on her way.

Carl Tate, the Morgans, and several others in Buckton, including Hank, had suffered great losses at the hands of Jed Ringer and his accomplices. For weeks, they had burned their way across town, destroying property and stealing mementos for some perverse reason. It wasn't until they'd been stopped in the act of torching Hank's workshop that they were locked behind bars. Between the evidence collected from Jed's trunk and Sam's courtroom testimony, which implicated all three of them in acts of arson, they'd been quickly found guilty as charged. Jed had been quite the sight on the witness stand, both of his arms and one leg encased in plaster casts as he slowly healed from the damage done by both Hank and Gwen. All three men had been sent to prison. It would be many long years before they were set free.

Rounding the corner past Elm Avenue, Gwen reached her destination. After years of cajoling his friend, Skip had finally managed to convince Hank to go into business with him. Their furniture store was set to open at the end of the week. Skip would deal with customers, taking orders for pieces that Hank would then build in his new workshop at the rear of the store. They'd also stockpiled a sizable inventory, which would be on display. As she approached, the two partners were out on the sidewalk, staring up at the sign they'd hung.

It read BUCKTON FURNITURE.

"Just in time to give your opinion," Skip said when Gwen joined them. "What do you think? Pretty eye-catchin' if I do say so myself."

"I like it," she agreed.

"Are you sure it's high enough?" Hank asked with a frown.

"It's fine!" Skip answered, playfully throwing his hands up in exasperation; clearly they'd been having a bit of a disagreement.

"I just don't want people to miss it."

"It's candy-apple red!" his friend exclaimed. "The only way it'd be more noticeable is if you put lights around it like a movie marquee!"

"Don't give him any ideas," Gwen said.

Just then, the telephone rang inside the store. Like a flash, Skip was moving toward it. "Could be a customer," he explained over his shoulder.

When the revelation of his innocence in his brother's death had been published in the newspaper, Hank had thought that Skip might be hurt. After all, even though they were best friends, Hank had never confessed his secret to him. But when Hank tried to apologize, Skip had waved it away.

"I don't care *how* the truth came out," he'd said. "Just that it did."

458

Once Hank no longer had a reason to avoid town, Skip had redoubled his efforts to get his friend to go into business with him. He'd argued, rather convincingly, that with his financial prowess and Hank's substantial woodworking skill, they could really amount to something. Since there was no one Hank trusted more, particularly when it came to money, he'd agreed. The people of Buckton had donated to those who had been affected by Jed's acts of arson; Hank had used his as a contribution to their new business. Now here they were, nearing the culmination of all their plans and dreams.

"I think it should be higher," Hank grumbled.

"You're worrying for nothing," Gwen told him. "Trust me."

"I just want everything to be perfect. Friday will be here before we know it."

"And everyone will say, 'That sign's just the right height!' "

"Smart aleck," he said, but they both laughed.

Looking at him, still finding him the handsomest man she'd ever laid eyes on, Gwen was convinced that Hank was about to propose to her. It was a feeling more than anything: glances shared between Hank and her father; the way he stared at her when he thought she wasn't looking, a smile curling the corners of his mouth; and especially the clumsy way he'd asked her what her ring size was, throwing the question out while commenting about a jewelry box Freddie Holland had ordered.

He needn't worry. If he asked — *when* he asked — she wouldn't hesitate.

The answer would be yes.

The almost-year they had been together had been the happiest of Gwen's life. Every day was a treasure, full of laughter, passion, encouragement, and even friendship. She wasn't afraid to be honest around him, to voice her worries and fears. Hank always seemed to know just what to say, building up her confidence or steering her in a slightly different direction. She tried to do the same in return; when he'd asked her opinion about Skip's business proposal, Gwen had told him to accept. They were building a future together, something to last a lifetime.

If that wasn't love, she had no idea what was.

"Did you have a chance to talk to your father?" Gwen asked.

He nodded.

"So how did it go?"

Hank's smile faltered but didn't completely vanish. The last ten months had been hardest on Myron. Having been revealed as the driver in the accident that claimed Pete's life was bad enough, but his allowing Hank to lie about it seemed to make things worse. Once, in the bank, Gwen had heard someone call Myron a coward; she thought the broken man would likely have agreed. Fortunately Sid Keaton had been right and the police declined to press charges. While Hank believed that his father wasn't drinking as much as he used to, it wasn't unusual for Gwen to smell alcohol on Myron's breath. But with the furniture business about to open, she'd suggested to Hank that he ask his father to help; maybe some time working beside his son would help him take another step in the right direction.

"He said he'd think about it," Hank answered.

"At least he didn't turn you down," she said in encouragement.

"How about you? Did you make your phone call?"

"I did."

"So what did he say?"

Shortly after she'd started working at the *Bulletin,* Gwen had begun writing a novel on the side. Freed from her restricting

461

relationship with Kent, strongly encouraged by Hank, back home and surrounded by friends and family, Gwen couldn't contain the words welling up inside her. She'd outlined some ideas, then fed paper into the typewriter and begun. As with all her other writing, she obsessed over the words, occasionally growing frustrated enough to consider quitting. But in those dark times, Hank had been there, refusing to let her give up so easily. Finally, through hard work and dedication, she had a manuscript she was proud of. Not knowing what she was supposed to do next, Gwen had decided to contact Dwight Wirtz, her old teacher back at Worthington.

"He gave me the names of a couple people he knows in the publishing business," she said. "He also asked if he could read it."

Hank's eyebrows rose. "Are you going to send it to him? I know how you can get. You'll be on pins and needles until he's finished."

Gwen smiled. "You're right, but I'm still going to do it." She nodded toward the furniture store. "It's like I told you when Skip wanted to open this place. Nothing ventured, nothing gained."

"The only thing I'm interested in gaining right now is a hamburger at Lafferty's," he said. "Sign hanging made me hungry."

"Did someone mention lunch?" Skip asked, stepping back outside. Pointing at Hank, he added, "And it's even your turn to buy."

"*I'm* buying," Gwen announced.

"What's the occasion?" Skip asked as he closed up the shop.

She slipped her hand into Hank's. "To new beginnings. For all of us."

Skip shrugged. "I'll eat to that."

"Give us a second, here," Hank said as Skip started down the sidewalk; his friend waved without looking back.

Once they were alone, he said, "Do you really like the sign?"

"Of course I do," Gwen answered.

"I just want it to be perfect. This is important for more than just me and Skip. This is about us, too. I don't want to screw it up."

Gwen stepped close, gently placing her hand on his arm; standing in the sun so long had made his skin warm to the touch. "You won't," she told him. "No matter what life throws at us, as long as we face it together, we'll be fine."

Hank grinned, then nodded. He leaned close, his lips brushing against her cheek. "I love you."

"Enough to jump into a river for me?" This question had become something of a running exchange between them.

"Again and again," he answered.

Gwen smiled. If he had to, she had no doubt Hank would do just that.

And that was why she loved him back.

ABOUT THE AUTHOR

Dorothy Garlock is one of America's — and the world's — favorite novelists. Her work has consistently appeared on national bestsellers lists, including the *New York Times* list, and there are over fifteen million copies of her books in print, translated into eighteen languages. She has won more than twenty writing awards, including an *RT Book Reviews* Reviewers' Choice Award for Best Historical Fiction for *A Week from Sunday,* five Silver Pen Awards from *Affaire de Coeur,* and three Silver Certificate Awards. Her novel *With Hope* was chosen by Amazon as one of the best romances of the twentieth century.

After retiring as a news reporter and bookkeeper in 1978, Dorothy began her career as a novelist with the publication of *Love and Cherish.* She lives in Clear Lake, Iowa.

You can visit her website at Dorothy Garlock.com.

FOR GRETCHEN
· ·

From the Author

DEAR READER,

I have no way of knowing who you are or why you picked up this book. If you are grieving, my heart goes out to you, and I hope you find some solace in these pages. If you are reading this because the title stirred your curiosity, perhaps my story will help you remember, when you need to remember, that you are not alone.

This book is no more (and no less) than one person's story of a struggle with grief. I am not qualified to tell you how to bear your own tragedies, so this is not a "self-help" book. In a Buddhist parable, a grief-crazed woman carrying her dead son in her arms is told to go and collect mustard seed from anyone she can find who has not suffered a terrible loss. At every house she hears a tale of woe and begins to see with her "deep mind" what she may have known, but only superficially, before: that every human's life is vulnerable to the shock of death. Reading this book, you might think of yourself as being at my doorstep listening to my tale. Mine is one of a multitude of stories, each as heart-wrenching as the next and,

as the story of the mustard seed suggests, comforting to those who are ready to hear.

I was poorly prepared for the tragedy that shattered my life. As a middle-class American with a good education and better-than-average luck, I had been temporarily insulated from death. I had no well-established religious beliefs, was not a member of a church, synagogue, or mosque. I was what you might call a spiritual loner, somewhat of a skeptic, and more comfortable with reason than emotion.

The sudden death of my twenty-one-year-old daughter, Gretchen, knocked me into a tailspin of spiritual, psychological, and emotional confusion. Like a dog suddenly kicked by a person who has treated him kindly for years, I was shocked to the core of my being. And I had no religious faith to fall back on. The well-intentioned people who spoke to me of God's love, of God's plan, of life after death and similar beliefs could not have known how incomprehensible (and at times infuriating) such statements were to me.

Because I love to read, I turned to books for help, only to discover that all the books on bereavement I could find were written either from a conventionally religious stance or from a New Age one. These books assumed belief in such things as immortality and the goodness of God, both of which I questioned. What I needed was not preaching, but companionship in grief and tolerance of my doubt and confusion. I kept searching until I found the kinds of stories, myths, poems, and personal accounts that spoke to me. I don't mean to imply that I didn't get and appreciate support from real live human beings: I did. But my late-night reading during the darkest months greatly expanded upon my personal experience. Books led me into a soothing stream of stories, ideas, poems, and emotions that flows through time from the minds and hearts of people of

all cultures and ages. The music of this stream sang tenderly to me and rocked me in its embrace. It still does.

Perhaps my words will join this stream. I hope so. And I hope that as you read, you will hear some of the music I heard.

Tom Crider

Give sorrow words; the grief that does
    not speak
Whispers the o'er-fraught heart and
    bids it break.
        —*Macbeth*, Act IV, Scene one

GIVE SORROW WORDS

A memorial service for Gretchen Erica Crider, who died in an apartment fire Saturday in Easton, Pa., will be held Wednesday at 2 P.M. at Christ Church here. Burial will be at the convenience of the family and there are no calling hours. . . .

Miss Crider, 21, a student at Lafayette College, died from smoke inhalation and burns when her third floor apartment at 106 Cattell St., Easton, caught fire. Easton fire officials believe the fire was started by several candles left burning after Miss Crider fell asleep.

She was pronounced dead at Easton Hospital after firemen removed her body from the small room shortly after 4 A.M. . . .

January
· ·

A new year begins as Earth moves through space, turning around the sun once again. Its orbit is not altered in the slightest by the sudden absence of my daughter.

· · ·

I wake up and lie in the dark. Her room is filling with smoke again. She gets up from her bed. The smoke is so thick! She stumbles toward the window and falls over a chair. This is where the firemen say they found her body.

When I see her stand up from her bed, I try to reach into the smoke and steer her to the door. "It's over here, Gretchen. Two steps away!" She can't hear me. She turns and goes toward the window, falls over the chair, and dies. Again and again.

· · ·

He doesn't understand how it is possible. A month ago he was asleep in his house on the hill with everything in its place and his immeasurably precious Gretchen in college. There was banging on the door, the dogs barked, and the police came out of the night to say that Gretchen had just died in a fire.

3

My dear, sweet Gretchen, my only child . . . dead?

. . .

He stands in a field of frozen grass, the sun above him a pale hole in gray sky, sucking warmth from the earth. At the edge of the woods, he looks for her in shadows.

. . .

In the mailbox is an envelope from Medic 9 Paramedic Services. It's addressed to Gretchen. Inside is a bill for what they did to try to save her. "Advanced life support aid was given for the following suspected problem(s): Cardiac arrest, burns, respiratory arrest."

The word *burns* startles him. He knows you don't treat burns if someone has stopped breathing; you do CPR. Was she alive when the firemen brought her downstairs?

I imagine I'm the paramedic, kneeling, tipping her head back, pinching her nose, putting my lips on her mouth. Two long breaths to fill her lungs, then I check to see whether her heart and breathing have started again.

Was it hard for the paramedic to put his mouth on her burned face? Did he see any life coming back to her? Did her eyelids flutter open?

He reads the bill several times during the day. Was the reference to treating her burns an error? Did they bring her back for a moment? Was she reaching up for life and air?

I'll call them and ask: Did my daughter come back?
Did she?

. . .

He and his wife, Mieke, waited in the hotel room for the funeral director. There was a knock on the door. A man came in and started speaking to Mieke, but she said she was not the mother and gestured to her husband. The funeral director handed him a maroon plastic box about ten inches long and six inches high, weighing less than five pounds.

Inside was his daughter's body, burned down to a small pile of ashes; not her really, but some of her molecules were in this ugly plastic brick he held in his hands. He was as close to her as he'd ever be again.

He placed her in a picnic basket, beside three roses. He knelt down on the floor and wept.

I weep thinking about it now. After a lifetime of pretending to be invulnerable, my tears amaze me. They are like jewels rising up from deep underground.

. . .

Awake again in the night, he stands in the dark in front of Gretchen's ashes (now removed from the plastic box and lying in a carved wooden box). He feels a strong urge to open the box, fill his hands with her ashes, and eat them.

Visions of things known and unknown torment him. He imagines her autopsy. Her body lies naked on a table, her burned face stares up, her body is being cut open, lungs peeled back, her vagina is examined for evidence of sexual activity. (There was none, according to the coroner.)

He told Peter, the boy she was with, the lucky one who for some reason woke up and stumbled out the door to safety, that he didn't blame him for not going back in to save her. Peter said he crawled back up the stairs with water in pans and a blanket over his head, but the smoke was too thick.

Looking into her room, he saw an orange glow through the smoke. He called to her, he said. He heard her fall down.

He heard her fall down.

. . .

The sky is a flat stone, the air frigid and still. He walks through the woods to the river and sits on a rock edged with ice. The trees along the shore stand, as always, silent and strong. They don't droop, as he feels they should. To him her death is a thunderous tragedy. To the rest of the world it is nothing.

A person is a vast thing, much bigger than the physical body. When a person dies, so much more is gone than the form you once could photograph or touch with your hand. In the eyes of those who love us, we billow high and wide, like parade balloon figures. The emptiness I feel at the loss of my daughter is so much larger than the space once occupied by a young woman five feet three inches tall, weighing 114 pounds.

What is it that makes her absence so big? Everything she said, thought, felt, and was. Everything she would have said, thought, felt, and been. All I imagined she was and would be. The effect she had on me and on everyone she met. The feelings I had for her when she sat beside me and the ones that stayed with me when she left. The hopes I had for her (and for me with her), the worries, the anticipation I felt when I knew I was about to see her. Even the anxiety and annoyance she caused from time to time. All this, so much more than her relatively small physical presence, has vanished, leaving a hole in the universe, and wisps of memory.

If I had known she was so large and that her leaving would create this arching emptiness, I would have fallen to my knees each morning and worshiped her. I would have strewn flowers at her feet, and I would have cherished every smile, every glance from her eyes, every word from her lips.

. . .

At night when he can't sleep, he reads books on death and religion. Some of them say she is not really dead. Some say God has other plans for her. He has never believed in a God who controls human lives or decrees their deaths, and he's always felt the idea of immortality was wishful thinking. Now, with his mind and emotions in turmoil, he seems to be scavenging for ways to keep her from having vanished. He finds himself ready to believe just about anything. He's like a beggar in winter, clawing through box after box of old coats, looking for one that fits.

I am not who I was. My reason, judgment, and all my defenses have dissolved, leaving me confused and terrified in a world turned suddenly strange.

. . .

Lying half-awake in the dark, too tired to get up, he dreams of paramedics trying to save her. A draft from the window ruffles his hair. It seems to be Gretchen, smoothing his hair, saying, "It's all right, Dad. Don't worry about me. I'm all right."

She was my child, my baby girl (or so it still seemed). But I feel like the child now—dazed, hurt, and afraid.

He sees death everywhere now. He knows other people aren't as aware of its presence. He didn't see it before either. He sailed through life as though death were on a far continent.

Of course he knew death could strike anyone at any moment. As a volunteer on the town ambulance, he had seen it happen many times. He thinks of the elderly lady on her way to the hairdresser on a sunny Thursday morning, hit by a gravel truck. He remembers the photo on her

driver's license, the lively smile that had once brightened the face of the body he had just pulled from the car.

But her death, and others he saw, had done nothing to prepare him for the death of his own daughter.

How can Gretchen—my amazingly alive child who was becoming a woman— how can she have completely vanished? Forever. This cannot be.

. . .

Nothing prevents his life from continuing as it did before: he has not lost his business, he has not fallen ill, his house is still standing, the sun rises, birds flutter in the bushes. He gets up in the morning and thinks, "I'm putting the same shoes on, just as I did before." He eats, works in his office, talks to people, even smiles.

My body moves on its own, through doors, past trees. I float above myself, watching myself turn like a leaf in a swirl of wind.

. . .

He reads a book on grief written by a Christian author whose wife died of cancer soon after they were married. As he reads, he feels the author's pain, but his theology is no help.

The wife's suffering and his own grief seem to make the author question his belief in a God who cares about human beings. He says, "If God's goodness is inconsistent with hurting us, then either God is not good or there is no God." The author concludes, predictably but unconvincingly, that God's goodness is *not* inconsistent with causing human pain.

Am I to believe in the goodness of a God who trapped my daughter in a burning room?

He stares through the window into the night. How small the moments of his life are in this vast dark. The selection of a shirt, the swallowing of soup, even the moments of pleasure or passion: how trifling next to the dark splendor of towering, magnificent death.

. . .

He imagines her removing the smoke alarm in her room, thinking, "I don't need this stupid thing." She was a know-it-all kid and no doubt thought she was immortal.

He recalls the only time he ever spanked her. A summer day when she and her cousin Betsey, both about four years old, had run down to play by the pond. He caught them walking back through the field toward the house, naked, muddy, and laughing. Overwhelmed with anger and fear, he spanked their bottoms and screamed, "You could have drowned!" When she was older, Gretchen laughed as she told the funny story of the only time her dad ever spanked her.

I'm angry at you now, too. You won't be telling funny stories this time, will you?

. . .

The only things in newspapers that interest him now are human tragedies comparable to his own and events geologic, or larger. Movements of tectonic plates, eclipses, comets. The vast and mysterious.

Illustrations in a newspaper article show how the earth's orbit changes shape in hundred-thousand-year cycles. Our path through space gets

more, then less, elliptical, slightly closer to the sun, before moving out in a wider arc. These orbital shifts affect the slow advances and retreats of glaciers at the North and South Poles. Geologists predict another ice age in a few thousand years.

The earth's axis, the article says, is not as steady as we think. It wobbles as a spinning top does when it loses speed. However reassuring it may be to imagine the earth as a sphere turning with precision in an exquisitely balanced solar system, it is more accurate to see it as a child's toy skittering about on the floor. A shocking image, and yet to him it is a confirmation of what he has learned—that nothing is as solid as it seems.

. . .

I dream I'm in the living room with Gretchen and Mieke. Gretchen sits in an armchair, turned away from me. I walk over to her and begin adjusting some kind of antenna that seems to be coming from her head. I look down on her as I fiddle with the antenna, and it suddenly occurs to me that she's going to die. I think, "I'm going to cry. I'd better go into the other room so she doesn't see me."

. . .

After meditating in the morning light, he turns and sees a distorted reflection of his face in a window. His head is caved in, and blood drips from the corner of his mouth.

Can my daughter, my only child, have been what is called a corpse? Can her precious body have been so cold and still? Did people around her whisper or make jokes —the hospital workers who wheeled her body to the morgue, the coroner who examined her, the man or woman who slid her small body into the furnace?

I never saw her, never saw her dead. I didn't see "it," her corpse. The coroner said her face and hands were burned. "You wouldn't want to see her," he said. I allowed myself to be persuaded, but now I wish I had seen her lovely-ghastly face, because I cannot understand how she could have been like that. She lived, she breathed, and I loved her. How could she have become what people call a corpse?

. . .

As the sun sets, he and Mieke go cross-country skiing on the low hills of a golf course. After a while he is far ahead of her, moving along the frozen river. As he approaches a footbridge, he comes up behind an old man with a cane who is walking as though each step is painful. He asks the man if he is all right. The man turns slowly and smiles, "So far, so good."

He skis on over the hills. It is almost dark when he suddenly feels weak and nauseated and has to lie down in the snow. He feels as though he might die, and he's not sure he doesn't want to, out there alone in the fresh snow with the sun's last redness on the horizon and the stars coming out. He lies, like a wounded animal, staring up at the stars until he can stand and make his way slowly back to the car.

. . .

He worries that Nancy, Gretchen's mother, will not be able to bear her grief. Living alone since their divorce, she has no one to share her suffering, no one to touch and comfort her. He has Mieke's support and yet still feels close to madness. He imagines himself coming home to an empty house, as Nancy does night after night, wandering alone through bleak rooms, hearing only his own movements hour after hour. When he talks with Nancy on the phone, her voice is thin, fragile, her cries are frail.

He wants to comfort her but knows there is nothing he can say to relieve her grief or her loneliness.

. . .

In the Bereaved Parents Group, he meets people for whom he feels an immediate, sad rapport. Their hearts have been broken by their children's deaths, too. They know.

After he describes Gretchen's death to the group, a woman says her daughter was also in college when she died. He asks how her daughter died. The woman takes a deep breath. "It's so hard!" She sobs, "Suicide!" and breaks into tears. A minute later she says, "It's the first time I've said it." Her daughter has been dead for two years.

The meetings are held in a Catholic church, and many of the people in the group talk about God as a benevolent being. He doesn't want to q⁻ tion their faith, but he can't understand how they can feel this way ab a God who found it necessary to kill their children. Do they, like t. author of a book he's reading, think of God as a kind of disciplinarian, who might take your loved ones away in order to teach you a lesson?

. . .

I am driven, like a nail, deep into myself, into a dark, stifling place where I can't see and noxious fumes poison my brain.

. . .

As he splits wood in the snow, fury hisses inside him like a raging cat. It feels good to crack logs open with blow after blow of the maul, but the fury is too deep to be released.

He'd like to have someone to kill for Gretchen's death. He understands

how revenge inflames those involved in wars, riots, revolutions. If he were a Palestinian, with Gretchen shot by Israelis, he would be a terrorist. If he were an Israeli, with his daughter blown to pieces by a terrorist's car bomb, he'd be a damned vengeful soldier.

As he works in his office, he hears his father-in-law, Arthur, bang in through the back door and stomp through the living room. He turns around to see Arthur standing in the doorway. The old man's face is red from the cold, his white hair stands straight up, his hands are black with grease.

"It's no damn good," Arthur growls and stares hard at him.

"You mean the car, or? . . ." he asks.

"You know!" Arthur says, still staring into his eyes.

"Yeah, I know," he says.

Arthur tells a joke having to do with the problems encountered by a man with an enormous sexual organ and laughs so loud that Ursa stands up and wags her tail uneasily. Bravado and humor are Arthur's ways of thumbing his nose at the anguish of life.

. . .

Late at night the sky is dark, moonless. Stars sit quietly in deep space. Alone in the stillness and cold, he waits for something. For the first few days after her death, he often felt she was near; not as a ghost, but as a vague presence. He hopes for this feeling to return. It doesn't come, but as he searches the stars there is the distant sound of her voice. Perhaps it's his imagination, or a lingering vibration in his auditory nerves. He hears, but he doesn't know what it is he hears.

He's never believed in ghosts or an afterlife, though he hasn't entirely disbelieved them, either. He has suspended judgement, thinking, "If these

things are going to present themselves to me, I'll believe them when they do." Now, as he longs to see Gretchen, and since he can't bear to think she has vanished completely and forever, he hopes she'll appear. He wouldn't care if the strength of his desire tricked him into seeing her standing among the trees.

Gretchen, please come back. Come, put your arms around me, and these tears will change to tears of happiness. Come back, Gretchen, please. I miss you more than my heart can bear.

. . .

His friend Alan suggests he try something called a Body Harmony treatment. It is supposed to relieve stress and provide other psychological and even spiritual benefits. While he lies on a table, the therapist lifts and holds his arm. Moving his arm slowly in a circle, the therapist asks, "Do you feel Gretchen's presence?" He says, "No." The therapist says, "I do. She's here."

A stranger feels her presence, when her father does not!

On his way out, after an hour or so of this, the therapist follows him to the door, whispering, "It's okay to be happy. It's okay to be happy."

. . .

He reads in the paper about the discovery of another mass grave in Timisoara, Romania. As the bodies were uncovered, friends and relatives of people still missing from the December uprising stood nearby waiting to identify their loved ones who had been buried there since shortly after Christmas. Among them was the father of a girl who had been wounded in the protests (the last he knew of her). When this man was led to his

daughter's stained body, he saw she had been tortured to death. He feels this man's anguish as he never could have before.

. . .

If she were alive, she would have called, or written me a letter, wouldn't she? I know she would, so she must be dead—the police said she was, I talked to the coroner, the firemen. Memorial services were held. I have what they say are her ashes upstairs on a shelf.

. . .

When Father Fred, the priest who came with the police that night to tell them Gretchen had died, stops by for a chat, he finds himself telling Father Fred about climbing a mountain in the Berkshires a few days after Gretchen died.

He wanted a strenuous climb to release the terrible tension in his body, so he took the steep trail beside the brook and waterfalls up through the hemlocks. When he had hiked past the highest waterfall and up the rocky outcrops above the tree line, he decided to perform a ceremony, to say good-bye to Gretchen up there, alone and near the sky. He left the trail and found a rock surface with a long view of lakes and gray hills. He sat in the snow next to a scrub pine and picked one of its weathered cones. With his pocketknife he cut his wrist and covered the pinecone with his blood. He let some of his tears fall on it before he scratched a hole in the earth and buried it. "Good-bye, Gretchen, good-bye. *Om shanti, shanti, shanti,* peace, peace, peace." He sat on the edge of the granite precipice looking into the horizon until the light began to fade; then he walked back down the mountain in the dark.

. . .

Hospital bills, with their cruel images of nurses and doctors trying to revive her, are still being sent to him by mistake. "Tube 14F 48, blood gas kit, diaphor electrode, pacemaker tray, cardiac manual vent, intensive treatment, code cart. $408.75."

He knows that special efforts are made to save the lives of young people like Gretchen. He did it himself—a young man, just Gretchen's age, had been holding a crane cable when it brushed against a high voltage power line. He remembers placing his own hands just above the holes blasted in the young man's chest by the electric current. Everyone on the ambulance crew knew it was hopeless, but they refused to give up on one so young, and so he had kept pushing rhythmically down, and down, and down on the young man's chest all the way to the hospital.

It may be that I need these hospital bills, this repeated evidence of her death. Otherwise I might be thinking even more often than I do that perhaps she's alive after all.

. . .

In the Waterbury Hospital Cardiac Care Center, he runs on a treadmill with wires stuck to his body. The nurse asks if he has any children. He tells her about Gretchen. She doesn't say any more. The treadmill picks up speed every couple of minutes until he's exhausted. The cardiologist says the EKG shows an "ST wave depression" in the thirteenth minute. It could be "an artifact," but he should have another more complete test soon.

He doesn't understand. He exercises regularly, keeps his weight down, eats a mostly vegetarian diet, and never has had a sign of heart trouble

before. Now he has attacks of weakness and his heart beats in an erratic rhythm. When asked whether this could be caused by grief, his doctor, a friend, says, "Not possible, Tom. Not something that shows up on the EKG."

. . .

As he lies in bed, memory and fantasy swirl around him, keeping him from sleep. He wanders through silent rooms and goes out into the night. Walking up and down the long driveway, he hopes to see her somewhere in the dark, or among the stars. "Gretchen, are you here?"

People tell him Gretchen is with God. Someone says, "She's in a better place."

James Russell Lowell wrote a poem after his daughter was buried. In it he acknowledges a friend's attempt to console him, but he says, "since the earth closed on her coffin, I keep hearing that, and not you."

. . .

Failing once again to concentrate on work, he goes out and walks down to the pond. Gusts of wind sway and knock the pines against each other. Looking up into a clear sky that seems endlessly deep, he thinks of Gretchen as being carried into its blue by this wind.

My little girl's body, now ashes and smoke, weeks ago risen from the crematorium, her self and spirit no longer cohesive, dispersing into the atmosphere and widening farther and farther out each day.

February

In the health club sauna, Leo is sitting on the upper bench as he comes in. When Leo asks how he's doing, he says, "It's hard, Leo, if you want the truth."

They talk about Leo's new career training people how to love. After a while, Leo gets up to leave, and says, "Gretchen had done what she came here to do, Tom."

"I wish I believed that, but I don't," he says.

"Know this, Tom," Leo says, shaking a finger at him, "It was her time. Her time had come."

He should have told Leo to stuff it.

He doesn't understand how people believe such things. Her time had come? Is there something he lacks, some facility that enables other people to understand what he can't?

. . .

Two months ago today, on a cold December night, the dogs' barking woke us just before dawn. At the window, I looked down and saw a police car, lights flashing, in the driveway. Below me, under the porch light, a stranger with a moustache looked

up, gesturing. I went downstairs and let them in. We stood in the living room. The
man with the moustache, who wore a priest's collar, turned to Mieke and said with a
groan, leaning toward her, "It is with great sorrow and regret that I must tell you
your daughter, Gretchen, died tonight in a fire at four A.M." He put his hand on her
arm, but she was moving toward me, her eyes wide.

. . .

After breakfast he takes a walk, hoping the cold will slap his mind
awake. In his office, he tries to work, but by the time he reads to the end of
a long sentence, he has forgotten how it started. In addition to the distraction of grief, the work he is doing—publishing a newsletter on com-
puters—seems unbearably trivial. He sits immobile at his desk, staring out
the window at dead leaves.

His friends John and D.J. want to help him get out the next issue of his
newsletter, and although he would rather not accept their offers, he brings
the work to them. Afterward he feels soothed by their kindness and by
this communal acknowledgment of the terrible thing that has happened.

. . .

Though rarely speaking of it directly, his father, a deacon in the Presby-
terian Church, had faith in the goodness of God. But one day, a few years
before he died, he had called to say that a young woman he knew had been
raped and murdered by three men while her children were locked in the
next room. "This makes me question my faith," he said in a quavering
voice.

After his father died, he had found a book on his father's shelf that
posed this question: "If God is good and He cares about us, why does he
let terrible things happen?" This author's answer was that God is not

responsible for such things because He hasn't finished the job of creating order out of chaos. We are living in the sixth day of creation and God is still laboring to make his work perfect. So when a stray bullet kills a little girl who happens to be walking down the street at the wrong moment, it's not God's fault. These things, the author says, "are not the will of God, but represent that aspect of reality which stands independent of His will, and which angers and saddens God even as it angers and saddens us."

This theory manages to avoid the problem of God's responsibility for the "bad things," but it assumes a God who cares about individual human beings. He finds this difficult to believe.

Are we really so important? I doubt it. This idea of a caring God seems to me a fantasy of the human ego, which sees itself as the golden child of creation.

. . .

How can a person live for nearly fifty years and be so shocked by death? By living in the mind, rather than in the world. And perhaps by being allowed to do so by America, which provides ways of hiding from many unpleasant realities. It is, in some ways, like the palace garden where Buddha's father confined his son because he wanted him to experience only the joys of life.

When the young Buddha finally snuck out of the garden, he was horrified by what he saw in the real world—an old man, then a sick man, and finally a corpse. He turned to his charioteer, who said, "Yes, Master, there is no escape. Old age, sickness, death—such is the lot of all men."

Years later, Buddha began his teaching with what is now known as the First Noble Truth: "Life is suffering." He urged everyone to understand this truth well. He was relentless on this point: "Birth is painful, old age is

painful, sickness is painful, death is painful, sorrow, lamentation, dejection and despair are painful."

To many people, Buddha's First Noble Truth must seem overly negative, but to me it seems a wise and honest assessment of the human condition. Perhaps if I'd been able to understand it more fully than I did when I first heard it years ago, I'd be better prepared for Gretchen's death.

On the other hand, words of wisdom are of limited value to those without experience, and I had not suffered much real hardship or tragedy in my life. If I had, I suspect I would not be as shocked, angry, and resistant as I am.

. . .

When you look through a camera at a loved one or friend, you may think when you press the shutter that you are preserving an image of the person at that moment in time. It isn't likely to occur to you that the image the face and body makes upon the film might outlast the person's living presence.

He had taken a photograph of Gretchen standing in front of a garden of orange chrysanthemums on a sunny day a month before she died, when he, his mother, and Mieke were visiting Gretchen at college. She looks happy and confident. Her brown hair falls forward over one shoulder. She had thrown her hair back on one side just before the picture was taken, revealing a dangling earring. Her eyes twinkle in a moment of feigned merriment as she tolerates her father's desire to take a picture of his daughter on her college campus. It's not a great photograph, not the one he would have taken had he known it would be his last, but she looks very alive, on top of the world, the way she liked to look. As he holds the photograph in front of him now, he asks himself, truly wondering, "How

can this lovely creature be dead? How can this familiar, smiling face be gone forever?"

He has given copies of this photograph to Gretchen's friends, and to members of the family. It stands on the mantel in the living room, too. He wants everyone to see it, to marvel at it, to be reminded of her and to know that it's all right to talk about her. He doesn't want people to come into the house and pretend nothing happened.

When Gretchen's friends come to visit, he draws diagrams of her room, showing where the candles fell over, where her bed was, and where her body was found. He hopes this will keep her death from being an abstraction to them. The details make things real, and he wants everyone to feel the reality, the terrible reality, of her death, as he does.

. . .

Writing in his diary, he sees himself as if from above, a small figure pulling words from his brain, and placing them before him, like a child playing with beads.

To write is to try to make an order out of things, an order that death's chaos shows to be false.

My daughter died in terror and all I can do is fuss with words. Instead I should be smearing my blood on this paper and all over these walls.

. . .

On his birthday he is glad he doesn't have time to think about what it means. He's too involved in Mieke's brother Jan's evening wedding in a darkened church. He and Mieke stand beside the altar photographing the children as they come down the aisle with their lighted candles. In the

front row, a young girl's face glows in the warmth of the candle she holds—the lovely light of a flame that, in other circumstances, could so suddenly kill.

Jan's face is flushed with pleasure as he and Mary say the words and do the slow dance—the fitting of the rings, the kiss, the turning to the congregation. He is surprised he can feel their happiness without being crushed by this formal demonstration that other people's happiness is still possible.

The next day Arthur asks him to go out to breakfast. "Just you and me," his father-in-law says, punching him in the shoulder with man-to-man punctuation.

He knows that underneath Arthur's rough manner there is a huge and tender heart, but as they sit by the window in a restaurant the old boy surprises him. He waits until they've each been served a plate of pancakes, then Arthur looks at him from under his white eyebrows and says, "You know, Tom, something's been bothering me."

"What's that?"

"I have nowhere to go to talk to Gretch," he says. He and Gretchen were buddies. She loved the jokes he whispered to her, as though the two of them were teenagers. "I need a place to go and talk to her," he says, his eyes filling with tears. One rolls down his cheek as he waits for a response.

He tells Arthur they'll be planting a tree in Gretchen's memory once he and Nancy have spread her ashes on the river in April. "Of course you'll be there, Arthur."

"That's that then," Arthur says. He picks up his fork and begins eating, without bothering to wipe away his tears.

A place to go and talk to her. To me she seems to be everywhere . . . and nowhere. How can she be in one place? She is in my heart and my thoughts, she floats like a mist around me everywhere I go.

. . .

Out walking about 6 P.M., it's already dark, and cold enough to keep him moving fast. As he goes up the hill, he notices the moon between branches, rising. Its shape is lopsided and leaning. Higher up the hill past the house, he sees it more clearly through an opening between trees. It is shaped like a head, not the round full-moon face, but a deformed head, bulging at the top, slanting down to a pinched jaw. There seems to be a mouth, too, howling. An Edvard Munch moon, screaming.

. . .

I walk through the valley of the shadow of death, but, unlike the psalmist, I fear evil everywhere.

It's deeper than fear, really, it's dread. He feels like a dog who's lived through being run over once and who jumps at the slightest sound to make sure nothing is coming at him again. When the phone rings, his heart bounds. He thinks someone else has died: Mieke, his mother, his brother, a friend. In a store or on a street, he hears a child scream, but instead of delight, he hears horror, and turns to see if the child needs help. Several times a day, spurts of fright splash up from a sea of dread.

In addition to the expected definition of *dread*—"to anticipate with anxiety, alarm, or apprehension; fear intensely," he finds this also: "fear mixed with awe or reverence."

Yes, there is awe in what I feel. It's what I imagine a mole might feel when the top of its burrow is scraped away by a grizzly. It comes from being one who is tiny in the presence of a greater, malevolent power. This power snatched my daughter Gretchen away from me. What will it do next?

. . .

Driving Gretchen to school one winter morning when she was thirteen, he hit a patch of ice on the road. Another car came toward them as they went into a spin. His turning of the steering wheel had no effect. They spun slowly, making a complete circle while skidding into the left lane. Just missing a head-on collision, they slid down the road sideways, looped back across the pavement, and bounced into a field, where they came to a stop.

"Boy, that was close!" he said. Gretchen was staring ahead through the windshield. She turned to him and said, "Dad, we're going to be late!"

"Don't worry," he said, and drove out of the field and on to school.

. . .

He sees the barn door open and walks across the field, drawn to this dark hole in the daylight, listening, as he walks, to the whisper of his feet crushing winter grass.

. . .

At the health club a guy asks him, "Do you have any children?" He hesitates before saying, "No." Would someone waiting to play racquetball want to hear what happened to Gretchen?

He feels the role of father, the silk robe he once wore, slipping from his shoulders. Everything it meant to be a father is gone, suddenly and for-

ever. When Gretchen was born, her infant life gave his a bright new purpose. She depended upon him for shelter, food, guidance, and love. Her development into genius or ignoramus, aggressor or peacemaker, may not have been entirely up to him, but it felt that way. And he believed he'd have some influence, through his child, her children, and her children's children, on the future of the human race.

Now, for him, in addition to his only child, his fatherhood and all that it meant has vanished. He has no daughter or son to care for and no lineage going out from himself into the future. He still has a lingering fatherly pride and love, but the object of it is gone, and he stands on a severed branch of the family tree.

. . .

He is running on the treadmill again, but this time, toward the end of the ordeal, a nurse injects a radioactive substance into his arm. He is then wheeled into another room. A nurse positions him under the eye of an X-ray machine. To this machine, his body is nothing. Its eye sees only radioactive dye flowing through his vessels and the chambers of his heart.

To myself I seem to be of some substance, to have size, weight, a palpable firmness. The machine sees me as light flowing in space.

. . .

He finds comfort in reading about a Nazi concentration camp, feeling a kinship with the people whose lives were destroyed and whose days were filled with horror. They had to endure much more than he, but he identifies with their suffering and their innocence.

The author says he survived the hunger, the cold, the pain and grief of Auschwitz by holding on to the love of his wife. She was in another concentration camp and he didn't know whether she was dead or alive, but his love for her gave his woeful life some meaning.

Do I have that bond with Gretchen, that bond between two human spirits, based on undying love? Yes, I do.

"Set me as a seal upon thy heart . . . love is strong as death."
   — Song of Solomon, 8:6

. . .

"She died in her sleep," the coroner said that awful morning in a deep voice, attempting to soothe. He held tightly to the thought that death had carried her off unaware. But later he talked on the phone to Peter and discovered the truth. The coroner had softened the facts. Peter said he heard her stumble across the room and fall. The truth twisted into his heart. She tried to get out!

The coroner may have been right to lie. He'll imagine her stumbling, falling, dying forever.

The truth raised agonizing questions: Why did she wake up? Was there a smoke alarm? Did she hear Peter yelling to her from the staircase? Why did she go toward the window across the room instead of taking three steps from the bed and out the door?

He had to find out as much about what happened to her as he could. The day after she died, he called the state cop in charge of the investigation and said he needed to know the facts. The policeman said, "I don't know why you want to know this, but I suppose you have a right."

Two days later he sat with Mieke and his brother-in-law Hank in an office listening to the fire marshal tell them his view of how the fire

started. The fire marshal placed several blackened candlesticks one by one on the desk and asked if they recognized them. The instruments of her death! He didn't want to look at them. The fire marshal said one of the candles must have fallen over and smoldered, perhaps on the upholstered chair, filling the room with deadly smoke.

The fire officials told them about questioning Peter after the fire. He and Gretchen had been at a party drinking beer. They went for a pizza with friends, then up to her room, where they fell asleep on her bed, both of them fully clothed. The fire marshal told them what Peter said about trying to get back into her room. Peter's nose and mouth were black with soot, he said.

The firemen took them to the house where Gretchen lived in the attic room. Plywood was nailed across a window in the roof gable. Other than this there was no visible evidence that a tragedy had occurred there. He would have felt better if the house had burned to the ground and nothing remained but a pile of charred beams.

The firemen led them past police barriers and up the stairs to her room.

Everything was black in that tiny space. This was where my dear Gretchen's life ended! Her body lay on this floor! The sickening odor of stale smoke. I can smell it now as I sit here three months later.

The fire marshal said they should take anything they wanted, but he thought, "What's the use? Do I want her clothes, the blackened books, her shoes?" Photographs of family and friends tacked to the wall by her bed had been curled by the heat and turned gray. The faces were gone; only shapes remained. He wanted to leave, but he couldn't turn his back on everything that was hers.

The smoke alarm was missing. If there had been one, he and Hank and

Mieke would not have been in that room filling boxes with her sad things, and she, instead of lying cold in the basement of the funeral home, would have been sitting at her desk studying, or out somewhere on campus talking and laughing with friends. He would have been home doing whatever inconsequential things he might have had to do—working on his newsletter, buying Christmas presents, splitting wood—and knowing, without thinking about it, that his daughter was alive.

But there was no smoke alarm to wake Gretchen up in time to save her life. So the next day, after receiving her ashes from the funeral director, they drove home with her belongings in boxes and the clothes from her body stuffed in a garbage bag.

. . .

A friend of a friend sends some pages from her journal. Her son was Gretchen's age, a college student. A truck driven by a drunken neighbor came around a bend and hit him as he stood in the street in front of their home. His father ran out and held his son in his arms as he died.

Oh how I wish I had been there to hold Gretchen, to stroke her, to kiss her, as she died.

The journal contains a quote from Victor Hugo, who said this to friends about his own approaching death: "As for you—if you should miss me—I am not really gone, just transformed, freed from the frail cloak, my physical body. 'But I will see you again and your heart shall rejoice.'"

At times he finds himself believing that Gretchen's spirit has flown from the "frail cloak" of her body and might visit him now and then. This soothes the ache, the painful yearning to see her. But the belief doesn't last.

. . .

Some mornings he feels as though he's been trampled by a heavy beast during the night. He can't work, think, or even make himself go for a walk. He limps through the day, dizzy and bruised, and he fears the beast who did this to him still lurks nearby. Whatever it is that killed Gretchen and wrecked his life has earned his profound respect.

Joseph Campbell says survivors of World War II saturation bombings in cities like Berlin and Dresden later described the experience as "sublime." This, Campbell says, is what one feels in the presence of awesome power. Not necessarily a "good" power, but a force capable of annihilating you and everything else . . . if it feels like it.

People who live close to nature, people unprotected by houses and health insurance, must be touched by the "sublime" quite often. This may explain why many of their gods are fearsome ones. Unlike religions that postulate the ultimate goodness of god, many "primitive" religions worship monster-gods who spring directly from their experience of thunderstorms, floods, volcanoes—the daunting power and energy of the universe.

Yes, I've felt this, too. With Gretchen's death, I've been struck by a force so impressive it feels "sublime." I could fall to my knees and worship it, purely for its power. I've felt its awesome presence, and this is enough for me. No religious concepts are necessary, or even relevant.

. . .

He recalls the afternoon he and Mieke went to the funeral home to get Gretchen's death certificates.

Should a father have to walk into a strange building, hear a stranger say, "I'm sorry," and be handed a garbage bag containing the clothes his daughter wore when she died? No, never.

He held the plastic bag away from him, afraid of what was in it. *These are the clothes they pulled from her body as she lay in the emergency room,* he thought. He looked around at the long, empty room. *Her body is in this building! Is it downstairs on a slab of marble? In a stainless steel drawer? Is it covered with a sheet or uncovered? Is it still and cold? Yes, her body is still and cold.* He didn't want to cry in such a place.

. . .

His stress test report says, "Subtle stress defect is demonstrated in the inferior wall" of his heart, and "question of previous inferior infarct identified." Dead heart muscle, the result, perhaps, of a heart attack.

He thinks of the survivors of Cambodia's Killing Fields, those who saw their children butchered, and later went blind. But in spite of the alarming language in the stress test report, the cardiologist says there's nothing to worry about.

. . .

A newspaper ad offered VIENNA FOR A SONG! A week in Vienna for a low price, airfare included. The idea of being in an old European city listening to timeless music overpowered him, and Mieke was easily persuaded.

In the old part of Vienna, an architectural relic of the Holy Roman Empire, they walk among magnificent buildings topped by gilded eagles and statues of mythical figures. They gaze up at Empress Maria Theresa, Joseph II, and many others, most of them on horseback, splendidly

attired, with noble expressions on their faces. The massive figures are regal, but he can't help thinking that the bones of these once powerful men and women lie crumbling nearby in Capuchin's Crypt.

They walk through narrow streets to St. Stephen's Cathedral, a towering gothic church, which took two hundred years to build, starting about 1304.

They enter the cathedral through the Giant's Doorway. The interior, with its high vaulted ceiling, is cool and hushed. The daylight is dimmed by the stained glass windows, and the human forms moving slowly about, and kneeling in pews, are shadows. Rows of candles flicker in the darkness. With trembling hands he lights one for Gretchen. This gesture in this place brings on waves of grief. His tears blur the candlelight, and he stumbles to a nearby pew. As he sits weeping, he feels as though a loving arm is placed around his shoulders.

It seems I came all the way to Vienna for this.

. . .

The next morning is sunny, and warm for February in Austria. They walk to the old part of Vienna and wander among the brass and marble likenesses of those who once led the armies and ruled the land. Men and women hustling to work with briefcases and umbrellas seem to press forward into time as legions of long-dead humanity watch them from behind.

Near the heart of the old city, in the center of a wide brick boulevard of fancy shops, stands a gold and marble pillar called the Pestsäule (the "Column of the Pest"). The column writhes with human figures, victims of the 1679 plague, their faces and bodies contorted in agony. Above them

are sweet-faced angels, who don't seem able to help. The devout Emperor Leopold I, who saw the streets of his city piled with bodies of men, women, and children, vowed to build this monument of thanks to God when the plague finally lifted.

In 1682, when the column was completed, Halley's comet appeared in the night sky, causing everyone in Europe to shudder. Was it a sign that the plague would return? Emperor Leopold wrote: "May God will that I do nothing wicked, for I know myself as a great sinner, and just now it is high time to appease the godly majesty, who shows his anger, for we see a comet that to all pious-minded people is clearly seen as a warning to make atonement before our new sins are punished with a well-deserved lash. . . ."

Sin, punishment, and atonement. All familiar, but to him quaint, even loony ideas. Did the emperors, empresses, and others whose likenesses stand in the squares of this city believe their actions affected natural events? He tries to imagine himself living then and believing (if Gretchen had died in the plague) that her death was punishment for his sins. The benefit of this belief, he supposes, would be that he would think matters of life and death were not entirely beyond his control.

How desperately we deny our helplessness.

At night they squeeze into a club with hundreds of people in costumes celebrating Fasching, the Viennese Mardi Gras. He and Mieke dance with devils, skeletons, and vampires, dozens of bizarrely disguised humans—all pretending to laugh at death.

. . .

The next day they walk under a blazing sun, which defines the buildings and statues with intense highlights and shadows, giving them a look

of remarkable solidity. As they move around and through these old structures, he feels the city gently stretching his consciousness, opening him to
the expanse of time and human aspiration.

Around the corner from a café, they are surprised by a mythological
scene, carved in marble, jutting into the sidewalk. Others who step around
it seem accustomed to brushing past Perseus as he swoops down from the
sky to save Andromeda from a sea monster, but he and Mieke stop to
marvel at it.

The man who carved this fanciful scene, Georg Raphael Donner, was
one of Austria's greatest sculptors. Though a favorite of the Hapsburgs, he
and his wife, a lovely young woman whom he often used as his model,
lived in poverty. He died shortly after completing the "Andromeda," of
lead poisoning, a particularly nasty way to die.

*Was Georg Raphael Donner weak and in pain as he carved the curve in
Andromeda's shoulder? Was he worried about what would become of his wife when
he died? He could not have imagined that 250 years later someone would care, but
reading about his life and work, I have the strange sensation that I am, through my
emotional connection with his struggle and his agony, helping him to triumph a little
over death.*

. . .

With groups of other tourists, they meander through palaces, vast halls
with gilded ceilings, rooms full of massive carved chairs, canopied beds,
marble washbasins — the trophies and prized possessions of royalty.

. . . always I ask whose is the skull
set in jewels grinning there in shadow
who thrust all this from him feverishly

as the white dove flew nimbly from the mouth
and the feathers made great onslaughts
against the mind, loosening, flattening himself,

to dive into the eye of the needle.
   —EDWIN HONIG, "The Quest"

March
. . . .

Home from Vienna, they've been greeted happily by their dogs and have hung their traveling clothes in the closets. The grand palaces of the old European city seem far away, both in space and time. Gretchen seems farther away, too, and he tries to refresh his memories, to keep them vivid. He can still hear her squeal, "Hi Ursie!" as she did whenever she came home and Ursa wiggled her plump black body up the walk to meet her. He also recalls the moody energy, which filled the house when she was there.

But I know the fog is moving in, making memories less clear. Her face, her eyes, her smile were once as precious and familiar as anything I've ever known. Can't love hold them fast?

. . .

In her room is a box of stones collected on a beach by Gretchen when she was little. He holds a smooth white one in his hand, trying to feel his way back to the day her eyes esteemed it and her eager fingers picked it from the sand.

The question rises again: How can it be? How can she be dead?

It's been three months since his daughter fell in that little room, and he is surprised by the persistence of this question. Even now he thinks that she might be alive somewhere, that she might have faked her death. After all, he never saw her body, never kissed her cold, burned face good-bye. His only proof of her death is the word of firemen, policemen, the coroner—all strangers.

He tells his incredulous self that many, many people die every day and that some of these deaths are as senseless as Gretchen's. Her death came when she was young and healthy, so it *should* not be. But it certainly *can* be. Is it that he can't accept what so clearly *should* not have happened?

He doesn't remember ever believing the universe to be fair, or that people get what they deserve. He took pride in facing the harsh truth: "As flies to wanton boys are we to the gods. They kill us for their sport." So it's not that he considers Gretchen's dying a violation of cosmic justice. His conviction that it should not have happened is more visceral than that.

She should not have died, a part of me insists, because she was my daughter!

This voice within him crying, "How can it be?" has the whiny, outraged tone of a child who believes that it, and all the objects of its love, are exempt from decay and destruction. His rational self would not, of course, say this, but Gretchen's death has shocked and angered another self—an infantile self, perhaps, an imperious character so blind to reality it thinks it has been orchestrating the good fortune he's had so far in his life. Like the baby convinced of its omnipotence by the arrival of a nipple whenever it screams, it's enraged when its wishes are thwarted.

Pain and grief have awakened a childish tyrant whose temper tantrums echo loudly in me. I'm shocked at how unaware I've been of this character who seems to live in my psyche, beyond the reach of reason or will.

. . .

Life in all its forms fascinates him as never before. Watching a chickadee cracking a seed on a branch, he hunches his shoulders in his jacket and wonders how it keeps its tiny body warm in the icy wind. He tries to imagine its life, seeking food from dawn to dark, sleeping in a bush at night, fluttering awake again in the morning. It does this for five or six years, he supposes, and one day it falls into the leaves and dies.

. . .

Jay, the attentive brother (and psychologist), calls to check up on him. "How's the anger?" Jay had warned him that he may turn the "anger component" of his grief against Mieke, since she's the most handy target. Good, sound professional advice, probably, but the assumption that a psychological formula can predict his emotions offends him. Is he a machine? Can his anger be measured with a dipstick and modulated by the closing of a valve?

. . .

His acute awareness of death fractures the appearance of order and peace in the world. Trees, snow, the gauges on the car dashboard, the cozy houses along the road into town — everything could be spattered with blood at any moment. His ambulance experience tells him there's some truth in this, and the taste of death in his mouth won't let him forget it.

If you listen at the doors of these neat white houses, you could very well hear a moan, or the rattle of a dying breath.

. . .

He is startled one morning by the sight of buckets hanging on sugar maples along the road. With the ground still frozen, can the sap be rising so soon? Can the trees have sensed the sunlight lasting a little longer each day? Are they already preparing for spring?

He is dismayed by this sign of an entire season's having passed since Gretchen was alive, this incontrovertible evidence that the gulf of time between then and now, between him and her, is ever widening. He longs to soar back over the days that have gone by and steer Gretchen away from her death, but he is carried onward, ever onward, by time.

He feels cursed by being human, by having a mind caught in the flow of minutes, days, and years. Change, decay, and death occur in time and, unlike ants and turtles, which presumably go about in blissful ignorance, we are conscious of its grievous effect on us. This, he thinks, is the principal cause of human suffering. Or, to be as precise as Buddha was, it's our *resistance* to time's changes that is the cause.

But how can I not resist the death of my dear Gretchen?

. . .

Listening to a sad cello in the dark, the sweet misery rushes from his ears to his heart. The music is a friend who knows how he feels, and together they cry.

. . .

Reading the Book of Job, he finds many poetic expressions of his own agony. Though he may not believe in the God of the Old Testament, he feels abused by a superior power and would like to protest to his tormentor, as Job does:

Thou art become cruel to me:
with thy strong hand thou opposest thyself against me.
Thou liftest me up to the wind;
thou causest me to ride upon it, and dissolvest my substance.
For I know that thou wilt bring me to death, and to the house
    appointed for all living.
    —Job, 30:21–23

He imagines poor Job at the end of the story, standing naked, his skin bursting with boils, the wind rising around him in a dark funnel. In a long lecture delivered from this wind, God responds disdainfully to Job's objections. All the wonders of the universe are of His making, He points out, and He mocks Job's feeble humanity:

Where wast thou when I laid the foundations of the earth? declare, if
    thou hast understanding.
Who hath laid the measures thereof, if thou knowest? or who hath
    stretched the line upon it?
Whereupon are the foundations thereof fastened? or who laid the
    corner stone thereof;
When the morning stars sang together, and all the sons of God shouted
    for joy?
    —Job, 38:4

Though he doesn't understand much of the Old Testament, this speaks to him. This God makes it clear that His powers are beyond human imagining and He isn't about to give us reasons for being what He is, or for doing what He does. His, Her, or Its ways are not to be questioned by the likes of us.

He loves the Book of Job for its long-suffering hero, its soaring poetry, and because it throws all theology out the window. The God in this story is not the Father who cares for human beings. Injustice, cruelty, and death are nothing to Him. The God who murdered Job's family and thundered at him from the whirlwind is pure power, without a hint of an anthropomorphic heart.

. . .

Mieke's brother Hank brings his boys for a visit. Their screeches and shouts ricochet through the house, causing their old dog Woody to crawl under a table. Mieke gets out the art materials and the boys paint elaborately armored warriors, one with a spiked club in raised hand, another with laser eyes, figures of superhuman strength. Later, playing pick-up sticks with Alex, he senses the boy is treating him carefully. Alex takes his shaky hand and moves it to another stick. "Here Uncle Tom, you can do this one."

I wonder what the boys think when they see Gretchen's picture on the mantel. Do they stand together when I'm out of the room and whisper about her? Are they frightened by her death, or are they convinced their magic armor will protect them?

. . .

His daughter's ashes lie in two wooden boxes on the shelf outside the bedroom door, waiting for the day he and Nancy will disperse them on the river. He sees them first thing each morning, and when he sits and meditates in the hall, facing out through the glass door, her ashes are behind him.

At times I imagine the ashes coming alive, and I expect to hear them shriek.

. . .

A friend tells him Gretchen had a wonderful childhood and a happy life, even though it was cut short. He agrees but inwardly complains that she's just trying to cheer him up with some so-called "positive thinking." On the other hand, he knows she has a point. As a child, Gretchen was a happy little butterfly. In her teens, she was like most adolescents—moody, self-centered, trying to be popular. She made friends, had some fun, caused a bit of trouble, but she made it through what can be life's most hazardous time and was beginning to flower into womanhood. This *is* worth remembering.

But when someone told him not long ago how wonderful she was— cheerful, smart, helpful, "a light"—he realized that he, too, is beginning to idealize her and that this will make her even more dead than she has to be. If this continues, he's afraid he'll lose touch with the real person she was and remember only an angel.

. . .

The once-thick winter ice is shrinking away from the shore of the pond. As it pulls back a little each day, it uncovers a rim of water between its lacy edges and the curled grasses of land. Beneath this water, past reflections

of sun and sky, dark shapes of dead plant debris lie, hiding the life that waits underneath.

. . .

He is pushed and pulled by conflicting impulses, different aspects of himself wrestling for control. Heart and mind, child and adult, a gaggle of mostly unfamiliar selves, all affected by her death, all struggling to react in their own ways. He cries at sloppy, sentimental music, is carried away by hopeful fantasies he soon rejects, and finds himself talking to her, though he knows she's dead and gone.

When he reads that Socrates espoused the idea of a human soul, his heart leaps like a puppy on a leash and pulls his mind reluctantly along.

As he was preparing to drink the fatal dose of hemlock, Socrates told his friends that the body, with its need for food, its diseases, its lusts and desires, is a "source of endless trouble." It hinders the soul in its search for knowledge, he said. So when we die and rid ourselves of "the foolishness of the body we shall be pure and hold converse with the pure, and know of ourselves the clear light everywhere, which is no other than the light of truth.

"And therefore," he said, "I go on my way rejoicing."

One of his friends, a man named Cebes, said he had a child within him "to whom death is a sort of hobgoblin," who needed to be persuaded to calm his fears.

Socrates answered, in part, "Shall we believe that the soul . . . whose nature is so glorious, and pure, and invisible, is blown away by the winds and perishes as soon as she leaves the body, as the world says? Nay, dear Cebes and Simmias, it is not so." A soul that seeks wisdom all its life will find it in death, he said.

Soon after this, the executioner handed Socrates a cup of poison. He drank it, and died.

. . .

A day of gloom begins with a dark morning of stranded thoughts and long sighs. It is possible, barely, to move, to make coffee and shuffle papers in his office. Through his window he sees Ursa's black form chase a squirrel across flattened brown grass to a bare tree. She runs into the distance noiselessly, as though at the end of a dream of his life.

No one can lift the stone from my heart, but I believe Mieke senses when such a day has taken shape for me. Knowing she is here, and that she feels some of my agony, provides me with a way of wordlessly leaning on her, even when she's in another room, or away on an errand. It may be that I imagine her awareness of my misery, but I feel we have a bond of shared bewilderment in a surprisingly brutal world. She has taken some terrible blows in her life and, although I have no right to be glad of them, I think the depth of her empathy arises in part from her own most painful experiences.

. . .

He reads and reads—in search of what? He doesn't know. But a parable from the teachings of Buddha touches him deeply.

A woman named Kisa Gotami is stricken with a terrible grief when her young son dies. She carries the dead boy around the village asking for medicine. People laugh at her, saying, "Where have you heard there is medicine for the dead?" She doesn't understand.

A wise man sees that grief has driven her mad. He tells her that the only person who might be able to help is the Buddha, who is staying nearby.

She takes her son to the Buddha and asks him for medicine. "You have done well to come here for medicine," he says. "Go from one door to the next throughout the entire city and ask for some mustard seed at every house where there has been no death."

Kisa goes into the city and at the first house asks for mustard seed. When the people there see her dead son and tell her their own stories of grief, Kisa says she can't accept seed from them. She goes from door to door, hearing many tales of woe, until finally she says to herself, "It must be the same for all the houses in the city. The Compassionate One who sent me here must have known."

Weeping, she carries her son through the city. "I thought you alone had been taken by this thing called Death," she says to her son. "But now I see that it is a law of mankind that death must come to everyone." She carries the boy to the place by the river where bodies are burned.

Later she returns to the Buddha, who asks whether she has gathered the mustard seed. "Done, reverend sir, is the business of the mustard seed!" she replies.

His consciousness, cracked open by pain, is ready for this parable. Though he feels he has a long way to go before he'll be done with the business of the mustard seed, the story helps him realize what he already knew, but needed to know more deeply.

. . .

A robin stands on the cold ground near the clothesline, his chest out, head back, looking (or is he listening?) for something to eat. The robin has just flown in to thawing New England from hundreds of miles to the south. As he watches the bird hopping around in the pale winter grass, he wonders not only where he's been, but whether he's one of the same robins

who were here last year. Did he find his way through the clouds, guided by hills and rivers or the seacoast, looking down at the earth for the one spot he considers his home—the tree near their clothesline?

It's possible. There are many records of birds showing up in the same place year after year. Sometimes on the same *day* each year. What is it that gives a bird the ability to navigate thousands of miles through winds and rough weather and arrive punctually at the hickory tree he left last fall?

In one study of bird migration, ornithologists banded some shearwaters, took them from their breeding colonies in England, and set them free along the coasts of North America and Southern Europe. Most of these birds easily found their way across continents and oceans back to their nests. They made what we might call a "beeline" for home. It only took twelve and a half days for some of the shearwaters to fly across the North Atlantic.

Not all birds can do this, but the long-distance migrators have extraordinary senses that enable them to find their way to the same piece of ground year after year. These birds seem to be guided by the position of the sun, adjusting for its daily movement across the sky. At night they steer by the stars, and possibly by hearing the low-frequency infrasound of oceans, even when they are hundreds of miles inland. They may even measure the angle between magnetic bands encircling the earth and the gravitational plumb lines between themselves and the ground below.

In view of all this, when he sees that robin again, he'll shout, "Congratulations!"

. . .

He knows Nancy must hate to call him, but she says he's the only one who knows the depth of her grief. Just before dinner, she tells him how much she misses Gretchen. Her agony goes straight to his heart. Crying as he stands in the kitchen, he wants to say something to soothe her, but all he can do is tell her of his own sadness.

He thinks of that awful morning when Dick drove him over to her house to tell her Gretchen had died. He hadn't seen her for months, and never visited her at home, so she knew when she saw him at her front door. "Nancy—" he said, and she screamed, "Oh, no! NO!" before he finished saying, "—Gretchen died last night in a fire." He sat with her in her living room, gasping out some of the details—the police coming to tell him, the coroner saying she died in her sleep, that there was a boy with her—everything he knew. The gulf that had developed between them over the years was forgotten as they grieved for the child they had made together. After a while, she got up, found a broom in the kitchen, and began sweeping the floor of the living room as she wept.

· · ·

A Tibetan tanka hangs on the wall at the top of the stairs. A blood-thirsty monster, probably the goddess Kali, drawn in gold on black cloth. Her lips are red with the blood of her victims and, he notices with a shock, she has flaming candles in her hair. This is the kind of god he can appreciate—a goddess of terror and destruction.

· · ·

The sitcoms on television seem to him insane. The people on the screen are like puppets, with unreal expressions and false gestures. They give no sign of having human hearts, no hints of having ever experienced tragedy

in their lives. He looks at them and feels estranged from their world and the audience for whom they have been created. He knows they represent, not life, not reality, but entertainment, diversion, relief from the strains of life. They don't entertain or relieve him, though. Instead, their antic gaiety mocks and disturbs him.

. . .

Another warm day draws him out of his office and into the garden. As he digs, a blazing red cardinal sings in the forsythia bush.

How strange that he is here, living on this sunlit hillside with a garden and a pond. A few years ago he was trapped, living in a dingy apartment, driving Allan Kern's yogurt truck to pay the rent, working day and night, besieged by bills.

So how did he get here, to this place and to these vastly improved circumstances? Some writing jobs came along. His idea for a newsletter took root and grew into a shining money tree. The bill collectors stopped calling. Credit cards came in the mail. He can buy new shoes, have the car fixed, start a retirement fund.

Suddenly he's in paradise. It's almost as though a deal has been made without his knowledge. "Give him the money, the wonderful wife, the house on the hill. Make him think he's got it all. Then take the girl."

. . .

Though snow still clings to the hills, spring equinox arrives. Night and day are now of equal length. The earth has reached the point in its orbit around the sun where the Northern Hemisphere no longer leans away from the light.

For thousands of years this point in time, determined by Earth's posi-

tion in space, has reassured the human mind, though it's of no significance to the grasses and trees, the insect larvae curled underground, or the animals, all of whom sense spring's approach in their own ways.

Centuries ago, our ancestors, careful observers of the heavens, built temples with stones positioned to catch the sun's rays as the seasons changed. Their ability to predict the return of the sun to the same point on the horizon year after year (which we now know as the earth spinning to the same point in space) must have made the universe seem less chaotic. They created an illusion we still cherish: that we are not victims of time — though we know in our hearts we are.

> The years like great black oxen tread the world.
> And God the herdsman goads them on behind.
> And I am broken by their passing feet.
>   —W. B. YEATS, "Countess Cathleen"

. . .

He reads accounts of near-death experiences with interest and hope. Could it be that she was not as frightened in that burning room as he imagines? Is it possible that she became detached from her body and observed its dying with a calm acceptance, as these reports suggest?

He longs to go back in time, to be with her for that moment, as he was with her in her childhood when she faced new and frightening experiences. Her first day at school, or in the hospital for an operation, or the first time she pedaled her pink bicycle down the street, around the corner, and out of sight.

He'd give anything to know that in that smoke-filled room her spirit passed willingly into the light.

. . .

He keeps seeing things around the house and loving them because they were there when Gretchen was still alive. The elaborately stacked woodpile he built last fall is in the same nearly finished condition as when she might have looked down on it from her bedroom window. A shirt in his closet that he last wore when Gretchen was home: she may have touched it. There could be traces of oil in its fabric from her fingers, he thinks, as he strokes the cloth with his hand.

After her husband died, Queen Victoria made the servants wait to clean up the bedroom where his body lay until after the scene had been photographed. She wanted to preserve every detail of the death scene on film: the prince's body in bed, ornate nightstands nearby, portraits of royal ancestors on the walls. For months Queen Victoria slept with Albert's nightshirt in her arms. She had a plaster cast of his hand on a nightstand, and on the wall over the empty side of their bed, she hung his portrait, framed with an evergreen wreath. Each night before dinner the queen asked servants to lay out clean clothes for the prince, along with a basin of hot water and a towel.

In the Victorian era, grievers sought comfort in ways that would now be considered ghoulish. People had photographs taken of their dead loved ones, in the casket, or even posed with the living. He recalls one image of a dead child lying on a couch with his head on his mama's lap. He wonders if this woman knew the photograph would help prove to her unbelieving heart that her son had really died.

. . .

On his morning walk through the woods, the earth, frozen solid the day before, gives way a little underfoot. The Northern Hemisphere leans

closer to the sun's warmth every day now. His path still takes him through landscapes of browns and blacks, and under leafless trees, but life is stirring underground. Beetles are waking up. Plasm is jiggling in the cells of buried seeds.

. . .

There is a news report on TV of a woman who had lived alone with her two children, both now killed in a fire that destroyed their home while she was away buying groceries. He sees her weeping in her front yard and feels a sudden swelling in his chest, then tears. He wants to touch her, stroke her hair, and cry with her.

April

. . . .

It's been four months now, and he thought even the most resistant parts of himself were yielding to the fact of her death. But a dream suggests he does not know much about his unconscious resistance.

I come up over a sand dune and see Gretchen playing on the beach with friends. They're throwing a large, multicolored ball by the ocean. I walk along the beach and see her again.

I go up to her and say, "What happened? I thought you had died?"

"It's in remission," she says.

Later I see her again and I go up to her. I fall down on my knees and put my arms around her legs. I look up into her face and ask, "Is it really true? I thought you had died!"

She looks down at me and says, "It's really true."

I weep and say, "I sure thought it was true." I wake up crying and hear myself saying again and again, "I sure thought it was true."

The enigmatic statements and questions in this dream tie his mind in knots. It seems that a powerful aspect of himself is still trying to alter the fact that she is dead.

. . .

A fine spring day it is, but its bright gloss is harsh and somehow menacing. To everyone else it must be beautiful, but my perception is skewed. Even in my own house I bump into things. Rooms at times fill with a disorienting light. The familiar is unfamiliar.

. . .

He rolls in bed hour after hour as the cries of spring peepers rise from the pond below the house. They seem to be calling him, and he finally goes out.

The warm night air quivers with plaintive peeps—tiny frog voices calling, "Here I am! Here! Here!" As he walks down to the pond, these cries echo loudly in the pines, but when he approaches the edge of the water, they stop. He stands looking at reflected stars and listening to the silence. After a while a voice across the pond chirps, and soon even the frogs in the grass at his feet lose their fear of him and join in. He feels welcome. He closes his eyes and it seems he's part of a chorus calling into the night, "Here I am! Here I am! Come to me! Come to me!"

. . .

The light lasts longer each day now, so his walks after work are in sunlight, rather than in darkness as they were in winter. The air itself seems to have more substance, as though its aromas are laden with infinitesimal seeds being spread over the land. As he walks down the hill, he imagines Gretchen's molecules carried on the breeze along with those of Shakespeare, Cleopatra, and all the previously living people whose names are now forgotten. Theoretically the atmosphere swirls with elements that

once belonged to them. Their briefly animate bodies sank down into earth, decomposed, and in time were lifted into the sky.

Gretchen is there, too, in that dispersed form that is no longer her. Most of her has risen up and up into the stratosphere, where she circles the earth. Some of her may have sifted down through the clouds by now, and as I walk I imagine her molecules energizing the trees and the grass.

When I take a deep breath, am I absorbing a little of what once was Gretchen, am I reusing some of the same atoms, the bits of ancient stars that once gave her life?

. . .

As every professional torturer knows, lack of sleep causes the mind to become unstrung. He never thought much about sleep before, but now that he suffers from its absence, he wonders why the mind needs, not to rest as the body does, but to run each night through a world of dreams. What the mind finds during its night journeys no one seems to know, but whatever it is, it has the power to heal all but the most grievous wounds.

Sleep is pain's easiest salve, and doth fulfill
All offices of death, except to kill.
   —JOHN DONNE

I long for this nearly dying as I never have before.

. . .

Above the trees this afternoon, the wind blows stray pieces of cloud across a ceiling of gray. The wispy shapes move like figures being hurried across a stage. As each fragment passes, it seems like the vanishing of a human life.

. . .

His nephew Travis reacted to Gretchen's death by trying to assure his place in Heaven. He begged his mother to ask their minister to baptize him immediately, even though he hadn't reached the required age. The following Sunday it was done.

He's read that children younger than Travis, those between the ages of three and five, do not see death as final. They believe it's a going away of one who may return. The one who has died is sleeping and can hear what is being said, and when buried, a dead person can feel if someone comes near the grave.

The child in me, the one who can't or won't understand the finality of it, sees death this way, too.

Studies show that six- or seven-year-olds tend to personify death as an angel, a skeleton, or "Death Man." At this age, children may say they have seen the face or form of Death or even that it has come into their room at night and tried to pull the covers off the bed. One child told psychologists that Death is white and has keys that can open any door.

At Travis's age, kids tend to accept scientific explanations. Death is the cessation of the heartbeat and other bodily functions, the end of life. When Gretchen died, it must have struck Travis that death really happens, even to young people, to someone he knows!

. . .

At times, writing in his diary seems pointless, an elaborate form of mumbling to himself. Of what use is it to write pages and pages of weeping words, tangled thoughts, wishes, cries, sentences drenched in

blood? The cathartic value alone is not enough to keep him going, so he imagines a listener, a reader. On a perilous voyage, you need companionship. He finds it when he reads the words of those who have been through similar storms, and when he writes it helps him to imagine a fellow sufferer by his side.

I talk to you, imagined friend. I gather pieces of life, search through thoughts and feelings, find words written by others, sometimes long ago, that seem to me meaningful, and I place them here for us to see, so that together we can try to understand.

. . .

The magnolia outside their kitchen door has flung open hundreds of glorious pink and white flowers overnight. Other trees are bare, and there are no flowers but these under the cold, colorless sky. He worries about these blossoms. This is the time of year when a capricious north wind could freeze them at any moment. Last year when the magnolia bloomed, its soft petals were covered with snow and were soon blown to pieces. But here they are again, bravely offering their beauty to the April air, while other trees wisely wait.

. . .

Alone in the house, carrying utensils from dining room to kitchen, he looks at a knife in his hand and thinks of suicide. An idea, not an impulse. "I could use this knife right now and bleed to death here on the kitchen floor." A curious possibility. A realization that the choice is his. He observes the idea, turning it over and over, as if studying an interesting rock.

His own death seems a doorway he could pass through without fear. If

Gretchen has done it, he can do it. As he was the second one to jump out of the plane in the parachuting class, where she has gone, he can follow.

In spite of his grief, he doesn't use the knife, but he asks himself why. Too messy. Mieke would find him lying in his blood. It would hurt people he loves.

The deeper reason is that I sense a certain momentum within me—a quiet but persistent force urging me onward.

. . .

What a sorry sight—a man and a woman, divorced, throwing their dead daughter's ashes into the river.

Standing beside the streaming water, he reads a passage from *The Prophet*, which ends with these lines: "For life and death are one, even as the river and the sea are one."

They scoop their daughter's ashes from the boxes and throw them out over the rapids, where they vanish in dark water. When the ashes are gone, they toss flowers. Yellow, white, orange, the blossoms ride downstream, pass under the bridge and around the bend. Nancy cries through all this, but he is too angry. He thinks how small they are and how feeble this gesture.

And what is it to cease breathing, but to free the breath from its restless tides, that it may rise and expand and seek its source unencumbered?

Only when you drink from the river of silence shall you indeed sing.

—KAHLIL GIBRAN, *The Prophet*

Is she singing now? "Yes," says his heart, but as he recites these words and imagines his daughter dead on the floor of her burning room, they do not describe reality.

In pain and confusion, we grope for meaning, but I can't convince myself that we have found it.

. . .

The next day at dawn the family gathers in the rain for the ceremonial planting of a weeping birch tree. They drop red roses in the hole before filling it with earth and the balled roots of the little tree.

After everyone is gone, he stands by the window, looking out at the tree. Except for the coming together of family and friends, the ceremony was sadly inadequate.

I wish instead I had built a bonfire on the hill so I could have leaped and howled around it all through the night.

. . .

Samuel Sewall, who lived a long and proper life in Puritan Massachu-setts, kept a journal for fifty-five years, starting in 1674. In it he recorded many events but little of his own emotions. His entry on the day of his newborn son's funeral listed the names of those who attended the service, but not a word of his own grief. Instead of lamenting his son's death, Sewall wrote, "The Lord humble me kindly in respect of all my Enmity against Him, and let his breaking my Image in my Son be a means of it," then added: "Considerable snow tonight."

When he first reads this, he thinks Sewall had no heart, or that the man's Puritan beliefs had turned what heart he had to stone. Judge Sewall apparently saw his son as an image of himself and thought the breaking of this image was God's way of teaching him a lesson. Was his wife made to carry a child for nine months only to have it die one cold night in order to teach Samuel Sewall some humility?

But as he thinks more about it, he realizes he, too, has been guilty of seeing an image of himself in his child and of making her death his own. Does Sewall's plea for the transformation of his anger into humility annoy him because his own ego, outraged by his daughter's death, refuses to bend to forces greater than itself?

But Samuel Sewall's prayer may have helped him attain some humility. Later he was the only judge in the Salem Witch Trial to admit he was wrong to convict nineteen "witches" and have them hanged. In 1697, five years after the trials, when the Massachusetts legislature held a day of public repentance, Sewall stood in the back of Boston's Old South Church while his admission of error was read aloud to those assembled.

. . .

The first turtle he's seen this spring is head and shoulders out of the water, about to climb up on the dock to sun himself. The sun is warm, and he imagines the turtle having just that minute risen from his winter sleep in the frozen mud. This would be his first sniff of air since . . . when? Last fall.

He identifies with this creature stretching its neck toward the sky, yearning for the sun's warmth. His blood, too, has been cold this winter. As he approaches, the turtle senses danger rather than kinship, however, and slides back underwater.

. . .

His college friend Steve Silverman shocked everyone who knew him by committing suicide at the age of twenty-six. Everybody loved Steve. They gathered around him for his jokes and his bittersweet, romantic view of life. He was their source of timely quotes. One of his favorites was from

Horace: "Happy the man, and happy he alone, / He who can call today his own; / He who, secure within, can say, / 'Tomorrow do thy worst, for I have lived today.'" But, only a few years after they graduated, Steve hoarded a secret supply of pills and, alone in his room on New Year's Eve, swallowed them all.

Steve had sometimes complained to him about feeling "low," but knowing little about depression himself, he did not take it seriously. At the cemetery Steve's psychiatrist stood among the tombstones several rows behind the family and friends, understanding that being young they would perhaps blame him. Since then, he's developed a respect for the dark power of depression. In its grip, even a person such as Steve can choose death.

Camus believed that suicide was the one truly serious philosophical problem, because it amounts to deciding whether or not life is worth living. "As soon as one does not kill oneself, one must keep silent about life," he said.

This morning, as I groaned at the thought of another day, I imagined Camus turning to me and saying, "If you're not going to shoot yourself, stop whining and get on with it."

. . .

Another ancient story beams through the ages to speak to him. It is from the *Mahabharata*.

The five Pandava brothers had been wandering in the wilderness for many days and were very thirsty. They sent the youngest brother to look for water. He came to a lake and was about to drink when he heard a voice say, "Stop, child, first answer my questions and then you may drink." He

didn't listen to the voice, drank some water, and died. A second brother came to the lake, heard the same words, ignored them, and died, just as the first brother had. Two more brothers came along, and soon there were four brothers lying dead beside the water. Yudhisthira, the oldest brother, arrived, saw the bodies, and began to weep. The same voice that had spoken to his brothers said, "Child, first answer my questions, and then I will cure your grief and satisfy your thirst." Yudhisthira turned and saw Dharma (meaning "the Way, the Law, or Reality") standing beside him in the form of a crane.

"What is the road to heaven?" the crane asked.

"Truthfulness."

"How does a man find happiness?"

"Through right conduct."

"What must he subdue, in order to escape grief?"

"His mind."

"When is a man loved?"

"When he is without vanity."

"Of all the world's wonders, which is the most wonderful?"

"That no man, though he sees others dying all around him, believes that he himself will die."

"How does one reach true religion?"

"Not by argument. Not by scriptures and doctrines; they cannot help. The path to religion is trodden by the saints."

Dharma, in the form of the crane, was satisfied. He revealed himself to Yudhisthira and brought the four brothers back to life.

Many of the questions in this story interest him, but the one about grief brings his crisis into focus. He's found that it's not his emotions—his heart—that he must subdue, but his mind. It's this aspect of himself,

the one he's relied upon all his life, that has not only proved unreliable, but seems to be conspiring with his ego to undermine acceptance of his daughter's death.

He sees in this ancient story an example of the inner balance he needs. The oldest brother, Yudhisthira, does not, in spite of great suffering, become self-absorbed as his brothers did (and as he himself has). Yudhisthira does not lose his ear for Dharma, his connection with Reality. He is able, even in agony and grief, to maintain a balance between his pain and his spiritual awareness. He listens when the crane speaks.

Yudhisthira represents a superhuman ideal, beyond his reach, but he feels this story urging him to turn toward the reality that lies beyond grief, beyond self, urging him to listen.

. . .

A breeze sweeps through the pines and across the field, bringing a humid, fertile odor, a sense of earth damp and ready. In the shadow of boulders at the end of a wall, two white anemones are blooming—the first wildflowers of spring. Surprised to see their luminous glow in the stone's shadow, he bends to examine their lovely petals and is moved by the improbability of their whiteness.

How does this lustrous radiance rise up from the depths of dark earth? If this can happen, then anything, absolutely anything, must be possible.

. . .

In his *(Old) Farmer's Almanack* he reads that a man named Joshua Slocum set sail on this day in April 1895, the first person to sail around the world alone.

I imagine a weathered man, a man who has since died but who was then in his prime of muscle and perspicacity, pushing his boat into the waves from a rocky beach. He lifts his sails, and the wind soon takes him far from land. I see him as a lonely speck of consciousness skirting death on wide oceans, moving day by day a little farther around the planet.

.   .   .

He thought time would heal him, that the agony would ease as the days passed, but he is learning that grief is a tide that ebbs for a while and then rushes back to drown you again.

Finding it impossible to work, he goes upstairs in a state of dumb sorrow, grabs ink, a brush, and watercolor paper, and lets his hand go where it wants, dipping the brush in black ink and water, moving it on the paper, filling one sheet after another with the same image: a figure hovering over a candle, one arm outstretched as if to ward off the flame. Each image is less distinct than the one before it, the figure enlarging, disintegrating, and spreading off the edges of the paper. After several hours of this, he lies on the floor among the scattered papers, the image floating on the ceiling above him.

Paddy cake, paddy cake, baker's man,
Bake me a cake as fast as you can.
Pat it and roll it and mark it with a G
and put it in the oven for Gretchen and me.

.   .   .

He reads in *Chuang Tzu, Basic Writings* about how the Chinese philosopher Chuang Tzu behaved after his wife died:

A friend came to visit and found Chuang Tzu sitting on the ground, pounding the bottom of a washtub and singing. The visitor was shocked at his cheerfulness and said: "It should be enough simply not to weep at her death. But pounding on a tub and singing—this is going too far, isn't it?"

Chuang Tzu said, "You're wrong. When she first died, do you think I didn't grieve like anyone else? But I looked back to her beginning and the time before she was born. Not only the time before she was born, but the time before she had a body. Not only the time before she had a body, but the time before she had a spirit. In the midst of the jumble of wonder and mystery, a change took place and she had a spirit. Another change and she had a body. Another change and she was born. Now there's been another change and she's dead. It's just like the progression of the four seasons, spring, summer, fall, winter.

"Now she's going to lie down peacefully in a vast room. If I were to follow after her bawling and sobbing, it would show that I don't understand anything about fate. So I stopped."

I see the wisdom in this, but it strikes me as a macho philosopher's story. Are ideas enough to quell grief? Informing a child about the law of gravity after he's fallen from a tree is not going to stop his crying.

"No," says another voice, "but if he understands such things, perhaps he won't believe that God broke the branch in order to hurt him."

. . .

Trees stand on the hill, their branches steady against passing clouds. He sees in them a quiet stoicism, a willingness to wait.

The plaintive sounds of spring peepers in the night have gone. Now the

booming of bullfrogs is heard. Thoreau said, "The bullfrogs trump to usher in the night. . . ." Crouched in dark weeds, they declare their existence and their eagerness to procreate. With their flashlights at the edge of the pond, he and Mieke see shiny yellow throats swelling as the bullfrogs sing.

They have it, too, somewhere inside them, that impulse, urging, urging, urging.

. . .

He and Gretchen spent hours playing, singing, and laughing together when she was little and he was working at home. They developed a certain chumminess, which changed when she became an adolescent but remained a bond based on good times remembered.

These memories soothe him now. They help him avoid the guilt he might have felt if he thought he had failed to love her enough. But an accusatory self points its finger and says, "You should have protected her!" He should have checked for smoke alarms and convinced her that she was not invulnerable. When he visited her a month before the candle fell over, he could so easily have installed a twelve-dollar gadget that would have saved her life!

In his delirium just after she died, he imagined he might be given a second chance. Surely time could be turned back and he could take his ladder and tools to her room and put an alarm on her ceiling. Then when the candle fell over and the room filled with smoke, the alarm would wake her and she would run to safety. The fire department would put the fire out, and he would hear her excited voice on the phone telling him about her narrow escape. "I almost died, Dad!"

Every parent would move danger from their child's path if they could,

but of course it can't be done; and most parents learn that if they try too hard, they smother rather than protect.

In a poem by Louis Simpson, a father worries as he puts his child to bed for the night.

> The lives of children are
> Dangerous to their parents
> With fire, water, air,
> And other accidents;
> And some, for a child's sake,
> Anticipating doom,
> Empty the world to make
> The world safe as a room.
>   —LOUIS SIMPSON, "The Goodnight"

Since we can't "empty the world," we are required by the counterpoised dangers of parenthood to both care and to restrain our caring, to hold on and to let go.

. . .

In the garden where he planted peas a few days ago, tiny green stems, most of them still bent, are pushing rocks and lumps of earth aside, seeking air and light. A few stand like small awakening dancers, bending and stretching in the sun.

. . .

Hot lava from the Kilauea volcano in Hawaii has been slowly inching toward the Pacific Ocean for the past four years. Now the lava stream is twenty miles long, a third of a mile wide, and fifty feet deep. It steams and

glows orange in the night. It creeps along, devouring roads, houses, trees, playgrounds. Yesterday it came down the street of the small town of Kalapana and engulfed another house. Now it's headed for the Star of the Sea Roman Catholic church and will swallow it, too, unless people lift and move the building out of the way in time. It cannot be stopped.

This is the kind of news that gets his attention. He sees the deadly lava as an aspect of the force that took his daughter away. He's awed by the forms it takes, and he looks for clues to its behavior.

Native Hawaiians say the Kilauea volcano is the home of the goddess Pele, the head of a family of fire deities. She was driven from her original home thousands of miles away in the western Pacific by her sister Namakaokahai, goddess of the sea. Pele fled across the ocean using her magic digging tool, the *paoa*, to strike through the earth's crust, making holes of fire where she could hide. Her sister pursued Pele, filling these holes with water, quenching their fires in great plumes of steam. Pele ran on and settled in Kilauea, where she spewed fire and smoke into the air, scaring her sister away. In her current home on Hawaii, Pele has been a moody goddess, stamping her feet, causing earthquakes, and sometimes destroying the land around her with flows of fiery lava, as she is doing now.

He was surprised to learn that this myth closely parallels the geologic history of the Pacific. Geologists describe the Kilauea volcano (Pele's current home) as the surface puncture through which a rising stream of liquid rock flows up from a hot spot below the earth's crust. The ocean floor has been moving slowly northwest for millions of years, crossing the hot spot and heaving up volcanoes, which cool into new islands as it goes. The Hawaiian Islands are a ridge of volcanic mountaintops (Pele's previous hiding places), which will eventually sink into the ocean and be succeeded by new volcanoes in the sea behind them.

May

. . . .

Eight years ago his father lay in an intensive care unit where his mother, his brother Jay, and he had been watching him grow weaker for more than a month. A nurse called one afternoon and said, "You'd better come now." They arrived just in time to see him, head back, mouth open, exhaling his final breath. The monitor above his head recorded his heart's last beat—a long, arcing line that looked like a wave good-bye as it moved across and off the edge of the screen.

Until that moment he believed his father would recover, that he *should* recover. Only seventy-two, he was reasonably healthy when he went into the hospital with a pain in his back. He lay in the hospital for days of tests. Then, very suddenly, he was rushed into emergency surgery for a burst aneurism of his aorta. This was hastily patched, and then his father lay for weeks in the intensive care unit while his life leaked away.

One evening he told his father, "Pop, you're going to get better." With a tired smile his father said, "Yes," and went on to tell him how his mother's quiet strength had helped sustain him during their life together.

One day he noticed the usual blood bag was not hanging beside the bed. When he asked about it, the nurse told him the doctor had changed his father's "code," thus removing all forms of life support. The family had not been consulted. He called the doctor and demanded that his father be given blood. This kept their hope alive for a few more days, but as he later realized, it prolonged his father's agony.

I was blinded to the reality of my father's dying by another self, a sly, stubborn defender of its own needs, an infantile self who refuses to see a world that is not the way it wants the world to be.

. . .

At sunrise he stands by the window looking out at the magnolia tree in the front yard, its small, young leaves moving under a shower of raindrops. At random moments a leaf bends and flings itself up in a burst of energy. The whole tree is alive with leaves dancing in the soft light of clouds.

. . .

His desk is covered with papers, bills, magazines, files, lists of things to do—software to test, letters to answer, articles to write, people to call, research to be done, records to keep—and the mail comes in as inexorably as the days go on.

As though on automatic pilot, he has always operated on the principle that the more money he made, the better, even though this meant working long hours. Now he wonders if there is a way to live on less money, and to make time for reading, walking in the woods, talking with friends, planting his garden.

After all, my daughter is dead and here I am alive, warmed by this benevolent sun, and feeling the preciousness of life so acutely I can't bear to think that I am wasting it.

. . .

Dr. K. shows him the images of his spine and points to two herniated disks and something called an osteophyte jutting into his spinal cord. One disk is squeezing the diameter of the cord, from twelve millimeters down to five. Dr. K. says he needs surgery, the sooner the better.

The pain he had last year has not returned, but Dr. K. says he may just be temporarily lucky. Soon he could have problems walking, controlling his bladder, his bowels. Or he could be paralyzed if he injures his neck again. Dr. K. recommends an "anterior laminectomy," which means cutting through the front of his throat to get at the offending disks. The risks of this surgery are minimal, Dr. K. assures him.

. . .

In the detergents aisle of the supermarket, an elderly woman he knows asks how he's doing. "Oh, I'm okay," he says. She is not convinced. As they talk, her old eyes fill with tears, and seeing hers, his do, too. Both embarrassed, they touch, say good-bye, and continue on, pushing their carts in opposite directions.

. . .

Mieke's laugh, a peal of gleeful music, comes from another room, making him smile, though he doesn't know what she's laughing at.

I love her laugh. It seems to spring from a readiness to play whenever life offers the chance.

. . .

A pear tree, stunted and bent, grows in the shade of larger apple trees. It's only slightly taller than he is, and it leans uphill, away from the other trees, trying to catch as much sun as it can. A few days ago there were a few blossoms on its branches, and he watched a honey bee crawl in and out of the delicate white flowers.

We see only the surfaces of things and pass by hidden worlds unaware.

Today he looks closely at one of the pear tree's flowers, now shriveled, and he notices a green swelling about the size of a pea under its dried-up center. This bulging thing is pregnant! Wanting to know more about how this happens, he consults his old botany textbook.

When a grain of pollen lands on the female part of the flower, the pollen develops a tube with sperm inside it. The tube elongates, probing downward into the flower as it seeks to fertilize the flower's "egg," a solid, roundish ball of tissue at the base of the flower. A tough skin covers this tissue, leaving a small opening to receive the end of the tube growing toward it from the pollen grain above. If the tube manages to find the opening, it enters and moves forward by digesting its way into the nucleus of the ovule. There it deposits its sperm cells, and fertilization occurs.

His botany book presents all this in a matter-of-fact manner because giddiness is inappropriate in textbook writing. But he's fascinated by the behavior of a grain of pollen. How does it "know" when it lands on its female counterpart rather than on another species of flower, or on the ground? What exquisite sense guides the probing tube down to the tiny opening that is the only place in the vast flower where it can reach its sexual fulfillment? His books don't answer such questions.

During the month of May this astounding feat of pollination occurs countless times, silently, all around the earth. When I think about how amazing this is, and how, if it failed to happen, the earth itself would die, I want to call for parades, music, fireworks.

. . .

Gretchen's dying has ruined his defenses against upwelling emotions— not only grief, but fear, sympathy, even gushing enthusiasms. His so-called "masculine" armor, built to keep things out as well as in, has been shattered. So he turns to other parts of himself, perhaps "feminine" ones, for help.

> Ulysses did this too.
> But only as a gesture,—a gesture which implied
> To the assembled throng that he was much too moved to speak.
> He learned it from Penelope . . .
> Penelope who really cried.
> —EDNA ST. VINCENT MILLAY, "An Ancient Gesture"

. . .

He sits with Arthur on the deck overlooking the pond at the end of the day. Usually Mieke's mother, Mimi, is there with him for "cocktail hour," but today she is down below on the opposite shore with a group of Cub Scouts and their parents, who are gathered for an annual award ceremony. There are squeals, shouts, and whistles as the boys explore the edges of the pond and run under the trees. Arthur, wearing a royal blue robe, his feet up on a stool, looks like a white-haired king observing from on high the initiation of young warriors. The wounded king. Suffering from a vertebra

he cracked in a mysterious fall, he winces in pain. The sunlight fades, and the scouts are called together for the start of the ceremony. The pledge of allegiance. An adult speaks. A song is sung.

Arthur is unusually subdued. He reminisces about the first time he held Mimi in his arms and danced with her. "Um, yum . . . That was it!" he says, smacking his lips. He goes on to talk about the good life they've had together and how much he loves her. They watch as scout leaders send a flaming arrow down from the dark trees to light a bonfire. The scouts cheer and clap. After Mimi returns, he walks back home wondering whether the mild stroke Arthur suffered a while ago was more serious than they know.

When he talked in that quiet way about his love for Mimi, was he telling me something to remember after he's gone?

• • •

In the morning, facing the open sunlit doorway, he does his Surya Namaskar stretches and thinks of the original purpose of these ancient yoga exercises. The movements are not meant as exercises only, but also as a series of bows and prostrations directed to Surya, the sun, which in the Rig Veda is the "soul of both moving and unmoving beings."

After years of doing the Surya Namaskar primarily for exercise, this morning it's as though he's joined the millions of human beings who, for centuries, have started their days by bowing to the sun, thanking the power in the sky that is the source of all our energy. He has a sense of kneeling in a cathedral, praying to Surya, God, Ra, Allah. It is a good thing to do, he thinks, to start each day with the movements of a lowly creature whose life derives from powers much greater than itself.

. . .

Memorial Day, the day for remembering all those who have died in the Civil War, the two World Wars, Korea, Vietnam, and all the other places where men and women of the United States armed forces have been sent into battle. He is reminded of them as he pulls weeds from the garden and hears a powerful roar behind him. Two jet fighters flying low, wing to wing, in formal procession shake the ground as they pass, in honor of those who died in wars.

There were hundreds of thousands of mostly young people killed in war—shot, drowned, blown to pieces, or otherwise extinguished before their time. And all their deaths were as awful for their parents, lovers, friends, as Gretchen's death is to me.

. . .

After an all-night rain, the pond is washed clean, and its surface shines. Reflected in it are yellow irises gleaming brightly on tall stems around the water's edge. As he approaches them in the morning, he notices a glitter of glassy wings. A slender damselfly is clinging to an iris leaf, drying its wings in the sun. Nearby, on another leaf, is what looks like an old brown grasshopper. When he prods it, it doesn't move. It is hollow, the empty skin of the damselfly's previous life-form, clinging to an iris leaf with dead legs.

. . .

Mieke and he have driven several hundred miles, and now sit reading magazines in the waiting room of a medical clinic with dozens of others who have come from all over the country hoping to meet the miracle worker who can cut and heal them. Since being told by Dr. K. that he

needs spinal surgery, he has read dozens of reports, medical journal articles, books. He has had a second opinion from another surgeon, and he has come to one of the world's finest clinics seeking a third.

He is shown to a small room, where he undresses and waits nervously. Mieke holds the notebook and pen. The surgeon, a young man with long fingers and a confident smile, examines him and says, as two others before him now have, that the herniated disks in his spine must be removed—and soon. When he asks about the risks involved in slitting his throat, pulling aside arteries and trachea, chiseling his vertebrae, and paring away the protuberances into his spinal cord, the surgeon says, "In my hands, less than one percent. Knock on wood, I've never had a serious problem."

This is the third surgeon who has said he needs surgery and who has warned that, without it, he is in grave danger. But in spite of this man's confidence, the operation frightens him, and the research he's done suggests that it doesn't always work. He leaves the clinic unconvinced.

The surgeons I've met are competent, I'm sure, and yet I suspect their egos may make them too quick to believe the solution to my problem lies in their hands. My incorrigible doubting has left me without much faith in God or man.

June

An oriole sings in the maple tree and buttercups bloom in the field, but even the warm glow of a June day is not enough to make him forget that in this glistening world there are dark rooms where such things happen.

Late at night, having had too much to drink, he sits alone in the living room and feels himself swelling with fury, his body bursting the walls of the house as he grows larger and larger, spitting blood and teeth into the heavens.

. . .

He remembers an old parable about a boatman crossing a river through the morning mist. The man sees a boat heading toward him, and he thinks he sees the figure of someone steering it. He curses and shouts, angrily demanding that the other boatman turn aside. The boat keeps coming straight at him, but he refuses to give way.

The point of this story, he thinks, is that if the man had realized the boat coming toward him was actually empty and driven only by the river, he would not have been angry and would have calmly given way.

He sees himself in this angry boatman. Outraged by Gretchen's death, he is unwilling to steer aside. In spite of his disbelief in a god who controls things, a part of him, a very stubborn part, takes his daughter's death personally.

. . .

American psychiatrist Elisabeth Kübler-Ross noticed little difference in the way religious and nonreligious people faced death. People who accepted it with equanimity tended to be those who had suffered and worked hard all their lives, she says. Others, who were accustomed to "controlling their environments," and had not been humbled by life, seemed to have more trouble. In other words, he concludes from this, what matters more than your beliefs is whether or not you have given up the notion that you can control your life. That infantile tyrant in you has to learn to bow to the inevitable.

The voice in me that keeps crying, "How can it be?" has the whiny, outraged tone of a child who believes that it shouldn't have to submit. This may come not only from my own foolishness, but also from living in a society that shields many of us from disaster. I doubt that people in Somalia, in Bangladesh, or in the ravaged parts of many American cities would believe life has such high regard for them. Their grief, I would guess, is not as contaminated, as mine is, by stubborn, angry resistance.

. . .

Arthur lies in the hospital dying of a stroke. He breathes in an erratic rhythm, steady for a while, then more and more deeply, until his breathing reaches a gasping crescendo, and stops. Everyone waits, and after a moment of silence that could be the end of him, it starts again, echoing down his throat.

The family can't see what the stroke has done to his brain, so his familiar face and florid complexion could fool them into hoping for his recovery and regretting the decision to keep him off life support. But they know he wouldn't want his life lengthened by drugs, pumps, and tubes. Arthur said many times, as though certain he'd have the power to choose the manner of his death, "I'm taking the express, not the local."

. . .

During his watch at Arthur's bedside, he listens to the old man's breathing and thinks about the dream Arthur had a few weeks ago. In this dream Arthur worked long and hard to plant a huge field of onions. One day he saw by their tall, green shoots that they were ready to pick. He pulled one up, but there was no onion attached. He pulled up another. No onion. He kept on pulling and pulling with the same disappointment, row after row, on and on throughout the whole field. No onions anywhere.

Arthur made fun of psychological theories and interpretations of dreams, but he was intrigued by this dream of his. He had worked hard all his life, but his business hadn't been going well recently and he was living on dwindling savings.

"You old fox," he says to Arthur in the bed, "You told us, 'When the money runs out, I run out!' and that's just what you're doing, isn't it?"

. . .

In the evening after rain, the damp air smells of the lilacs blooming in the dark just beyond reach of the porch light. Birds are nowhere to be seen or heard as he walks through the pines along the path to Mimi's house. As he approaches the wooden footbridge Arthur built last fall, there is an explosion of sound in front of him, something huge and quick leaping in

the darkness, crashing through branches. He stops and strains to see the thing that may be looking back at him. But the moonlight is too dim, and he moves on.

. . .

When he arrives at the hospital to take over for Hank at Arthur's bed-side, the room is quiet and Arthur's cheeks are gray. He puts his hand on Arthur's not yet cold forehead and says goodbye. The body lies still, with Arthur's face, but without Arthur.

In that plain yellow room there is no visible or audible evidence that a man has let go of his life, no sign of his spirit drifting off into a tunnel of light, or of the agony in their hearts. Only the daylight angling through the window, nurses' voices in the hall, and Arthur's body lying with its thick white hair sprayed out on the pillow.

. . .

Every morning at dawn the songs of birds come through the open bed-room window. Most are either piercing, territorial, or cheerful to the human ear, but as he wakes he listens for one melody, heard in intervals between the others, the soulful notes of a lonely heart out there some-where in the trees.

In the swamp in secluded recesses,
A shy and hidden bird is warbling a song.

Solitary the thrush,
The hermit withdrawn to himself, avoiding the settlements,
Sings by himself a song.

Song of the bleeding throat,
Death's outlet song of life, (for well dear brother I know,
If thou wast not granted to sing thou would'st surely die.)
    —WALT WHITMAN, "When Lilacs Last in the Dooryard Bloom'd"

. . .

As he works in his office, he hears high, mournful cries coming from
Mieke in another room where she is working. When she cries, he feels the
grief rising in his own throat and he turns away from his desk to look out
the window, past the barn and into the woods.

We are together, but we are alone.

. . .

He looks again at a card he sent friends telling them of Gretchen's death
and at the sad black silhouette against the deep blue sky, a painting by
Matisse entitled "Icarus." He chose the card without noticing the title. The
tragic pose of the figure, its arms bent like broken wings, appealed to him,
as did the red spot in its chest, which he saw as a hole resembling the one in
his own heart. Now he realizes this is not a hole at all (or not only a hole),
but the sun, which Icarus flew too near despite his father's warning. The
sun melted the wax his father, the clever inventor, had used to make the
wings. The feathers came apart and the boy plunged to his death in the sea.

The unhappy father, a father no more, cried out: "Icarus!" "Icarus," he
called. "Where are you? Where am I to look for you?" As he was still calling "Icarus" he saw the feathers on the water, and cursed his inventive
skill.
    —OVID, *The Metamorphoses*, trans. Mary Innes

Breughel also painted Icarus' fall from the sky. The painting seems at first an ordinary landscape, with a ploughman at work, large in the foreground, on a hill overlooking a bay. You have to look closely to see the boy's legs disappearing into distant waves. The ploughman has turned his back to the water where the boy has fallen, as has the shepherd, who stands with his sheep nearby. Even the ship not two waves from the plunging boy sails away from him, apparently unaware.

In a poem inspired by this painting, W. H. Auden praises Breughel's insight into human suffering:

> . . . how it takes place
> While someone else is eating or opening a window or just walking dully
>   along;

When Gretchen died that night, people were brushing their teeth, driving cars, buying Lotto tickets. Even I, her father, slept, and did no more than perhaps roll over on my back. And what of the neighbors, near the house where the candle burned in Gretchen's room? When they heard the sirens, the roar of fire trucks, it was someone else's disaster.

> . . . the ploughman may
> Have heard the splash, the forsaken cry,
> But for him it was not an important failure; the sun shone
> As it had to on the white legs disappearing into the green
> Water; and the expensive delicate ship that must have seen
> Something amazing, a boy falling out of the sky,
> Had somewhere to get to and sailed calmly on.
>   —W. H. AUDEN, "Musée des Beaux Arts"

. . .

Arthur laughed at death, calling it "the big kick in the ass they save for the end." He said that when he died he wanted them to flush his ashes down the toilet. But they ignore his orders and hold a memorial service at sunset, with poetry readings outside on the deck where he loved to sit.

Among other things, they read from Eliot's *Four Quartets:*

Home is where one starts from. As we grow older
The world becomes stranger, the pattern more complicated
Of dead and living. Not the intense moment
Isolated, with no before and after,
But a lifetime burning in every moment
And not the lifetime of one man only
But of old stones that cannot be deciphered.
There is a time for the evening under starlight,
A time for the evening under lamplight
(The evening with the photograph album).
Love is most nearly itself
When here and now cease to matter.
Old men ought to be explorers
Here and there does not matter
We must be still and still moving
Into another intensity
For a further union, a deeper communion
Through the dark cold and the empty desolation,
The wave cry, the wind cry, the vast waters
Of the petrel and the porpoise. In my end is my beginning.
  —T. S. ELIOT, "East Coker"

After the readings they all walk down to the edge of the pond. Jan, Mieke, and Cathy paddle the canoe out to the deep water, where Cathy sets her father's ashes afloat inside a wreath. The children push toy sailboats bearing lighted candles out from the shore. They all watch in silence as wavering lights move out on the water and Arthur's ashes sink.

. . .

Bees fly in to work on nearby azalea blossoms, and he puts his book down on the terrace to watch them. Too late he sees an ant running into its descending shadow. The book crushes her flat. She may have been on her way to report a discovery of food to the other ants, but her plans, her journey, her life, are all cut short by his impulse to stop reading. To her he is as a force of nature might be, striking down a running boy with lightning, spreading a deadly ice slick on the road, or melting candle wax in such a way as to cause a candle to fall over in the night.

He is sad for the ant he killed, but nature, though beautiful, is, he believes, remorseless. The tranquillity of skies, the loveliness of lilacs, could easily lead him to romanticize nature, to mistakenly interpret beauty as kindness. But the universe doesn't love. It won't grieve for a dead ant, just as it won't miss him when he dies. But neither will it murder him with intent.

The ant and Gretchen and I and all living things seem to have been let loose to run among everyday dangers at our own peril, while the unblinking eye of the universe looks on, and on.

. . .

Summer solstice. The sun rides high and warms the earth through 93 million miles of space. Trees that were stark bones this winter have come alive. Butterflies, bees, ants, beetles, and birds swarm, buzz, and flutter at the peak of their life energies. The sun powers them all. And today marks the height of the sun's arc over this northern half of the earth. After today the daylight will begin its gradual declension toward another season of cold and death. This is no longer a fact of great interest, though it was to our ancestors, who appreciated the sun's rising and feared its disappearance.

If, at sunrise today, you stood by the altar stone at Stonehenge, the place built by our anxious ancestors, and you looked along the axis of the structure, through the opening in other stone configurations, your eye would come to a point on the eastern horizon a little to one side of where the sun was rising. From the same spot in 2000 B.C., someone looked precisely at the sun's rising point, but because the earth wobbles in its rotation, the axis of Stonehenge is now a little off. Perhaps in a few thousand years the earth will lean back to the angle it assumed when the stones were so carefully maneuvered into place.

. . .

Mimi raises her glass and toasts, "To Arthur and Gretchen." Smiling at him, she says, "I know he's found her by now and they're laughing together."

Not knowing whether it is true or not, we play with this notion of immortality, and it makes us feel a bit better.

. . .

Gretchen's birthday. Her cousin Kirstie and husband Tom join them for a hike and help him not to brood over the meaning of this day. He wonders whether now, six months after her death, he should be steering his thoughts away from her. Is writing in his diary, for instance, a way of holding on to grief?

Since Gretchen died he's been paying attention to his thoughts and emotions, observing them with unaccustomed interest. For most of his life he ignored his emotions, especially the painful ones, thinking them of little use, and somewhat dangerous. They were annoying strangers, appearing now and then as though from a foreign country. Snub them, don't offer them a chair, he thought, and they'll go away.

Now grief, agony, anger, desperate fantasies, are familiar and, in a strange way, friends. He welcomes them because they connect him with Gretchen. If the emotions were to leave, all he'd have would be the memories.

In Shakespeare's *King John*, a mother who has lost her son says:

Grief fills the room up of my absent child,
Lies in his bed, walks up and down with me;
Puts on his pretty looks, repeats his words,
Remembers me of all his gracious parts,
Stuffs out his vacant garments with his form;
Then have I reason to be fond of grief.

I love that image of her touching her dead son's clothes, of her grief filling them out with his presence. It's true that this emotion, with its strong needs and its whirling confusions, can make you feel, for a moment, that you once again possess what you have lost.

. . .

He looks into Ursa's warm brown eyes, loving her more because he knows that somewhere behind them, in a corner of her dog-mind, is a memory of Gretchen. Gretchen's form and scent, the sound of her voice, would be instantly familiar to Ursa. If Gretchen were to step out of her car and come running to the house, Ursa would wag her tail and wiggle with glee. And Gretchen would call, "Ursie! Ursie!" as she always did when she came home.

I search Ursa's eyes for some sign of sadness, but I see none. She doesn't seem to know that Gretchen will never come home again.

. . .

In his on-and-off practice of meditation over the years, what brings him back to it again and again is his sense that it is a way to the quiet center of his being, a part of himself that lies beyond thought and emotion. It is the peaceful refuge he seeks now every morning. An inward place that could be the very source of breath, it also seems to open out into everything there is.

In the *Four Quartets*, Eliot speaks of the "still point of the turning world." The poet's reference is as wide as time and the universe, but may also refer to the inward center that is sensed in meditation.

At the still point of the turning world. Neither flesh nor fleshless;
Neither from nor towards; at the still point, there the dance is,
But neither arrest nor movement. And do not call it fixity,
Where past and future are gathered. Neither movement from nor
   towards,
Neither ascent nor decline. Except for the point, the still point,
There would be no dance, and there is only the dance.
   —T. S. ELIOT, "Burnt Norton"

These are merely words preserved in ink on paper, but though written years ago by a man now dead, they illuminate something that I, too, have sensed, a vague perception clarified by another human being in another time.

. . .

Time carries me in its stream, swiftly moving. There she is on the shore, her figure fading, and yet she rides the current with me. She's a breath of wind, a wave, both there and here.

July
· ·

Two years after her father's death, Emily Dickinson wrote to a friend, "I dream about father every night, always a different dream, and forget what I am doing daytimes, wondering where he is."

In her grief she seems to have had some of the same type of crazed ideas he's had about Gretchen returning.

The distance that the dead have gone
    Does not at first appear;
Their coming back seems possible
    For many an ardent year.

And then, that we have followed them
    We more than half suspect,
So intimate have we become
    With their dear retrospect.
    —EMILY DICKINSON, Untitled

· · ·

A robin watches from a branch as he walks down the driveway through the pines. When he gets near, the robin flies to a rock and seems to wait for him. He walks on, the bird fluttering just ahead, looking at him now and then as though trying to make sure he sees it. "It's Gretchen!" The thought can't be stopped. The robin stands for a few seconds in a patch of sunlight and stares at him with a wide open eye. Apparently satisfied they have made contact, it flies off down the length of driveway and into the dark pines.

It's not the first time he's had such a fantasy. He's often felt she was looking down on him or saying hello from a star. Is there some aspect of him that believes this? Of course his mind says, "Nonsense," but he's more tolerant of nonsense than he used to be.

After the death of his young son, Thomas Huxley, the nineteenth-century scientist, wrote to a clergyman who had tried to console him with thoughts of immortality. Huxley said he did not believe in immortality, but he also did not think we should disbelieve something solely because we don't understand it or because it seems too amazing to be true.

> No man who has to deal daily and hourly with nature can trouble himself about a priori difficulties. Give me such evidence as would justify me in believing anything else, and I will believe that. Why should I not? It is not half so wonderful as the conservation of force, or the indestructibility of matter. Whoso clearly appreciates all that is implied in the falling of a stone can have no difficulty about any doctrine simply on account of its marvelousness.
> —THOMAS HUXLEY, letter to Charles Kingsley

Huxley went on to say that although his mind was open to the marvelous, he would not believe in immortality simply because he liked the

idea. As a scientist, he was wary of adopting views that conformed to his preconceptions. "My business," he said, "is to teach my aspirations to conform themselves to fact, not to try and make facts harmonise with my aspirations."

I wonder if I could expand upon Huxley's approach by making a truce between the heart's hopes and wishes and the mind's insistence upon what it calls facts. Why not allow the heart to sing and play with its aspirations while the mind watches, tolerant and bemused?

. . .

In a conversation with his friend George about the recurring gloom, George says, "You haven't lost hope, have you?" The question confuses him. For a moment he thinks George means hope for her return. "No," he says, when he realizes George means a more reasonable hope, "I haven't lost hope."

But what do I hope for, if not her return?

. . .

In his mother's living room, the most prominent painting is an Impressionist landscape in soft lavenders, greens, and yellows. A low wall is in the foreground, with lilac bushes behind it, then green fields, and a mountain in the distance. She tells him, as they sit having tea, that when she's alone she looks at the painting and imagines going for a walk within it. First she gathers together all the dogs the family has ever had. His mother stops to say, "I know this is silly." He says, "No, please tell me the rest."

She says his father, who died nine years ago, appears, and they follow the dogs through the opening in the wall, between the lilac bushes, and into the first field, where Gretchen is waiting for them. Gretchen greets all

the dogs with a hug and leads them up to the higher, more distant field. She goes up the mountainside to the peak, where she stands with both arms outstretched. Then she goes over to the other side. They all follow her, one by one, until they disappear.

"You mean Gretchen waves to you before she goes over?" he asks.

"No, her arms are out, welcoming us, and we all follow her," his mother says.

He has just been listening to a tape of Eliot reading the *Four Quartets*, and these lines come to him now:

> We die with the dying:
> See, they depart, and we go with them.
> We are born with the dead:
> See, they return, and bring us with them.
> —T. S. ELIOT, "Little Gidding"

. . .

Up as usual at 4 A.M., he reads a newspaper article about a man in Chile searching for the body of his son. He's been looking for seventeen years, ever since he was told that his son was one of the students executed during the coup against Salvador Allende. Now a mass grave has been unearthed in the desert near the ocean, and he has come to the site hoping to find his son. Twenty-one bodies are in the grave, but his son's body is not there.

A photograph shows the old man, dressed in a suit, tie, and hat, pacing back and forth in the desert, crying, "Michelito, where are you? I'm looking for you and I can't find you!"

. . .

His mother has told him she often talks to his father. She consults with him and he guides her, she says. He wonders how real these conversations seem to her and decides to try to find out. He sits quietly for a while and . . .

Gretchen?

Yes, hi, Dad.

Is this really you . . . I had a dream . . .

I know.

How are you, Sweetheart?

Not so hot really, but it's worse for you.

I think about you all the time.

I know, me, too.

I don't suppose you could come back.

I don't know.

I love you Gretchen. You know that don't you? I worry that toward the end we weren't as close as we were when you were little.

It's okay.

But are you . . . in pain, or disappointed . . . what can I do?

It doesn't matter. I'm here now and you're there.

I don't like it this way. I want you to be here with me.

Dad.

Yes, I know.

You can talk to me.

Yes, but it feels odd. I don't know how to picture you. I see a vague nothingness really, not you. Or you seem to be above and behind me.

(no answer)

You know, I die every time I think about you in that room. I worry that it was

awful for you, your last moments, in the dark, choking . . . Gretchen, I can't stand this.

I have no body now.
We cremated your body. They said I wouldn't want to see your face.
It doesn't matter. You loved me.
Yes, and I still love you. (He cries.)
Dad, I'm crying, too. It hurts me to see you cry.
I wish I knew where you are.
I'm just here.
Where is here?
With you.
Will you stay with me?
Yes, don't worry, I'll stay.

. . .

The bullfrogs have stopped calling in the night, and he goes down to the pond to see what has happened to them. They are still there, squatting silently in the weeds, facing the water. Have they all mated? He's read that male frogs watch over their young, know their own tadpoles from the others, and will protect them until they are big enough to fend for themselves. "Are you waiting for your kids to be born?" he asks one green fellow who squats in the mud. Seemingly unaware of his approach, the bullfrog waits until the last moment to jump—just before the finger reaches his back.

. . .

In talking with her, I entered a dreamlike state where she seemed nearby. I talked and listened for her response, my ear tuned to the frequencies of mind and memory.

I felt a flood of love for her, and I cried as I would have if she had been sitting there holding my hand, looking at me with unburned eyes.

. . .

His mind, tormented by questions about death, also yearns to know about life. What is it that Gretchen lost in the moment of her dying? What flame went out in her that still glows in him?

In spite of all we've learned about how the world works, we still don't know what life is or how it began. Biologists say lightning probably started it about three billion years ago by synthesizing amino acids from an atmosphere of hydrogen, methane, ammonia, and water vapor. There are other theories, too, but none of them is conclusive. We're not much closer to understanding this mystery than were the early Scandinavians, who believed the first human was formed when a cow licked a frozen rock into life.

We don't know much more than they did about death either. During emergency medical training, the people in his class were told that "clinical" death occurs when the heart and breathing stop: when you can't feel a victim's breath on your cheek, see his or her chest rise and fall, or find a pulse, the person is clinically dead. But final "biological" death doesn't come for another five minutes. Something inside that body can be coaxed back to life, if you act quickly.

People who have been brought back from the edge of death say that consciousness lives on past the heart's stopping. Sounds are heard, understood, remembered. Eyes closed, breathing stopped, the brain is still aware. A nurse's voice shouting, "Hurry with that face mask!" is heard and recorded, and later, if the blood starts moving again, the memory may be recalled.

In some cases, the spark of life survives beyond the five-minute limit. There are reports of people reviving in morgues, of soldiers coming alive inside body bags. Children have been pulled up from the bottom of frozen lakes after being underwater for half an hour or more—and have lived. For one thing, cold seems to slow the dying process. Brain and body cells preserve the essence of life, and when warmth, oxygen, and blood flow resume, they revive. In his emergency training class, they were taught to keep going with CPR when the body temperature was low. A person is not dead until he or she is "warm and dead."

He reads that biologists observing a cell under a microscope find it hard to tell when death has occurred. Since he thinks of the cell as the place where life might hide from death, this intrigues him. Normally, a cell is busy absorbing, secreting, and moving substances around inside its membrane. These movements are, to the observer, the most basic signs of life. For years biologists thought that when none of these activities was taking place, the cell could be said to have died. Now they've found that some cells appearing to be dead in this sense can revive, given the right circumstances. Viral cells, for instance, often go for long periods without showing any indications of life, but when they're put inside other cells, they respond by reproducing themselves. Fungal and bacterial cells also seem to perk up miraculously. Dead in one environment, they come to life in another, more hospitable one.

I read this with more than normal interest, as though I'm trying to follow Gretchen, to discover where she's hiding by peering deep into the tiny corners of life, almost into the invisible. But the secrets of life and death remain beyond my reach.

. . .

Out for a hike on a sunny afternoon, the boys run ahead of the adults, yelling, breaking branches, throwing rocks. To them the woods are an amusement park. When they are found stuffing stones into a hole at the base of a tree, Mieke points out that this is an animal's home. "I'll poke this stick in and kill it!" says Travis, but he knows better than to do it in front of them.

The trail winds steeply up through large outcroppings of rock, a perfect spot for the kids to ambush the adults, making sounds of laser swords. But the adults fight back, waving dead tree trunks over their heads and roaring.

When they sit on an overlook to eat lunch, he sees Alex squash an ant walking across a nearby rock. He asks Alex why he did it. Alex shrugs.

"Imagine what his life is like," he says to Alex, fumbling for the right words. "His brothers and sisters might be over there sleeping under the leaves and he's come out looking for something to eat. Now it's all over for him."

This isn't really what he meant to say, but Nick gets the idea and brings a horned beetle cupped in his hands. He puts it in the grass, where it topples over on its back, legs moving in the air. The kids laugh and push each other to get close to it. Nick uses a stick to help the beetle right itself, and it stands, waving long, jointed antennae. Travis notices its pincerlike mouth parts and says it would be okay to kill it because it bites people. He tells Travis that beetles feed on rotten wood and need those pincers, not to attack people, but to chew food. Travis presses the point. "But it'd be okay to kill him. They don't have feelings."

How do you answer a boy whose body is growing strong and whose hormones urge him to dominate, even to kill? His response to Travis is feeble. "We don't really know whether they have feelings or not, so why kill him if he's not bothering you?"

As they walk after lunch he tries to think of a better response. He could have said that beetles break down dead wood into food for new plants, and asked, "Did you know that if all the beetles and other insects died, most life on earth would die, too? But if you and I and all human beings became extinct, life would go on as though nothing happened."

That might have made Travis wonder, but the moment has passed, and the boys are off hooting in the trees.

. . .

Mieke gets up at six and paints until ten, when she starts to work on more practical things. Her paintings express her agony. One depicts a fledgling bird struggling to fly up from flames. Mieke calls it "The Accident." Now she's painting a grim self-portrait, her head turned as though she's about to leave the room. She looks back with a wide, anguished eye. She asks him whether she really looks this morose. She does, he says, but she's capable of looking merry, too.

We try to live with the pain of death, Mieke by painting, and I by writing—our attempts to drag grief out into the open where we might, if not dispose of it, at least give it a more or less coherent shape.

. . .

He doesn't know how to sing the blues or play a sad cello, but he can go into the woods and groan. No one should hear this, so he goes far from the house, up on the hill in the midst of trees. He begins with deep breaths and long, exhaling sighs. As they continue, the sighs gather sound, pulling it from every part of his body. It's as though he's drawing grief from his feet, his bowels, his blood, gathering it in his chest and

giving it form as he pushes the sound out through his throat. The sounds can become alarming, even to him. These are the sounds he might make if he had arrows in his back. But after a while he becomes intrigued by the tones, as if he were strumming the instrument of his body, flinging a wordless song into the astounded trees.

. . .

He aches for a good night's sleep, but exhaustion does have its compensations. He sits out in the morning sun with a cup of tea in a shaking hand. He feels weak and defenseless. In this condition, the shapely andromeda bush beside him seems a thing of perfection, a graceful being extending its leaves into the space around it. The plant's presence and growth seem quietly inevitable, and inspire in him a feeling very close to love for simply sharing with him the same morning, in the same light, here in this place on earth.

I try to imagine what it would be like to grieve in a city, without being able to sit among plants or walk under the trees, without being able to watch the breeze sparkle across the pond. How does a woman in a ghetto live through the months after the death of her baby? How does the man whose wife lies starved on a barren Somalian roadside not go mad? Will future generations have to bear their grief on a parched earth or in bleak cities, and if so, at what cost to the evolution of the human heart?

. . .

Often when he reads it's as though the writer is a friend speaking to him personally. Even when the writer is long dead, the writer's words, meanings, and emotions seem to come from someone by his side. William Stafford wrote this after the death of his son, Bret:

When I run what am I running from?
You turned once to tell me something,
but then you glimpsed a shadow on my face
and maybe thought, Why tell what hurts?
You carried it, my boy, so brave, so far.
Now we have all the days, and the sun
goes by the same; there is a faint,
wandering trail I find sometimes, off
through grass and sage. I stop
and listen: only summer again—remember?
    —WILLIAM STAFFORD, "A Memorial: Son Bret"

.   .   .

People say humans are the only animals on earth graced with intelligence, which gives us dominion over the dumber beasts. It enables us to build the fanciest nests and to move about at great speed without exerting ourselves, but it has its drawbacks. Thanks to our brains, we may be the only creatures on the planet who know that our friends, parents, sons, and daughters, and we ourselves, will one day die.

There is an Iroquois legend that has to do with the tragic loss by human beings of blissful ignorance. The story begins long ago in the region above Earth, where humanlike beings lived in long lodges facing the sun. They lived in a state of contentment, never weeping and never seeing anyone die. In one of the lodges a brother and sister were sequestered, forbidden to leave their rooms on opposite sides of the lodge. But each day, after the others went out, the sister would cross the lodge to visit her brother and tend to his hair. One day it became apparent that the girl was pregnant. No one could imagine who the father was. As her belly grew

larger, her brother began to sicken, and as he lay in bed he told his mother that he was about to die. She didn't know what he meant by this. No one in their land had ever died. But her son told her that his breathing would stop and his body would never move again. He said when this happened she would weep. This, too, she didn't understand, because she had never seen tears. She watched as her son's breathing ceased and as she closed his eyelids, she found herself weeping, as did the others who were present. And so, the legend says, we all will weep when someone we love passes away.

This story is similar to myths from all over the world, stories of the first humans who violate divine law and acquire knowledge. Their punishment, which seems to result directly from their knowledge, is eviction from Paradise. From then on, human beings must live in a world outside the blissful garden, a world in which change, decay, time, and death await them.

The problem with human knowledge, these myths suggest, is that it involves the perception of distinctions. A bird is seen as different from a tree, now is not the same as then, and the self is separate from the rest of the universe. "Behold but one in all things; it is the second that leads you astray," says the Sufi poet Kabir. In duality the state of oneness experienced in Paradise is lost, and human beings, fallen or expelled from the garden, live in a separate, painful world.

I imagine the human mind thousands of years ago dreaming up these stories, and it seems he or she or they were as troubled as I am. Even then, when human beings walked barefoot through meadows and squatted by streams, even then they felt the ache of separateness in their hearts.

. . .

After a hot, humid day, the air cools in the evening, but when he and Mieke lie on their backs in the driveway after dinner, the sun's heat, trapped in the dark asphalt, rises into their skins. Above them is the powdery arc of the Milky Way, the gigantic swirl of matter in space. Its bland name belies what astronomers using infrared telescopes have recently discovered—a violent storm at the center of our galaxy, a collapsing maelstrom of gases and astral debris plunging into a black hole. But on this summer night he and Mieke can only see a silent spray of lights in the high darkness.

.   .   .

A disease is killing bees throughout New England, so he is happy to find one fumbling energetically inside a squash blossom. It appears to be healthy and still able to perform the surprising bee feats he's read about recently. Lewis Thomas writes in *The Lives of a Cell* that in studying bee navigation, biologists wanted to train bees to fly from their hive to a distant place. Thinking bees rather dumb, they first put a plate of sugar a short distance from the hive. After the bees found it, the biologists moved the sugar twice the distance from the hive, then twice that distance, continuing to place the sugar farther and farther from the hive. At one point, though, the scientists found the bees waiting for them at the next location. The bees have done this in several separate studies, and no one quite knows what to think of it. Biologists say this doesn't mean bees are intelligent or can read human minds, but they say it warrants further study.

Beekeepers of the last century had great respect for bees. They felt, for instance, a need to tell the bees when their owner died. They believed that if this was not done, the bees would be offended, and might fly off or die.

The preferred way to break the news was in rhyme:

Honey bees, honey bees, hear what I say!
Your Master John has passed away.
But his wife now begs you will freely stay,
And still gather honey for many a day.
Bonny bees, bonny bees, hear what I say!

In some parts of England it was customary to decorate the hives with black crepe and to put a plate of food from the funeral feast near the hive.

. . .

I hardly thought about my love for you. It lay as unnoticed as my heart moving in the darkness of my body. I did not bear you as a mother does, and yet you were always in me and you carried me in you. My love followed you, my child: smiling, worrying, urging, watching you running from me and back into my arms again, as an echo follows a call.

. . .

After work he lugs rocks through the pines and up a steep incline to the edge of the driveway, where he plans to build a stone wall. A wall isn't needed there, but he wants exercise, and the process of carrying stones and gradually building a simple structure appeals to him.

Magical power,
    marvelous action!
Chopping wood,
    Carrying water . . .
    —Zen saying

As a result of this afternoon's effort, eight large stones of different shapes lie on the ground waiting to be put into place. Tomorrow eight or nine more, and each day after that, slowly, stone by stone, I will build a wall.

. . .

John calls every few weeks from Pittsburgh to check up on him, and each time he wonders how John could know that he still needs encouragement. He is surprised at how much some of his friends understand about the persistence of this agony. He assumes they expect him to have recovered by now, so he apologized recently to Alan and Suzin when he digressed once again to the subject of death as they had dinner together. Suzin said she'd give him at least a year to talk about it.

Like wolves and other pack animals, we need to run and huddle with our kind, especially when wounded. Our pain is our own, but the warm presence of others soothes us. He felt this last April, when Irene and Vin showed up in the rain to help landscape around the tree they had planted in Gretchen's memory. And when George, Jerry, Linda, Bill, and others who live far away dropped what they were doing in midweek to attend Gretchen's memorial service. They understood the value of coming together in a tragic moment. They knew, as he now knows, that when agony is spread among sympathetic hearts, its poison is diluted.

. . .

While swimming in the pond, he feels a fish nibbling at his side. He thinks of Arthur, whose ashes are in this water. He imagines Arthur laughing, "So you thought it was a fish, huh? Ha, ha!"

There's an old saying that goes something like "If the dead are truly dead, why is it that they still walk around in my heart?"

August

Standing by Gretchen's weeping birch tree, he wonders how he would feel if her body were buried here. He thinks he would imagine her lying in a coffin beneath his feet and would feel close to her. He would, he imagines, feel this in spite of knowing she was never her body, even when alive, and least of all now.

During Greek Orthodox funerals a priest sprinkles wine and dirt on the body, saying, "The earth that fed you now will eat you." The lid is put on the coffin and it is lowered into the ground. But her body is not in this ground; her body was burned. Her arms, her legs, her hair, her eyes were reduced by heat and flame to their basic elements and went up the crematorium chimney as vapor and smoke.

The air you breathed is breathing you now.

. . .

Dr. R., a neurologist, examines him and says he may have multiple sclerosis. This could explain his gimpy leg, shaky hands, and abnormal reflexes,

which surgeons had attributed to the herniated disks in his spine. The doctor says if tests confirm that he has MS, he may not need the surgery others have recommended.

. . .

The weather has been hot and dry for weeks, and the river is shallow now except for a deep channel out among the rocks, where I sit in the sun watching it go by. The river is an ages-old metaphor for time, the stream of minutes, days, years, the passing of a life. Fascinated by the flow of water over stones, for the first time in my life I wonder, what is the difference between now and then?

When human beings began to see the present as different from the past, the linear concept must have helped make sense of events and seasons that seem to come from the future and flow by us into the past. This is a practical way of looking at it, good for planning and scheduling. But most of the world's religions suggest that the concept of time is an illusion. Past, present, and future are one, they say. The Hindu god Shiva is often shown poised in a graceful dance that simultaneously creates and destroys the universe. With arms outstretched, Shiva holds a drum representing the steady beat of seconds, minutes, days, and years, while another hand holds a candle whose flame burns through this concept, this illusion of time. In Shiva's hair a skull and a new moon signify death and birth, the old and the new, past and future, all of them present in Shiva's dance of the eternal now.

He has hung a photograph of a statue of Shiva on his wall where he will see it every day and, he hopes, absorb some of the meaning of Shiva's dance.

. . .

How uneventful life can seem on days like this. What did you do today, Tom? I meditated before breakfast, worked for a few hours on the newsletter, walked down the driveway to get the mail (dogs following), took a look at the lettuce on the way back, picked a few slugs off the broccoli plants, returned to my office, worked some more, and so on . . . a day like many others, in which nothing much appears to have happened.

. . .

In a dream he is looking for some shy creatures who live in a meadow far from the noise of humans. He finds them on a grassy ridge near a tree. They look like woodchucks, or prairie dogs standing on their hind legs. He sneaks up behind the tree so as not to scare them. Suddenly he is close to them and feels friendly toward them. He walks among these furry creatures and notices some of them look quite human. They ask him his name. He says, "Tom Pain." They say, "Why Pain?" He says, "Because I live in human society." He thinks about it more, then says, "No, it's because it hurts so much when you love someone who dies."

. . .

His daughter's death has destroyed his resistance to sentimental music. Eating breakfast in a busy diner, he cries when he hears the mournful words of a song through the chatter: "I don't want to lose you, I don't want to lose you, I don't want to lose you . . . forever."

. . .

Memory is a roiling sea in which the light and the dark stir and shine, rise and sink. There was the awful afternoon when he told Nancy he wanted a divorce. He went upstairs to Gretchen's room to tell her. She was

eleven years old. When he came into her room she was sitting at her little school desk doing homework. He told her that he couldn't live with her mother any more and explained that he would be moving out in a few days. She tried to ignore him, to keep on writing, but she couldn't stop the tears from running down her cheeks. "Sweetheart, I love you—you know that don't you? I'll always love you and be with you." But how could he comfort her when he, too, felt the world falling apart?

· · ·

He looks through a photo album and comes to a picture of Gretchen sitting cross-legged on the floor of her room at college. She is looking at him with a half smile that says, "Okay, Dad, take your picture and let's go to lunch."

He must have been sitting on her bed, or standing near it. The Georgia O'Keefe flower poster is on the wall to the left, and the door to her closet stands open in the foreground. The room is lit by the camera flash, and outside through the window behind Gretchen, sunlight shines on yellow leaves. Gretchen is, he notices with horror, sitting in the very place the firemen found her body. Next to her is the desk chair they said she fell over in the dark.

· · ·

Carrying stones uphill to the wall, he has another attack of weakness. The stones roll away down the slope as he slumps down in the pine needles. As betrayed as Caesar by his body, his old friend, he lies helpless, wondering if this is a heart attack or multiple sclerosis, swift extinction or slow disintegration.

. . .

In the diner he and his friend Dick have apple pie and coffee. He asks Dick how things are going, and Dick replies: "Surely goodness and mercy shall follow me all the days of my life." Dick is a devout Episcopalian, so it's not meant as a joke. "You really believe that, don't you?" he asks. Dick replies, "Yes, I do." "How could Gretchen's death possibly be goodness and mercy?" he asks, and Dick says, "Who am I to ask more of the universe than it can give?"

Feeling foolish, he realizes that he still questions the rightness and the reality of Gretchen's death, that he *is* asking more than the universe can give. Buddha said human suffering is caused by tanha, which means "selfish craving," or "blind demandingness." As he understands it, this refers to the subconscious human demand that the impermanent be permanent, for the universe to be what it is not. Ever since Gretchen's death, a part of himself that lies beyond the reach of reason has been asking, pleading, even insisting, that things not be the way they are.

When Buddha said "life is suffering," he used the Sanskrit word *dukkha*, the origin of which is a word for a defective axle in a wagon or chariot. The flaw in the human axle is the inability to accept reality. From this comes the mistaken belief that we and the things we hold dear are permanent, when in fact everything changes and passes away, even the things we want most fervently to stay.

I know this, as any idiot knows this, and yet I do not completely accept it, as Dick seems to. When I try to understand my failure, it seems to be my ego that refuses to face what other aspects of myself see quite clearly. Who, other than ego, behaves like a childish tyrant so in love with control that he can't see he's already lost it? Could

there be any clearer proof of my helplessness than the fact that I could not keep my daughter from dying? What more does this dimwit need to convince him?

. . .

Disturbed by the lawnmower, yellow jackets swarm from a hole in the grass, just as they did one day when Gretchen was a little girl playing barefoot in the yard. She screamed, "Daddy, Daddy!" and he picked her up and ran around to the other side of the house, both of them getting stung, running, running.

. . .

A quiet summer evening. In the sky to the south is one bright star. Behind him, through dark trees, a rising, nearly full moon. Fireflies glimmer soundlessly in the meadow at the bottom of the hill, and above him in the trees, tiny sparks, hundreds of them, glowing and then vanishing in the dark.

Beauty and terror both are here. But at this moment the beauty is most apparent, and it croons softly to my heart, persuading me with its harmonies that somehow, in spite of the other, all is not lost.

. . .

On a camping trip with Travis, Nick, and Alex at Lake Waramaug, they set up tents and go to the beach where the boys splash and dunk each other and swim after Canada geese. Before dark everybody climbs the big rock behind the campground and hikes up into the woods to gather firewood. After dinner they sit around the campfire. What do the kids want now? A scary story.

He can't tell them the real horror story of Gretchen's death, but he makes one up about kids left alone at night in a house with a "forbidden room" at the end of the hall. It works. Alex, the youngest, climbs into Mieke's lap and covers his ears at the climax, when the horrible thing (that the children in the story have themselves let loose) stands over the little boy's bed.

He and Mieke have been taking the children to the woods as often as possible, hoping they will develop a love of nature. Is he defeating that purpose now by telling them horror stories? The kids are already afraid of the dark woods and the animals they imagine are hungry for their blood ("Raccoons bite, don't they Aunt Mieke?"). But it may be that a horror story relieves their fear. While they are involved in the story their hearts pound, but when it's over they're safely sitting with their aunt and uncle by the fire. They've encountered the terrible and survived.

. . .

The first day back on ambulance duty since Gretchen died, he gets a call to go to a girl who has tried to commit suicide. His hands shake on the steering wheel as the ambulance speeds to her house. Fortunately the number of pills she has swallowed isn't lethal. When asked why she took them, she says she was bored and wanted something to happen. She got it. There are two police cars, the ambulance, flashing lights, and the neighbors standing in the street watching as she is wheeled out. He looks into the dilated pupils of her insolent eyes and has to turn his head away. Even if she were willing to listen, there isn't time for him to tell her about Gretchen.

Driving the ambulance, he realizes he has forgotten things that were second nature to him a few months ago. He can't remember the codes to

use when talking on the radio to the dispatcher, and he drives too slowly, imagining an accident around every corner.

. . .

One night, a week or so after her death, the urge to have some contact with her had overpowered his better instincts, and he had opened one of Gretchen's diaries. After reading about a sexual experience she would have wanted to keep secret, he shut the diary, ashamed of himself for violating her privacy.

He remembers coming into the living room one day when she sat on the couch writing. She turned toward him with an apprehensive look and quickly closed a notebook, saying, "Hi, Dad!" Now that she's dead, her secrets can't embarrass her. But if she is to live on in him and in those who remember her, he should allow her the privacy he would grant her if she were still alive.

. . .

The butterfly counts not months but moments, and has time enough.
—RABINDRANATH TAGORE, "Fireflies"

Children can't imagine the time when they will be old. Even in middle age we think of death as a vague and distant thing, nothing to worry about right now. We have time, we're sure, to do many more things, to carry out plans, fulfill dreams, mend ways. We measure our lives in minutes, days, and years, which seem to us manageable, but these units of time are scaled to the human notion of what is long-lasting and what is brief.

Stephen Jay Gould points out that the time of the clock and the cal-

endar are not the only ways to measure a life, and perhaps not the most accurate. Biologists believe the number of breaths or beats of the heart are better predictors of how long a mammal will live.

As a rule, mammals breathe about 200 million breaths in a lifetime and have four times that many heartbeats. Smaller animals breathe faster and live shorter lives (if measured in days, months, and years) than larger mammals. The mouse lives a year or two at most but gets in as many heartbeats as other, much larger, longer-lived mammals.

Humans are the exception, as is often the case. By the heartbeat clock, we tend to live three times longer than we should. But even this is only an instant when measured in geologic time. If the life of the earth thus far is considered as a single twenty-four-hour day, human beings as a species have only existed for a minute before midnight. In spite of this, a ninety-year-old human who can remember the smell of horse manure on the city street will have the impression he or she has lived for aeons.

In 1844 an evolutionist named Robert Chambers suggested that the human sense of time may cause us to misjudge the universe. He proposed that we imagine what a mayfly—who lives in its adult form for only a day—might conclude about the nature of a tadpole. The mayfly in the air above a pond would see the tadpole in the morning, and perhaps again in the afternoon. As evening came and his own life ended, the mayfly might die believing that a tadpole was merely a tadpole. It would be inconceivable to him that the gills of the tadpole would one day drop off, that lungs would form inside its body, and that it would sprout legs and feet, crawl up on land, and hop about as a frog.

. . .

A letter from Dr. R. gives a definite diagnosis of multiple sclerosis, based on analysis of his spinal fluid, magnetic resonance images of his brain, and other tests, all cited in the letter. Strangely, this does not disturb him. It may be the abstract nature of the test results and the fact that he doesn't feel sick. There is also the pleasant distraction of houseguests, whose children are frolicking in the pond. In any case, he knows there's not much that can be done about the disease, which has so far baffled medical researchers.

. . .

Working in the garden barefoot, he disturbs an anthill near the lettuce. One ant stings his ankle, and others hurry toward him, their antennae waving. He has read that ants communicate with airborne chemicals called pheromones and by stroking each other in certain ways. "Watch out, here comes the enemy!" "I'm hungry, please give me some food." They're so sensitive to vibrations in the soil that when an ant is trapped by a cave-in, it can use its legs to drum a distress signal that brings fellow ants to its rescue. Several of them could be calling for help in the earth below his foot. He steps back, and though he knows they are not good for the garden, he lets them stay.

. . .

Every year eight million people in the United States suffer the loss of a family member. Eight million people whose father or mother, wife or husband, sister or brother, son or daughter dies, some after long illnesses, others without warning. Psychologists say the death of a loved one is the most severe of life's stresses, and that such loss can increase the risk of mental and physical illness in the survivors. Every year death leaves about

800,000 people in the United States without their spouses. Some 400,000 children under age twenty-five die each year, too.

That's more than a thousand children a day in the United States alone. How many are dying at this moment? If we could make our misery visible, the sun would shatter and blue sky would go black.

. . .

The damp wood of the chair chills his bare legs as he sits in the dark at the edge of the pond waiting for dawn. He is so tired it feels as though his breathing would stop if he failed to force each breath.

The soft light of dawn dissolves the darkness around him. The surface of the pond, the pine trees along one shore, and the tall maple on the other are slowly made visible. Mist rises from water and vanishes into the warming air. An hour later the sun is up and the world is bright again, and busy. A damselfly, its body an impossible blue, sits on the back of his hand. Its wings glisten as it waits. A shocking thought occurs to him: *Is it such a tragedy after all that I continue to live and breathe in this glittering world for what amounts to a few moments more than she does?*

The damselfly lifts off toward the water.

. . .

They say we grieve many times in our lives, that we mourn nearly every loss, even the small ones—a crushed toy, an absent friend, a missed opportunity. Some suggest the word *grief* evolved from Sanskrit words meaning "heavy, weighty." He imagines heartstruck human beings—rejected lovers, drought-stricken farmers, distraught parents—groping for the word they needed to express what they felt: "I feel . . . heavy." He thinks about the

word evolving over the course of centuries as grieving people found weight to be the right metaphor. Generations of saddened people have grafted an emotional meaning to the word that once was used only to describe solid objects that are hard to lift.

. . .

Disturbing thoughts rise like fumes in his brain: As he hangs up Mieke's nightgown, he thinks of himself doing this just after she has died. Sitting with his overweight friend Hubie eating breakfast, he notices a blood spot in Hubie's eye and imagines him lying in his coffin with flowers around him.

At times he feels victimized by such thoughts, but he knows he is not a victim of his thoughts any more than he is of clouds that darken the sky. Thoughts are cerebral events, not unlike external ones: the sound of a dog barking, the flight of a cardinal. He can choose to pay attention to them, to relish them, or to let them pass. Though he can't control them, he can achieve some distance from them by observing them as he observes external events. And when he does this, when he is the "witness," he can separate himself from them. "Oh look," the witness says, "another thought about death. It comes up, and now, see, it fades away."

Walt Whitman described his witness this way:

Apart from the pulling and hauling stands what I am,
Stands amused, complacent, compassionating, idle, unitary,
Looks down, is erect, bends an arm on an impalpable certain rest,
Looks with its sidecurved head, curious what will come next,
Both in and out of the game, and watching and wondering at it.

Backward I see in my own days where I sweated through fog with lin-
   guists and contenders,
I have no mockings or arguments. . . . I witness and wait.
   —WALT WHITMAN, "Song of Myself"

. . .

In the old man's boat they drift on Bantam Lake and watch a long-
legged heron catch more fish than they do. Kronid, his neighbor, tells him
fishing has always been his way of calming down. "When I thought if I
went to work I'd smack someone, I'd call in sick and go fishing until I felt
it was safe to go back." Kronid has been trying to get him to go fishing for
months, and now he realizes this was Kronid's way of trying to help him.
They drift and talk, bait hook, cast out, wait.

He asks Kronid, a retired sea captain, if he knows how Magellan died.
Kronid says he doesn't quite remember. He tells Kronid about his surprise
at reading that Magellan did not, in fact, sail around the earth.

Just a few years after Columbus made his voyages to America, Magellan kissed his young wife and child good-bye, bid farewell to his
astrologer (who refused to go, believing the trip would be disastrous),
and set out from Spain. Magellan crossed the Atlantic and sailed down
the coast of South America, probing each bay of what was thought to be
a narrow strip of land. He had to ride winter out with scarce supplies and
he had to quell a mutiny, but with iron determination he finally found
the strait at the tip of South America that led his ships into the Pacific.
Magellan wept for joy and named the cape at the west end of the strait
Cape Deseado ("Desired"), for, as one voyager wrote, "we had been desiring
it for a long time."

As they tried to cross this unexpectedly vast ocean they ran out of food.

They boiled and ate their sails, and many of his men starved to death as the ship lay becalmed in the bright blue water. A year after leaving Spain, having reached the beach of the tiny island of Mactan, Magellan and his crew were attacked by natives with spears and poisoned arrows. Magellan stood his ground while his men ran back to their boats. Though he was wounded many times, he turned again and again to see if they had reached safety. Finally the arrows and spears overcame him, and he fell face down in the sand.

Magellan's bravery, his suffering, and his heroic death inspire and sadden me. But the sadness has a curious sweetness to it.

An Italian journalist who survived the voyage and saw Magellan fall wrote, "Thus they killed our mirror, our light, our comfort and our true guide."

That word mirror, *strange as it is in this context, hints of ego taking vicarious pleasure in heroism. My own shameless ego, believing itself of cosmic importance, may see no difference between Magellan and itself. It is certain the universe shook when Magellan fell, when Gretchen died, and will shake upon my death as well.*

. . .

Even when he comes to it nagged by thoughts of business things undone, working on the stone wall at the end of the day calms him down. Sometimes he tries to hurry, to carry thirty stones uphill before it's dark instead of the usual twenty or so, but he soon asks himself, "What's the rush?" and slows down, moving them at the only pace it's possible to sustain. His desire for accomplishment, the sooner the better, is forced to adjust to weight, time, and the limits of physical endurance.

Each afternoon he starts by carrying several stones up along the now-worn path and dropping them on the ground near the unfinished end of

the wall. When he has a workable group, he places larger ones on the bottom, fitting shapes together, following the basic principle of one on two, two on one for stability. Working with shapes is not a rational left-brain activity. He has to look over the stones lying on the ground, allow the forms to impress themselves on a little-used part of his mind, then step over to the one that seems right and lift it into place. Often his selection is wrong and he has to turn and flip the stone, or set it aside and walk down the hill for one with a better fit. He has trained himself, or the wall has trained him, not to be annoyed by the delay and to continue looking for the right shape or, when it can't be found, to pull the stones apart and rebuild.

I love this work, not only because it gives me exercise, but because it seems to fulfill the need, when everything has fallen apart, to piece something together, to give something form, even a structure as unnecessary as this wall. This putting together is symbolic only, and yet it fools a part of me that sorely needs to be fooled.

. . .

The more he reads about multiple sclerosis, the more it seems a kind of mysterious roulette. His immune system, governed by cells that normally know what they are doing, becomes confused and attacks the myelin sheathing of his nerves, apparently mistaking it for an invading enemy. His nerves are, in effect, killed by "friendly fire." If the attack hits an optic nerve, he will go blind; if it hits nerves to the bladder he'll be incontinent; if it hits nerves to the leg muscles, he won't be able to walk. There's no telling where or when this will hit, and there's no known way of stopping it.

Even with this illness, though, it seems to him his situation is not so different from the shifting probabilities of disaster that everyone faces. We all

wake up each day to a world full of danger and go about in it at some risk. The chance of injury or death increases when we get into a car, decreases when we get out, increases if we play football, decreases if we watch the game instead. The odds of his being struck down have increased, just as they have for those who work as firefighters or who tend the sick in Calcutta. We ignore all but the most imminent dangers, believing our good luck, our personal magic, or a guardian angel will see us through.

In the *Mahabharata*, the crane asks, "Of all the world's wonders, which is the most wonderful?" and Yudhisthira answers: "That no man, though he sees others dying all around him, believes that he himself will die."

When Gretchen put a lighted match to the wick of that candle, she thought nothing of it.

. . .

Carl Jung was on a tour of the American Southwest when a Pueblo chief told him that white men frightened him because their faces were pinched and sharp and they seemed restless and always after something. "We do not know what they want. We do not understand them. We think they are mad."

"Why?" asked Jung.

"Because they think with their heads."

"Of course," said Jung. "What do you think with?"

"We think here," the chief said, pointing to his heart.

I, a white man who has always thought with his head, am now afraid of my own mind. Its restlessness disturbs me. It roams, as outlaws, trappers, and gold diggers roamed the West, and I don't really know what it wants. It was, I suspect, a mistake for me to allow my mind to dominate for so much of my life.

In spite of going to Sunday School as a child, singing in the church choir, and even being entranced for a while by Billy Graham's evangelical Christianity, I became skeptical. As an adolescent flexing my new intellect, I balked at belief in miracles and at what I saw as foolish leaps of faith. I told myself I was too intelligent for that, but emotion and ego were working behind the scenes here. To me reason seemed more powerful, safer, more my own. Reason gave me the impression that I was in the driver's seat steering my own life.

Now, after decades of trust in the power of my mind, I feel betrayed. In the worst crisis of my life, my mind has been useless. Worse than useless. It torments me with its vain efforts to figure everything out, to find reasons for the unreasonable, to understand. Based upon its few minor achievements, my intellect struts about like a boxer who's won a few matches and is unaware of his limitations. It seems now that this part of myself may be good for nothing more important than learning to fix leaky faucets.

Tagore said, "The mind all mind is like a knife all blade, it makes the hand to bleed." The heart may be soft at times, but, as the Pueblo chief suggested to Jung, it is more friendly, not only to others, but to its owner as well.

. . .

Yesterday a tornado in Illinois killed twenty-eight people as it cut a seven-hundred-foot swath through houses and cornfields. The National Weather Service failed to detect it until it was too late to issue warnings. Several people died when the tornado sucked them up into the sky and then dropped them in nearby fields.

I imagine hearing cries in the wind, and wonder: was a little girl snatched from her wading pool by the dark swirl? Was a man pulled from his house as he tried to close his back door? Did he, for a final moment, hold the child in his arms as the terrible wind roared in their ears?

September

. . . .

At the end of the day he has to drag himself out from the office to work on the stone wall. He knows he needs this exercise, but he's tired, he still can't get a full night's sleep, and he's felt very low the past few days.

Am I, like other survivors of disasters, troubled not only by grief, but by guilt at being the one who lives on? Do I feel I deserve this agony?

Author Judith Viorst believes this is common. She writes:

It seems from what I have read and from the tears that I have seen shed over daughters and sons dead many years ago, that parents—including women and men with loving, productive lives—may never give up grieving for their lost child.

Indeed, holding on to grief may feel like fealty to the dead, while giving it up may seem like a betrayal. "I'm proud of myself," says Vera, whose twenty-nine-year-old daughter June died seven years ago, "when I can say her name without a tremor." But, she quickly adds, "I'm *horrified* when I can say it without a tremor."

—JUDITH VIORST, *Necessary Losses*

What horrifies me is the suspicion that, like the uncaring world, I, too, might one day go on living as though nothing had happened.

. . .

After walking heartsick in the shade of tall pines, he sits to rest for a while and feels a touch of warmth on his cheek. In his weakened state, it occurs to him that this beam of sunlight reaching through a gap in the dark evergreens is an attempt to comfort him.

He goes back to the house and looks for a statement he read years ago about the healing power of nature. After searching through several books, he happens upon this, written by Black Elk, an Oglala Sioux holy man:

> We should understand well that all things are the works of the Great Spirit. We should know that He is within all things; the trees, the grasses, the rivers, the mountains and all the four-legged animals, and the winged peoples; and even more important, we should understand that He is also above all these things and peoples. . . . We regard all created beings as sacred and important, for everything has a *wochangi*, or influence, which can be given to us, through which we may gain a little more understanding, if we are attentive.

"If we are attentive." These words have the persuasive force of a message straight from Black Elk to me. My grief has curled me inward, but the warm light on my cheek reminded me that I am alive and still in the world, where, Black Elk says, I can receive the wochangi *if I can be attentive to nature—the trees, the sky, the light touching my face. "Look, Tom, look for the* wochangi. *It's there for you, everywhere, if you allow it to enter your heart."*

. . .

He is getting tired of his rusty old car and thinks of buying a new one. But with his heightened appreciation for how brief life can be, it occurs to him that the cost of a new car, refrigerator, and other things ought to be stated in terms of how much time you have to give up for it. The price tag ought to tell you how many days of work it will take to possess the shiny new thing you think you need. How many days you *can't* spend hiking, playing, or doing whatever you like. The sticker on the new car might say, "Base price: $20,000 (for someone earning $15/hr, 167 days, or 33 working weeks—1,333 hours of life)." He'll try to stop dreaming of a new car and keep driving the old clunker.

If I hadn't been so damned focused on making money when Gretchen was alive, I would have spent more time with her, taken her on more trips, written those ruminating letters to her that I meant to write.

He has the luxury of being his own boss, so he escapes from his office whenever he can now. Today he ignored the objections of his business-person self and took a couple of hours to sit in the shade and read the *Bardo Thödol*, known also as the Tibetan Book of the Dead.

A spiritual guide to the experience of death, the *Bardo Thödol* was written to be read out loud by a relative, friend, or spiritual teacher while the person is dying—and for days afterward, in the belief that the dead one still hears. According to the Buddhist Tantric tradition, a few very holy people pass immediately into Nirvana upon dying. The rest of us go into a dreamlike swoon during which the soul passes through a series of stages, or passages, where it encounters fantastic creatures, some beatific, but most of them terrifying.

At one point the dead person is confronted by wrathful deities—terrible, blood-drinking monsters. But the *Bardo Thödol* is reassuring. "Fear

not. Be not terrified. Be not awed. Know them to be the embodiment of thine own intellect."

The *Bardo Thödol* describes death as another phase of existence, a fantastic adventure through one's own illusions, and an opportunity for liberation. In his foreword to the book, the Tibetan lama Anagarika Govinda says the *Bardo Thödol* provides essential advice for the living by helping us avoid the most basic human error:

> the identification of the individual with his temporal, transitory form, whether physical, emotional, or mental, whence arise the mistaken notion that there exists a personal, separate egohood of one's own, and the fear of losing it. If, however, the disciple has learned, as the *Bardo Thödol* directs, to identify himself with the Eternal, the Dharma, the Imperishable Light of Buddhahood within, then the fears of death are dissipated like a cloud before the rising sun.
>
> —ANAGARIKA GOVINDA, foreword to *Bardo Thödol*

. . .

Carrying rocks at the end of the day, he's startled by the sight of a dead butterfly lying in the driveway. A dark wing points up from its squashed body and waves in the breeze. He comes closer and sees it's not a beautiful thing dead, but a twisted leaf. When hungry you can mistake the word *take* for *cake*. He still sees Gretchen driving cars and waiting in lines at checkout counters.

. . .

A quiet September morning. He sits on the porch eating a bran muffin with orange marmalade and sipping from a cup of dark, steaming coffee. Light shimmers on the pond below him, illuminating the leaves of a wild rose bush across the water.

Concentrate and sense the world out there. Only the world out there.

He eats and looks around him, feeling as though he should be content.

. . .

With the words of a poem by Dylan Thomas ringing in his brain, he walks down through the hemlocks and sits by the river to reread and try to understand what the poet meant in his disturbing poem "A Refusal to Mourn the Death, by Fire, of a Child in London," which might have been written about Gretchen's death. How could you refuse to mourn the death of a child?

In the poem, inspired, he assumes, by the news of a child dying in a fire, Dylan Thomas insists he will not mourn "the majesty and burning of the child's death." When he rereads the poem, he begins to see that Thomas felt anything he or anyone else could say about the girl's death would betray its sacred nature. "I shall not murder the mankind of her going with a grave truth . . ." Even the customary elegies of innocence and youth are blasphemous, he says. So he ends his poem without praise or pity, by directly confronting death's cold reality:

Deep with the first dead lies London's daughter,
Robed in the long friends,
The grains beyond age, the dark veins of her mother
Secret by the unmourning water
Of the riding Thames.
After the first death, there is no other.
    —DYLAN THOMAS, "A Refusal to Mourn the Death,
      by Fire, of a Child in London"

As I sit beside our river, I reread the poem out loud, and the tumbling of the "unmourning water" adds its music to the words.

At first the poem only aroused my grief, but as the poet's insistence on accepting death in its own "majesty" seeps into my consciousness, I gain a little courage. The poet was not the father of the girl who died in the fire, so it was easier for him to be philosophical. Even so, the connections he makes between the dead daughter, the living mother, and all those who have died before help me to feel Gretchen's death as part of an ongoing human continuum.

. . .

Wednesday is his day for ambulance duty. The radio he wears on his belt could announce at any moment that a child in his town has been struck by a car, a man in the supermarket is having a heart attack, a woman has been found unconscious. The wearing of this radio always caused him some anxiety, but now its every crackle makes him jump. In his calmer moments he thinks of it as being an EKG attached to humanity. When something goes wrong with the collective body, the sensors pick it up and alert him. But his gut says it's more like tracking the activities of a demon who lurks in the shadows and strikes people down without warning. A demon he greatly fears.

. . .

How moved I am when Amanda walks beside me and slips her four-year-old hand in mine. She drops it just as suddenly to run up the hill after her brothers.

Run little girl, up through high grass, hands flashing, feet flying past startled beetles. Sing as you fly bright-feathered into the trees, through light and shadow, filling your heart with this new time.

. . .

Years ago, when he took a course in drawing, the teacher said not to think about what they were drawing, because if you think "An eye is an oval with a dot in it," you won't see the real eye in front of you with the shadow made by its drooping lid. He returns to the *Four Quartets*:

. . . There is, it seems to us,
At best, only a limited value
In the knowledge derived from experience.
The knowledge imposes a pattern, and falsifies,
For the pattern is new in every moment
And every moment is a new and shocking
Valuation of all we have been.

In the search for answers to questions about life and death, Eliot sees "no secure foothold" and finds we are "menaced by monsters, fancy lights, risking enchantment." Even old age, he says, does not bring us wisdom.

The only wisdom we can hope to acquire
Is the wisdom of humility: humility is endless.
    —T. S. ELIOT, "East Coker"

Is humility really less elusive than wisdom, as Eliot suggests? I look in my dictionary and find it defined as "the quality or state of being humble in spirit: freedom from pride or arrogance." The word comes from humus, *the earth, ground, soil. There is a hint here, but not one that ego likes very much.*

. . .

An Indian summer night on the island of Martha's Vineyard. He and Mieke sit by a campfire with Irene and Vin, the friends who last winter thoughtfully, tenderly, removed Gretchen's ashes from the ugly plastic brick and placed them in carved wooden boxes. Now they sit together watching the gleam of red coals and talking of what a pleasure it is to sit by a fire at night.

Ancient forms of worship were responses to the magical quality of light—in fire, stars, the sun. The oldest gods in human history were the gods of ancient India called devas, whose name in Sanskrit is derived from the word for brightness. These gods, whose praises were sung in early sacred hymns, represented the radiance of the world. The worshipers apparently did not seek explanations from these gods for the way things were. Unlike the gods of later eras, the devas were not thought to have created order out of chaos, they were not good or evil, they were nothing more or less than the shining splendor of the universe.

Near our campsite, behind us in the dark, is the field where Gretchen once lay on a blanket as we searched the sky for constellations. "Do you see a bear, a swan, a queen on her throne?"

. . .

On Katamah Beach, the ocean rolls against the windy stretch of bright sand. Not long ago he taught little Gretchen to body surf in these waves. She held her head up, eyes squeezed shut, and squealed as the water carried her to the shore. He can see her now, dancing in the gleaming sand, the water shining on her sun-browned shoulder.

Before she was born he had hurt his back fighting the big waves. Later he learned that the way to enjoy the ocean is to respect its superior force,

to allow the meanest waves to submerge you, to go under willingly, to bend and roll with them.

He and Mieke lie in a sandy valley between soft sand dunes that shelter them from the ocean wind. The sun's energy penetrates the cool September air, gently spreading warmth through his body.

He reads about Mato-Kuwapi, a Sioux whose name means "Chased by Bears." Mato-Kuwapi resisted missionary efforts to convert him to Christianity, and just before his death in 1915, he talked about the old beliefs of his tribe, which he still held in his heart.

> When a man does a piece of work which is admired by all we say that it is wonderful; but when we see the changes of day and night, the sun, moon, and stars in the sky, and the changing seasons upon the earth, with their ripening fruits, anyone must realize that it is the work of some one more powerful than man. Greatest of all is the sun, without which we could not live. . . .
>
> We talk to Wakan tanka and are sure he hears us, and yet it is hard to explain what we believe about this. It is the general belief of the Indians that after a man dies his spirit is somewhere on the earth or in the sky, we do not know exactly where but we are sure that his spirit still lives. Sometimes people have agreed together that if it were found possible for spirits to speak to men, they would make themselves known to their friends after they died, but they never came to speak to us again, unless, perhaps, in our sleeping dreams. So it is with Wakan tanka. We believe that he is everywhere, yet, he is to us as the spirits of our friends, whose voices we can not hear.
>
> —*Touch the Earth,* comp. T. C. McLuhan

Here, it seems to him, is the statement of a man who made peace with uncertainty. This old man admitted he knew little about the god Wakan tanka or about the spirits of the dead. He believed in something, but he didn't try too hard to define it.

> I hear and behold God in every object, yet understand God not in the
> least
> —WALT WHITMAN, "Song of Myself"

. . .

Life is not lost by dying, Stephen Vincent Benét said, it is lost in every passing minute, day by day, "in a thousand small uncaring ways." A lifetime is a string of moments: dying moments when you are uncaring or uninvolved in what is happening; living moments when you care.

Buddha was approached by a stranger who asked, "Are you a king?"

Buddha answered, "No."

"Are you a priest?"

"No."

"Are you a god?"

"No."

"What are you then?"

"I am awake."

This is what *Buddha* means: the Awakened One.

Gretchen's death should have slapped me awake, but I still let many moments, hours, even days of my life slip by. If I'm going to be here for a while longer, I want to keep my eyes open. I feel I owe it to Gretchen to be awake to the life around me and within me, but still I nod off, and moments die, gone forever.

. . .

There are mirrors in the house, but he hasn't really looked at himself for months. He shaves without stepping back, brushes his hair quickly, anywhere. The light is weak in their bathroom, and when he brushes his teeth at night, the details are dim. So when, in the bright light of the barbershop, he sees his face in clear, sharp focus, he is appalled. Who is that old, sad man wrapped up to his chin in a sheet? This fellow's mouth droops to one side, and his eyes have the look of someone on an operating table.

Has depression drained the life out of me? It feels as though I'm still alive, sickened by grief and fatigue, for sure, but capable of recovery . . . I think. On the other hand, why do I still wake up in the dark, just about the time that fire started? Why do I weep so easily and see dead bodies in the road where there are only shadows?

. . .

Autumn equinox arrives, bringing clear skies. Midmorning he leaves his office to walk up the hill and get his blood moving. High in the blue a pair of hawks ride the wind, flying south. After walking through the woods for a while, he stops to sit on a rock in the pines. The sun illuminates a group of golden ferns nearby. Their graceful shapes glow in the light between long shadows of the trees. This lovely scene somehow reassures him. Nature doesn't grieve with him for the loss of his daughter, it enfolds her, drawing her into itself as it does every living and dying thing. But his mind is stilled by its beauty, and something in him, something very deep, senses a bond, almost a kinship.

Thoreau enjoyed most of his solitary life in the woods, but one day when he felt lonely, he wrote:

In the midst of a gentle rain while these thoughts prevailed, I was suddenly sensible of such sweet and beneficent society in Nature, in the very

pattering of the drops, and in every sound and sight around my house, an infinite and unaccountable friendliness all at once like an atmosphere sustaining me. . . . Every little pine needle expanded and swelled with sympathy and befriended me.

—HENRY DAVID THOREAU, *Walden*

This flight of imagination, which bestows human emotions on trees, clouds, flowers, and other things of nature, is an example of what has been called the *pathetic fallacy*. Ever since John Ruskin used the term to deride Romantic poetry, writers who employ such phrases as *cruel sea, angry storm*, or *devouring flame* have risked being charged with having lost their balance. Ruskin said such thoughts were signs of "reason . . . unhinged by grief."

It may be pathetic in the modern, derogatory sense of the word, but the habit persists, I suspect, because human beings do feel a sense of communion with nature, and whether the emotions flow both ways or not doesn't much matter.

. . .

When she was little they played at turning tears into laughter. After a nasty fall, she sat on the floor crying. "What happened Sweetie?" he asked. "I hit my head on the wall!" He slapped the wall, saying, "Bad wall!" and she giggled. He hit it again, and she laughed and laughed, with tears streaming down her round pink cheeks.

. . .

The pines are dark against the night sky as he and Mieke walk home from dinner at Mimi's. After a period of cool autumn weather, a summerlike warmth has returned, and at their feet are tiny lights glowing here and there in the grass: fireflies, knocked down by the cool air of recent

days, too weak to fly now, and no doubt dying. He picks one up, and it moves slowly in his hand. It still has enough life in it to respond to warmth, to light itself up in a desperate attempt to attract a mate before the final cold descends.

. . .

In the morning he walks up and down his driveway, tormented by a mind that chatters like a radio left on after everyone has left the room. He's been reading too many books that try to explain the unexplainable. He doesn't seem to be able to stop indulging the foolish self that keeps trying to figure things out.

In a Zen story, a monk asks the master, "What is mind?"

"Mind."

"I do not understand, Sir."

"Neither do I."

He senses the truth in this, and yet there is someone in his crowd of selves who keeps an ear out for the hint of meaning that might make sense of it all.

Another story from the Zen tradition tells of a monk who was agonizing over the question of immortality.

"How can I escape the bondage of birth and death?" he asked.

The master replied, "Where are you?"

. . .

The radio on his hip speaks: "The ambulance is needed at Twenty-two Platt Road for an infant convulsing." He drives too fast, hands shaking, mind orbiting on rocket fuel. The baby lies on the living room rug while the young mother sobs, "My baby! My baby is dying!" He, too, chokes

with emotion as he and Terry sponge the chubby legs and heaving belly, though he knows this baby will live.

. . .

His psychologist-friend Bradley, who was on the phone with his astrologer when he arrived, chides him for his doubts about astrological readings and other such things. When he first told Bradley that he has multiple sclerosis, Bradley said it may have been caused by grief. There is metaphoric validity in this idea: instead of going into the woods and shooting himself, his immune system turns its guns against his own body. He doesn't doubt the mind can affect the body and that there are psychological factors in some diseases. If he had inoperable cancer he would probably pursue the converse notion that love and hope can be curative. But he questions whether grief could cause the sheathing of his nerves to be eaten away. He wouldn't say it's impossible, he just doesn't know, and he can't see how anyone could know such things for certain.

He tells Bradley about his dream of meeting Gretchen on the beach and not knowing whether she was saying she was alive or dead. Bradley suggests he's on the verge of accepting the paradox of her being both. Drop that either/or thinking and accept the possibility of both/and. "Well, yes, she is both dead and alive in the sense of still walking around in my heart, but really alive?" Bradley raises an eyebrow.

I may be wrong to be skeptical; not wrong in a rational sense, I don't think, but wrong because I am missing out on the reassurance that must come from believing in angels or personal guidance from the stars. I occasionally sense a yearning to embrace some of these beliefs, but my mind says yearning is not enough. Though I'm more aware than I've ever been of my mind's limitations, I can't ignore it completely.

. . .

I am "mind," "heart," "child," "ego"—a bickering family of characters. That is one way of describing my internal conflicts, but these "characters" conspire and even blend personas. Mind may be the one who angrily rejected the idea of a caring God, but it seems controlled by ego, as when "reasons" are self-serving, which they often are. And then there are the masquerades—mind acting the father, restraining and protecting foolish heart; then turning cruel and locking heart in the closet. It's been hard for me to find out who it is that won't admit the reality of Gretchen's death. Is it the child who wants too much or the ego who can't tolerate so blatant an example of its lack of effect in the world? And who is it that knows she is gone forever?

When I sit by the pond, I hear a voice saying, "It's time to get back to work," but another one says, "Stay here and watch the light dance on the water awhile longer." Who decides?

. . .

His brother-in-law Jan comes to pick up a crib and other things for the baby, due in a week or so. As he helps him load the car with boxes of tiny clothes and toys, he thinks of saying, *Next time I see you you'll be a father,* but he holds back, fearing that if he says it the baby will die, or Jan will die, or some other tragedy will prevent it from happening.

As Jan drives away, he leans out the window and yells, "The next time you see me I'll be a father!"

October

· ·

He remembers the day a year ago when he, his mother, and Mieke visited Gretchen at college.

They toured the campus, met a few of Gretchen's friends, and saw her sunny little nest of a room at the top of the stairs, above an apartment shared with two other girls. They were pleased to see her so happy with her courses, her work at a home for troubled kids, and her social life.

After dinner Gretchen told them about a dream she had in which a vampire approached her, trying to recruit her into his service. She agreed, she said, in order to save her friends. He told her to set herself on fire, and assured her it would be all right. She lit the fire, legs first, but when the flames came up her body, she changed her mind and ran away.

Though she planned to major in psychology, Gretchen scoffed when he said she might want to think about this dream. A few days later he wrote her and asked why she thought she had to save her friends. Was this a role she needed to play? "Remember how your friends at school used to call you Mom?"

Now, as he reads the diary entry about that October visit, he's struck by

how oblivious they were to the tragedy that was waiting to happen a month later. Like partyers in a train rushing toward a collapsed bridge. He knows he shouldn't be surprised at this, and yet, when he looks back, it seems strange that such a huge disaster, so near to them, would be hidden from their sight.

But was it completely hidden? Could Gretchen's dream indicate that some part of her knew what was coming? An intriguing thought, but he decides that his urge to believe this is based more than anything on a wish that it be true, a wish to exalt the powers of human consciousness.

> As for the future, your task is not to foresee, but to enable it.
> —ANTOINE DE SAINT-EXUPÉRY, *Wisdom of the Sands*

. . .

His mother, concerned about his lack of comforting beliefs, gave him a popular book on spiritual matters. It is full of lovely notions:

> The process of dying is this: a soul's intent in a human lifetime has been fulfilled and the soul considers whether it wants to remain and begin something else or not. It does not matter how old or young a person is chronologically—this is the process.
>
> The soul ultimately decides, "I've done all I can with this particular circumstance. From here on in it will be unfruitful in some manner and that will not serve Perfect Love. So I choose to come home."
> —*Emmanuel's Book II,* ed. Rodegast and Stanto

The writer apparently believes the soul decides when and how the body it occupies will die. When it thinks it's time to come home, it arranges for an illness, an accident, a murder.

I hear a voice saying, "Wouldn't it be nice to know Gretchen wanted *to die?"
But my mind recoils. How can anyone know this? I might feel better if I believed
Gretchen's soul had decided it was time to go, but when I search within myself, I
find nothing much more than a yearning that this be true. Other people may
have found in themselves a sense of certainty about such things, but that is not
my experience.*

*Knowing would satisfy my need for order. Certainty would give me a sense of
control, which would be welcome now, when I feel I have almost none. But do I
want to do what Thomas Huxley warned against: distort reality to suit my needs?*

The poet John Keats described a human quality he called negative capability,
*which he defined as ". . . capable of being in uncertainties, Mysteries, doubts, without
any irritable reaching after fact & reason." This, I think, would be a quality worth
cultivating. If I can convince my ego-mind to curb its "irritable reaching," perhaps I'll
be able to live peacefully with the mysteries I find all around me.*

. . .

While reading a book by a Vietnamese Buddhist monk, he recalls two
searing images from the Vietnam War. The first is a young girl on fire,
trying in vain to run from the burning napalm that clings to her body.
The second is a Buddhist monk seated in the lotus position, engulfed in
flames of his own making, the can of gasoline by his side. The image of
the girl is pure human terror: she may just have been looking for a piece of
papaya for breakfast. Suddenly flaming jelly is burning her skin, her hair.
The monk, who ignited himself, sits as though the flames mean nothing.
These two images remain with him, his mind's eye seeing one and the
other, and then mixing them up—the little girl sitting calmly in flames,
the monk screaming and running.

. . .

The fact is, even though it shouldn't have, it happened—she died. My sweet, lovely daughter, Gretchen, died in a fire. There's no way to deny it, and I would do well not only to accept it, but to hold this awful truth before me always. In having death's reality illuminated for me with such power, I am perhaps oddly privileged. I sense that I must treat it with respect by not trying to make it something other than it is, and that if I can face it straight on, it will not destroy me. On the contrary, it might then become the glass through which I can see more clearly, the lens that helps me recognize what is real and what is of value.

. . .

Muhammad said, "Die before ye die." Jesus said, "Whosoever shall seek to save his life shall lose it; and whosoever shall lose his life shall preserve it." A similar message threads through the Heart Sutra.

What would it be like to live as though you had already died? There is a story about a monk in a Tibetan town where soldiers were disemboweling all the monks they could find. When the monks in the monastery heard about this, they fled to the hills—all but one monk, who stayed behind. When the soldiers arrived, he stood waiting in the center of the courtyard. The soldiers broke down the main gate, and the general strode into the courtyard. He drew his sword and threatened the monk, but the monk did not move. The general glared into the monk's eyes and said, "Do you know I could take this sword and slice your belly open and rip out your guts without blinking an eye?"

The monk was silent for a moment, then said, "Do you know I could let you slice my belly open with your sword and rip my guts out without blinking an eye?"

To "die before ye die," as he understands it, means the death, not of "you" the living organism, but of "you" the ego, the self that believes itself to be separate from the rest of the world. The death of the ego, like the death of the physical body, involves a kind of merging of what was, or was perceived to be, an individual, with the universe as a whole. Dead and buried, the ego decomposes, loses itself, blending into the earth. Humus.

He's read about meditations that can ease your reluctant self into accepting death: lie still and imagine you have just died. See your body lying motionless, eyes closed, no breath entering or leaving your mouth or nostrils. As time goes by your skin turns yellow and gradually becomes violet as your body bloats. Worms and beetles come, birds pick bits of your dead flesh away. Fluids ooze out, the flesh deflates. More of your body is eaten, revealing bones, teeth, empty eye sockets. Slowly, slowly your body loses its form completely and rots, becoming earth.

Some say this meditation is most effective if done while lying in a coffin.

. . .

He tried to quit smoking many times but always failed, until one day when Gretchen was five or six. As he was lighting up he imagined himself in the hospital dying of lung cancer. In vivid detail he saw Gretchen visiting him for the last time and saying in her little girl voice, "Good-bye Daddy, good-bye." He closed his eyes. The sound of her voice and the image remained, powerfully real. He *was* lying there amidst a tangle of tubes, struggling to breathe. Little Gretchen *was* standing by his bed, her small hand on his arm. He wouldn't live to see her grow up. He would never see his little girl again.

He had put the cigarette out, and from then on, whenever the urge to

smoke arose, he recalled the hospital scene and the desire faded. When he had tried to stop before, he had talked to himself, repeating the reasons for quitting: lung cancer and/or heart attack, the rising cost of cigarettes, nasty breath, morning cough, and so on. But reason was no match for his addiction. That image of little Gretchen saying good-bye to him drew upon something stronger and deeper, the same something he hopes can help him now.

. . .

Illness, he has read, can be used as an exercise in awareness, in the power of "mindfulness."

So he lies in bed with the flu, concentrating on every swallow as it burns his throat, the ebb and flow of aches and pains—not rejecting, not fighting, but observing them.

As tai chi masters observed, the crane strikes at the snake with its beak, but the snake survives by giving way, bending, curling, dodging the attacks. He can feel, as he observes the pains of the flu, an easing of mental and physical resistance. And something else—a kind of separation of himself from his bodily sensations.

Gretchen was not her body, and I am not mine either. Whatever I am, I am not an aching leg muscle or a sore throat. I feel pain, I feel anger, I feel my body, but I am none of these.

. . .

The clocks have been turned back an hour, darkening the days too soon. As the light fades, dimming the few gold leaves left on the maple tree, he can't bear to be inside. He stops working, sometimes in mid-sentence, to go outside just before the sun goes down.

I hurry out, as though late for a plane, to be there in time, before the sky lets go of another day.

There is no way to hold on to light or to jump the horizon and follow it, but there's time for one last spin in the bright air, and to not be there, to not be bathing in its sweet fade, would be to miss the good-bye in a dying loved one's eyes.

Many people feel the loss of sunlight as much as he does. The Eskimos, when they see the sun swinging lower on the horizon, foreshadowing the long night of winter, sit with loops of string, playing cat's cradle. With hand movements learned from their elders, they weave ever more complicated patterns, with which they hope to entangle the sun, keeping it with them for a few moments more.

· · ·

The elderly woman weeps as they put her on the gurney. She says her husband died seven years ago. "It's so hard to be alone," she sobs, not looking at him, though for the moment he is the only one in the room with her. "It must be very hard," he says, putting his hand on hers and imagining himself without Mieke.

But I know I am alone, as we are all alone with our pain and fear. Others can commiserate and hold our hand, but life will surely lead us to a place where they are left behind and we are facing the flames on our own.

· · ·

At the pond no frogs call, no insects fly. The iris plants, once tall yellow flames, have fallen into the water, spilling their ruby seeds in the mud. Multicolored leaves float on the water's surface, pushed by breezes through patches of reflected sky. The damselflies have laid their eggs in

tightly sealed cases and flown away to die. The painted turtles who sunned themselves on the dock all summer have hatched their young and dug into cold mud, where they will lie, barely alive, through the winter.

And yet, for the first time in months, I am full of energy. With death and destruction all around me, my body, for no reason I know of, is humming with life.

. . .

I accept them all now, God the Father, Yahweh, Odin, Zeus, falcon-headed Horus, Vishnu, and all the lesser gods and goddesses, the lordly faces, the flowing robes, the golden elephants, the multiarmed whirlers. I see them and embrace them as images shaped by humans afraid of chaos and dazzled by the light. All the myths, gospels, and theologies, I accept as pointing toward something having more to do with hope than reason.

Saint Thomas Aquinas said, "The divine essence by its immensity surpasses every form to which our intellect reaches; and thus we cannot apprehend it by knowing what it is." But we try because not knowing is hard on us. Months ago I was angry at what I thought was the sheeplike stupidity of people who believed in a God who cared about them. Enraged by Gretchen's death, I could not understand how people, especially those whose children had died, could believe they were loved by God. Having myself grown up with that image of the fatherly taskmaster, I needed something to blame, something to hate for what had happened; and there He was, still present in my memory, somehow alive under layers of consciousness. Shortly after Gretchen died I saw a woman driving a car with a bumpersticker saying GOD LOVES YOU, and I felt like running her off the road. I saw the same message the other day and shrugged.

Now that my anger is subsiding, I see Him and all the other gods as not unlike my own "pathetic fallacies," the fantasies of minds and hearts unhinged by grief. I

may not believe what others do, but I have experienced the desperate longing to understand, and I know I, too, am one of the sheep. So I don't begrudge anyone a belief that can help them through the day.

. . .

When they arrive in the ambulance, they find a scruffy fellow lying outside a house on the deck, where he had come to die in view of his ex-wife and daughter, who can be seen through the sliding glass doors, sitting in the living room and trying to ignore him. It is a cold afternoon, and the young man is pale and shivering. They have been warned by the dispatcher that he may have AIDS. In answer to their questions, he mutters that he has consumed large amounts of alcohol and drugs, but refuses to cooperate further. They manage to get the woman to come out and talk to them, but she expresses no interest in his welfare. "You'll take him away and make sure he can't come back, won't you?" And he whines to her as they lift him, "I took more than last time! This is worse!" His daughter remains sitting in the living room with her back to her father.

. . .

A Zen master, whose students asked him to write some words of wisdom on the board, wrote, ATTENTION. Asked to explain, he wrote, ATTENTION ATTENTION.

To one stunned by grief, attention is a potent concept, a way of waking, of establishing through all the avenues of awareness a connection to reality. Depression can wall you off from the world; attention punches through. And, perhaps most critical in my case, attention is an antidote to self-absorption.

I have heard from Black Elk, Thoreau, and others that if I can be attentive, espe-

cially to nature, I can receive a healing influence. Now I read Thich Nhat Hanh, who says every act is a rite, no matter where you are, even the washing of dishes. "Does the word 'rite' seem too solemn?" he asks. "I use that word in order to jolt you into the realization of the life-and-death matter of awareness."

. . .

He has always loved to run. As a boy he ran through fields, along roads, sidewalked or not, often with his dog, who would lope ahead, glancing back now and then to be sure he followed. Later in his life, when unnamed fears and too much thinking bunched and knotted his muscles and nerves, a good, long run smoothed them out. Even now, slowed to a walk by doctors' warnings, his body is so grateful for movement, expression, and heat that he feels sure there remains in his body the memory of being a grazing or a hunting animal, moving across savannahs, leaping rivers.

Every day he makes the effort, sometimes considerable, to push away from his desk and go for a walk or work on the wall. There is always a struggle between the business robot and the self who knows the antelope can't live in a pen, but after a few steps up the hill, a look at the sky, a whiff of breeze, the animal is ascendant and the robot's chatter fades.

. . .

During a talk with his psychologist-friend Bradley, he describes the drawing he made one morning after meditating. It has the shape of a seed split open, with something like a comet circling in the sky above it, connecting the parts. He asks Bradley for paper and pen and draws the image for him. "This is wonderful," Bradley says. "I see this as a clear sign of personal growth, don't you?"

"Yes, I guess. . . . Well, maybe . . ." he stammers, but feels a surge of grief,

and begins to cry. He feels like a child handed a present wrapped in the skin of someone he loves. "How can I use Gretchen's death for my own growth? How can I be happy because she's died!"

Am I such a fool that I had to lose my daughter to learn how to live? How can I accept such "growth"?

. . .

The odor of smoke rises from the file folder marked GRETCHEN. The papers retrieved from her room are brown. The folder contains her bank statements, student loan papers, insurance forms, a letter in which she tells him she likes her professors, copies of the death certificates. He takes one of these out and reads her name, sex, social security number, date of death and date of birth (in that order), place of death, race, occupation, marital status, address, informant (himself), funeral home, and finally, at the bottom of the page, "Immediate Cause of Death: a. Carbon monoxide poisoning and burns b. house fire." Signed, "Joseph F. Reichel, Coroner."

"How can it be?" the voice asks, still fighting what it doesn't want to be true, and I say, "I don't know." It's all right not to know. "The only wisdom we can hope to achieve is the wisdom of humility. Humility is endless."

Why did she have to die? I don't know. Did her life have a purpose? I don't know. Does mine? Where is she now? Is there a God who cares? I don't know.

A flame in the night,
alive by her hand,
burns in her sleep,
a lovely light,
dancing to the rhythm

of breeze or breath,
or to its own wild tune
heard in the God-aweful
heart of the sun,
it dances and shines,
reaching for the moon,
whirling on and on,
gathering all in its
radiant embrace,
without stopping for anything,
even love . . .
and suddenly one so young
never was old;
time, punctured,
poured in on itself,
a deluge of moments
converged into one,
the last became the first,
and the first forever the last.

· · ·

At dawn he lies looking out the window at the softening sky, thinking about the dream in which he met Gretchen on the beach. For months he's tried to understand what she meant when she said, "It's true." Was it true that her death was "in remission," as she said earlier in the dream, or did she mean it was true that she was really dead? And when he asked her, "Is it true?" what did *he* mean? The questions twist back on themselves.

It occurs to him that the dream is a puzzle similar to a Zen koan and

that its purpose, if there is purpose to dreams, may have been to force his mind to run through the alleys of a labyrinth until it fell down exhausted. Certainly this has been the effect. The dream suggests what D. T. Suzuki called "the reason of unreason." The problem becomes a nonproblem. He simply has to accept the unreason of her statement, the mystery of it all. "It's true."

Light eases into the shadows of the window curtain. He feels tension flowing away and a blessed relief washing through him.

I don't know if it's ego, mind, both of them, or something else in me that is finally ready to stop fighting. Whatever it is, some stubborn son-of-a-bitch inside me is sighing, "All right, that's how it is. I can't figure it out and there's nothing I can do to change it." At last I can admit my helplessness in this encounter with "towering, magnificent death."

This may be defeat, but it feels more like liberation.

. . .

Halloween, the day of ghosts, antic skeletons, and pumpkin faces glowing with candlelight. He reads that in ancient Britain and Ireland, this day marked the end of summer, the start of a new year. It was a time of transition: the harvest had ended, the herds had returned from their pastures, and the supernatural forces of nature had to be placated. The Celts held festivals and built huge fires on hilltops to scare away evil spirits. They believed the dead escaped from their graves on this night and roamed the countryside seeking vengeance on the living.

As darkness falls, he and Mieke creep around Hank and Sharon's house waggling their masked faces in the windows and making what they hope will be heard by the children inside as eerie sounds. Travis leans out the

back door and yells with dramatic boredom, "Aunt Mieke and Uncle Tom, we know it's you."

Later at a party in a dimly lit old house, someone, he can't figure out who, keeps coming up to him wearing a white plastic face, a face without expression. The underlying human refuses to say a word. There are many people at the party whom he doesn't know, but this one taunts him with such persistence that the blankness of the mask hides, he is quite sure, the face of someone he knows well.

He has a long talk with a woman whose husband died about the same time Gretchen did. She says her husband had elective heart surgery so he could enjoy the things he loved—hiking, leading bird walks. He sought out one of the best surgeons in the country, but something went wrong and suddenly he was dead. She has come to the party with large black spiders stuck to her clothes, in her hair.

As they did in Vienna, for the second time in this strange year he and Mieke dance late into the night among people in disguise, and the person in the deathly white mask dances, too, continuing to bedevil him.

November

. . . .

In Mexico people are celebrating Dia de los Muertos with festive music,
special foods, and ceremonies. This is the day for beautifying graves,
hanging painted skeletons from trees, and eating *pan de muerto*, bread
shaped like bones and covered with icing. Unlike the Celts who built fires
to scare the dead away, Mexican families gather to welcome the dead back
home. Pathways of marigold petals lead them to the house, showing the
way to the *ofrendas*, altars with photographs of the dead surrounded by
flowers and the dead ones' most prized possessions.

In *The Labyrinth of Solitude*, Octavio Paz says, "To the inhabitant of New
York, Paris or London, death is a word that is never uttered because it
burns the lips. The Mexican, on the other hand, frequents it, mocks it,
caresses it, sleeps with it, entertains it; it is one of his favorite playthings
and his most enduring love."

. . .

The ambulance goes to help a seventeen-year-old girl run over in a
parking lot. She was walking with her sister when an elderly man backed

into her, knocking her down and under the car. The man heard her screams, shifted into drive, jammed his foot on the accelerator, and ran over her again. His car shot forward, up an embankment, through a light pole, and into a tree.

This was too much for me. I left the ambulance with its flashing lights on, draining the battery. As it turned out, she wasn't as badly hurt as I imagined, but I would have been useless if she had been. Instead of treating her injuries, I wanted to hold her in my arms. Dave had to do all the thinking, and most of the work. I drove erratically to the hospital and nearly hit another ambulance as I backed up to the emergency room.

These accidents tap directly into a fear that shoots up and blows my circuits. I can't think straight and I feel as though the world is falling apart again. I'm going to have to quit ambulance duty for a while and hope that in time I will learn that although there is danger, it doesn't lie around every corner.

• • •

Mieke's eighty-five-year-old aunt Noenoe, who has been about to die, or so everyone has thought, for years, lives in a New York apartment but has been brought to the country for a visit. The tiny old woman, crippled by arthritis and strokes, sits hunched in her wheelchair glaring out the window and declares in the booming voice of a field marshal, "Those birds are too big!"

• • •

A young African woman named Fannely Zulu, of Chimbunda Village in Zambia, looks at him from a news photograph on his bulletin board. Sitting gracefully on the ground in the doorway of a small hut, her head is

shaven and her gaze has a look of beatific exhaustion. Her shaven head signifies bereavement for her baby who died of AIDS.

Fannely Zulu has been on his bulletin board since April, when he thought of her as one of those from whom he could not accept mustard seed. The article with this photo says Mrs. Zulu, who is twenty years old and looks healthy, though tired, has AIDS herself. A hospital worker expressed the hope that she would die quickly.

. . .

On the way to the neurologist, he stops at a department store to use the men's room. A man in a wheelchair is struggling at the door to a stall. He offers to help, and as he lifts the stranger to the toilet, the man says he has multiple sclerosis. "I have MS, too," he says. The man turns in his arms and looks up at him, "You must be in remission!" Then, through the closed stall door, the man says, "I was your age when I got it, but don't worry too much, you can learn to live with it."

In the clinic, neurologists examine him and ask him about bladder and bowel control, sexual function, memory, speech, and paralysis. He is oddly flattered by their intense interest in him. The chief neurologist, a man highly respected for his research, says they don't know how to cure multiple sclerosis yet, but they believe in "aggressive" treatment of its symptoms. The doctor gives him his card and says to call immediately if he suffers an attack.

He leaves the clinic wondering why he isn't more worried. He hopes it's not because he still believes he can make things turn out the way he wants.

Chuang Tzu tells of a sage who became severely crippled:

Yet he seemed calm at heart and unconcerned. Dragging himself halt-
ingly to the well, he looked at his reflection and said, "My, my! So the
Creator is making me all crookedy like this!"

"Do you resent it?" asked Master Ssu.

"Why no, what would I resent? If the process continues, perhaps in
time he'll transform my left arm into a rooster. In that case I'll keep watch
on the night. . . . Or perhaps in time he'll transform my buttocks into
cartwheels. Then, with my spirit for a horse, I'll climb up and go for a ride.
. . . I received life because the time had come; I will lose it because the
order of things passes on. . . ."

—*Wandering on the Way*, trans. V. H. Mair

*If MS crumples my legs and makes me piss on myself, will I be able to laugh and
say, "I guess the Creator has decided to make a jellyfish out of me now!"*

. . .

Frost sparkles in the grass, and the morning sky is clear as a mirror.
Out early for a walk, he picks up a leaf, mottled brown and yellow, drying
and full of holes. The hand holding the leaf shakes as he watches the sunlight dazzle in tiny crystals of ice before melting them away.

His daughter's death has both beaten him down and cracked him open,
so that now he looks a little longer, and with greater fondness, at such
things.

. . .

Putting on a black jacket before leaving for the theater, he hesitates,
imagining an accident on the road tonight. Should he wear a lighter color
so he can be seen in the headlights of oncoming cars as he tries to drag
Mieke's bloody body to safety?

What if . . . the lights that should not do strike them in the night? The wet road shines with her blood and there are more lights coming, coming, as I try to pull her broken body to the side. Shouldn't I dress for the theater in my ambulance jacket, a reflective vest? And shouldn't she wear a helmet instead of that flimsy ribbon in her hair?

. . .

Listening to a tape as he drives, he is startled by Joseph Campbell quoting from the Thomas Gospel. "The Kingdom of the Father is spread out upon the earth, and men do not see it." He assumes this refers to the human failure to see reality, the fogging over of it with our wishes and preconceptions, while the world, as it is, is wonderful enough. Did Jesus really say this?

He gets a copy of the Gnostic scriptures and reads that Jesus poked fun at those who thought of the "Kingdom of God" as being somewhere in the great beyond. Jesus said, "If those who lead you say to you, 'Look, the Kingdom is in the sky,' then the birds will arrive there before you." The disciples didn't understand, or didn't want to. They kept asking when the new world would come. Jesus said, "It will not come by expectation. It will not be a matter of saying 'Here it is,' or 'There it is.' Rather, the Kingdom of the Father is spread out upon the earth, and men do not see it."

I identify with the disciples' reluctance to be satisfied with this. I see the wisdom in Jesus' words, but there are aspects of myself that are unable, unwilling, or too afraid to completely accept them. I look out at the leaf-strewn yard, with dead plants fallen in the garden, our black dog curled in the driveway by the car. Can this be the Kingdom of the Father?

At the moment I know it is. And yet I soon forget.

. . .

I cringe when Nick uses the word awesome *to describe a toy warrior. How, I wonder, will he find a word with enough majesty in it when he encounters something that truly is?*

. . .

A baby boy is born to Jan and Mary. The birth of another child, wriggling as Gretchen did in his arms. Another gathering of stardust, brought together, reverberating in a new form.

Astronomers discovered a galaxy recently, the largest ever detected, with more than 100 trillion stars. It is over six million light years in diameter—sixty times the diameter of our Milky Way. This huge swirl of suns lies in the center of a cluster of about a thousand other galaxies, called Abell 2029.

The discovery raises again a question that has long puzzled astronomers: why does the material of the universe clump together into galaxies (or human beings) rather than spreading evenly out as in a well-stirred soup? There doesn't seem to be enough matter in the universe to account for the gravitational forces binding things together, so astronomers suggest a large part of the universe may consist of "dark matter," something as yet unseen.

He and Mieke are asked to be baby Daniel's guardians. They gladly accept.

. . .

I am immensely grateful to the weavers of papyrus, the cutters of stone, to geese who surrendered their quills, to Gutenberg, to whales whose deaths provided illumination for writers, to the sweaty inkers of presses, and to the multitude of humans

who wrung words from their hearts, creating waves of thought and emotion, undu-lating through language and years, touching others, who added their words to the flow, creating the stream of messages from those now dead to those of us who are here now, to me, one of the living. I have found dear companions in books—many who have suffered as I have and more, those who have told me their sorrows and secrets, passing them on through time.

. . .

What about this word God, *so repugnant to me when I thought it always meant "God the Father"? I now see it as a word of a thousand meanings. It's a word I don't reject in anger any more. I can accept it in my own way as referring to the unnameable mystery that lies behind visible reality. This vague definition (or should I say nondefinition?) is one that my peculiar family of mind, ego, heart, and other selves can live with. Other people have come up with their own meanings or have chosen to adhere to the gods of their religious traditions, and I wish them well.*

Sometimes I think I might not be as out of step with others in this regard as I once thought. Perhaps even those who believe more or less in the anthropomorphic image of God may use this image because they want something easier to contemplate than the infinite, the eternal, the unknowable. Such abstractions are elusive and emotionally unsatisfying. Stories, myths, images of kings, dragons, and many-headed monsters, appeal to us in ways that abstract concepts cannot.

In a poem by Yeats various animals are overheard talking about God, each in the image of its own kind.

I passed a little further on and heard a peacock say:
Who made the grass and made the worms and made my feathers gay,

He is a monstrous peacock, and He waveth all the night
His languid tail above us, lit with myriad spots of light.
   —W. B. YEATS, "The Indian Upon God"

If it helps the peacock to imagine God as a great bird, or humans to
think of God with a human face, what's the harm in it, even if God is
none of these? Or not one of these, but all of these?

*I've begun to think of all terms and images of the divine as masks behind which the
unknowable hides. I grew up with the fatherly Christian god mask, so it was a handy
target for my anger when Gretchen died. But, though I half believed in God the Father
when this image provided me with someone to blame, I now see all religious images as
fantastic and feel free to take what insight and comfort I can from them.*

*When a bereaved parent tells me it was God's will that her son died, I look past
whatever she might believe about God's purposes and see what we might have in
common—the need to acknowledge a greater power than oneself, and to submit to
that power. "Hallowed be thy name. Thy will be done . . ." Perhaps what some refer
to as God's will is not so different from saying, "The Way It Is," or "Reality," or, as it
is called in the Buddhist mustard seed story, "The Law."*

*I now hear in the beginning of the Twenty-third Psalm a statement of submission to
the reality of human existence. "The Lord is my shepherd; I shall not want." I interpret this as saying, "Reality is my guide (or my law); I shall not want what cannot
be, and what is shall be enough for me." This may not be the interpretation I might
hear from a minister or a rabbi, but it satisfies me to believe that the poetry of the
Old Testament, the words so many people in my culture live by, also speak to me.*

. . .

Howard, one of Gretchen's best friends, comes for a long, tearful visit.
He says Gretchen called him shortly before she died and left a message on

his answering machine, which he saved but hasn't had the heart to listen to yet. When he broke up with Kristen, a close friend of Gretchen's, a couple of years ago, Gretchen said if he waited ten years, she'd marry him. They joked about this, saying, "Only eight years to go, ha, ha!" He tells Howard about his dream of seeing Gretchen on the beach. Howard, a proud young fireman, says he dreams of saving her.

She wasn't just mine, was she? Or our family's. There were others who loved her, and whom she loved.

. . .

In rebuking Job for his impertinence, God asks:

Doth the hawk fly by thy wisdom, and stretch her wings toward the
   south?
Doth the eagle mount up at thy command, and make her nest on high?
Canst thou lift up thy voice to the clouds, that abundance of waters
   may cover thee?
Canst thou send lightnings, that they may go, and say to thee, Here we
   are?
—Job, 39:26–27

Unable to answer such questions, Job concedes that God does not have to give reasons for pain, suffering, or anything that happens in the universe, and Job sees something he hadn't seen before:

I have heard of thee by the hearing of the ear: but now mine eye seeth
   thee.
—Job, 38:34–35

I can imagine myself saying the same thing if I were Job. As I read his story, I feel as though I've "seen" God, too. Not the Old Testament God perhaps, and one more felt than seen, but a force so awesome that it has brought me to my knees and made me perceive its unquestionable majesty.

A new translation of the Book of Job says,

> I have heard of you with my ears;
> > but now my eyes have seen you.
> Therefore I will be quiet,
> > comforted that I am dust.
> > —Job, 42:5, trans. Stephen Mitchell

Job's questioning stops, and his surrender, his comforting surrender, begins.

. . .

Carrying rocks at the end of the day, he notices as he comes up the hill that his wall is almost done. He rakes leaves away from it so he—and others—can see it better. Its rough order of shapes, though less than perfect, satisfies him. The wall is substantial, a heavy, pleasing structure well placed on the earth, but he knows how gravity pulls, animals dig, frost heaves, the earth shudders, and even the best-made walls eventually fall apart.

It will outlast me, though. It will be here along the pine trees after I'm gone, and some man or woman will stand here and think, "I wonder who built this wall, and why. It serves no useful purpose here." Perhaps they will let it stay—though they won't know the desperate urge behind its making—simply because it is beautiful.

• • •

In a dream, Gretchen is cutting away folds of flesh that have grown in my right armpit. She uses scissors, but the cutting isn't painful because the growth is more or less dead flesh anyway.

• • •

The Japanese Zen writer Kenko wrote:

If man were never to fade away like the dews of Adashino, never to vanish like the smoke over Toribeyama, but lingered on forever in the world, how things would lose their power to move us! The most precious thing in life is its uncertainty.

As I grow old, if I am to grow old, I imagine you getting older yourself and watching me as someone watches from a window a person carrying packages on the street below. I hope you will continue to love me in spite of my failings. Though you were a child when you died, I'm sure you had already discovered how hard it is to be human. If you ever want to encourage me as you see me struggling along, please throw open the window and shout.

• • •

Thanksgiving was the last time they were with her. During the five-hour trip to the family gathering, she told them she loved her professors and talked at length about what she had learned that semester. Her enthusiasm lifted his spirits. He had worried that college was only feeding her love of parties. As they drove, he and Mieke and Gretchen had a lively discussion for the first time in months, and he saw what he'd been hoping to

see in her—a growing interest in the world beyond her own life and circle of friends. He had tried to encourage this himself, but his attempts seemed clumsy efforts to convey his own curiosity about things she usually found "boring."

In the photo album is a picture of her smiling in the candlelight as she sits next to her grandmother at Thanksgiving dinner. After dinner Mieke and Gretchen sang some songs. One of them went: "Farther along, we'll know all about it / Farther along, we'll understand why / Cheer up my brothers, live in the sunshine / We'll understand it all by and by."

. . .

Down by the river this morning, I sit on the dark, shaded side looking across the water at sunlit trees, noticing a difference. Not in them, but in me. Months ago their silence disturbed me. I saw them as coldly indifferent to Gretchen's death. They should have been shaking with agony, as I was. Now I see them as possessing a quiet strength, almost a courage. The tall hemlock leaning over the water asks for nothing, makes no judgements about what should or should not be, and unlike me, it has never wished for life to be different than it is.

. . .

A year ago today he went about his usual routines, working, eating, letting the dogs in and out of the house, without any awareness of what was about to happen to Gretchen. She had just returned to college after Thanksgiving with them and was preparing for her exams. He recalls feeling happy that day about the person she was becoming.

He ordered a Christmas present for her from a catalog—a tiny pocket-

knife with a blade, scissors, nail file, toothpick, tweezers, and her name imprinted on it. After she died he couldn't throw it away. He now carries it in his pocket and pulls it out almost daily, her name, GRETCHEN, in silver on black, unexpectedly in his hand along with quarters, dimes, and pennies.

December
· ·

This morning the trees stand in the cold with their dark branches stiff against the sky. And there is the sun, my dear, low and distant through trees, rising with the same promise of warmth as on that morning a year ago when you last woke to its light.

Do you know where the bees have gone to hide from the cold? I don't know exactly where, but not far from here, maybe up the hill in an old tree, they are huddling in a dark hive, flexing their wing muscles, making heat for their queen and keeping the precious honey soft. A few weeks from now, soon after winter solstice, the queen bee will lay her eggs for the next generation of bees. And then, when the earth has tipped back toward the sun, the young will hatch and fly from the hive into the fragrant air of spring.

· · ·

December 2, her "death day."

It hovers between autumn and winter, with an overcast sky and the air cool enough for rain or snow. As they walk, he and Mieke are silent; this is to be a meditative climb. They cross a little brook, pass up through a field

and into tall hemlocks at the base of the mountain. Here a stream, coming from high up, from where they are going, pours through rocks and trees, swirling with the force of its sharp descent. The path they follow quickly becomes steep.

He tries to clear his mind of thoughts—the error in the printing bill, the need to get gas before heading home—by looking at the stones and roots on the trail. The knuckles and sinews of the mountain. There is, he soon notices, something strange here. Every few yards there are gray-brown hairs clinging to the knobs of roots and sharp rocks in the path. After a while he realizes these hairs tell of a deer shot and killed higher up on this mountain, its still-warm body dragged down this trail. He thinks it is not fair to present him on this day with reminders of vibrant life suddenly extinguished. But there they are. He points them out to Mieke, then picks up some hairs and puts them in his pocket.

They cross the stream on unsteady rocks and continue up the trail on the other side. He tries again to clear his mind, to think only of Gretchen, or of nothing. Just walk, one step, then another. Foot over root, now down between rocks, up on the fallen tree, and over. The trail climbs steeply up beside the brook and turns left into a slope of old hemlocks, where they leave the sound of rushing water behind. The air is still, except for their breathing and the sounds of their boots hitting ground. They stop to rest and silently pass the water bottle before moving on. The trail winds higher up the side of the mountain and returns them to the stream. They stand on a boulder looking up at a high, narrow fall of water dropping through light into a rocky pool.

Hours later, above the source of the stream, he crawls up a long, angled surface of stone, his vision blurred by tears. Soon he's on top of the mountain, in the open area of scrub pines and low, wind-bent birches where he

cut his wrist and "buried" her a year ago. He recalls how he needed to exhaust his restless body with the climb, to be high up in the wind and light, as close to the sky as he could come without dying himself. Since then he's imagined her up here, lying under the stars and riding the backs of deer. With its view of hills and horizon all around, this could be the peak in the Dakotas that Black Elk called "the center of the world."

On the windy outcrop of rock, he sits where he sat last year when the pain of her dying was still tearing his heart and he couldn't think what else to do. Below and far away, a small lake curls beside low hills. A voice in him is sobbing, "Oh, it's been hard, so hard." He takes a deep breath and looks out over the hills into the sky. It seems quite possible she is out there somewhere. The wind blows across his face. He breathes it in, slowly, deeply, and the waves of grief gradually subside. In the rhythm of his breathing he hears another voice: "I'm here, my love, I'm here."

Notes

. . . .

Through all the seasons of my grief, a morning walk in the woods or a few minutes beside the river or under the night sky would gently coax me out of self-absorption. Some of my favorite writers on the beauty and mystery of nature are Henry David Thoreau, Aldo Leopold, Annie Dillard, and Lewis Thomas.

I also recommend reading the works of poets, both ancient and modern, whose word-music soothes and heartens.

Further Reading

· ·

Agee, James. *A Death in the Family*. New York: Bantam, 1983.

Becker, Ernest. *The Denial of Death*. New York: The Free Press, 1973.

The Book of Job from the Old Testament of the King James Version of the Holy Bible.

Bowker, John. *The Meanings of Death*. Cambridge: Cambridge University Press, 1991.

Burtt, Edwin A., ed. *The Teachings of the Compassionate Buddha*. New York: New American Library, 1955.

Campbell, Joseph with Bill Moyers. *The Power of Myth*. New York: Doubleday, 1988.

———. *Joseph Campbell and the Power of Myth: With Bill Moyers*. Audio- and videotapes by Mystic Fire Video in association with *Parabola* magazine, 1988.

Evans-Wentz, W. Y., ed. *The Tibetan Book of the Dead*. New York: Oxford University Press, 1960.

Frankl, Viktor E. *Man's Search for Meaning*. Boston: Beacon Press, 1959.

Huxley, Aldous. *The Perennial Philosophy*. New York: Harper & Row, 1970.

Kabat-Zinn, Jon. *Full Catastrophe Living: Using the Wisdom of Your Body and Mind to Face Stress, Pain, and Illness*. New York: Dell Publishing, 1991.

Kübler-Ross, Elisabeth. *On Death and Dying*. New York: Macmillan, 1969.

Kushner, Harold S. *When Bad Things Happen to Good People*. New York: Avon Books, 1983.

Levine, Stephen. *Who Dies?: An Investigation of Conscious Living and Conscious Dying*. New York: Doubleday, 1982.

Lewis, C. S. *A Grief Observed*. New York: Bantam Books, 1980.

Mair, Victor H., trans. *Wandering on the Way: Early Taoist Tales and Parables of Chuang Tzu*. New York: Bantam, 1994.

McLuhan, T. C., comp. *Touch the Earth*. New York: Penguin Books, 1971.

Moffat, Mary Jane, ed. *In the Midst of Winter: Selections from the Literature of Mourning*. New York: Vintage Books, 1982.

Nhat Hanh, Thich. *The Miracle of Mindfulness!: A Manual of Meditation*. Boston: Beacon Press, 1976.

Prabhavananda, Swami and Christopher Isherwood, trans. *Bhagavad Gita: The Song of God*. Hollywood: Vedanta Press, 1944.

Sogyal, Rinpoche. *The Tibetan Book of Living and Dying*. San Francisco: Harper, 1993.

Robinson, James M., ed. *The Nag Hammadi Library in English*. San Francisco: Harper & Row, 1988.

Suzuki, Shunryu. *Zen Mind, Beginner's Mind*. New York: Weatherhill, 1970.

Thoreau, Henry David. *Walden*. New York: Grosset & Dunlap, 1910.

Viorst, Judith. *Necessary Losses*. New York: Simon and Schuster, 1986.

Text Credits

. . . .

This diary would have stayed within the covers of a notebook if it hadn't been for the help and encouragement I received from many wonderful people. First of all is my wife, Mieke, who read with patient and sensitive attention each of my many attempts to deepen and clarify the manuscript. The manuscript was much improved after careful readings by Linda Donn, Nancy Adams Malone, and Violet Skorina. My gratitude also to caring family members and many stalwart friends for their support through this time of anguish.

And to Peter Workman, Shannon Ravenel, and Elisabeth Scharlatt, who believed my story was worth putting into print.

Published by

ALGONQUIN BOOKS OF CHAPEL HILL

Post Office Box 2225

Chapel Hill, North Carolina 27515-2225

a division of

WORKMAN PUBLISHING

708 Broadway

New York, New York 10003

For permission to reprint poems and excerpts in this book, grateful acknowledgment
is made to the holders of copyright, publishers, or representatives named on page 175,
which constitutes an extension of the copyright page.

Library of Congress Cataloging-in-Publication Data
Crider, Tom, 1941–
 Give sorrow words : a father's passage through grief / by Tom Crider.
  p. cm.
 ISBN 1-56512-116-3
  1. Bereavement—Psychological aspects. 2. Grief. 3. Death—Psychological
aspects. 4. Crider, Tom, 1941– . I. Title.
 BF575.G7C75 1996
 155.9'37—dc20   95-42238
                    CIP

10 9 8 7 6 5 4 3 2 1
FIRST EDITION

GIVE SORROW WORDS

A Father's Passage through Grief

TOM CRIDER

ALGONQUIN BOOKS OF CHAPEL HILL 1996

wanted to discuss the matter once more with Hitler. It is not
certain whether he could not get in touch with him for techni-
cal reasons. He may have preferred a personal conversation to
a telephone call or radio contact, giving him greater freedom
to explain his misgivings. There are indications in Weizsäcker's
diary that Ribbentrop particularly wanted to avoid the obli-
gation not to make peace separately, since it would exclude a
separate peace with Britain.[47]

However this may have been, Hitler decided probably on
November 28 and definitely by December 4 to meet the Japanese request. But now the Germans were not satisfied with
the exchange of simple promises with which the Japanese
would have been content. The Germans demanded a formal
agreement based on reciprocity. They apparently thought it
possible that a German-American war could come sooner
than one between Japan and America. When this war came
on December 7, the agreement had not yet become effective,
so once more a decision had to be made. Hitler could have
avoided a declaration of war on formal grounds, particularly
because the advantage he had been seeking, namely, the reduc-
tion of the danger of American intervention in Europe, was
now won in his view. He could also have declined the Japanese request to enter the war against America in the same way
that Japan had declined the German request to enter the war
against Russia. He could even make his earlier request a condition of Germany's meeting the Japanese request.

Instead he decided once more for war. But he did not declare
it immediately. He insisted on concluding what has been called
a no-separate-peace treaty beforehand. He must have attached
great importance to it, for he read and stressed the treaty
prominently in his speech to the Reichstag. We may call this
treaty the price to be paid by Japan for Germany's entering
the war.

Viewed from this perspective and against the background

of his general considerations and the situation in December 1941, Hitler's decision becomes comprehensible. His failure to win a quick victory over Russia amounted to a failure of his concept of war in general. The war that he had envisioned as a series of lightning campaigns (*Blitzfeldzüge*) was now becoming a war of attrition just as the war of 1914–1918 had been. Then Russia had collapsed in the fourth year of the war and had had to accept the Treaty of Brest-Litovsk, with the result that Germany had gained immense lands in the east. Even so, in Hitler's view Germany had lost the war in the end for internal and external reasons, the latter referring to the American intervention, and he had since concentrated on overcoming these factors. The internal reasons had been removed by his racial policy. The external reasons were, as we have seen, Hitler's main concern in 1941.

It is a reasonable assumption that Hitler foresaw in December 1941 a development of the Second World War similar to that of the First: Russia could be defeated and America would intervene. But Germany did not have to lose the war if Japan took part in it. Japan could prevent America from all-out intervention in Europe by diverting that part of the American and British forces which so very narrowly had determined the outcome in 1918. In order to guarantee this sequence of events, Japan had to do more than enter the war. It had to be kept from pulling out before victory had been won in Europe. It had to be kept from concluding an early peace as it had done with other opponents in 1895 and 1905, in each instance in the second year of the war.

The treaty of December 11 to which Hitler attached so much importance, just like the earlier draft agreement of December 5, was to serve that precise purpose. In return for entering the war, Germany received the promise that Japan would not leave it. From Hitler's point of view this was not an unreasonable idea and there is no need to assume irrational motives. The declaration of war against the United States was an adequate step toward winning a war that essentially was and remained a war of conquest against the Soviet Union, in spite of the failure of the campaign of 1941. That war was madness, yet there was method in it.

5

Hitler and the Germans

Only rarely did Hitler and the Germans call each other by their proper names while they were contemporaries and made history together. Hitler usually did not address them as Germans, but as German folk comrades, and when he referred to them, he preferred to use the collective form and spoke of the German people or the German. He would say, for instance, that a German youth must be "as tough as leather and as hard as Krupp steel."[1] Or that "for the German soldier nothing is impossible."[2] The Germans, for their part, almost without exception called him the führer (even though they greeted each other with the phrase "Heil Hitler"), and the prescribed form of address was "my führer." The more intimate appellations applied to many statesmen were not at all commonly used, and it would have been unthinkable for a cheering crowd to shout "Adolf."

This seems to point to a rather impersonal relationship. But regardless of whether Hitler and the Germans loved each other or feared each other, what they thought of each other and, above all, how the one could emerge from the other are questions that can find their answers in a historical analysis.

Hitler always kept in mind what he had written in his book *Mein Kampf:* "The basic foundation for establishing authority is always popularity."[3] He immediately qualified that sentence and saw "in power . . . in force" the other principal basis of all authority.[4] Nevertheless, no saying of his has been handed down to posterity that even remotely resembles the words engraved on Napoleon's tomb: "May my ashes rest on the banks of the Seine near the people whom I loved so dearly." That Hitler loved the Germans is a dubious proposition; indeed he did not even want to be buried on the Spree, but in Linz on the Danube.[5]

Just as Alexander the Great was not a Greek, Napoleon not a Frenchman, and Stalin not a Russian, so Hitler came from the outside, at the least from outside the boundaries of the German national state created by Bismarck, and he spoke of the Germans in a distant manner, as if he didn't really belong to them. "Here too I am as cold as ice," he remarked during the war. "If the German people are not prepared to do battle for their self-preservation, then fine, let them perish!"[6] Even in public speeches he made these comments, as on December 18, 1940, to a group of officer candidates: "This nation will fade away" if it fails to assert its claim to existence.[7] Then "it should vanish," he declared to a foreign statesman on November 27, 1941.[8] Moreover he would "not shed a tear for it."[9] To be sure he wanted to make Germany great, greater than it had ever been in history. But he was less concerned with Germans as individuals—with their well-being and their fortunes— than with German blood, which he shed coldheartedly in order to expand the nation.

The Germans, by contrast, loved him rather than feared him. Even though we must verify the general truth of this statement and will indeed do so, this much is indisputable: Under Hitler the Germans never doubted, despaired, or revolted as they might have under a tyrant. Forces from abroad had to take him away from them, and only then was the spell that had bound them to each other for over twelve years broken, and it was broken immediately. Perhaps nothing characterizes the relationship of the Germans to Hitler so aptly as a phrase that was making the rounds in those days and went like this: "If only the führer knew about that!" Being applicable and indeed applied to the petty nuisances of daily life as well as to the great horrors of the regime, it absolved the führer (who after all could not concern himself with everything) of responsibility for specific events and also elevated him to the ranks of the unimpeachable.

One example can serve as evidence. When the mentally ill were being put to death by the tens of thousands at the beginning of the war, the district leader of a Nazi women's organization (certainly no enemy of the regime) wrote to the wife of the chief justice of the Nazi party on November 25, 1940: "People are still clinging to the hope that the führer knows nothing about these things, that he can't possibly know, otherwise he would stop them." And again, "The matter must be brought to the attention of the führer before it is too late and there must be a way for the voice of the German people to reach the ear of its führer."[10] A twofold deception! Naturally, Hitler knew what was to be brought to his attention. After all, it issued from his mouth and figured as his command. But far more important, the horrified reaction of the people not only reached him; he even listened to it, rescinded the order, and ended the operation.

In general, the relationship of the Germans to Hitler rested on deception, conscious deception on his part and self-deception on their part. He concealed his plans from them, although he knew exactly what he wanted, and they failed to recognize in him a causal agent even when he translated his intentions into action. They rewarded his deception with trust and, even under the worst circumstances, did not believe that they were being deceived but rather that he was being deceived.

In the beginning he had been open about his intentions. During the 1920s he repeatedly stated and wrote that a new war had to be waged in order to secure living space (*Lebensraum*) for Germany, and he had precisely articulated the domestic and foreign policy measures necessary to prepare the way. He had also repeatedly stated and written that the Jews had to be done away with, and he had noted that such a process was and would continue to be "a bloody one."[11] He had even mentioned poison gas in that context.[12] All this appeared in a book that had a distribution of hundreds of thousands of copies before 1933.

But it is also beyond doubt that the Germans did not grant him power in order to implement that program. Beginning with the memorable Reichstag elections of September 1930, when for the first time so many Germans voted for him that the chancellorship came within reach, Hitler deceived the Germans and the world. He had to remain silent about his war plans, if only to avoid alerting his adversaries. This, in turn, does not imply that the Germans themselves remained completely in the dark. That pluralistic party democracy was to be abolished and replaced by a rigid one-man rule was something the Germans well knew, and those who voted for Hitler favored that plan. That Hitler stood as an enemy to the Jews was something they also knew, put up with, or even condoned.

Hitler's rise to power may be controversial, but the numbers of Germans who voted for him is, by contrast, easy to determine. About every third German who went to the ballot box gave Hitler a vote at least once. One third—no more, no less. Even when he was in power, during the March elections of 1933 (which were no longer free yet still allowed alternatives), far more than half of all Germans did not vote for Hitler. How they viewed him after that can hardly be captured by statistics. From time to time public referendums were held, but there was nothing to vote for between the registers of "yes" and "no." Even the officially announced election results, which very early recorded up to one-quarter "no" votes in some places, are unreliable, for falsification of election results is clearly documented in many cases.

But even when a nation is no longer polled, can no longer vote, and has lost the right to express opinions freely, public opinion still exists and can, within limits, be investigated. Even a dictator—especially a dictator—is in his own interest eager to know what his subjects and above all his enemies among those subjects think of him. Under Hitler, a kind of comprehensive polling of public opinion arose from the police surveillance and control of so-called ideological enemies and was incorporated into an extensive set of reports. These reports, which were collected and evaluated by several agencies but with especial zeal by the SD, the security department of the party, tell us more about public moods than about opinions. For the regime wanted above all to know whether morale was good or bad. It was not disposed to heeding the opinions of the populace; it intended to rule, and for that it needed popularity, as Hitler himself had stated.

It goes without saying that the utmost care must be used in drawing conclusions from reports on morale. Not that things were glossed over in the reports; that would have made them worthless. In the end they so dismayed the leadership that Bormann prohibited them in the summer of 1944.[13] But there is a certain arbitrariness inherent in them. Statistical evidence of any precision is missing; reports often pertain only to certain parts of the Reich, and the spies did not, of course, find out what people were afraid to say. The result is an impression, not a definitive conclusion; a portrait of moods, not of opinions.

Generally speaking, one can say that morale fluctuated in a peculiar way. It was lowered principally by the economic cares of daily life, but then bolstered by foreign policy successes and later by military victories. Perhaps these responses were all too human, but still it seems to have been characteristic of this regime that it was more likely to win approval from the populace by diverting its attention from misery than by actually ameliorating conditions. Diversions of an intoxicating kind (presented in exactly that fashion) were abundantly available. Rarely has a generation been exposed to so many sensational new things in so few years.

The "Olympics, Spain, and the result of the London talks," states a report of August 1936, "are having a salutary effect on the morale of the populace and are helping us to smooth over all sorts of unpleasant things."[14] In the following year, when relatively little happened, morale evidently reached a low point. "A sense of discontent among the people is stronger than ever," stated a report of May 1937. "The National Socialist government is being held responsible for the shortage of raw materials."[15] The annexation of Austria then sparked "jubilation and joy." During the Sudeten crisis, "fear of war" reigned supreme, and after Munich there was once again "an elated mood."[16]

It is well know that the outbreak of war was greeted with little enthusiasm and with great apprehension. Nonetheless, a report on the events of June 1940 states that the victory in the west brought about "a degree of solidarity never hitherto achieved among the entire German people."[17] After this high point, things went slowly downhill again. The uncertainty of the course of the war, the increasing food shortages, and the air raids on German cities prompted a pessimistic mood that set in during the summer of 1942 and, after the battle of Stalingrad, shaded into doubt and resignation and finally into a still hopeful fatalism. The daily struggle for existence and survival displaced politics and dominated all other considerations. It should be noted, however, that the assassination attempt of July 20, 1944, was not only, with few exceptions, "unanimously" condemned but even contributed to a strengthening of the "bond to the führer."[18]

This, then, is in general the other predominant view, and with that we return to the fundamental issue: Whatever criticism may have been aired, Hitler was almost always spared it. Nearly every one of his speeches raised the general morale. People were disappointed if those speeches were not carried by the radio. They felt the need, as was reported during the war, "to hear, once again, the voice of the führer."[19] They wanted to see him too. A report of November 1940 stated, "we have almost reached the point where a newsreel without pictures of the führer is considered inferior. People always seem to want to see what the führer looks like, whether he appears serious or is laughing."[20] Similar sentiments were expressed even more emphatically in April 1943, when pictures of the führer had become rare. "A picture of the führer from which one could determine that, contrary to rumor, his hair had not turned completely white has a more positive effect on the mood of the people than a whole raft of battle slogans."[21]

Neither admiration, nor respect, nor even fear seems to characterize perfectly the attitude of the Germans toward Hitler. What they felt for him, especially during the war years, was an almost childlike devotion to a beloved father, a devotion that could easily dissolve into compassion. According to reports on morale, the general reaction to Rudolf Hess's flight to England was a "deeply felt sympathy . . . for the heavy blow that had struck the führer, 'who is not spared the cruel strokes of fate'."[22] Up to the very end, this reaction recurred whenever signs of defeat, disloyalty, or betrayal appeared— not least on July 20. "The führer is really spared nothing" was a phrase that functioned as a code word, much like the phrase "If only the führer knew about that!"

These observations do not correspond to what became the prevailing opinion after 1945, and the quotations cited above may therefore elicit indignant protest, especially among those who lived through those times. It is true that there was always dissent and even resistance: The reports on morale offer clear evidence of that. But it is also true, unfortunately, that this resistance (honorable and courageous though it was) receives an emphasis that may well be morally justified but that somewhat stretches the actual historical facts. When a German schoolbook dealt with National Socialism a few years ago under the rubric "Persecution and Resistance," that may well have been pedagogically salutary, but it did not represent the truth. On the other hand, this pessimistic view cannot and should not lead to a blanket moral condemnation of the Germans living at that time, for they were as a whole no worse and no better than the generations before and after them. But they were subjected to ordeals and to temptations that others escaped.

If one proceeds on the assumption that the Germans did not suddenly become criminals, then unusual circumstances must have led them to support the criminal that Hitler undoubtedly was. The nature of these circumstances is a significant question if we intend to go beyond superficial description to a historical analysis of the relationship of the German people to Hitler.

At the time of Hitler's rule, the vast majority of the German people were denied the kind of information that ordinarily builds the foundation of public opinion. Nothing shows this more clearly than the countless and often quite extravagant rumors that made the rounds in those days and were dutifully recorded in the reports on morale. Not infrequently those rumors had been put into circulation by Goebbels himself. The free expression of diverse opinions was replaced by a form of propaganda that twisted everything. Many fell victim to that propaganda out of sheer ignorance; those who voiced criticism publicly were persecuted by the police.

It must once again be emphasized that Hitler's rule over the

Germans did not in any way rest solely or even predominantly on the use of terror. That aspect of the regime has been too heavily stressed since 1945, for understandable reasons. Not even the crimes of the time can be explained in this way. Orders of a criminal nature were, as a rule, carried out not because of the threat of coercion, and rarely because people derived some kind of pleasure from committing a crime, but because of obedience, out of blindness, or for the sake of some advantage. Not one case is known in which a person's life was in danger or in which a person suffered serious consequences by refusing to participate in a crime, such as the murder of unarmed people. By the same token, membership in the Nazi party was a distinction that promised advantages and was thus not forced upon anyone, especially not on an unreliable person (a fact that is usually misunderstood or not mentioned these days); quite to the contrary, many people had their membership taken away from them. The party could in fact easily have had more members in the beginning than it actually had. Thus, the attitudes of the Germans under Hitler and to Hitler cannot be explained away by terror (except in the case of the persecuted).

Much more complicated and (for good reason) more controversial is the question concerning the circumstances that made Hitler's rule over the Germans possible. It would be easy to fill a book with nothing other than a list of the various explanations that have been proposed to date. The Versailles treaty and the Great Depression figure most prominently among them, but here too valid objections and refutations can be made. The Weimar Republic had almost succeeded in overcoming the financial impositions occasioned by the war before it collapsed, and the Great Depression hit the United States harder than it hit Germany, yet there it did not undermine democratic institutions. For a time a more literary approach to German history was very popular. Historians combed the writings of Bismarck and Frederick the Great and went back to Luther and even Arminius in their search for authoritarian predispositions in the German people, and both the romantic period and the Wilhelminian era yielded various interesting points.

Hard upon this analysis of intellectual currents came social and economic analysis. Capitalism, heavy industry, and the middle class were held responsible, and in recent years so-called theories of fascism (which have become ever more complicated) are held in high esteem. Yet at the same time there are also serious historians who, for well-founded reasons, attribute the rise of Hitler to the failings of individual figures. This business becomes completely hopeless when attempts are made to explain the origins of National Socialism through polemical allusions to one's own political or ideological adversaries. Such biased efforts are not only unscholarly but in most cases thoroughly contemptible.

The confusing array of serious explanations results not least from the fact that there is still no consensus on what exactly is to be explained; in other words, How should Hitler's rule be defined? For a long time, it had been viewed as a totalitarian or authoritarian dictatorship of great internal cohesiveness. But recently the many contradictory forces in it have received emphasis, for example, the so-called polycratic structures under which Hitler, in the final analysis, appears as a "weak dictator," a person driven by events rather than shaping them. Let us now review and reconsider the points discussed in earlier chapters.

A good description is, without doubt, the precondition for a good explanation. It is clearly insufficient simply to point to certain facts such as the Versailles treaty or the Great Depression, or even to intellectual currents. For there is no rational reason why such things should have led to Hitler's seizure of power and not, say, to a military dictatorship, a revolution, or to some altogether different phenomenon. The process deserves more careful investigation.

My explanation begins with the assumption that the regime that came to power in Germany in 1933 differed strikingly from the preceeding one and from earlier forms of government because it was a monocracy. For now we will take that to mean that all vital political decisions were made by one person, in this case Hitler. Yet this definition of the term is not really adequate. Military dictatorships are, in my view, not true monocracies, for the military dictator rules in conjunction with the military, and his power remains circumscribed by the extent to which the military is willing to support him. By the same token, monarchies, despite the linguistic contradiction, are also not necessarily monocracies of the kind meant here, especially in cases where the monarch depends on the nobility, derives his power from it, and is thereby also held in check by it.

Our monocrat, if I may put it in this way, rules in a vacuum as little as anyone else does. He too needs support. He does not receive it from one group alone but from several, which —and this is the decisive face—have entirely differing and even opposing interests, and also have differing and even opposing expectations about his rule. His power rests on being able to play these groups against each other. Every ruler does this to a certain degree while still remaining dependent on the factions supporting him. But for an autocrat, the support of different and opposing groups constitutes the actual source of his power.

These types of monocracies, which were probably described for the first time by Karl Marx and Friedrich Engels, may be rare in history, but they do occur. Examples in modern history are the absolute monarchies that played the various estates against each other, and the reigns of Napoleon I and Napoleon III, who maneuvered their way between the upper and lower bourgeoisie, or between the bourgeoisie and the workers. The special conditions under which such autocracies emerged have been convincingly analyzed in some cases, and it can be useful to draw upon such analyses as analogies for explaining Hitler's rise to power, assuming, of course, that he was actually a monocrat. Description and analysis thus go hand in hand.

As we have seen, Hitler came to power as the head of a coalition government. If the Nazi party had had a majority in the Reichstag, he would to a certain extent have been dependent on it. The support he received from his own following and from the Conservative party (two groups with wholly different interests) provided the preliminary basis for his monocracy. The creation of the government had not been guided by parliamentary procedure, if only because the two coalition partners together did not constitute a majority in the Reichstag. Moreover, this had been preceded by an intrigue in which the industrialist Wilhelm Keppler, then Hitler's economic adviser, had persuaded the banker Kurt von Schröder to arrange a conference between Hitler and Franz von Papen in Schröder's house in Cologne. The meeting took place on January 4, 1933, and the result was that Papen induced President Hindenburg to name Hitler chancellor of a coalition cabinet. We saw in chapter 1 that this story in reality is much more complicated than our brief summary. It passes over the motives of those participating in the intrigue, leaves open the question of whether they acted under instruction from specific groups, and says nothing about negotiations with other parties. Moreover, the intrigue of January 4 was of special importance, but it was not the only one of importance in those agitated weeks.

Again, we can briefly summarize what we have learned. Hitler did not come to power as the authorized representative of a specific group, but because of the support of several differing groups and persons who expected different things from the new chancellor. In that respect, his accession resembled a transfer of power rather than a seizure of power. The seizure of power and the establishment of monocracy took place when Hitler played the different groups supporting him against each other, as well as the groups that opposed him or stood on the sidelines. It was then that he revealed the distinctive nature of his regime. Once again, some briefly sketched examples must suffice.

Hitler flattered the conservatives by opening the new Reichstag in Potsdam and even led them to hope that he would restore the monarchy. At the same time, he promised work and bread to his followers, spoke of a "national revolution," yet shied away from tampering with property arrangements, although he allowed his private army, the SA, a free hand for the first anti-Jewish pogrom. He promised armament contracts to big business, new tasks to the army, protection to civil servants—in short, everything to everybody. On May 1, 1933, he gave the working classes the Labor Day holiday they had demanded in vain for decades; the next day he abolished the trade unions. In July he concluded a concordat with the Vatican and thereby put an end to the political power of the Center party. In September he bestowed on the farmers the Hereditary Estate Act, which guaranteed the unencumbered intergenerational transfer of small farms. On June 30, 1934, he sacrificed his party army, the SA, and thereby bound the regular army to him, but not without simultaneously strengthening his own police force, which then persecuted his remaining opponents.

Clearly Hitler was not the representative of any single group or class but of many groups at the same time. He served or threatened them all, giving something here and taking something there, always steering a middle course, even between the mutually hostile dental surgeons and dentists. He had no other choice if he wanted to stay in power, for no group was so powerful that he could base his power on it alone. His only hope was that the various factions would cripple each other.

Monocrats come to power through a stalemate, and this, as we have seen, is the fundamental fact, if not the decisive fact, about the Weimar Republic.

The stalemate appears on a superficial level in the contrast between the republicans and the supporters of the old regime. In parliamentary terms, the Weimar coalition, that is, the Social Democrats, the Democrats, and the Centrists, stood against a massive opposition force consisting of Conservatives and many former National Liberals, who either flatly rejected the new constitution or accepted it only grudgingly as an unfortunate fact of life. But is is only through the social structure that the contrast can be fully understood. On the one hand, there were those groups or classes that had served as the backbone of the old authoritarian state—those in large landed property and in business, the more prosperous bourgeoisie, the army, and the civil service. On the other hand there were those who had been excluded from the state and who had repeatedly been attacked as enemies of the state, that is, the working class and petit-bourgeois classes, which were constantly growing in the wake of industrialization.

In the upheaval surrounding the defeat of 1918, the former ruling class moved temporarily into the political opposition without losing its social and economic power. For property relations, the general economic order and even the state apparatus changed very little, if at all. That led to the unequal, or to be more accurate the equal, battle that characterized the political controversies in the Weimar Republic and increasingly assumed the character of a stalemate. One element in German society was no longer strong enough to control the government and the other element was not yet strong enough, indeed the less so since a third faction comprising the Communists and later the National Socialists proved itself incapable of forming a coalition either among themselves or, until 1933, with one of the other two factions.

This situation did not result simply from the lost war or

even the Versailles treaty. The main cause of the stalemate was a shift in the German social structure created primarily by the rise of the working class, whose growth had become politically manifest through the steady growth of the Socialists, which had furnished the strongest Reichstag delegation as early as 1912. The origins of this shift went back to the nineteenth century, long before the First World War led to the major problem of the inner structure of German society.

This problem suddenly erupted after the military collapse and led, with even greater bitterness, to the conflict that created the stalemate. That stalemate, in turn, found its most conspicuous expression in the breakup of the coalition of March 1930. Thereafter, no majority government whatever was formed, although that would have been perfectly possible given the distribution of power in the Reichstag. The majority were simply incapable of building a consensus, and the Republic thereby became parliamentarily ungovernable. Although we now know that the coalition government could have held out through the worst period of the Great Depression, the Reichstag was prematurely dissolved, and in the September elections of 1930 Hitler achieved his first great breakthrough. The numbers of his voters rose from 800,000 to 6.4 million, and those of his parliamentary representatives from 12 to 107. Hitler owed his victory to the inability of the Reichstag majority to build a consensus. This lack of consensus may have been triggered by problems related to the Great Depression, but it reflected a more fundamental failure of German society to reach a consensus.

Despite his victories, Hitler was by no means in power yet. He received more than twice as many votes in the Reichstag elections of July 1932 as he did in 1930, namely, 37.3 percent, but in the elections of November 1932, his percentage sank to 33.1 percent. Only after this defeat, in which two million voters deserted him or failed to return to the polls, did power come into his hands. He did not seize it, as he always maintained and as many still hold today. Neither a parliamentary majority nor revolutionary force brought him to power. Power was transferred to him through a confusing play of forces. There was the formal designation by the Reich president, the coalition with the German Nationalists, and above all the negotiations between public and private individuals. These negotiations and the intrigue behind them could only succeed because the parliamentary system was no longer functioning, primarily because the constitutional parties had abdicated. The political decision-making process was thereby displaced to the realm of extraparliamentary affairs; the effect of that displacement was to bestow on a wide array of forces a freedom and influence that had not been foreseen in the constitution.

This was not a political development that saw the light of day only in the last phase of the Weimar Republic. Since neither of the two leading factions of German society dominated the government, a development took place that can be described as the growing autonomy of the state apparatus. Left without clear political directives, the army, the bureaucracy, and the judiciary for a long time had been acquiring power of their own that expressed itself in actions of unprecedented arbitrariness. In the resulting power vacuum, officials bound to accept direction freed themselves from control.

The fundamental state of the Republic bestowed, indeed imposed, growing influence on generals and high officials as well as on individual politicians and business leaders. Certainly they all had their own interests, as everyone does. But one can also assume that they worried about a state that no longer functioned properly. There was one fear that united all the propertied classes, regardless of their differences of opinion in other matters, and that was their fear of a social revolution, of communism. The Communist party grew nonetheless. In the Reichstag elections of May 1928 it received 10.6 percent of the vote; in September 1930 13.1 percent; in July

1932 14.3 percent; in November 1932 16.9 percent. Its electoral share, unlike that of the Nazi party, did not decrease, and it preached expropriation and promised sovietization. Hitler, on the other hand, gave reassuring promises and openly courted the industrialists. Whatever else one might have thought of him, he was certainly a passionate anticommunist. Moreover, he had at his disposal millions of largely poverty-stricken (and therefore dangerous) followers and possessed such a charismatic appeal for them that he seemed in a position to make them serve the state. It was true that he spoke without much restraint and that he intended to abolish the constitution. But had not this very constitution, an exceedingly unpopular one at that, led to the present dilemma? And was it not possible to control the risk of transferring power to him by taking him in, binding him to a coalition, fencing him in, and taming him?

This was the train of thought of the political powers in the winter of 1932-1933. However briefly the process has been described here, it nevertheless offers an explanation for Hitler's rise to power. Unable to exercise power in their own right, the property holders of Germany, led by industrialists such as Keppler, bankers such as Schröder, and conservative politicians such as Papen, secured political power for a charismatic hero of the masses in the hope that he would at least protect their economic power and ward off a social revolution. To put it concisely, this constituted a pact with the devil: political power for economic stability. One was sacrificed to secure the other. And this plan did not, after all, fail completely, even though catastrophes of unimaginable extent followed and in the end buried the state.

Hitler could rule as he wanted so long as he did not seriously antagonize any of the differing and opposing factions that had helped him rise to power, neither his indigent followers nor his propertied stirrup holders, nor any of the other great social forces (such as the churches) whose institutions he was not in a position to destroy. This was the hallmark of his monocracy, its strength as well as its weakness, and Hitler fully understood his position. He was always haunted by the fear of being pushed off the throne.

There is much to be said for the view that Hitler, like the two Napoleons, turned to foreign adventures in order to preserve his political power. The way in which he ran state finances essentially allowed only a choice between bankruptcy or war. On the other hand, his foreign policy was not improvised, but followed a rigid plan that Hitler had designed long before coming to power and had incorporated into his world view. This plan, furthermore, was not wholly incongruent with general developments and its realization was therefore ensured. Late imperialistic territorial conquest was presaged in the development of Germany, just as it was in the development of Japan and Italy. All three states had entered world politics at the same time, around 1870, met disappointment in the result of World War I, and allied themselves subsequently. Thus Hitler, notwithstanding his own great personal responsibility in shaping events, was no more than the executer of a longstanding tendency.

With the accession of Hitler, however, German society had deprived itself of the opportunity to determine, according to its own interests, whether and how the path inherent in its development was to be taken. There were attempts, above all through military resistance, to prevent Hitler from taking the path to war or at least to complete defeat. Nevertheless, neither the military nor any other group that had made Hitler's accession possible was strong enough to win back its power of co-determination once it had abdicated it. Hitler led them all, up to the bitter end, to the destruction of their state.

The most horrifying thing is also the most difficult to explain: the murder of the Jews and of the often forgotten gypsies. Here too Hitler's personal responsibility was great.

Certainly, there are convincing answers to the question why minorities are persecuted. During a crisis, the majority often sees in them the guilt that it cannot recognize in itself or in the circumstances. But this wasn't even, in the final analysis, a gigantic pogrom. The vast bureaucratic process of a cold-bloodedly organized and mechanized mass murder—one without historical precedent—simply cannot be attributed to the kind of atmosphere that led to pogroms, much as that might explain what happened. The rational power of language becomes paralyzed in the face of that event.

Our historical analysis of Hitler and the Germans may perhaps sound more rational than the subject would warrant. Even the sober historian who becomes absorbed in the attempt to understand the past knows that there are more things in heaven and earth than are dreamt of in his philosophy. He also knows that he can count on more applause if he tags the guilty with some weighty value judgments. It is easy enough to name crooks and criminals; they are, moreover, palpable and especially visible after the fact. Yet they have also always existed and will continue to exist. The task of scholarship is therefore to try to explain why they sometimes exist on the fringes of society, and sometimes stand at its very center.

The Germans have been liberated from Hitler, yet they will never be free of him. He himself will never return, and even the danger of another monocracy like his is remote in view of current social developments. That quite peculiar constellation of circumstances that made his rule possible cannot, in my view, recur within the foreseeable future. What other dangers threaten us is a question that cannot be addressed in this context. But it is important to note that even the dead Hitler will always remain with the Germans, with the survivors, with their descendants, and even with the unborn. He will be with them, not as he was with his contemporaries, but as an eternal monument to what is humanly possible.

Notes

CHAPTER I

Bibliographical Note
The preceding essay represents a continuation of three earlier articles. Although partly out of date, these articles deserve mention because they cover issues that I cannot address again here. The first describes above all what my interpretation owes to the path-breaking writings of Karl Marx and Friedrich Engels.

Jäckel, Eberhard. "Wie kam Hitler an die Macht?" In Karl Dietrich Erdmann and Hagen Schulze (eds.), *Selbstpreisgabe einer Demokratie*. Düsseldorf, 1980.

———. "Hitler und die Deutschen." In *Hitlers Weltanschauung. Erweiterte und überarbeitete Neuausgabe.* Stuttgart, 1981.

———. "Der Machtantritt Hitlers—Versuch einer geschichtlichen Erklärung." In Volker Rittberger (ed.), *1933: Wie die Republik der Diktatur erlag.* Stuttgart, 1983.

The following is an alphabetical list of the most important studies on which I have drawn.

Bracher, Karl Dietrich. *Die Auflösung der Weimarer Republik.* 1955. Königstein, 1978.

———. *Die nationalsozialistische Machtergreifung.* Cologne, 1960.

Dorpalen, Andreas. *Hindenburg in der Geschichte der Weimarer Republik.* Berlin, 1966.

Eschenburg, Theodor. *Die improvisierte Demokratie.* Munich, 1963.

Hamilton, Richard F. *Who Voted for Hitler?* Princeton, N.J., 1982.

Hubatsch, Walter (ed.). *Hindenburg und der Staat.* Göttingen, 1966.

Huber, Ernst Rudolf. *Deutsche Verfassungsgeschichte seit 1789.* Vol. 6, *Die Weimarer Reichsverfassung.* Stuttgart, 1981.

Kershaw, Ian. *Der Hitler-Mythos.* Stuttgart, 1980.

Kuhn, Axel. "Die Unterredung zwischen Hitler und Papen im Hause des Barons von Schröder. *Geschichte in Wissenschaft und Unterricht 24* (1973): 709ff.

Merkl, Peter H. *Political Violence under the Swastika: 581 Early Nazis.* Princeton, N.J., 1975.

Milatz, Alfred. *Wähler und Wahlen in der Weimarer Republik.* Bonn, 1965.

Neebe, Reinhard. *Großindustrie, Staat und NSDAP 1930–1933.* Göttingen, 1981.

Passchier, Nico. "The Electoral Geography of the Nazi Landslide." In Stein Ugelvik Larsen et al. (eds.) *Who Were the Fascists*. Bergen, 1980.

Schulze, Hagen. *Weimar: Deutschland 1917–1933*. Berlin, 1982.

Stachura, Peter D. (ed.). *The Shaping of the Nazi State*. London, 1978.

Turner, Henry Ashby, Jr. *Faschismus und Kapitalismus in Deutschland: Studien zum Verhältnis zwischen Nationalsozialismus und Wirtschaft*. Göttingen, 1972.

———. "Das Verhältnis des Großunternehmertums zur NSDAP." In Hans Mommsen et al. (ed.). *Industrielles System und politische Entwicklung in der Weimarer Republik*. Düsseldorf, 1974.

———. "Großunternehmertum und Nationalsozialismus 1930–1933." *Historische Zeitschrift* 221 (1975): 18ff.

———. "Hitlers Einstellung zu Wirtschaft und Gesellschaft vor 1933." *Geschichte und Gesellschaft* 2 (1976): 89ff.

Vogelsang, Thilo. *Reichswehr, Staat und NSDAP.* Stuttgart, 1962.

Weber, Hermann (ed.). *Die Generallinie: Rundschreiben des Zentralkomitees der KPD an die Bezirke 1929–1933*. Düsseldorf, 1981.

Weßling, Wolfgang. "Hindenburg, Neudeck und die deutsche Wirtschaft." *Vierteljahrsschrift für Sozial- und Wirtschaftsgeschichte* 64 (1977): 41ff.

Wheeler-Bennett, John W. *Der hölzerne Titan: Paul von Hindenburg*. Tübingen, 1969.

1. The most recent and detailed explication of the constitutional aspects is by Ernst Rudolf Huber in *Deutsche Verfassungsgeschichte seit 1789*, vol. 6, *Die Weimarer Reichsverfassung* (Stuttgart: Kohlhammer, 1981). The relevant documents are published in his *Dokumente zur deutschen Verfassungsgeschichte*, vol. 3, *Dokumente der Novemberrevolution und der Weimarer Republik 1918–1933* (Stuttgart: Kohlhammer, 1966).

2. Andreas Dorpalen. *Hindenburg and the Weimar Republic* (Princeton, N.J., 1964). I have used the German translation: *Hindenburg in der Geschichte der Weimarer Republik*, trans. Charlotte Dixon and Margareta von Eymern (Berlin: Leber, 1966), p. 409.

3. See Helga Timm, *Die deutsche Sozialpolitik und der Bruch der grossen Koalition im März 1930* (1952; Reprint Düsseldorf: Droste, 1982).

4. See the important works by Henry Ashby Turner, Jr., listed in the Bibliographical Note.

CHAPTER 2

1. Eberhard Jäckel, *Hitlers Weltanschauung*, enlarged and revised ed., (Stuttgart: Deutsche Verlags-Anstalt, 1981). An English translation was published under the title *Hitler's Weltanschauung* (Middletown, Conn.:

Wesleyan University Press, 1972) and reprinted as *Hitler's World View* (Cambridge, Mass.: Harvard University Press, 1981). It should be noted that the two English books are identical and based upon the first German edition. The second German edition made use of new material published in Eberhard Jäckel and Axel Kuhn (eds.), *Hitler: Sämtliche Aufzeichnungen 1905-1924* (Stuttgart: Deutsche Verlags-Anstalt, 1980).

2. See Wolfgang Wippermann, *Die Bonapartismustheorie von Marx und Engels* (Stuttgart: Klett-Cotta, 1983).

3. A good selection of materials on this subject may be found in Gerhard Hirschfeld et al. (eds.)., *Der "Führerstaat": Mythos and Realität* (Stuttgart: Klett-Cotta, 1981); see particularly the essays by Tim Mason and Hans Mommsen.

4. Ernst Rudolf Huber, *Verfassungsrecht des Grossdeutschen Reiches* (Hamburg, 1939), p. 160.

5. Hans Mommsen, "Nationalsozialismus," in C. D. Kernig (ed.), *Sowjetsystem und Demokratische Gesellschaft*, vol. 4 (Freiburg: Herder, 1971), p. 702.

6. See Harold C. Deutsch, *Hitler and His Generals: The Hidden Crisis, January–June 1938* (Minneapolis: University of Minnesota Press, 1974).

7. See Klaus-Jürgen Müller, *General Ludwig Beck* (Boppard: Boldt, 1980).

8. Marlis G. Steinert, *Hitlers Krieg und die Deutschen* (Düsseldorf: Econ, 1970), p. 156.

9. Generaloberst Halder, *Kriegstagebuch*, vol. 2 (Stuttgart: Kohlhammer, 1963). p. 49.

10. Hans-Adolf Jacobsen, "Kommissarbefehl und Massenexekutionen sowjetischer Kriegsgefangener," in Hans Buchheim et al. (eds.), *Anatomie des SS-Staates*, vol. 2 (Olten: Walter, 1965).

11. Nuremberg Document L-221, *Der Prozess gegen die Hauptkriegsverbrecher vor dem Internationalen Militärgerichtshof*, vol. 38 (Nuremberg, 1949), p. 88 (hereafter cited as IMT).

12. Notes by General Liebmann, published in *Vierteljahrshefte für Zeitgeschichte* 2 (1954): 435.

13. Nuremberg Document PS-386, *IMT*, vol. 25, pp. 402ff.

14. Adolf Hitler, *Mein Kampf*, vol. 2 (Munich: Eher, 1927; reprint 1930), p. 579.

15. See Bernd Wegner, *Hitlers Politische Soldaten: Die Waffen-SS 1933–1945* (Paderborn: Schöningh, 1982).

16. Helmut Heiber (ed.), *Hitlers Lagebesprechungen* (Stuttgart: Deutsche Verlags-Anstalt, 1962), pp. 63ff.

17. Ernest Fraenkel, *The Dual State* (New York: Oxford University Press, 1940).

18. Winston S. Churchill, *The Second World War*, vol. 1 (London: Cassell, 1948), p. ix.

CHAPTER 3

1. The two principal comprehensive works still are Gerald Reitlinger, *The Final Solution* (London: Valentine, 1953), and Raul Hilberg, *The Destruction of the European Jews* (Chicago: Quadrangle, 1961).

2. Christopher R. Browning, "The Decision concerning the Final Solution" (unpublished lecture, Paris, 1982).

3. Martin Broszat, "Hitler und die Genesis der 'Endlösung'," *Vierteljahrshefte für Zeitgeschichte* 25 (1977): 739–775. See Christopher R. Browning's reply, "Zur Genesis der 'Endlösung'," ibid. 29 (1981): 97–109. An English translation of Broszat's article is available in *Yad Vashem Studies* (1979), Vol. 13, pp. 61–98. The most recent functionalist interpretation is Hans Mommsen, "Die Realisierung des Utopischen: Die 'Endlösung der Judenfrage' im 'Dritten Reich'" *Geschichte und Gesellschaft* 9 (1983): 381–420.

4. For more details see my book *Hitlers Weltanschauung*. (Stuttgart: Deutsche Verlags-Anstalt, 1981).

5. Eberhard Jäckel and Axel Kuhn (eds.), *Hitler: Sämtliche Aufzeichnungen 1905–1924* (Stuttgart: Deutsche Verlags-Anstalt, 1980), pp. 88-90.

6. Adolf Hitler, *Mein Kampf*, vol. 2 (Munich: Eher, 1927; reprint, 1930), p. 738.

7. Ibid., p. 772.

8. Jäckel and Kuhn, *Hitler*, p. 280.

9. Gerhard L. Weinberg (ed.), *Hitlers Zweites Buch* (Stuttgart: Deutsche Verlags-Anstalt, 1961); English translation: *Hitler's Secret Book* (New York: Grove Press, 1964).

10. *Akten zur deutschen auswärtigen Politik 1918–1945, Serie D: 1937–1941*, vol. 12, 2, p. 838 (hereafter cited as *ADAP*).

11. Hugh R. Trevor-Roper (ed.), *Hitler's Table Talk, 1941–1944* (London: Weidenfeld, 1953), p. 79.

12. Rudolph Binion, "'Der Jude ist weg': Machtpolitische Auswirkungen des Hitlerschen Rassengedankens," in Josef Becker et al. (eds.), *Die Deutsche Frage im 19. und 20. Jahrhundert* (Munich: Vögel, 1983), pp. 347–372. See also Binion's earlier work, *Hitler among the Germans* (New York: Elsevier, 1976).

13. Lecture in Hamburg, March 23, 1938. Max Domarus (ed.), *Hitler: Reden und Proklamationen 1932–1945*, 2 vols. (Neustadt a.d. Aisch: Schmidt, 1962 and 1963), p. 839 (hereafter cited as Domarus).

14. June 6, 1938. *Droste Geschichts-Kalendarium*, vol. 2, 1 (Düsseldorf: Droste, 1982), p. 451.

15. Conference, October 14, 1938. Nuremberg Document PS-1301, *Der Prozess gegen die Hauptkriegsverbrecher vor dem Internationalen Militärgerichtshof*, vol. 27 (Nuremberg, 1948), p. 163 (hereafter cited as *IMT*).

16. *ADAP*, vol. 5, nos. 84, 88, 89, 91, 92, 95, 97, 98, 101, 103, 107, 127, 652, 664, 665.

17. Conference, November 12, 1938. Nuremberg Document PS–1816, *IMT,* vol. 28, pp. 538–539.

18. *ADAP,* vol. 4, p. 293.

19. Helmut Krausnick, "Judenverfolgung," in Hans Buchheim et al. (eds.), *Anatomie des SS-Staates,* vol. 2 (Olten: Walter, 1965), p. 338.

20. *ADAP,* vol. 4, p. 170.

21. Krausnick, "Judenverfolgung," pp. 342–343.

22. *Stenographische Berichte des Reichstags* (1939), p. 16(B).

23. Jochen Thies, *Architekt der Weltherrschaft* (Düsseldorf: Droste, 1976), p. 115.

24. Krausnick, "Judenverfolgung," p. 351.

25. Hans-Günther Seraphim (ed.), *Das politische Tagebuch Alfred Rosenbergs* (Munich: Deutscher Taschenbuch Verlag, 1964), p. 99.

26. Nuremberg Document PS-686, *IMT,* vol. 26, pp. 255–257. Cf. Robert L. Koehl, *RKFDV: German Resettlement and Population Policy 1939–1945* (Cambridge, Mass.: Harvard University Press, 1957).

27. Werner Präg and Wolfgang Jacobmeyer (eds.), *Das Diensttagebuch des deutschen Generalgouverneurs in Polen 1939 – 1945* (Stuttgart: Deutsche Verlags-Anstalt, 1975), pp. (hereafter cited as *Diensttagebuch*).

28. Reitlinger, *The Final Solution,* p. 46.

29. To Colin Ross, March 12, 1940, *ADAP,* vol. 8, p. 716.

30. "Denkschrift Himmlers über die Behandlung der Fremdvölkischen im Osten (Mai 1940)," *Vierteljahrshefte für Zeitgeschichte* 5 (1957): 197.

31. Krausnick, "Judenverfolgung," p. 355.

32. See Eberhard Jäckel, *Frankreich in Hitlers Europa* (Stuttgart: Deutsche Verlags-Anstalt, 1966), pp. 46–58.

33. Paul Schmidt, *Statist auf diplomatischer Bühne 1923–45* (Bonn: Athenäum, 1952), p. 485.

34. *Diensttagebuch,* p. 252.

35. Jäckel, *Frankreich,* pp. 81 and 128–129.

36. *Diensttagebuch,* p. 284.

37. Ibid., p. 327.

38. Letter from Lammers to Schirach, December 3, 1940, Nuremberg Document PS-1950, *IMT,* vol 29, p. 176.

39. Krausnick, "Judenverfolgung," p. 358.

40. *Diensttagebuch,* pp. 335-337.

41. See Helmut Krausnick and Hans-Heinrich Wilhelm, *Die Truppe des Weltanschauungskrieges: Die Einsatzgruppen der Sicherheitspolizei und des SD, 1938–1942* (Stuttgart: Deutsche Verlags-Anstalt, 1981).

42. Krausnick, "Judenverfolgung," p. 371.

43. Reitlinger, *The Final Solution,* p. 28.

44. *Diensttagebuch,* p. 336.

45. Ibid., p. 386.

46. For example, in a letter of July 5, 1943, Himmler called Sobibór a *Durchgangslager,* as did other SS officials in the ensuing correspondence. Adalbert Rückerl (ed.), *Nationalsozialistische Vernichtungslager* (Munich:

Deutscher Taschenbuch Verlag, 1977), pp. 176–178.
47. To Marshal Kvaternik, *ADAP*, vol. 13, 2, p. 838.
48. Alfred Streim, *Die Behandlung sowjetischer Kriegsgefangener im "Fall Barbarossa"* (Heidelberg: C. F. Müller, 1981), pp. 74–93.
49. Józef Marszalek, *Majdanek* (Reinbek bei Hamburg: Rowohlt, 1982), pp. 24–26.
50. *Diensttagebuch*, p. 389.
51. See Yisrael Gutman, *The Jews of Warsaw, 1939–1943* (Brighton: Harvester Press, 1982), and Raul Hilberg et al. (eds.), *The Warsaw Diary of Adam Czerniakow* (New York: Stein and Day, 1979).
52. Nuremberg Document PS-710, *IMT*, vol. 26, pp. 266–267. That the authorization was prepared by Heydrich in advance and was written by Eichmann: Rudolf Aschenauer (ed.), *Ich, Adolf Eichmann* (Leoni: Druffel, 1980), p. 479. That Heydrich went to see Göring is confirmed by an entry in Göring's appointment book: *Vierteljahrshefte für Zeitgeschichte* 31 (1983): 366–367.
53. Goebbels diary, August 20, 1941, quoted by Broszat, "Hitler," p. 750.
54. See Martin Broszat (ed.), *Kommandant in Auschwitz: Autobiographische Aufzeichnungen von Rudolf Höss* (Stuttgart: Deutsche Verlags-Anstalt, 1958), p. 153, and Jochen von Lang (ed.), *Das Eichmann-Protokoll* (Berlin: Severin und Siedler, 1982), p. 69.
55. Hans-Heinrich Wilhelm, "Wie geheim war die 'Endlösung'?," in *Miscellanea: Festschrift für Helmut Krausnick* (Stuttgart: Deutsche Verlags-Anstalt, 1980), p. 137.
56. Robert M. W. Kempner, *Eichmann und Komplizen* (Zürich: Europa Verlag, 1961), p. 87.
57. Note by Rosenberg, Nuremberg Document PS-1517, *IMT*, vol. 27, p. 270.
58. Nuremberg Document PS-709, published in Rückerl, *Nationalsozialistische Vernichtungslager*, pp. 99–100.
59. Document 203 AR 690/65, Zentrale Stelle der Landesjustizverwaltungen, Ludwigsburg; quoted by Broszat, "Hitler," p. 749. On SS-Sturmbannführer Rolf-Heinz Höppner, who signed the letter, see Martin Pollack, "Jäger und Gejagter," *Transatlantik*, November 1982, pp. 17–24.
60. Bradley F. Smith and Agnes F. Peterson (eds.), *Heinrich Himmler: Geheimreden 1933 bis 1945* (Berlin: Propyläen, 1974), pp. 169 (Oct. 6, 1943), 202 (May 5, 1944), 203 (May 24, 1944), and 203–204 (June 21, 1944).
61. Louis P. Lochner (ed.), *Goebbels Tagebücher aus den Jahren 1942–43* (Zürich: Atlantis, 1948), pp. 142–143.
62. Kempner, *Eichmann*, p. 97.
63. *Vierteljahrshefte für Zeitgeschichte* 11 (1963): 206–209.
64. Browning, "Decision" (see note 2).
65. Broszat, "Hitler," p. 764.
66. Helmut Heiber, "Aus den Akten des Gauleiters Kube, *Vierteljahr-*

shefte für Zeitgeschichte 4 (1956): 67–92.

67. Seev Goshen, "Eichmann und die Nisko-Aktion im Oktober 1939," *Vierteljahrshefte für Zeitgeschichte* 29 (1981): 74–96.

68. Keesings Archiv der Gegenwart 1942, p. 5705.

69. Adolf Hitler, *Hitlers Politisches Testament: Die Bormann Diktate vom Februar und April 1945* (Hamburg: Knaus, 1981), pp. 70 and 122.

70. Felix Kersten, *Klerk en beul* (Amsterdam: Meulenhoff, 1948), p. 198.

CHAPTER 4

This chapter is a revised version of an essay originally published under the title "Die deutsche Kriegserklärung an die Vereinigten Staaten von 1941," in *Im Dienste Deutschlands und des Rechts: Festschrift für Wilhelm G. Grewe* (Baden-Baden: Nomos, 1981), pp. 117–137.

1. *Akten zur deutschen auswärtigen Politik 1918–1945, Serie D. 1937–1941*, vol. 13, 2, pp. 817 and 812–813 (hereafter cited as *ADAP*).

2. Max Domarus (ed.), *Hitler: Reden und Proklamationen 1932–1945*, 2 vols. (Neustadt a.d. Aisch: Schmidt, 1962 and 1963), pp. 1794–1811.

3. *ADAP*, vol. 13, 2, p. 813.

4. See once more my book *Hitlers Weltanschauung* (Stuttgart: Deutsche Verlags-Anstalt, 1981), and Axel Kuhn, *Hitlers aussenpolitisches Programm* (Stuttgart: Klett, 1970).

5. *ADAP*, vol. 11, 1, pp. 175–176.

6. Hans-Adolf Jacobsen (ed.), *Kriegstagebuch des Oberkommandos der Wehrmacht*, vol. 1 (Frankfurt am Main: Bernard and Graefe, 1965), p. 328.

7. Walther Hubatsch (ed.), *Hitlers Weisungen für die Kriegführung 1939–1945* (Frankfurt am Main: Bernard und Graefe, 1962), pp. 103–104.

8. See Peter Herde, *Pearl Harbor* (Darmstadt: Wissenschaftliche Buchgesellschaft, 1980).

9. *ADAP*, vol. 12, 1, pp. 317–324 and 374–378.

10. *Foreign Relations of the United States, Diplomatic Papers*, vol. 4, *The Far East* (Washington, D.C., 1956), p. 933.

11. Andreas Hillgruber, "Japan und der Fall 'Barbarossa': Japanische Dokumente zu den Gesprächen Hitlers und Ribbentrops mit Botschafter Oshima von Februar bis Juni 1941, *Wehrwissenschaftliche Rundschau* 18 (1968): 312–335.

12. Leonidas E. Hill (ed.), *Die Weizsäcker-Papiere 1933–1950* (Berlin: Propyläen, 1974), p. 258.

13. Gerhard Wagner (ed.), *Lagevorträge des Oberbefehlshabers der Kriegsmarine vor Hitler 1939–1945* (Frankfurt am Main: Bernard und Graefe, 1972), p. 263.

14. Nobutaka Ike (ed.), *Japan's Decision for War: Records of the 1941 Policy Conferences* (Stanford, Calif.: Stanford University Press, 1967), p. 60.

15. *ADAP*, vol. 13, 1, p. 34.

16. Wagner, *Lagevorträge*, pp. 264–265.
17. *ADAP*, vol. 13, 1, p. 95.
18. ADAP, vol. 13, 2, p. 834.
19. Wagner, *Lagevorträge*, p. 286.
20. Genraloberst Halder, *Kriegstagebuch*, vol. 3 (Stuttgart: Kohlhammer, 1964), p. 219.
21. *ADAP*, vol. 13, 1, p. 413.
22. *ADAP*, vol. 13, 2, pp. 497 and 499.
23. Ibid., p. 547.
24. Ibid., p. 586.
25. Ibid., pp. 653 and 610 n. 4.
26. Ibid., p. 653.
27. Ibid., p. 660.
28. Ibid., p. 665.
29. Ike, *Japan's Decision for War*, pp. 241–242.
30. Department of Defense, *The "Magic" Background of Pearl Harbor*, vol. 4 (Washington, D.C.: U.S. Government Printing Office, 1978). See also Peter Herde, *Italien, Deutschland und der Weg in den Krieg im Pazifik 1941* (Wiesbaden: Steiner, 1983), where the Italian documents are used as well.
31. *ADAP*, vol. 13, 2, pp. 708–710.
32. Department of Defense, *The "Magic" Background*, p. A-383.
33. Ibid., p. A-388.
34. This is evident from several sources. See Guenther Blumentritt, *Von Rundstedt: The Soldier and the Man* (London: Odhams, 1952), p. 114.
35. Domarus, *Hitler: Reden und Proklamationen*, p. 1788.
36. Department of Defense, *The "Magic" Background*, p. A-389.
37. *ADAP*, vol. 13, 2, pp. 781–783.
38. Ibid., pp. 779–780.
39. Ibid., p. 781.
40. Hill, *Die Weizsäcker-Papiere*, pp. 278–279.
41. *ADAP*, vol. 13, 2, pp. 799–800.
42. Domarus, *Hitler: Reden und Proklamationen*, p. 1793.
43. Wagner, *Lagevorträge*, p. 327.
44. *ADAP*, vol. 13, 2, pp. 807–812.
45. Ibid., pp. 812–813.
46. Its official title, as published in the *Reichsgesetzblatt* of February 13, 1942, was "Abkommen zwischen Deutschland, Italien und Japan über die gemeinsame Kriegführung gegen die Vereinigten Staaten und England."
47. Hill, *Die Weizsäcker-Papiere*, p. 274.

CHAPTER 5

This chapter was originally a lecture and was later included in the second edition of my *Hitlers Weltanschauung* (Stuttgart: Deutsche Verlags-Anstalt, 1981).

1. Speech of September 14, 1935, at Nuremberg. Max Domarus (ed.), *Hitler: Reden und Proklamationen 1932–1945*, 2 vols. (Neustadt a.d. Aisch: Schmidt, 1962 and 1963), p. 533.

2. Speech of May 4, 1941, before the Reichstag. Domarus, p. 1704.

3. Adolf Hitler, *Mein Kampf*, vol. 2 (Munich: Eher, 1927); reprint 1930), p. 579.

4. Ibid.

5. Albert Speer, *Erinnerungen* (Berlin: Propyläen, 1969), p. 113. In an earlier will Hitler had wished to be buried in Munich; see Gerhard L. Weinberg, "Hitler's Private Testament of May 2, 1938," *Journal of Modern History* (1955): 415–419.

6. Adolf Hitler, *Monologe im Führerhauptquartier 1941–1944* (Hamburg: Knaus, 1980), p. 239.

7. Domarus, p. 1639.

8. *Akten zur deutschen auswärtigen Politik 1918–1945, Serie D: 1937–1941*, vol. 13, 2, p. 705.

9. Ibid., p. 708.

10. Marlis G. Steinert, *Hitlers Krieg und die Deutschen* (Düsseldorf: Econ, 1970), p. 156.

11. Hitler, *Mein Kampf*, p. 738.

12. Ibid., p. 772.

13. Heinz Boberach (ed.), *Meldungen aus dem Reich* (Neuwied: Luchterhand, 1965), pp. XXVII–XXVIII.

14. Steinert, pp. 76–77.

15. Ibid., p. 62.

16. Ibid., pp. 77–79.

17. Boberach, p. 77.

18. Steinert, pp. 469-490.

19. Boberach, p. 191.

20. Ibid., p. 116.

21. Ibid., p. 384.

22. Ibid., p. 146.